"A darkly comedic story with hijinks that will leave you torn between shock and horrified laughter. Casale has tackled a heartbreaking topic with the dexterity and nuance it deserves. I don't condone murder, but I would like to join the Lockdown Ladies' Burial Club now, please!"

—Jesse Q. Sutanto, author of *Dial A for Aunties*

"*The Best Way to Bury Your Husband* is poignant, funny, and warm, but also dark, searing, and downright heart-breaking. Beautifully written with a perfect blend of humor, pathos, and important, hard-hitting messages."

—Andrea Mara, international bestselling author of *Someone in the Attic*

"Warning: You won't sleep until you've finished this book. It's utterly unputdownable. Tense, funny, moving, and strangely cozy at the same time. Casale writes about domestic abuse with clarity and urgency, and yet with humor, farce, and warmth. You'll weep as these four survivors find solace and homecoming as they share their stories (and tips on dismemberment). Not to be missed. Read it now!"

—Holly Bourne, international bestselling author of *It Only Happens in the Movies*

PENGUIN BOOKS

THE BEST WAY TO BURY YOUR HUSBAND

Alexia Casale is a British-American author, script consultant, and course director of the MA in Writing for Young People program at Bath Spa University. This is her adult debut. Alexia has over a decade of experience as an editor specializing in the field of male violence against women and girls, having been an executive editor of an international human rights journal. She holds two master's degrees from the University of Cambridge and a PhD from Essex.

Penguin Reading Group Discussion Guide
available online at penguinrandomhouse.com

THE BEST WAY TO BURY YOUR HUSBAND

ALEXIA CASALE

PENGUIN BOOKS

PENGUIN BOOKS

An imprint of Penguin Random House LLC
penguinrandomhouse.com

LIBRARY OF CONGRESS CATALOGING-IN-PUBLICATION DATA
Names: Casale, Alexia, author.
Title: The best way to bury your husband / Alexia Casale.
Description: [New York] : Penguin Books, 2024.
Identifiers: LCCN 2023035375 (print) | LCCN 2023035376 (ebook) |
ISBN 9780593654606 (trade paperback) | ISBN 9780593654590 (ebook)
Subjects: LCGFT: Black humor. | Novels.
Classification: LCC PR6103.A79 B47 2024 (print) |
LCC PR6103.A79 (ebook) | DDC 823/.92—dc23/eng/20231027
LC record available at https://lccn.loc.gov/2023035375
LC ebook record available at https://lccn.loc.gov/2023035376

Printed in the United States of America
1st Printing

Set in Iowan Old Style
Designed by Sabrina Bowers

For all the women who fight for other women.
And all the women who make my life wonderful.

(PS: You'd better believe the pledge of corpse-burying
assistance is legit. Naturally, I expect this to be a
reciprocal bond of love, devotion, and,
if necessary, dismemberment.)

THE BEST WAY TO BURY
YOUR HUSBAND

1

Granny's Skillet

One of my earliest memories is Granny making Welsh cakes in a cast-iron skillet. It was age-blackened even then, though carefully tended.

I remember the first time she let me hold it, hand hovering beneath mine because its size belies its weight. I remember the day she taught me how to wash and temper it so the patina would stay forever like silk. Each memory is washed in golden light, though her tiny galley kitchen had no windows for the sun to stream through.

She bequeathed the skillet to me in her will.

"Like an heirloom," sneered my father. But then love never was in his gift.

Jim offered to buy me a new one when we moved in together. He laughed when I cradled Granny's close at the very suggestion.

Now it sits amid the wreckage of breakfast, one edge poking over the lip of the counter. Blood drips from the rim.

There's only one thought in my head as I stare at the skillet: If I'd died today, how would Jim have explained it?

Would he have started with this morning? The Lockdown? The day we met?

There's a blurry photo of that moment in our album—me at seventeen, him at twenty-four. We're at a house party awash with nineties fashion and alcopops in celebration of my best friend turning eighteen. Janey was my second-most-favorite person in the world after Granny.

In the previous five minutes I'd comforted a girl crying over a boy-band breakup, joking her back to watery laughter . . . then swung a tottering guy twice my height into an armchair so he could pass out safely . . . then rescued the whole household from an inferno sparked by four drunk teenagers trying to light eighteen candles on a small, lopsided cake.

The fire-starters, led by the birthday girl, had been calling for me to come and help, but the crying-girl and toppling-guy delayed me long enough to arrive just as a candle tipped off the edge of the cake into the nest of napkins set thoughtfully to the side. Before anyone could blink, I had the smoking mess in the sink with the tap running.

As I stood back to take my bow amid wild applause, a shadow fell over me.

"That could have ended badly," someone said. And there was Jim.

I will never forgive myself that instead of seeing what was right in front of me—a man oozing resentment at a life already thwarted by his own mediocrity—I let myself believe that here was someone no one else took the time to appreciate: a good soul dismissed because of indifferent looks and an awkward manner.

That makes me sound like a silly little fool, but none of what followed would have happened if I hadn't felt so unkind when Jim suddenly slipped an arm around me, pressing in close, and I froze in horror . . . only to realize that Janey was standing in front of us with her brand-new camera, snapping pictures of the crowd around the cake.

Why'd I want a photo with a no-hoper like you? sneered the voice in my head. Appalled by the ready cruelty of my thoughts, I felt my cheeks burn with shame.

"Gotta ask for a copy of that."

Guilt stabbed me as my skin crawled with revulsion at his over-jolly leer, though I could see he'd been aiming for jokey charm.

I thought I was the one with all the power—couldn't conceive that there could be any danger. So when Granny died a month later and suddenly there was nowhere to run from my mother's misery and my father's venom, it seemed like nothing less than a miracle that there was Jim, with a salary and parents willing to provide the down payment for a mortgage. There was no way I could ever have followed Janey to university—what would someone like me do with a university education and the debts that came with it? I'd still end up stuck at home, paying my father rent instead of being able to save for a deposit—moving in with a boyfriend would remain my only prospect of getting away for years.

I couldn't wait that long. Not when there was the promise of a safe home right there in front of me. And so what if I was young? I told myself that the universe owed me a stroke of luck and here it was: my way out.

We got married three weeks after the end of school.

Janey used the excuse of passing over my wedding bouquet to whisper, "Sally, are you sure you want this?" but I just laughed as if she were joking, and off we went down the aisle.

When Dad lifted my veil at the altar, he stopped and, taking out his handkerchief, began to scrub at a nonexistent smudge on my face, exchanging a commiserating glance with Jim even as he left a red mark, like a bruise, on my cheek. My mother looked pointedly away, busying herself with excavating her handbag as if something needed rescuing from its depths.

Did she know I was heading straight for a life like hers? If she did, she didn't tell me. Just held me a little too tight as she wished me luck before Jim led me out of the church under a barrage of rice and flower petals.

Now I blink and half expect to be back there, because anything would make more sense than standing in my kitchen, in my home, with Granny's skillet bleeding onto the floor.

But maybe it's not my life that, in an instant, has become unrecognizable. Maybe it's me. Because instead of feeling as if I'm wrapped in a nightmare and just need to wake up, for the first time in over twenty years I am awake.

Suddenly I can see that it isn't just the skillet that makes no sense. It's the pain in my wrist and the bruises from yesterday and the day before and the day before that. It's the fact that my life in Lockdown is barely different from my life before.

How did I let my world become little bigger than the confines of the house, with all my friendships fading into the past, and even my contact with the kids dwindling? I know the answer, of course. The problem was that before today I refused to ask the question.

Now realization rushes at me so that for a second I stumble, but it's still level linoleum under my feet, still the quiet kitchen around me. The roar in my head is twenty years of memories reorganizing themselves into a completely different story from the one I've been telling myself.

Like my last visit to the local book club five years ago. At the time I didn't know that's what it was, or that it would mark the end of any regular socializing at all. I was too distracted by how everyone laughed that I'd turned up in a cardigan on a blistering summer's day. Underneath, fingerprint bruises patterned my arms forget-me-not blue over fading marigold, but I didn't let myself dwell on it, too busy pretending to laugh along because I just wanted it to be nice, to be easy—an hour of smiles and laughter. And it was. The sheer relief of it sent me singing my way home. Only when I let myself in there was Jim, back early from work with a headache. And I told myself that what happened next was my fault: that he had a migraine—couldn't see straight. It wasn't as if he meant to pour the boiling kettle over my hand.

Just like he didn't mean to shut my fingers in the cupboard door, or elbow me so hard my ribs hurt for a month. They were just accidents. Only accidents.

So many accidents.

But the kids were nearly through school, so I couldn't leave yet—had to hang on a bit longer. Only then came uni and they wanted a home for the holidays and, after all those years, what was a few more in exchange for having them under the same roof again for weeks at a time, my last chance before they were gone, flown the nest . . .

Charlie graduated, found a job, and moved out just as Amy's graduation came round, bringing her back home while she saved for a deposit so she could move in with her boyfriend. Then she was gone too, just before Christmas, and by the time I was sure it would stick . . .

Lockdown.

And there we were. Just him and me. All through March and past the end of April with no sign of a letup in sight . . .

So you can see how I got here, to this morning, with me taking Jim a cup of tea at the kitchen table and him glancing at it—a shade too light—and the look on his face . . .

His hand clamped white around my wrist as he yanked me over to the counter so roughly I stumbled, smacking my head against the oven hood. Fumbling for something to hold myself up, my hand closed on the edge of the hob, fingers brushing the handle of the skillet. Beside me, Jim grabbed the kettle, spattering my hand with hot water. My flesh seared with the memory of the last time we stood at the counter like this.

How long will he hold me there this time? Even the voice in my head quavered with fear because, in Lockdown, with no one to know and no one to see, there was also no one to stop him if he chose to just keep pouring and pouring . . .

Like everyone else, I'd read stories in the papers about women who fought back, but I couldn't even begin to understand those women. For years they seemed like a different species. I used to wonder if it was a type of desperation I'd yet to experience, or some inner store of strength and courage—and, if so, where I could get some.

Then I went and smashed Jim's head in with Granny's skillet.

2

A Pot of Petunias

You understand now I've explained, don't you? Not just how it happened, but why. And if you understand why, you'll know it was an accident. Because it was definitely an accident.

Kind of.

A Jim sort of accident anyway.

At the very least you can see that I didn't mean to do it—it wasn't planned. I didn't even think, my hand just . . . moved on its own.

More or less.

Anyway, self-defense isn't anything to criticize a person for. I mean, it's not just legal but perfectly proper and correct: morally A-OK.

I look over at the skillet. Another drop of blood falls from the rim.

I watch it splat onto the floor next to Jim. He's on his front, face turned away. He could just have decided to take a nap down there but for the spreading pool of blood around his head.

"See what you made me do?"

I thought the words would come out spiteful and gloating, but my voice is a whisper, hollow as an echo. There's despair instead of triumph burning through my veins.

I stagger to the counter, pick up the phone, and dial 9. And again. My finger hovers . . .

I slam the phone into the cradle, then stumble out of the back door into the garden.

Outside, everything is normal. So terribly normal: normal sounds, normal sights, normal smells for early May in suburban southeast England. The sky is overcast but not dark, the sun a white glare behind the clouds. In Nawar's garden next door the cherry tree is dropping the last of its blossom, while the magnolia is coming into its own. Everything goes on as it did before. Except that behind me, in the kitchen, Jim is dead.

Hidden behind the watering can, a colorful pot of pansies catches my eye. I snatch it up, cradling it to my chest, hand pressed over the message printed on to the side—*Best Mum Ever! Love, Amy and Charlie x*

"I'm so sorry," I whisper, chest constricting with grief till it hurts to breathe and every pulse feels like agony. Tears spill on to my cheeks as I squeeze my eyes shut. "I'm sorry, I'm sorry, I'm so sorry . . ."

My hand strokes the cold ceramic glaze while the pansy leaves brush my fingers as if trying to comfort me.

I stumble back inside. Averting my eyes from the floor, I set the flowers gently in the middle of the table, where I'd wanted them from the start. Jim had said they were in the way, seizing the pot and slamming it down outside the back door so that one of the cheerful pansy faces tore off against the brickwork. I found it later, discarded on the ground.

I force myself over to the counter and pick up the phone again. Gritting my teeth, I stab the 9.

My eyes drift back to the pansies. From this angle, the message on the pot is just visible. I want to turn away, but that would mean facing what the *Best Mum Ever* has just done to her children's father.

In my hand, the phone quivers, the 9 on the screen blurring. Then it blinks away, timed out.

I press it again, then stall anew.

Once I call the police, my kids lose both their parents.

How could I let it come to this? I've failed them so much, in so many ways, but this isn't failure: it's ruin.

Slowly, I slot the phone back into the charger. Sinking into a chair, I turn my back on the kettle, the skillet, the phone, Jim, staring instead at the glorious colors of the pansies. The little faces seem to peer smilingly back. The blue one, tilted at an angle, looks almost sympathetic, like a friend waiting to listen to my troubles.

Janey, my heart says. *I want Janey.*

But even if I hadn't destroyed our friendship, how could I bring her into this?

"I always wanted to try talking to the wall like Shirley Valentine," I tell the patient little pansy, the cheeriness of my voice making the world distort with unreality, "but I guess it makes more sense to kill two birds with one stone . . ." I glance at Jim. "As it were." I turn away again. "And they do say plants flourish when they're talked to, unlike, say, walls or . . ." I resist the urge to look at Jim once more.

"I shall call you Petunia because Jim would hate it. He hated silliness. And ignorance. And me."

I brush a fleck of dirt off the side of the pot. "You probably think that was obvious, but I've been a bit slow on the uptake."

The violet and blue faces on the left may look positively indulgent, but the magenta one in the middle has a decidedly disbelieving expression.

"OK, so it's been twenty-odd years," I snap. "But at least I'm up to speed now."

I can't help but look back at Jim then. The blood seems to have stopped spreading, which is a relief: it's going to be hell to scrub out of the grouting.

Which is a bad thought. The wrong thought. But there we go.

"I know I have to call the police, but I just don't want to, Petunia," I hear myself say. "I don't want to go to prison now I'm finally free."

By my elbow, Jim's newspaper is wall-to-wall Covid Lockdown.

"Well, obviously I can't go anywhere or see anyone, but I could . . . have a piece of cake."

Since Jim can no longer tell me I'm a fat lump, I pad over to the counter, opening the cupboard above. A wall of baked beans stares back. My eyes go to Jim, then to the baked beans. A moment later I'm dragging over the bin, about to scoop the whole lot in, then I pause. Fetching a bag, I load them into that instead.

"The food bank is welcome to them, Petunia, but I am never eating sodding beans on toast again."

I set out a knife, plate, fork, then pause and, with a defiant look at Jim, start eating straight from the cake tin. No one snatches the food from me and stuffs it into the bin because I am disgusting and undeserving. For a moment nothing bad happens at all.

Then the doorbell rings.

Dead ~~Dear~~ Deer?

freeze, buttercream souring between my teeth. My eyes go
to the window, expecting to see horrified neighbors goggling
over the fences to either side, perhaps a policeman creeping
up the garden path . . . but there's no one, not even a bird fishing in the lawn for worms.

*Do they know or just suspect? Should I try to hide Jim or stay quiet
and hope they go away?*

The doorbell rings again. Resignation washes through me
as if my veins have been injected with lead.

Prisons aren't like they used to be, I console myself. *They've got
electricity now. And libraries. But the food is probably . . .*

My eyes fall on the bag of baked beans. Before I can give in
to the urge to turn and run hopelessly out the back—they've
probably got an officer waiting in the alley behind the house—
I shuffle into the hall. The front door looms ahead and, behind
it, the end of everything.

It's only as I flick the latch to pull the door open that I realize I'm still holding my fork. Perhaps it will help me mount an
insanity defense.

I blink at the masked young man standing on the mat. For a moment, I forget the pandemic and wonder if he's about to barge in to commit burglary and, if so, what he'll do when he finds Jim.

"Need a signature," he says, holding out a touch pad.

"Murgh?" I ask him as I look past his shoulder for the police.

The street is empty but for the little post cart with its drooping bag of mail.

"Didn't mean to interrupt your elevenses. Something nice today, is it?"

I follow his gaze to the fork in my hand. "Cake," I explain. "I'm having cake. Do you like cake?" I sound unhinged.

"Mm," he says warily, proffering the touch pad again.

I watch my hand come up, finger extended; it makes a swirly pattern on the screen. Is that my signature? It doesn't seem to matter because the postman wipes the screen with a cloth, dumps a parcel at my feet, then hurries away.

I stand there, fork aloft and mouth open. The curtain in the front room of the house opposite twitches, but absolutely no one comes to arrest me.

After a while, I totter backward, swinging the door shut. For a moment I stand staring at it, then at the fork, then the door, then the fork again. I wait to dissolve into laughter or tears, but when neither happens I shuffle back down the hall to the kitchen.

I feel better once I've demolished the rest of the Victoria sponge, though my brain keeps presenting me with bad memories associated with cake and parties. My father throwing my seventh-birthday cake against the wall and Granny picking me up, though she was too old and I was too big, and taking me back to hers for a week. The party where I met Jim. Our wedding cake. And yet it's the parties I wasn't even at that my brain keeps coming back to. I've missed so many over the years, but Janey's twentieth was the first.

I'd spent weeks making sure Jim would have no trouble looking after Charlie—our son when it suited, mine when it came to anything tiresome. But at eight months, Charlie was finally taking two feeds of formula a day without fuss, so I figured I could go for a few hours at least.

Singing under my breath as I skipped downstairs, my favorite heels in hand, I shucked my slippers on to the mat with glee—it felt like the first time in forever.

Then I looked up and there was Jim, looming in the living-room doorway, and the look on his face as his eyes swept up and down my body . . . I hitched my dress higher over my bust, but his eyes darkened. Upstairs, Charlie began to cry.

I waited for Jim to slip past me to comfort our son. Instead, he turned and went back into the living room, snapping the door closed. Charlie's cries soared into full-on screams. And I just stood there, staring at the door, willing it to open again, willing Jim to be the man I thought he was . . .

Moments later my slippers were back on, heels abandoned on the mat as I trudged upstairs.

That was the first big crack in my relationship with Janey. I knew it then, but I told myself there would be time to make it up to her.

A month later she helped organize my father's funeral as I'd once helped with hers, and for a few weeks it seemed as if everything would be OK . . . Only I kept canceling plans. Kept getting worse and worse at returning phone calls. Kept letting the time between catching up get longer and longer. Kept failing her. Failing myself.

Kept letting the distance between us get bigger and bigger till I was so lonely for her I ached, but it seemed impossible to do anything about it with Charlie so small. I thought things would ease once Charlie was in preschool, but he was only ten months old when I found out I was pregnant again because Jim and I had the worst luck with condoms. So *then* I told myself . . .

My brain stops, reverses.

 . . . *I was pregnant again because Jim and I had the worst luck with condoms* . . .

The truth spills on to my cheeks, though the realization isn't fresh and raw but dull and rotten.

I knew. Of course I did. Even I'm not as stupid as Jim always said I was.

When I could no longer pretend my period was just late, I knew that no one was that unlucky with condoms, but I was so busy accepting that I was pregnant again it was easy to push aside the truth of what Jim had done. And why.

Somewhere inside I knew that he'd done it to trap me, but the terror that this was the man I was tied to not just by marriage but by two children was so immense it felt like numbness.

But even then it wasn't only terror and desperation, it was love.

I hadn't chosen to be pregnant with Charlie, or again with the baby who would become Amy, but from the second I knew, I loved them, so I couldn't regret them. There was no decision to make about it: I loved them, and that was that. It was the only part that was easy. And God did I need one thing that was because it's only now, with it finally over, that I can look back and see why I folded instead of marching myself out the door to Janey's birthday party, despite Charlie's screams and Jim's sullen silence from behind the living-room door.

The hatred blisters through me as if I've been caught in a wildfire . . . then just as suddenly it's gone, leaving me cold and tired in the kitchen, with Jim still dead on the floor.

But the front door is shut, and the delivery man long gone, so no one is any the wiser.

"I really thought that was it," I tell Jim. "Off to prison: do not pass go, do not collect . . ." The urge to laugh makes me light-headed. I grip the edge of the counter and breathe the panic from my lungs. "Maybe I could collect *something* first . . . ice cream! I could collect some ice cream." I turn to Jim. "Did you hear that, dear? Cake for lunch and ice cream for dessert. A last hurrah before it's back to beans on toast—for life."

I flick on the radio to fill the silence. "I Can See Clearly Now" comes on. Instinctively, I open my mouth to sing along . . . then glance at Jim and close it. Maybe I should save the singing for a last shower—though a long soak in the bath is probably more fitting for a pre-prison bucket list. Perhaps it'll be even harder to call the police when I've just reminded myself of all I'll be missing, but I need *some* pleasures, however small, before I lurch from one nightmare to another. I know I can't stay in the limbo between killing Jim and facing the consequences forever.

But the bit of me that picked up the skillet isn't quite done. I know I should feel only grief and despair, but somehow, madly, there's this strange sense of . . . hope.

Maybe it's madness or shock, because there is no fixing Jim's brains spilled across the kitchen floor.

But I don't feel defeated.

For the first time in longer than I can remember, I feel powerful.

4

The Last Bath

Cracking the seal on a bottle of fancy scented oil I've been saving for years, I pour a luxurious amount into the water, then top up the bubbles too before lying back, wineglass in hand. It's only supermarket-brand cooking wine, but recently I've truffled out a few decent ones so I can allow myself the odd drink without risking a side order of black-eye from Jim for wasting his hard-earned cash.

Petunia sits on the edge of the sink, peering down at the mountain range of bubbles rising around me. For a moment, I consider sliding down under the water and not coming back up, but drowning's not how I want to go. Not even to escape prison.

Suddenly I hear Janey's voice, bright and happy and mocking, as if she's in the room with me. "Hey, Courage, where's your courage?" A catchphrase we nobbled, then adapted as our own after a particularly boring history lesson at the start of secondary school.

Over the years, I shouted it at her when she froze at her big moment in the school play. She yelled it at me when I balked at the zip-wire challenge when her mum took us to an adventure park for her sixteenth. We screamed it hoarsely across the school playing fields when they made us run laps. Whispered it before exams. Howled it between laughs whenever either of us answered the phone—"Who's calling?"—to have the other scream back, "Hey, Courage! It's Courage!"

How can I have let it be so long since we last spoke? Part of the answer lies below in the kitchen, but only part.

Longing surges like a rising wave of tears, but I can't afford those right now so I take a fortifying sip of wine, then dangle the glass over the side of the tub the way I've seen women do in movies. It's incredibly uncomfortable.

Putting the glass on the floor, I curl my hands into the hot water instead, squeezing bubbles between my fingers.

"I'm still not thinking sad thoughts, Petunia," I admit as I raise a foot out of the water, waggling my frothy toes. "And I just don't think I'm going to, because I've realized how happy I am."

Petunia's little faces are comfortingly unperturbed by my confession.

"If it weren't for the whole prison issue, this would be the one good thing to happen to me since the kids left. But I can't tell the police that, can I? I mean, I could, but it'd definitely end in tears—mine, the kids', everyone who still loves me . . ."

I intended the words to come out with a huff of laughter. Instead, my throat tightens.

I feel my eyes growing hot but can just about make myself believe I've got soap in them.

Taking another sip of wine, I reach along the floor until my fingers find the bowl of crisps I set there earlier. "But what"—*scrunch*—"am I"—*crunch*—"going to tell the police? Especially now Jim's been chilling out—Ha! Chilling! Literally—on the kitchen floor for hours? If"—*munch*—"there was a chance for them to believe me, I've probably blown it with the cake and now . . . this."

Eventually, I drag myself out of the bath. When I've toweled off, I pause as I reach for my ratty old robe. Dropping the towel, I pick up Petunia and the wine bottle and parade naked into the bedroom. I have to climb on a chair to fetch down the box from the back of the cupboard above the wardrobe. I draw out the silk dressing gown I bought two years ago in a vain attempt to give myself a boost, only to realize I was too afraid of Jim seeing me in it to ever wear it.

The fabric runs through my hands like water. When I slide my arm through one sleeve, then another, it's like wearing quicksilver. The chill in the silk makes me slide on a pair of knickers underneath.

"Yes, I know they're boring and basic," I tell Petunia. "I'll have to get myself some better ones later."

It stops me in my tracks. There won't be new knickers unless they're prison-issue.

My feet carry me down to the kitchen. "If you could only see me now, dear," I tell Jim as I pass. "Pity you're too busy decomposing." I want to sound light and airy, but the words come out hard and sharp, like my voice has been tuned wrong.

My phone buzzes with a text from Charlie: a YouTube link to "Here Comes the Sun." There's no message. There hasn't been since the start of Lockdown. Stuck in the house together all day, every day, Jim started demanding to see every message as it arrived. It took me four days to realize he was deleting half of

Charlie's texts before I'd even seen them, replying to the rest with a stream of criticism. The only type of message that was safe was song links since Jim could never be bothered with music.

My finger hovers over the link. How can I accept my son's comfort with his father lying dead three feet away?

On the counter, the red dot of the landline's power button glares at me. It's time to call the police and admit my crime, not swan about listening to music.

Here comes the sun, the voice in my head teases.

And, just like that, the decision is made.

"I'm not going to call the police at all, am I?" I whisper to Petunia. "I've already served my time, taken my punishment. Now the shoe's on the other foot." I toe at Jim's ankle.

His slipper falls off.

"I'll just have to hope fortune favors the desperate as well as the brave, because I'm not sorry it's you instead of me."

I turn my back, taking Petunia and the wine bottle over to the table. "The only thing I'm sorry about is the skillet—I'm going to have to re-temper it and that's such a faff, even without a corpse to dispose of."

I try to laugh, but all that comes out is a breathless huff.

"It's not like I can take you down the dump." I pause with the wineglass halfway to my mouth but dismiss the possibility. The dump's been closed for a fortnight and breaking in with a body won't end well. "They'd surely understand the urgency, but I expect they'd still frown on the whole corpse issue."

I stare at Jim hopelessly. "Even if I put you in the garden, it's going to take a while to dig a deep enough hole, and you can't stay where you are till then, starting to smell." Tilting my head thoughtfully, I grab my mobile and start tapping away in the search bar.

"How . . . to . . . dispose . . . of . . . a . . . dead . . . deer? Not quite the way I'd describe you, dear, but it'll have to do."

5

The Secret Ingredient

Desperate times, and subsequent desperate measures, were proving rather a local theme as, less than a mile away, Samira paused midway up the stairs, arms full of laundry as her life crumbled around her.

She'd been on her way to deliver a load of freshly washed towels to the bathroom when the tone of her husband's voice from behind the bedroom door stopped her in her tracks. He hadn't shouted, or hissed a command, or even clicked his tongue in the way that usually signaled imminent pain. And yet she'd known, before she even caught the first word, that disaster was closing in around her, the same way his hand had closed on her throat the night before when she'd fought to keep his explosion of temper from reaching their daughter.

From behind the door came a scratchy, hissing noise, then a second voice crackled ominously through a tinny laptop speaker turned up to the max. A minute later her daughter's future was decided. But unlike the conversation that had set her own marriage in motion, there would be no carefully orchestrated meeting between the two young people before the *nikah* was performed. Leila wouldn't see her future husband and feel her heart lighten with hope at his smile, then quicken as she took in his features, the pleasing lines of his figure. She wouldn't be nervous yet excited to meet the man she'd heard so much about—the man all the people who loved her best in the world said would be her perfect match. She wouldn't prepare for the *walima* surrounded by joyful family, filled with the belief that this was the start of happiness, of safety, of a good life.

For Leila, there would be only misery, dread, and the bitterness of betrayal. Where Islam demanded the consent of both bride and groom, Leila's would not be given—and yet the marriage would still be performed. Instead of railing against this wrong—against God and their daughter both—her father would sign the *nikah* on her behalf, not to show his support for her and the marriage, but to prevent her from even being present to voice her refusal.

As for the *walima*, Samira had read a story in the paper where the bride—just a child, younger even than Leila—was medicated so she didn't know what was happening. Would Leila one day sit staring at a video of her wedding celebration and see herself smiling instead of fighting? What would she think seeing her family assembled to pretend they were witness to a true marriage, even though every cell in their bodies should have rebelled at betraying her and their faith so shamefully?

"It is for the groom to pay his bride the *mahr*, not for me to pay his parents the price twice over!" her husband shouted on the far side of the door.

"A small cost to restore the respect and reputation of our family, Yafir," crackled the voice at the other end of the call. "She is lucky to have such a match. You will not find better for her."

Yafir heaved a sigh of assent. "As soon as international travel resumes, we will journey over. There must be no delay in conducting the marriage once we arrive."

Samira sagged against the banister, their voices blurring into white noise. When they returned from that trip, their daughter would not just be married by contract, but by consummation—if they returned with her at all. Because Leila wouldn't accept her fate obediently: she would rage and fight, and when they tried to beat the willfulness out of her, she'd fight some more until the price of such defiance was death. If she hadn't already taken matters into her own hands.

Samira felt her eyes flutter closed against memories of stories in the news about the girl who'd drunk bleach to avoid a forced marriage. She'd survived her injuries only for her parents to murder her some months later.

Below, in the living room, Samira could hear her daughters talking quietly. What would bleach do to Leila's rich, deep voice? What would her husband do to her when she fought him rather than going obediently to his bed because, to her mind, they were not truly married at all and she had no such obligation to him or, through him, to God?

This is the moment I could have stopped it, she'd say to herself a month, a year from now, when she had only one daughter left to hold.

Her hands clenched so tightly around the laundry her bones burned with the pressure.

As early as tomorrow, plans would be underway to ensure the marriage could take place as soon as they were able to travel. As early as tomorrow, everyone would know—including Leila. As early as tomorrow, it might not matter that there would be no way to prevent the journey, prevent the marriage when they got there. As early as tomorrow, Leila would refuse for the first time.

One way or another, by her father's hand or her own, by tomorrow her daughter's life would be over.

And all because of rumors. Nothings. A girl giving a rose to her daughter in the far background of a school Valentine's Day photograph. Why should anyone believe it was more than friendship just because their hands were touching? As if Leila would be part of such public impropriety. How could this simple, tiny thing be sufficient to unravel their lives, and yet . . .

This is the moment it happens if I don't stop it.

Her head resounded with the echo of the thought, then quieted, her terror and panic draining away until all that was left was a ringing calm and a single thread of pure purpose.

She arranged the towels in the bathroom, carefully smoothing them into place with gestures so tender she might have been soothing her children to sleep. Even as her hands busied themselves, her thoughts whirled from one idea to another. But the panic was gone. In fact, suddenly she didn't seem to feel anything much at all. There wasn't time with so much to do.

Creeping downstairs, she tried the front door, unsurprised to find it locked, the key missing from its usual hook. The hall stretched into infinity then snapped back to normal as she stepped into the kitchen. The back door was locked too, the key no longer under the mint pot on the windowsill. But the little side door into the garage opened under her touch. Even in the half-light she could see the control for the garage door was gone from the nearest shelf, but still she let her fingers confirm it, brushing over the smooth plastic of mold sprays and stain removers, the sharp edges of a rusted mousetrap, the thick cardboard of a box of rat poison, then on to a bottle of drain cleaner and another of bleach.

Her mind went again to the girl who had survived the bleach only to be murdered.

This is the moment it happens if I don't stop it. There wasn't any way out of the house. Arguing would only end in injury, and fighting back was worse than pointless.

"You catch more flies with honey than vinegar." She'd heard that once on TV, and now it floated up from her memory. There were few enough ways she pleased her husband, but cooking had always been one of them.

Soon she was back in the kitchen, letting the familiarity of chopping, slicing, grinding push away thoughts of the task that lay at the end of it all. Pots hissed and saucepans bubbled as she stirred and seasoned, filling the air with the scent of garlic, onion, and spices. With her sleeves rolled up, the bruises mottling her arms could almost have been mistaken for a patterned undershirt.

"Are you listening to me?" Leila demanded, appearing at her side. "Cousin Huma heard them talking and she said they're already discussing where we'll live until I'm eighteen and he can get a spousal visa to come here. They're not just trying to find me someone—they're a day away from having it all agreed!"

Leila let out a choked noise when Samira didn't look up, just kept stirring, stirring.

"You don't believe me, and it's going to be too late—"

"Let me feed your father then—"

"Then what? I'm not going to just stand by and let him marry me to some stranger. You know what he's going to do to me when I say no, but I can't just go along with it!"

"He won't touch you."

"Look at your arms! You'll try to protect me, but you can't. Not unless I agree to the marriage. I want you to be safe—of course I want that—but I can't marry someone I don't . . . I can't . . . When I refuse, he won't just hurt you, he'll *kill* you, and then he'll kill me! We need to run. We need to get out of this house and—"

Samira lifted a lid. Richly scented steam wafted through the kitchen. "The front door is double-locked, and so is the back. He has all the keys," she said, stirring some more. The spoon dripped red sauce back into the pan. "And where would we go in this Lockdown?" She shook her head. "We just need to get through the meal, then you will take Maryam upstairs to do her homework and I will sort things out with your father."

"Even your chicken Lahori can't work miracles," her daughter said, her slender neck bowed in despair.

"We shall see. Now, go fetch your sister and make sure she washes her hands."

"Mum, please . . . If we can just get out, we can go to the police, social services . . ."

"We will have lunch now, Leila," Samira said, her voice as clinical as the edge of her favorite knife. She wouldn't let Leila's terror drag her from the gentle embrace of the strange calm that had come to her on the staircase. For now, all her focus belonged to keeping her children safe. Because she would keep them safe. Whatever the cost.

"Go fetch your father," Samira ordered. "Then hurry back to help Maryam lay the table. Only ill will come of making trouble before we eat."

Leila wrenched away with a sob. As her daughter's footsteps faded down the hall, Samira turned to the crowded spice rack. Squashed in behind the cinnamon bark and the black mustard seeds was the extra-special ingredient she'd brought in from the garage to add to her husband's plate.

The visible corner of the packet showed a skull and crossbones.

6

The Watcher at the Window

R osemary! Fancy finding you here." I beam as I lift the little bay tree down from the "reduced" shelf in the DIY shop, popping open the child seat in the trolley and settling the pot there. "Petunia has been asking when she could have a friend over."

I saunter on down the pet aisle, humming along as "Feeling Good" belts over the tannoy. Pulling out my phone, I text a YouTube link for the song over to Charlie.

"You can find out anything online now, Rosemary. For instance, if you have a corpse you can't move, like a dead mouse in a wall cavity, one way to get rid of the smell is to pour in cat litter. It dries the body out and stops it stinking—genius!"

I lug a jumbo bag of cat litter into the trolley then, after a pause, add a second.

"Apparently vinegar and bicarb of soda set nearby can also help, but we've got those at home," I tell Rosemary as I turn past a rack of newspapers. The headlines helpfully inform me that *Domestic violence has soared in lockdown!*

How many other women stood at their kitchen counters today, their husbands gripping their wrists as the kettle roared to a boil?

Whatever happens next, I'll never be that woman again.

In the next aisle, a child of about seven is sitting on the floor tapping away at a handheld game. There's no one beside her, but when I look further along I see a teenager wearing glorious purple boots to match her hijab—clearly the older sister. She's looking through a rail of shower curtains printed with photos of far-flung destinations—a jungle, a beach, a cave behind a waterfall.

"What am I going to say?" she hisses into the mobile held nearly to her lips. "'Oh, I'm sorry, Uncle Ayaan, my father's wrapped up in Bali right now.'" She glances around self-consciously, flinching when she sees me.

I give her the brightest smile I can muster, hoping it shows in my eyes even if she can't see my mouth under my mask. "Take care now," I call cheerfully as I walk by, sneaking a look into her trolley as I go. I wonder what a teenager wants with rope and gaffer tape, though I'm reassured to see two large bags of cat litter too. I was worried mine would be suspicious, especially with my other seemingly random purchases, but maybe odd combinations of items are the new normal, given the pandemic.

It leaves me with a sense of déjà vu, but I'm soon distracted by the sheer scale of the display of saws. Who knew there were so many types? I peer at the labels, but none offers anything helpful like "ideal for dismemberment." There isn't even one that says "suitable for wood and bone."

With a sigh, I pick one with a wooden handgrip and a blade

as long as my arm. After a moment, I add a little hacksaw, swapping at the last minute from one with a blue grip to a deep red. "So it doesn't get stained with the"—I glance around—"rust."

I add a third saw for luck.

When I finally reach the tills, I'm so busy thinking about the horrors that lie ahead it's only as I park myself on one of the socially distanced queueing marks that I realize the girl with the matching trolley is standing in the next lane, staring blankly down at her mobile. She jumps when her younger sister barrels up and throws a packet of sweets into the trolley. It is promptly taken back out.

The child opens her eyes wide and beseeching. "If Dad's self-isolating in the garage, he won't find out. Ple-e-ease, Leila!"

Leila turns back to her phone.

"A girl in my class says that her mum says that the world's ending," her sister continues, undaunted. "This is Plague and then there's Famine. If there's going to be Famine, we should all eat sweets while we can."

Leila doesn't lift her eyes from the phone.

"It's not fair!" her sister whines, kicking out at the wheel of the trolley. "Ow!" she squeals, clutching her foot.

"You know how you were asking what instant karma meant the other day? That," Leila says, pointing, "is it. Right there."

The woman behind me clears her throat noisily. Realizing my till is free, I hurry forward and start unloading.

"Wish I'd thought of a tarp," says the cashier dolefully.

I nearly drop the coil of rope as I spin to stare at her.

A frown crosses her face when she sees my expression. "For under the litter tray, when you're toilet training, right? Or are you getting a Lockdown cat rather than a puppy?"

"A cat!" I cry. "Yes! I'm getting a cat! Kitten! Cat!"

The woman looks at me as if I'm mad. Then my collection of saws sails down the conveyor belt.

"They're not for the cat! Obviously. Ha-ha," I say brightly. Then I realize I said the "ha-ha" out loud. "It's . . . They're . . . for a bush," I hurry on desperately. "I've got to do some pruning. Bush pruning."

The cashier is still staring at the saws. "Most people use secateurs," she says faintly. "I could get someone to fetch you a pair if you'd like?"

"Yes! Secateurs. Lovely! Thank you!"

She puts out an assistance request, looking as if she'd prefer to be calling for a straitjacket. "And, um, did you need a litter tray?" she asks tentatively.

"Litter tray?"

"For the cat," she says, looking pointedly at the massive bags of cat litter.

"Oh, yes! I mean, no. I mean, I'm all set."

The woman reaches to take back the saws, but I hastily start packing them in with the rest. "I'll keep these anyway. Can't ever have too many tools, can you? And I've got all of Lockdown to figure out what to use them for, right? Who knows what I'll be able to fix."

AS I HAUL CAT litter out of the car twenty minutes later, the curtains twitch in the front room of the house opposite. Reaching back into the boot, I hunch over the bag with the saws sticking up at one corner. With difficulty, I fumble the keys into the lock, so I can set the bag behind the front door without showing my cargo to the street.

It does beg the question of how I'm going to move Jim past the eagle-eyed gaze of Edwina, the neighborhood's unofficial Covid-regulations inspector, who lives opposite. Maybe if I do enough weird stuff in the run-up, no one will suspect a thing when I move into the body-disposal phase of my life as a secret widow.

"She may never have met a person she can't alienate on sight," I tell Rosemary as I retrieve her from the passenger seat where I'd belted her in for the drive, "but she's no dummy. If only she were senile, even if she did see something dodgy no one would believe her."

Glancing over at Edwina's energetic curtains, a movement at the corner of my vision draws my attention.

A woman is struggling down the street, puffing under the weight of four overstuffed shopping bags. Even so, she steps down into the road as a pair of teenage boys approaches.

"Afternoon!" she calls as they pass.

One boy flips her off while the other, busy pushing a sweet wrapper into a hedge, ignores her completely.

I sigh, making a mental note to fetch the litter after I've finished bringing in the shopping, but the woman is already plucking it out of the leaves. Folding it into a tissue, she tucks it away in her pocket.

Something about it tugs at me—I know nothing about this woman and yet, in that one moment, we might have been the same person.

It makes the house feel even lonelier as I let myself in and join Jim in the kitchen once more. *I will be alone in this forever,* I think as I set my new saws on the counter.

Before today, Lockdown was a disaster, turning my life into a waking nightmare. Now it's a reprieve—but one that won't last. By the time the world goes back to normal, I need to be rid of Jim for good.

7

The Art of Desiccation

Any thoughts?" I ask Rosemary and Petunia, as I stare down at Jim and the tarpaulin stretched out beside him. "I suppose I could roll him, but . . ."

I don't want to see what Granny's skillet did to his skull if there's a way to avoid it. Just the thought makes my stomach roil, but I can't leave him where he is.

Pulling on a pair of rubber gloves, I crouch by his feet and lift them, only to shriek and scramble away, shocked by how pliant the body is. For a horrible second, I expect him to just dissolve, like in a horror film. When nothing happens, I edge forward again and poke his leg.

"I thought you'd be stiff as a board," I tell him. "Does rigor mortis come later?" I glance at my phone. "Yet another thing I'd better not google. The dead deer was one thing, but it can't look like a pattern."

Taking a deep breath, I lift his feet once more and set them down on the tarp before shuffling up to his waist. "Lift with your legs," I remind myself as, with a grunt, I manage to shift his middle over. I reposition myself by his shoulders, close my eyes, and heft his torso up.

A scrunching noise forces me to open one eye, then the

other. Jim's forehead, trailing just above the floor, is wrinkling up the edge of the tarp.

With a whimper of disgust, I raise his shoulders high enough for clearance, then set him face down on the tarp. Repeating the process from top to bottom, I gradually shift him sideways until his whole body is a comfortable three feet from the edge.

I nearly gag at the mess where his head was. Pulling myself together, I take up the cloth and bleach I set out earlier and get to work, attacking the grouting with Jim's toothbrush till there's no sign that anything untoward happened. Well, ignoring the body on the tarp.

Afterward, I put the cloth, toothbrush, and rubber gloves next to Jim's feet and help myself to a large glass of cooking sherry and most of a block of Brie.

"I need something to soak up the alcohol," I tell Rosemary and Petunia, who wisely say nothing.

Next, with a lot of heaving and shoving, I manage to get the jumbo bags of cat litter lined up next to the tarp. I attack the top of the first with a kitchen knife, leaving a ragged gash in the plastic.

Scooping pellets into a measuring jug, I raise it over Jim's feet, then freeze.

This is the point of no return: the minute the cat litter goes on him, the police are never going to believe it was an accident or self-defense. It would look bad that I've taken so long to call them, but I still could. If I do it now.

I look over at the phone, then down at the jug in my hand.

Would he have killed me if I hadn't hit him with the skillet? What if I'd called the police when I first realized how bad Lockdown was going to make it? What if I'd called them the day

Amy moved out? What if I'd left years ago? Taken the kids and gone . . . or not been with him in the first place.

But without Jim there would be no Charlie, no Amy.

I stare down at their dead father. How do I fit those pieces together—my love for my children and what I've done? Maybe it's impossible. But it's equally impossible to change it, and anything is better than my children finding out the truth of who their parents are. This is the only way I can protect them now.

Letting the dizzying sense of unreality sweep me away, I raise the jug once more.

Just do it, I tell myself. *You don't have any other option, so just tip that jug and pour the cat litter on your husband's corpse.*

A snort escapes me, then a laugh. Alice is well and truly down the rabbit hole, but if going a bit mad is the only way I can do what needs to be done, then so be it.

"Bottoms up, dear," I say, and tip the jug over my husband's feet.

A mist of dust billows up, sending me stumbling to the back door to waft it out into the garden. When the air clears, I snap on a mask and return to decanting the cat litter—in a slow, steady trickle—over Jim's ankles, calves, knees, thighs. Once the bag is half empty, I heft it into my arms, staggering under the weight as I pour it over his waist and back, then finally his head.

I repeat the process with the second bag, then snap off my gloves and cross to the cupboard, pulling out every packet of rice and salt I have, then sprinkling them over the top. If you put wet phones in rice to rescue them, it must do the same sort of thing as cat litter. And the salt should keep any bugs at bay.

"Just like our wedding day!" I say as I scatter my husband with rice. "Only now all the violence is already behind us."

With that happy thought, I flap the short edge of the tarp over Jim's back before crouching beside the body, one hand on his shoulder and the other on his nearest hip. If the cat litter and rice are to do their work, I need Jim parceled up nice and airtight. And if the cat litter and salt don't work, it'll be even more important to stop the smell and the likely . . . seepage.

Staggering over to the sink, I splash cold water onto the back of my neck until the nausea subsides. It is all I can do to force away thoughts of what will soon be happening inside the tarp to Jim. My husband. My children's father. Who was alive yesterday and today is dead because I killed him, and is now about to be parceled up like the world's most appalling present.

I focus on the task at hand.

"This is quite the exercise routine," I huff as I slowly lever Jim up high enough on to his side that I can rock him back and forth till gravity takes hold and he tumbles on to his front, safely encased in a roll of tarp so I don't have to see any of the grisly details.

Several repeats later, Jim is a neat little parcel tied carefully with rope and secured with gaffer tape at every edge. I fetch a glass of wine and sit massaging the heel of my hand into my eye socket, trying to push the images, sounds, and sensations out of my mind before they can become memories.

Dragging over my shopping-list notepad, I flip to a fresh page.

Get Rid of Jim, I write at the top, then underline it, and add **Item 1: Wrap and leave to desiccate.** I draw a big tick next to it.

My headache pulses, so I try pressing my knuckles into the other eye instead. That doesn't help either.

Item 2: Set out vinegar and bicarb of soda dishes. Another tick.

Dragging myself to my feet, I fetch a soup bowl, slosh some vinegar into it, and set it by Jim's head like an offering. Then I fetch the open bicarb of soda from the fridge and place it beside his feet.

Item 3: Find somewhere to dispose of body.

Ticking this off will have to wait, as I've no idea where I could put him—and whether I'll even be able to move him.

"I'll come up with something," I tell Rosemary and Petunia defensively. "Won't I?"

There follows a long, long silence.

8

If You Go Down
to the Woods Tonight

Two hours later I have a lot of crossed-out notes and absolutely no solutions.

"If I can't put you in the garden, where could I bury you deep enough that a dog or fox won't dig you right back up? It needs to be somewhere I won't draw attention while preparing such a big hole," I tell Jim as I work my way through a dinner of ice cream followed by more ice cream.

As I go to toss the carton into the paper recycling, I pause then peer closer at the folded newspaper on the top: the front page shows a group of volunteer gravediggers hard at work in a field. The headline proclaims, *Covid death toll surges: funeral and burial services unable to keep up with demand.*

My eyes travel to Jim, then back to the paper. There are an awful lot of fresh graves around. Would anyone notice if one too many was filled in? Probably. But what if I dug one down just enough to pop Jim in then cover him over? Surely once the intended occupant was put in on top no one would ever find him.

I write a note, then circle the line with a flourish.

Despite being so tired my eyes keep crossing, I stuff myself into Jim's coat and hat and take myself off to the local churchyard to scout the terrain. A second outing, even in the middle of the night, is a risk given the restrictions, but surely it's an even greater one to leave Jim on the kitchen floor a minute longer than I have to.

Slipping through the ancient lych-gate, I start down the narrow path between the oldest gravestones, but soon falter to a stop as I realize how far it is to the field that houses the newer residents. There's no way I can carry or even drag Jim this far. Could I bring him in a wheelbarrow?

I nearly shriek as light falls on the side of my face. Spinning round, I find I'm standing in front of the vicar's cottage. A warm yellow glow gilds the opening magnolia buds on the tree nestled against the wall that separates garden from graveyard.

The vicarage window opens and a voice calls out, "We're happy to talk if you're in need of comfort."

Bog off! shouts the voice in my head, but I manage to clamp my lips shut before the words can escape. After all, it would be a lovely gesture if it hadn't scuppered my only half-decent corpse-disposal plan.

"All good, thanks! Just getting some exercise!" I shout back as cheerfully as I can while fighting the urge to scream every swear word I've ever heard. "Sorry to disturb you!"

"Stay safe!"

Yes, I think to myself. *Yes, I am safe now. That's the whole point.*

"*Porca miseria!*" I mutter under my breath as I scuttle away. I have no idea what the words mean: Janey taught them to me after her family went to Italy one summer when we were about ten.

Janey, says the ache in my chest.

Does she still remember it? The pair of us giggling on the wall of the playground. Even if we were still friends, she probably wouldn't. That moment was nothing to her, but to me her return was the world grown suddenly bright again after a gray fortnight spent trudging the woods alone to avoid the alternate silence and shouting at home.

The night air is warm and heavy with the scent of May blossom. Something about the quietness—everyone at home, only a few distant cars audible—makes the night feel safe, even though it's past twelve and I'm all alone as I slip from the churchyard on to the street and then into the woods, winding my way between the trees into shadow. Moonlight falls through budding branches, making trelliswork of the ground.

Roots trip me and branches dangle brambles that tear at my clothes. No kindly dryad appears to show me an old abandoned well or mineshaft, or even a handy, recently vacated animal burrow large enough to fit a human.

Filthy, scratched, and ready to fall asleep against a tree, I finally admit defeat and turn back. There are no solutions to my situation here.

A few streets from home, I round a dark corner and go flying over a food-recycling bin tipped on its side at the edge of a driveway. A pair of glowing eyes looms out of the darkness.

I scuttle backward then stagger to my feet, but nothing rushes at me. Instead, a thin young fox edges out of the shadows and trots away, a chicken carcass hanging from its mouth.

A few feet away, a wooden bench sits under a thin, listing tree. I sink down onto it, only to flinch as something leaps up beside me.

"*Maoh?*" says the green-eyed cat, nuzzling hopefully at my hand.

"You think I'm going to pet you when you've just given me

a heart attack?" I ask, but my hand lifts all the same and starts stroking the cat's back. It arches into my touch, purring so loud and hoarse it makes me think of Jim's electric shaver. Only that didn't purr so much as buzz with a threatening undercurrent. It always made me think of wasps and the way their low vibration suddenly explodes into sharp nearness no matter how quietly you walk, how still you stay, like an ordinary morning shattering into stinging pain, into bruises and burns because of the wrong word, wrong tone, wrong place to set the cup down, *why did you do that, you stupid—*

If Jim is a wasp, he's a dead one now, I remind myself.

The only danger is how I dispose of his corpse. I am not going to get Jim out of the house unseen, let alone into an illicit grave, in one piece. It's just not possible without being caught.

"I really am going to have to dismember him, aren't I?" I thought the words would die on my tongue, but they come out smoothly, calmly.

The cat eyes me disdainfully then pushes its head into my palm, asserting its right to more diligent petting. The world goes on turning and no thunderbolt strikes me dead. What lies ahead won't be fun, but it's survivable.

"I suppose it can't be any worse than having to live with him," I tell the cat. My eyes fall on the food bin.

"He definitely counts as compostable, even desiccated," I say consideringly, "but I'd have to cut him up into an awful lot of pieces to fit him in one of those. And with those flimsy biodegradable bags . . ."

The cat swivels its head away from my fingers, peering eagerly into the darkness.

"Well, what's your suggestion?"

The cat springs away. A moment later there's a skirmish in the bushes. Something squeaks, high and plaintive. The cat emerges with a shrew hanging limply from its mouth. It watches me as if waiting to be told off.

"I can't exactly criticize, can I? But no, I'm not going to take a leaf out of your book and eat Jim. Thank you all the same."

When the cat throws itself down and starts making horrible crackling-crunching sounds, I head for home, but I've barely turned the corner when something else makes me stop. For a moment, I can't figure out what caught my attention. Then I hear it again: a sob, quickly stifled.

Straining my ears, I catch the sound of harsh breathing from the left. Creeping forward, I follow it to a fence and press my eye to a knothole in the planks.

In the garden beyond stands a woman, face tilted to the sky. I can't make out her eyes, but the moonlight paints the lines and curves of her brow, cheek, jaw. The darkness of her skin is a drop of warmth in the night where my own fingers, hooked into a fence strut at eye level, look almost greenish.

The sound of a door opening signals the patio light going on, bathing the woman in brightness. In the second before she turns away, I see the side of her face that had been in shadow and register, with a jolt, that something is wrong. One eye is smaller than the other, the lid puffy and . . .

Mingled familiarity and unfamiliarity lance through me. I'm used to blue-green bruises submerged by ivory makeup. This woman bears a reddish-purple glow under dark brown foundation.

A muffled shout rings out from the house. The threat in it tells me the bruise is no accident.

The woman hurries back up the path.

My pulse beats in my throat as I stare into the garden beyond the fence. Should I call out? What would I say?

I wait, straining anxiously after sounds of violence in the house, but soon the patio light goes out again. All remains quiet. Reluctantly I head home.

As I let myself in, the curtain twitches in Edwina's front room.

9

Home Sweet Home

A few streets away, Ruth pulled her bedroom curtains closed on a dim view of the garden, wishing she dared run back out to the safety of the darkness. But now her husband had called her in, in she would have to stay.

Lionel slammed open the wardrobe, throwing a fresh set of pajamas onto the bed. "How's the eye?" he asked gruffly.

"Already better," she lied, turning the unbruised side of her face as she smiled over her shoulder at him.

"I just wasn't expecting you to start in is all. Not right then. Knowing I'd just been on with the bloody tax office and . . ." He grabbed a pillow, pounding it into shape then tossing it down and seizing the next.

"I thought it would help to have two incomes again."

"Thanks for the vote of confidence. Ten years I've been providing for us, and you can't give me a break with a pandemic on."

"Lionel . . ." Moving away from the window, Ruth put her hands pleadingly over his as he grabbed another pillow. "You know that's not it. They're desperate for nurses," she said, sounding equally desperate herself. "I can't bear knowing I have all these skills and I'm just sitting here at home."

Her husband shook her off to grab the duvet. Sighing, Ruth went to the other side and together they lifted it for shaking, Lionel jerking the fabric so hard it ripped from her hands.

"I can't believe you'd guilt me over that too. You willing to chalk us up as another pair of statistics? You've seen the news—people of color twice as likely to die—and you want to go to a place that's guaranteed to be full of Covid. Your sainted mother would be so proud of you, killing your husband and yourself to boot—"

"She'd want me to help," Ruth pleaded. "I can take precautions—wash as soon as I come in, leave my bag and coat in the hall, put my clothes in the wash every day. I could even sleep on the sofa, then—"

Lionel crossed his arms over his chest so his muscles bulged menacingly. "Oh, so I'm going to be given the plague *and* denied having my wife in my bed? You looking for an excuse to stop me touching you?" he asked, moving closer. "Because you've been playing some games recently and I'm about done—"

Since she was already wearing the consequences of backing away, against every instinct Ruth reached out. "Of course not!" Cupping his cheek in one gentle hand, she drew herself to him. "I just meant if you were worried about the germs—"

"If I'm worried about the germs, I get a cold bed. That's a nice piece of blackmail."

"You know I didn't mean it like that. You're just twisting—"

He shoved her away so roughly she stumbled back against the bureau, grazing the fragile skin along the underside of her arm. "*I'm* twisting?" His eyes narrowed. "What's this 'second income' stuff really about? Why'd you want to make me feel bad we had to pinch a few pennies the last month? What's really going on?"

He stalked toward her, trapping her against the wall as he pushed his face into hers. "It's that woman from the hospital—the fat one with the frizzy red hair. Always sticking her nose in—inviting you here, inviting you there: trying to get you to stop out at night like some slut."

"It was just a few people having dinner, and that was *weeks* before Lockdown. You can't still be—"

"A few people, yeah?" he snapped.

She turned her face as spittle misted her cheek.

"Not 'the girls' after all then. That fancy boss of yours from before—he there?"

Ruth's eyes widened. "You *know* I'd never cheat. You know that." Swallowing her fear and the revulsion, she reached for him tenderly. "You've nothing to worry about."

And though there were tears in her eyes and her voice cracked on the words, he lent in for a kiss that quickly roughened as if she were bright-eyed and eager. Catching her own eyes in the mirror as his hands went to the buttons of her shirt, she heard herself sob at the despair in the face that looked back at her.

Lionel laughed, low and full of heat as if she were gasping with lust instead of weeping, and it felt like madness. Because he had to know . . . but what could she do other than pretend? And whose fault was it then?

She looked from her own face to the shadow of his reflection, and that felt like madness too. Because it couldn't be her, couldn't be him, couldn't be real. Just something happening over there, in the mirror.

But how she wanted to help that woman. She'd never been someone who looked away from those in trouble: never been one to stand by and do nothing. And yet now she froze, unable to move, as if she'd lost control of her body or stepped outside it somehow. She knew she needed to fight her way back to it so she could stop what was happening to the woman in the mirror. But she knew too that she'd fail.

The despair held her immobile. What was the point in fighting when there was no hope of winning—when all she would do is make it even worse?

But what happens when there's no worse for it to get? the woman's eyes seemed to ask. *What will you do when there's nothing left to lose?*

10

The First Day of
the Rest of My Life

When I accidentally catch sight of my reflection in the oven door at lunchtime, I have to stop and look closer. Maybe it's wishful thinking, but I seem younger. I certainly look an awful lot happier. I glance down at Jim, then back at my reflection. Yup, still happier, corpse and all.

"If money buys cake and cake is a type of happiness," I muse to Rosemary and Petunia as I give them a drink from the jug Jim's parents gave us as a wedding present but which he would only allow to be used at Christmas, "it follows that I need much, much more cake. And cheese. I need all the cheese. And not a single sodding baked bean," I add as I sit down to start a shopping list.

Biscuits. Wine. Crackers. Wine. CHOCOLATE. I underline the last twice to be on the safe side. Then I add a title: Be Happy List.

"Maybe the whole retail therapy thing isn't such a joke after all." I brush my fingers through Rosemary's leaves, letting the heady scent fill the air. "But maybe sticking to food is thinking too small."

New clothes, I write, then squish the word "happy" in at an angle after "new."

Next on the list goes **karaoke machine**.

"This house is going to be full of song," I tell Rosemary and Petunia. I glance down at the Jim-parcel. "Get over it."

As if on cue, a text chimes in from Charlie. For a moment I dither, then I think about why we're reduced to texting love through song: why all the music, fun, and laughter of his childhood happened when Jim wasn't there.

How early in my children's lives did the refrain of "Daddy has a headache," "Daddy's very tired today," "Daddy just needs a little peace and quiet" become "Dad's home," with nothing more needing to be said? I don't even remember. Too early. I used to tell myself how lucky I was that they were such considerate children, but I knew it wasn't normal.

They weren't quiet for Jim, but for me. I can see that now— see that even though Jim never hit them, rarely yelled, they knew I wasn't just concerned for their father. That alone wouldn't have kept Charlie from playing music, wouldn't have stopped Amy's nonstop clattering and chattering. They knew I was afraid, so they were quiet when their father was home, gentle with doors and stairs and furniture, as if the house itself needed pacifying.

I saw it, but I never let myself think about it because I was too focused on how different their childhood was to mine to see all the ways it was the same.

What did they know about me and Jim? I want to believe it was nothing, but somehow, in that "out of the corner of my eye" way, I've always known that's not true. The proof is in my hand—Charlie sends me a song every day because I don't dare call him and he doesn't dare call me.

"Why are you afraid of telling him to stop interfering with your phone?" he asked after the second time he and Jim fought over Jim answering my phone.

"You're making too much of it, Charlie," I said, with a "come on now" laugh. "I *have* told him not to, but he's just so bored in the Lockdown."

"Then how come last year you told me to call, not text, so Dad and I couldn't get into it over him reading my messages? It's really weird, Mum. Do you honestly not see it?"

"I know it irritates you, darling, but all families get on each other's nerves sometimes, wanting to be in on their children's business. He just feels left out."

I told myself Charlie dropped it because I'd soothed his worries, but did I believe it, even then?

I hit the latest song link and the opening bars of Kelly Clarkson's "Because of You" fill the kitchen.

I almost turn it off again but draw my hand back. Soon this won't be my only connection with my son. But not if I let myself get lost in the past. There will be time for that later. For now, I need to remind myself of everything I will lose if I don't find a solution to getting rid of Jim.

I return to my *Be Happy List* and add, **Get a cat once Jim is out of the way.** With a sigh, I add, **Find alternative home for cat in case of ending up in prison.**

I stare at the words, the music suddenly discordant and eerie. Finally, I scratch out the line and add a better one: **Don't end up in prison.**

———

TWITCH-TWITCH GO THE CURTAINS in Edwina's front room as I trudge into the drive two hours later, laden with shopping. Can she really just sit there all day *and* all night? Did she die and leave behind an extremely nosy ghost?

I peer nervously at the Jim-parcel as I stuff ice cream into the freezer, but there's no apparition hovering by the bread bin. Still, I can't help wondering what sort of ghost Jim would be: a wan little shadow trailing cat litter, or even more vicious and dangerous than when he was alive. The thought sees me edging my hand carefully round to grasp the kettle's handle as it comes to the boil in case it suddenly tips itself over my wrist as if Jim is still here, still able to hurt me. I close my eyes against an image of him looming over me, weight pressing me against the counter, clawlike, spectral hands grasping at me . . .

I force the image away, replacing it with the memory of a rainy afternoon sprawled across Janey's bed, teaching ourselves how to do French braids as she spun ghost stories from thin air. For a moment, I smile, remembering the feel of her hair in my hands, the warmth of the handknitted blanket we huddled under as rain gusted against her window.

A second later, the comfort of the memory washes away on a riptide of grief for all the time and anger between us. With Jim dead, what was the point in losing my best friend?

Janey, says my heart.

My gaze goes to my phone. I deactivated my Facebook account ages ago so Jim wouldn't be tempted to interact with anyone "on my behalf."

What is Janey doing now? How is she spending the Lockdown? The last time we saw each other was at my mum's funeral five years ago, and though I'd hoped it would be like Dad's—something that would bring us back together—the awkwardness between us felt unbridgeable. By the time I'd found the courage to talk to her, she was gone and that was that. She didn't call me again, and I didn't call her.

I know she's still in touch with the kids—sends them birthday cards and presents. I want to believe she's still in their lives as a way of being in mine, but even if it's just for their sake I'm grateful to know they didn't lose her too.

I pick up my phone. It's cold to the touch.

She'll either be willing to talk . . . or not.

Unable to bear the thought, I put the phone down and grab the bleach out of the shopping bag. Nothing quite punctures the temptation to get lost in thought (good or bad) than cleaning the loo, so I take myself off to do just that.

Yet as I scrub all I can think about is whether Janey still lives only a few miles away. After Jim is gone and the restrictions ease, what would happen if I went over? Could I bear it if she slammed the door in my face? Even after five years it's Janey whose name turns me inside out, whereas I didn't even flinch this morning when I walked past Jim's corpse to make breakfast. Perhaps I should feel guilty about that, but I don't. His loss feels like relief. And though I'm not yet ready to face it, the thing I'm afraid to let myself start mourning is not him at all, but everything he took from me.

Pushing the tangle of misery away, I head back outside to bring in the recycling bins. The wheels insist on getting stuck in every crack and hole. I'm dragging the last one into the corner of the drive when Edwina's door opens.

I hunch into myself as she comes marching over. Is she just

extra bored or could she have put two and two together and twigged that she hasn't seen any sign of Jim?

I'm just working myself into a panic when I realize she's not looking at me. I spin round to find my next-door neighbor climbing out of her car.

"Good afternoon, Nawar," Edwina calls across the street, every inch the retired headmistress. "Is everything quite all right? Only I noticed that you were out earlier today too, and we *are* only allowed one shopping trip and one hour of outdoor exercise per day, you know."

Although I feel bad for leaving Nawar to it, I whisk myself back inside.

"Yes, I know it's a lot of cake," I tell Petunia's yellow face, which takes on a judgmental cast as I unload the rest of the shopping onto the counter. "But I've got a lot to do."

Then, to prove it, I finally bend over my notepad and add the task that should have been number one on my *Be Happy List*: *Get a job.*

The pen nearly pierces the page as I dig into the curve of the G, then goes faint on the downward stroke of the J as if the ink has run dry.

I still remember the day I showed Jim a job advert in the paper, only for him to throw it straight in the bin—"For goodness' sake, Sally! The kids are too young!" Only nothing changed when they moved from primary to secondary. And what did I do? Pretended it didn't matter—that I was content and fulfilled and didn't need independence or self-worth or other adults in my life who might have seen me differently: who might have helped me see myself differently.

It was the pretending that destroyed everything with Janey.

She probably thinks I still don't understand, but the truth is that I did from the start. She thought that if she could just shatter the warped mirror I was holding up to my life then I'd be able to walk away. When that failed, she showed me how it was done by walking away from me. I tried to believe it was an act of cruelty but knew the truth was that she couldn't stand to watch as my world got smaller and I got smaller to fit. I'd lived it with my own mother so of course I understood, but I wasn't ready, wasn't able, wasn't willing . . . wasn't whatever I had to be to leave.

Looking down at Jim, I expect to feel weak—drained by all the years that led me here. But I don't. I feel strong. Not in the big, bold way that I always thought was what I lacked, but in a small, quiet way.

After all these years, there it is.

When this is all over and Jim is gone—not just from the land of the living but the kitchen floor too—I am going to get myself a job and then I am going to call my best friend and tell her. And if she won't talk to me, I'll write to her. Even if she doesn't ever write back, I need her to know how much I love her.

Needing more comfort than cake can provide, I head upstairs and fetch the fluffy cat slippers Charlie got me as a joke but which Jim hated too much for me to ever wear. I've barely stepped back into the kitchen when my foot snags on the bottom of the Jim-parcel, sending me tripping into the counter as if to punish me.

"You're done giving me bruises," I hiss at him, narrowly resisting the urge to kick him, as he so often did to me.

The fresh wave of memories drives me into the garden, but still the images hang before my eyes like cobwebs. Then a robin swoops down on to the lawn just a meter or so away, cocking his head at me, and I realize that the air is sweet with the scent of lilac blossom and the sun is shining—wanly, but shining all the same.

I'm not out of the woods yet, but I've had a good morning: the best in a long time. I've chosen my clothes to please myself. I've eaten what I wanted. I've sung when the mood took me. And I've spent not a single minute wondering how I could make sure that today Jim didn't hurt me.

11

All the Lonely People

When I head out for some exercise (and to see if wandering around will give me some fresh disposal-site ideas), I am surprised to find Edwina standing by the little patch of scrubland—a tangle of brambles, weeds, and spindly self-seeded trees—that stretches along the end of the street.

"Enjoying your outing for the day?" she calls. "What does your husband think about you going out so often?"

"Absolutely nothing," I tell her truthfully. "Doesn't even notice these days."

Edwina's eyes narrow. "Didn't he used to do all the shopping at the start of Lockdown? If he's showing symptoms, you're both required to self-isolate, you know. Creeping out at midnight is no solution if he's ill. Don't deny it," she says, wagging a finger at me. "I was getting a glass of water late last night and there he was, scuttling off around the corner."

The flash of irritation that she spotted me is quickly tempered by the realization that not only have I accidentally hit on a way to double the number of times I can leave the house each day, Edwina is now witness to "Jim" being alive and well the night after his death.

"Jim is showing no symptoms whatsoever," I tell her truthfully. "He's just . . . having a quiet time." My eyes fall on a bucket, trowel, and pair of secateurs beside a little patch of cleared ground next to a small cherry tree. Bulbs are sending up shoots from between the roots. "I didn't realize you were working on a project here. Are the bulbs daffs?"

"White narcissus and black gladioli," Edwina says with a sniff. Then her expression shifts, but she turns to look at the tree before I can pin down what emotion I'm seeing. "Every year I clear another foot, add a few more bulbs. It's seven years now since I started with the cherry and the winter aconites. I'll never manage to clear the whole area, but at least I can make a little patch of color."

As I watch, she shifts her sights to a woman approaching with a pram. The woman's eyes widen as she clocks Edwina. Ducking her head, she crosses the street and scuttles past.

For a second, Edwina's face morphs into a mask of misery, then she turns away with a tut.

It hadn't even occurred to me before, but as a widow she must be even lonelier than normal in Lockdown. Has she spoken to *anyone*, apart from the neighbors she's told off? Suddenly, all the scoldings and nosiness take on a different tone. And with that comes the germ of an idea. Plus two new items for my *Be Happy List*: **baking** and **gardening**.

I used to love growing things with the kids. There's a picture on the bookcase of Amy and Charlie dwarfed by a towering sunflower. In an album hidden at the back of the shelf above the wardrobe there's one almost exactly the same of me, Mum, and Granny. I'd planned to keep up the tradition, but Jim complained that it was cruel for me to stuff our garden full of flowers when he suffered from hay fever. The next year I only did a few trays of seedlings, then the year after just the sunflowers. The year after that, when the kids didn't mention it, I pretended to myself that they were too big and didn't want to bother anymore. But Charlie made sure the Mother's Day card they drew for me that year was of sunflowers. There's been a similar card every year since.

Suddenly I want to rush home and order Charlie a bunch of sunflowers, but of course I can't. It would practically announce that something huge has happened, and the last thing I need is Charlie coming round in a worry about what it could be. Still, I could order some seeds so that when this is all over we can restart our tradition.

There's nothing I can do about all those lost years, but perhaps if I plant some seeds now, by the time they bloom everything will be different.

AN HOUR LATER, I wave to Edwina through her front window as I balance a tin of freshly baked shortbread on her wall. Maybe it'll cheer her up—or maybe she'll decide it's a hanging offense. Either way, I've got to do *something* if I'm to get a body past her.

I hurry to explain myself when she opens the door, then brace for impact, but she just nods.

"Thank you. That was a kind thought," she says tightly.

I try not to believe the words pain her, but it does look more like she's just sucked on a lemon than tried out a smile.

"But don't think you can mollify me with this then break the rules," she adds sternly.

"Actually, it was an advance thank you. I was hoping you might help me with a few gardening tips. If I'm going to be stuck at home, I want to spruce the back up a little and I thought maybe you could be my guide to the wonderful world of not killing things?"

I wince as the words come out, but Edwina, of course, is thinking of dead plants, not people, as purpose kindles in her shrewd gray eyes. Guilt flutters unexpectedly in my stomach. Maybe my plan for distracting Edwina from my corpse-disposal endeavors needs to include a little companionship. It would be nice to be useful.

While the *Get Rid of Jim List* is necessary and the *Be Happy List* hopeful, what I really need is some bigger, better purpose. Befriending Edwina is a small enough thing, but it's not the world's worst place to start.

As I lie in bed that night, I try to think heartwarming thoughts about bringing the neighborhood together. Maybe we could raise some money for a community project, or we could throw a street party when the Lockdown ends. I imagine tables marching down the middle of the road, paper tablecloths rippling in the wind, every front garden overflowing with blossoms. And yet as I fall into sleep I dream the wind whips up, blowing the petals off the flowers until every branch and stem is bare. It blows the tablecloths away, then the tables too, rolling them over and over till they crash into Edwina's cherry tree, snapping its slender trunk and strewing its limbs across the street.

And still the wind blows, sending me tottering down the street and round the corner into the road where I grew up, as if the two towns have twined into one. On I walk, turning then turning again, but everywhere I look the fences and walls are papered with posters showing every injury Jim ever gave me.

Frantic, I double back, only to find a woman standing in my path, staring up at the sky as she cries blue-white tears over the red-purple bruises that glow under her skin.

Despair rushes up my throat.

I wake with a sob.

12

Favorite Ghost Stories
for Infants

On the other side of town a very, very tired new mother nearly wept as she woke to the sound of her baby beginning to grizzle in the way she knew promised imminent screaming. However, this was only a footnote problem; as she rolled toward the edge of the bed, ready to pull her aching body out of the warm sheets, her husband put out his foot and kicked her to the cold floor.

"Get that shrieking little fuck out of here," he mumbled, pulling his pillow over his head.

The very, very tired new mother stumbled over to the Moses basket, gathering her daughter into her arms. The rocking chair in the corner beckoned, but she lumbered into the hall, only to stand swaying at the top of the stairs before gravity got the best of her and she slumped down onto the top step.

A shadow loomed in the bedroom doorway. "Why are you so fucking useless?" her husband spat. "Can't you fuck off downstairs at least?"

"I'm too dizzy. I'll fall," whispered the very, very tired new mother, curling her daughter protectively away from his fury.

"Good riddance, the pair of you," he told her, then slammed the door.

The baby redoubled her yells.

The very, very tired mother tried rocking her, then burping her, then checking her nappy, then offering a breast.

"Please, darling," she croaked. "Please stop crying. Daddy doesn't mean it. He's just very, very tired. We're all so very, very tired."

The baby, of course, paid absolutely no attention and continued shrieking.

"At least it's a fierce sort of screaming, isn't it, my love? A demand, not a whimper." Her voice broke on the words, tears spilling onto her cheeks. "Well, fearsome little girls get stories to match, so why don't you quiet down and I'll tell you a tale of witches and ghosts and murder—all the best things in life. At least that's what my best friend used to say when I told her this story."

The very, very tired new mother sniffed as the longing for her oldest friend—as lost to her as her mother was to dementia—forced fresh tears to her eyes. Neither could rescue her now, even if she asked for help. But maybe if she just hung on a little longer everything would go back to the way it was. It would all be fine if they could just go back.

They'd been so happy. Truly happy. Then he'd said, "Let's have a baby," and she'd thought, "Well, it's now or never, and maybe I do want that." Only she'd wanted it with the marriage she thought they had. Nearly five years came apart in the first two months of pregnancy. The nausea and exhaustion set in almost immediately, upending expectations that city breaks and their usual hectic social schedule could carry on as normal until at least the fifth month. The canceled restaurant reservations, theater tickets, and party invitations were bad enough, but when her interest in sex was replaced by a near-constant urge to vomit, Keith's frustration festered into something darker. Soon bored squabbling became shouting, but she told herself it didn't matter if sometimes it seemed that they didn't even like each other anymore. It would pass.

Only, instead, it got worse . . . then suddenly it was something else entirely. But she told herself it was just temporary. Just the stresses of impending fatherhood . . .

But the stresses of new fatherhood proved even worse. And then Lockdown arrived and it was like a different person had slipped into her husband's skin. A nightmare from her most ghoulish stories.

"How did I get here?" The words dissolved into the darkness.

Perhaps it would have been easier if there were regrets to shout into the night, but all she had was grief for the life she thought she'd be living, with the man she thought she'd married.

Swallowing away the wash of loneliness, she propped herself against the newel post and tucked the baby close, offering her breast once more. The baby mewled but, after some fumbling, latched on.

"There we go," the very, very tired new mother whispered. "Now, are you lying comfortably? Good, then I can begin. Our story starts with a sailor rejected by the girl he loved. He tried to forget her, but she haunted his every dream until he became convinced she had him under a spell. The tale soon spread till all along the coast people were whispering that she was the witch who walked the cliffs on stormy nights, calling ships to their doom."

The baby turned her head away from the nipple, face scrunching up.

"All change, is it?" whispered the very, very tired new mother, presenting the other breast. "Well, what do you think the superstitious villagers did?" she continued, when the baby was feeding once more. "They ambushed the girl on the way home one night, dragging her down to the beach and abandoning her there as the tide came in. But the girl was clever and brave, so, as the water came up, she fled into the caves that wove through the cliffs. Only soon she found herself lost in utter darkness, with not a speck of light or hope."

Starlight spilled through the window as the very, very tired new mother stared up at the glow of the moon behind the clouds.

"But never fear, my love, for the moon watches everything that happens in her realm, and when she saw the girl's courage she smiled down, lighting up the night. Deep in the caves, the girl caught a glimpse of silver glinting off water and followed it out to a hidden cove on the far side of the cliffs. Overjoyed, the girl threw herself down on the warm, dry sand. Then a shadow fell across her, and she realized someone had been waiting for her."

The very, very tired new mother looked over at the bedroom door, but no line of light shone around the hinges. All was quiet in the darkness beyond. The softness of the bed tempted her, but she knew that what truly waited in the deceptive glow of her husband's warmth wasn't ease but anger, pain, and misery.

13

The Meter Man Cometh

lthough I'm draped warmly in Granny's shawl, the lingering threads of the nightmares that kept me tossing, turning, then starting awake every hour through the night keep painting themselves across my vision. The doorbell is a welcome summons. I'm expecting the sunflower seeds, or the new dress I bought yesterday as part of my daily inroads into the *Be Happy List*, so I'm smiling as I hurry down the hall.

Instead of a delivery, I find a gas-and-electric meter-reader on the mat. I waste precious seconds registering that he isn't a cardboard box, that it's very odd anyone is here to check the meter in a pandemic, and, finally, that if I let him in I'll end the day in prison.

"Kitchen, isn't it?" He makes to stride past me while I stand there, frozen.

"Wait! You're-not-wearing-a-mask!" I blurt, throwing up a desperate hand.

"Got one in the van. If it's necessary."

Over his shoulder, I see Edwina's front door open and relief floods through me, which isn't a sequence of events I ever thought possible.

"It's necessary," I tell him truthfully. "My neighbor is very strict about the rules. She'll definitely report you otherwise . . ." I trail off with a frown. "Are you even allowed to do meter readings right now? Isn't it against social distancing?" I do my best Edwina impression, arching one brow and trying to look down my nose at him. It's surprisingly hard to do with someone taller than you. I make a mental note to ask how she manages it. "Anyway, didn't we have a smart meter installed? Isn't the whole point that no one needs to come out to check it?"

"First check's gotta be done in person within six months," insists the meter man. "I could come back in two weeks."

It may be a complete lie, but I've no way to check—at least not this instant. Two weeks would give me time to hide Jim, but do I really want to have blocked a workman from coming inside when I've no reasonable excuse? Won't it look suspicious if there are questions later?

"Is everything quite all right?" Edwina calls from her front doorstep.

How does she make her voice carry like that without raising it? Is it connected to the looking-down-her-nose magic?

"He has to read the meter because it's newly installed. He's just getting a mask," I call back.

Edwina turns her deceptively mild stare on the meter man, who scuttles to his van.

"I'll get my husband out of the way!" I squeak, then slam the door shut.

Sprinting to the kitchen, I grab the foot of the Jim-parcel and, heaving and swearing, try to drag him out of the way. It doesn't work.

Heart hammering in my throat, I move to the top end and

heave again. Jim jolts a few inches across the floor. Every muscle and joint screaming, I yank him along, slowly realizing that a gentle side-to-side motion helps him slide more easily.

A sharp knock sounds at the door.

"Coming!" I call.

Heave. Another foot.

Drag. Another foot. Pulllllllll . . .

Another knock, more aggressive than the last.

"Just a sec!"

With Jim finally out of the way, lying by the washing machine, I grab the laundry basket, dumping the contents over the top. It's probably the most hopeless attempt at disguising a body the world has ever known, but it's the best I can do.

Tottering back into the hall, I snap on my mask and open the door.

The meter man brushes past, leaving me to follow in his wake as he lets himself into the kitchen.

I plant myself in front of Jim and the washing machine. "Sorry I kept you. My husband's not moving very swiftly these days. Couldn't get him out of the way."

The meter man takes out a machine and a torch, shining the latter on the meter, then tapping something into the former. "All done," he says. "Lotta fuss about nothing."

A high-pitched giggle escapes me. I hope he translates it as an attempt to be girlish rather than hysteria.

"Couldn't bother you for a glass of water?" the meter man asks instead of leaving.

I leap to fetch it for him.

He takes his mask off and stands gulping it down while I shift from foot to foot, internally chanting, *Go away, please go away, just GO AWAY GOAWAYGOAWAY*, on repeat until it gets so loud that, for a horrible moment, I think he's going to hear it.

"Ta," he says, bashing his glass down on the counter. He turns to pick up his bag, then stops.

Turns back.

Looks at the pile of laundry.

My muscles lock with fear.

It's such a mad situation that I've been on the verge of laughter since I opened the door to him, but there's nothing funny about the prospect of life imprisonment. Nothing funny about what it'll do to my children. If he goes to look under the laundry, can I tackle him? Bribe him?

"Might want to make a start on that before something crawls in and dies under there," the meter man says. He turns away again, carelessly throwing out an elbow as he grabs his bag. He catches the side of Petunia's pot and sends her smashing from the table to the ground.

"Sorry, love," he says. "Bit close to the edge that was."

My hands clench into fists as tears flood my eyes.

"I'll, um, show myself out."

Thump, thump, thump down the hall goes the meter man. A moment later, the front door opens then slams, making me and half the things in the house jump.

Dropping to my knees beside Petunia's shattered pot, I try desperately to scoop up her soil and straighten the broken necks of her smiling faces. Tears stream down my cheeks. Swiping at them, I smear dirt across my chin. I know I should stop, take a deep breath, then do something that will actually help—find a new pot, a dustpan and brush, a tissue . . .

Crumpling forward over my knees, I give into tears, howling into the linoleum as Petunia wilts over my fingers.

I'VE LURCHED UP TO the edge of tears so many times over the last two days—fine one moment, then frozen with fear the next, then forcing myself into sunny cheer. I just want to stop. Give in. Let the feelings wash through me so that maybe one day they wash out again. But there isn't time to cry twenty-odd years of tears now.

I give myself ten minutes, then pull myself together and re-plant Petunia in a broken teapot.

"I know you've had a horrid time, but you'll be fine now. Better than ever," I promise as I set her back beside Rosemary. Then I lean the shard of ceramic bearing the message *Best Mum Ever! Love Amy and Charlie x* against the side of Petunia's teapot. I press my fingers to my children's names, then look down at Jim.

"Don't go getting comfortable down there," I tell him. "I *am* going to be rid of you."

Then suddenly the full weight of my stupidity hits me.

Getting rid of him isn't enough. Lockdown isn't going to last forever. Soon I'll need to explain where he's gone—and do so in such a way that it makes sense when he never comes back.

More than *that*, whatever I tell people will have to persuade not just his colleagues but Amy and Charlie, and the police too, because people don't just disappear off the face of the earth without the police being involved.

How could I think I'd ever get away with it? I might as well have let Jim—

"No." The word comes out quiet but firm.

On the table, sunlight glints off the piece of Petunia's pot with the message from my children. They can't ever find out the truth.

Somehow, I have to make sure *no one* does.

I BLINK AND FIND myself still sitting at the table, hand against the shard from Petunia's pot.

The light has changed, falling low and golden through the kitchen window. The laundry pile has slipped to one side, letting the sun gleam off the smooth surface of the gaffer tape holding the tarp closed around my husband's corpse.

Instinctively, I start to turn away. Then I stop and, instead, face Jim fully, making myself look down at the parcel. For a moment I can't understand why my mind goes to the day when, too afraid to ask my father for new shoes, even though mine had sprung multiple holes, I woke to find it had snowed but school wasn't canceled. My toes were numb before I reached the school gates. Skiving off assembly, I hid in the library to dry the shoes on the radiator. The slow prickle as life came into my flesh . . . that's how I feel now. How I've felt ever since I realized that Jim was dead. Like I'm slowly thawing.

I suppose it was one thing not to be thinking clearly on the first day—surely it's fair enough to blame that on shock. As for how I managed to waste the whole of yesterday not twigging that I can't just hide Jim's body and expect that to be the end of my troubles . . . I've spent twenty years letting him slowly take control of my life. In the Lockdown it became every waking moment, but I told myself it was "just" this, "just" that, "just" the other—separate moments of control and violence and misery. The numbness made it possible never to put the pieces together to see the full picture . . . until that moment when he was holding my wrist and I knew what was coming and knew it wasn't going to stop there, knew it wasn't ever going to stop.

For the first time I saw the truth.

And maybe that does make me as stupid and pathetic and useless and weak as Jim always said I was . . .

Only I'm not letting myself be any of those things anymore. And, yes, I'm bad at being clever. Bad at being useful. Bad at being strong. But I'm getting better. In only two days I've done so much. Changed so much.

Two days ago, I was numb, and now I am thawing.

Two days ago, I had a corpse bleeding on to the floor.

Today I've got a desiccation parcel, and now that I've finally put the pieces together I can get to work on solving not just the disposal issue but the disappearance. I could sit around beating myself up for how long it's taken me, calling myself all the names Jim would if he were still alive, or I can work on proving him wrong. Maybe one day soon I'll be able to push through the shame and phone Janey and . . .

My eyes fly wide.

"HIS PHONE!"

I've been assuming the fact that Jim's on furlough means no one will be trying to contact him, but what if there's some weekly check-in at work? Today's Wednesday—if someone emailed on Monday, how long will it be before they notice he's unreachable?

I rifle frantically through the mess on the table, then on the counter—nothing. Hurrying upstairs, I look in the bedroom, then the study. *Where is it?*

"No," I whisper as I thud heavily downstairs. "No, no, no . . ."

Horror washing through me, I crouch by the Jim-parcel. Then, screwing up my face and averting my eyes, I start pawing at where I think his pockets must be. For a second, I feel something solid and rectangular, but it's far too small—part of his belt buckle probably. I shudder as I realize this must mean he's lying face up. I don't know why, but it makes a cold sweat break out across the back of my neck.

Then I grasp what an utter moron I'm being. Scrambling to my feet, I grab my phone, flicking through my contacts then tapping Jim's name.

The phone in my hand rings . . . but there is no answering chime. Is his battery dead?

I look around in the vain hope the phone will be sitting out on the side and, in my panic, I've not even noticed. No such luck.

With a sigh, I head upstairs to search my way through the house.

If I am going to have to open the parcel, it'll be when it's the only place left to look.

14

Friendly Obstacles

A painstaking search of the upstairs turns up a pair of earrings I'd thought lost, £2.47 in loose change, several pens and paper clips, but no phone. I'd rather go to bed with the hope that the phone's somewhere downstairs than try to sleep after tackling the parcel, so I decide to start again in the morning. Although no one in the street seems to be stirring as I check the locks, I find myself pausing as I peer out into the garden. The alley may not be safe from Edwina's eagle eyes during the day, but perhaps at midnight . . .

Hoping to end the day solving at least one problem, I grab Jim's coat and hat from the peg by the door and tiptoe across the lawn to the gate. Reaching out, I ease the latch up and . . . *SQUEAK!*

"Who's there?"

This time the squeak is mine as I whirl around, looking for Edwina. *Does that woman never sleep? Why is she lurking in the alley behind my house?*

There's no one in the garden with me, or visible through the gap in the gate.

"Hello?" pipes the voice, and I realize it's coming from behind the fence separating my garden from Nawar's.

"Nawar!" I gasp. "What are you doing out here in the dark?"

"Drinking," she says glumly. "Hi, Sally."

I ease the gate closed and cross to the fence, wondering whether I should climb up onto one of the horizontal bracers so we can see each other, then deciding against it. It'd probably violate the Covid restrictions and I don't doubt that would summon Edwina somehow.

"Are you OK?" My heart twists in my chest as I register how small and desolate her voice had sounded. "Is it . . . is it your husband?"

"Not especially," she says matter-of-factly. "We've just been together, the four of us, every second, of every day, for the last billion years and I can't even go to the loo without at least two people talking to me through the door."

I lean my back against the fence as relief wars with disappointment, my stomach souring with the realization that though I was dreading a yes to my question, part of me had hoped for it too.

There's a loud *glug* from the other side of the fence.

I almost laugh, then almost cry as she continues in the same flat tone, as if all my carefully constructed calm isn't about to break apart because I thought, for a moment, that maybe someone else understood what Lockdown had been for me after all.

"My dad's alone, up near Bedford, but I can't get him into a home because they're all full of Covid, and it's too far to drive without staying over and that's not allowed. And I know how lucky I am—I do," Nawar is saying, "but the longest stretch of work I managed today was seven minutes and twenty-three seconds."

I'm going to tell her Jim's dead. That I killed him.

I let the fantasy dance through my mind—let myself imagine the relief—then I put it in a box and shove it to the back of my mind.

"Is there anything I can do to help?" I ask on autopilot, then suddenly realize how much I want her to say yes. I need to do something good to set against everything with Jim. But it's more than that. Apart from the kids, there's no one I matter to. I have to change that. And while I doubt I can be much use to a woman like Nawar, who has friends, family, and a career in environmental consulting, to be any help at all would be *a whole lot more than nothing*.

"Something is a whole lot more than nothing" was one of Granny's phrases to live by. I'd forgotten, but maybe it's time I gave it a go.

Behind the fence, Nawar heaves a sigh. "It's impossible without breaking the rules, and if Edwina tells me off one more time I'm going to have to kill her, so unless your offer includes impromptu grave digging . . ."

"No graves!" I squeak. "No murder!"

"Figures," comes the dejected reply.

"I could cover for you with Edwina if you went to visit your dad. I could say the car's in the garage, then I could go round the alley and let myself in, and turn on the lights and TV for a bit in the evening then turn them off again before bed."

"She'd never believe it. Nothing gets past that woman." She takes another gulp of her drink. "I came out here for five minutes alone, but when I sat down a whole bunch of things went crunch and now there's slime seeping into my knickers and I think I might have committed a snail massacre with my bum." She sniffs wetly. "If sitting in the dark at the bottom of the garden is going to be my pandemic coping mechanism, I'm going to need a lot more Baileys."

"Same," I say morosely, trying not to despair over the fact that, in her own way, Nawar is shaping up to be just as much of an obstacle as Edwina.

I'll end up burying Jim in the garden after all, I think dismally as I trudge upstairs later, only to trip on the top step, as if the house itself is determined to become a stumbling block.

15

Head over Heels

Four blocks away, Ruth took a deep breath as she reached the bottom of the staircase, then scuttled along to the kitchen as quickly and quietly as she could. She'd averted a mid-afternoon disaster over a punnet of floury pears with cold beer and a basket of battered plantains. Now she fetched out garlic, onion, cloves, brown sugar, pimento, thyme, cinnamon, orange peel and the heap of other ingredients that made up her mother's pepperpot. Usually it was a "special occasions" recipe, though weekends always included a "family meal" from either her side or his: a touch point of joy for the week—and a way to raise his spirits if he'd been short of work.

Soon the kitchen windows were cheerfully fogged with steam as spices crackled in oil, the radio crooning in the background on low, safely tuned to Lionel's favorite channel.

The air grew fragrant and warm, comforting as a worn blanket. On the wall, a print of her mother's favorite painting—the clear blue of a jungle waterfall set off against the burnt umber of a flamboyant tree—watched over her. They had played a game when she was little of trying to spot hummingbirds hidden in the fronds and branches, but it was impossible to tell from a print what might be a bird and what was simply the grain of the oil paint.

"*Mwen kontan*," her mother would say, whenever she looked at the painting. *I'm happy.*

"I'm happy," Ruth whispered hopelessly.

A vibration against her thigh prompted her slip her phone from her pocket. Casting a wary eye behind to check that the kitchen and hallway were clear and the TV was still blaring from the living room, she tapped in her PIN and called up the message.

Cursing as liquid spat onto the stove as a pot boiled over, she sandwiched the phone between her ear and shoulder, reaching to turn the hob off.

A hand on her shoulder, hot breath in her hair.

She jumped, sending the lid of the pot clattering onto the hob. The phone was plunked away, a strand of hair catching on Lionel's watch so that she flinched back with a little cry, hand flying up to press against the smarting skin behind her ear.

"Oops," Lionel said. "Sorry. Just looked like you were about to have an accident. Didn't figure you wanted the phone in the pot."

"Here," she said, wiping her hands on a dish towel then reaching for the phone. "I'll put it out of the way."

Lionel quirked an eyebrow as a tinny voice from the phone instructed them to press one to repeat. "Twelve new texts too. Aren't you the popular one?" He made a show of taking his own mobile from his pocket and checking it. "Nothing new on when we can have my brother's funeral and who's to be left out because of the restrictions, so how come your phone's blowing up like a teenager's?"

She shrugged, reaching for the phone again, but Lionel twisted away to lean against the table as he started scrolling through her texts while, in the background, Corinne Bailey Rae's "Put Your Records On" gave way to Sade's "Never as Good as the First Time."

"It's just some friends—you know, the old nursing crowd from the hospital," she said, trying to keep her tone light. "Come on. Put that down and give me a kiss," she coaxed, but Lionel raised a hand, keeping her back.

"Nursing crowd, huh?" His eyes narrowed. "You mean that red-haired bint with the face like a smacked arse, not the randy consultant, right?"

"Why would I still have his number?" she asked, gently trying to tug the phone from his grip. "Come on. Give me it back. It's just girl-talk. You know—what our kids are doing, menopause stuff."

That wrinkled his nose. Hand going around her waist as if he were about to pull her close, he moved to set the phone on the table.

Then suddenly he snatched it back with a cheeky smirk and tapped twice. "Always wanted to be part of some girl-talk."

"You have one new message," the phone announced on speaker. "New message. Received today at 4:15 p.m."

Ruth felt her pulse quicken till it beat threateningly in her ears.

"Just me again. Look, I know you always planned to come back to work—well, now's the perfect chance. We need you, and I can't believe you're happy to just sit at home, watching it all on the news. I *know* you, Ruth. You've never stepped back from anyone in need . . . I just don't get it."

"See? It's just Prudence. You remember—her mum's Dominican. Knew my mum back in the day. We started at the hospital together, so it'll just be her wanting to talk about old times. Nothing exciting. I'll listen to the rest later." Ruth reached for the phone once more, but Lionel shook his head, holding it up, out of her reach.

"What's going on, Ruth?" the phone asked worriedly. "It's just not like you. Is it your husband? Is he the one stopping you?"

The smile slipped off Lionel's face. His free hand clenched into a fist.

She'd known the day would end in disaster one way or another, but she'd expected the type of bruises that came with overcooking dinner or saying the wrong thing when he told her the latest about the delays to his brother's funeral.

Now, as Lionel's mouth thinned into a line, she knew no disaster that had come before had prepared her for what would come next. Not daring to back away, Ruth slid one foot behind her, slowly settling her weight onto it.

"Look, I'm sorry. I'm probably just being stupid but . . . call me, OK? Just so I know you're all right." A beep. "Press one to listen again," said the phone.

Lionel tapped the screen, silencing it.

Ruth waited for him to look up, to shout, to lunge, but he was still, so very still.

The air in the kitchen beat like a pulse.

She bolted round the far side of the table, racing into the hall. Ricocheting off the wall, she threw herself around the banister and thundered upstairs, her only hope to reach the safety of the bathroom—the one room with a door that locked.

A hand closed on the trailing end of her cardigan five steps from the top. Flinging her arms backward, she let it pull off her shoulders then grasped for the newel post at the top of the stairs to propel herself round the bend. A fist smashed into the middle of her back, punching the breath from her lungs and sending her tumbling face first onto the stairs.

Her chin hit the edge of a riser, teeth cutting into her cheek and flooding her mouth with blood. Her shins and shoulders seared with pain as they struck the edges of two lower steps.

A hand clenched around her ankle just as her own locked frantically around the bottom of the newel post. She kicked out wildly, hoping to buy just enough time to crawl up those final few stairs and scramble into the bathroom.

Her foot made contact, the uneven surface she'd hit crumpling under her slipper. A howl of pain filled the hall. The hand ripped away from her ankle, then a weight buffeted the balustrade, making the staircase shake. There was a gentle creaking, a soft gasp of surprise, followed by a breathless hush.

Then a thunderous crash from the floor below sent vibrations through the whole house. The letter box snapped open and shut. Something rocked ominously then fell with a smash.

For a moment Ruth stayed frozen, waiting for danger to loom over her once more, but it never came.

Finally, she turned to peer between the banisters.

Lionel lay crumpled on the hall floor, legs incongruously—ridiculously—stretched up the wall as if he'd been attempting some strange backward handstand.

His head was turned to the side, resting at an impossible angle. His eyes stared into hers.

She knew she should fight her way to her feet and get to the bathroom while she could, but her body was locked in pain and fright.

Lionel just kept staring, but he wouldn't stay stunned for long. Soon he'd be up again. She needed to get a locked door between them before the staring turned into fury.

She waited for the blink that would show he was coming back to himself, but he just kept staring and staring.

Slowly her breathing calmed and her muscles untensed while Lionel stared on, unblinking.

When she realized she was squinting because the hall was growing dark, she wondered briefly if it were about to storm. The air felt right for it—thrumming with pressure.

When night fell, she finally accepted that there was no need to wait any longer.

Her body didn't feel like her own as she floated downstairs and knelt beside her husband. Softly, she brushed his eyes closed.

16

Hope and Weeds Spring Eternal

My eyes snap open early the next morning, mind already flooded with fears about the messages that could be piling up on Jim's phone. Even if there's time before someone follows up in person, when I try to explain away his disappearance after I've disposed of the body, questions will be raised about when he really went missing unless I sort this out *now*.

Dragging myself out of bed, I stuff myself into the nearest clothes then stumble downstairs, determined to throw myself into the task and not stop until it's done, even if that means opening the Jim-parcel.

As I step down into the hall, my phone buzzes then chines with Charlie's song of the day—"All by Myself"—and I realize there's one last thing I can try. Jim loved to keep his phone on silent, so maybe it's not off or out of battery after all. If I'm right, I just need to be right on top of it to hear the vibrations, so if I go foot by foot . . .

I start by the hall table, hitting Jim's contact on my phone, then crouching as I strain my ears.

Nothing. Stepping into the living room, I listen by the book-case. The call goes to voicemail, so I redial. Not by the TV. Not on either side of the sofa. But as I step toward the armchair there's the faintest sound, just before the voicemail kicks in once more.

This time I'm ready, kneeling over the chair as I hit redial. Every muscle in my body tightens as I wait . . .

And then I feel it—something moving in the chair. It's not under the cushions and I feel under the seat with no luck, but when I fish down the side . . .

Soon I am holding the phone aloft as if it is the magic sword at the end of a mythical quest. I feel triumphant. Victorious. Ridiculous.

I lower my arm as I see the battery is down to the dregs. Hurrying to the kitchen, I plug the phone in before it dies. While I wait for it to charge, I make tea, then carefully type in the same PIN as the one Jim programmed into my phone—not because I couldn't figure out how to do it myself, but so he could check my texts whenever he wanted or answer my calls. He'd say it was because I looked tired or had my hands full, but really it was just another way to discourage anyone, even the kids, from call-ing me, since they could never be sure who'd answer.

Hitting the last number, I grin when the lock screen is re-placed by the home menu.

"This is what you get for being controlling," I tell the Jim-parcel as I start checking his texts—all junk, thankfully, but now junk that his phone has interacted with.

I don't know whether to feel relieved or wretched that not only are there no messages from friends or colleagues, there aren't even any from the kids.

"Turns out your life was even sadder and smaller than mine," I tell the parcel. "Not that I've talked to most of my friends for . . ."

Grabbing my notebook, I add an all-caps entry to the *Be Happy List*—RECONNECT WITH OLD FRIENDS.

"Assuming they want to reconnect with me," I whisper, then pull myself together. "Well, if they don't, I'll join a choir. Hell, I'll *join a choir* anyway."

I add it to the list and feel that prickly tingle in my chest again as I thaw a little more.

AFTER MAKING MYSELF A list of local choirs, I head out for fresh provisions (somehow I've run out of cake), WD-40, snail pellets, and Baileys.

Finding a single bag of flour on the supermarket shelves, I try to see snaffling it as a triumph rather than a sign that the world is ending. If it were, that would rather sort out my dead-husband issues. Instead, it stubbornly keeps existing.

Jim died three days ago and I've made no further progress with the *Get Rid of Jim List*, though I have been ticking things off the *Be Happy* one. Today's progress is discovering that I don't even need a karaoke "machine"; as an extremely helpful Amazon reviewer explains, *YouTube has loads of songs with the lyrics up on screen to sing along to*, and I'm perfectly happy pretending random kitchenware is a microphone.

Two rounds of "All by Myself" later, the shopping is put away and the *Be Happy List* updated. Letting myself out into the garden, I march across the lawn then chuck the snail pellets over the hedge, hopefully onto Nawar's patio rather than the flower-bed. Good deed done, I spray the hinges of the back gate with WD-40, working it to and fro until it moves silently, then repeating the process with the latch and bolt. Maybe Nawar will still hear me if I creep out at midnight, but at least I've done *something* to try to solve the problem of how to get out of the house unnoticed.

Next, I tackle the bigger obstacle of Edwina. Step one is to bake a lemon cake.

An hour and a half later, I parcel up a generous slice and take it across the street. Placing it on Edwina's mat, I stand well back as I wait for the door to open. "To thank you for your help making the meter-man put his mask on," I tell her brightly when she peers out at me.

Edwina picks up the Tupperware and wipes it down with the cloth and disinfectant spray that apparently live beside her front door. "I suppose this isn't breaking any rules. Though you should sterilize the box when I return it to you," she adds sternly. "Since you're here, I'll take the opportunity to give you your first gardening lesson. I'll be splitting my irises today so I'll drop a few bulbs over later—though I need to be sure you'll put them somewhere suitable. I'm expecting you to nurture them, not kill them off."

I flinch.

"Don't be wet, Sally," Edwina says tartly. "You just need to put them in a sunny spot, with well-drained soil. And for goodness' sake water them for the first week—first thing in the morning, mind, not in the middle of the day when they'll get scorched."

"Sunny, well drained, water in the morning," I dutifully parrot, and produce a hopeful smile.

"Are you waiting for applause?" She shakes her head. "I will also bring you a few aquilegia seedlings. They'll come up again next year if you let them go to seed rather than getting impatient when the petals fall and just taking the heads straight off."

She frowns as I grimace at the words. There's probably going to be plenty of head removal in my near future, since dismembering Jim will almost certainly involve decapitation. What will it feel like to saw through his neck?

"Please don't tell me that's too much to remember, Sally. I shan't believe you," Edwina says, bringing me acerbically back to the present. "Though clearly it's past time to start exercising that brain of yours more often. I've always thought it was quite a good one, despite your determination to let it go to waste. I hope I've not been mistaken."

A week ago I'd have hunched my shoulders miserably and spent the next ten hours thinking of all the ways I'm stupid and useless. But people who have decapitation on their horizons can't afford to be wimps, so I raise my chin and square my shoulders. "Just taking it all in," I tell Edwina.

Could that be the hint of a smile? It's almost more unnerving than the thought of detaching Jim's head.

"Your flowerbeds will thank you for it. Now, there are a few things you'll need to buy if you're really serious about getting your hands dirty."

As Edwina reels off a list of tools and other gardening supplies, I try to focus on how lovely it'll be when her advice blossoms into a home surrounded by flowers. Maybe the pruning and trimming will help bury the memories of what it'll take to reduce Jim to parts.

———————

COME MIDNIGHT, I PULL on Jim's coat and hat, then pad across the garden to the back gate. It opens silently under my touch. I pause, listening, but all is quiet in Nawar's garden.

Slipping out into the alley, I hurry to the corner, where I press myself against the hedge and peer into the street. I can just make out Edwina's house. All the lights are off. Carefully, I edge out, branches prickling into my back.

The curtains stay still. The lights stay off.

Out I edge, further and further . . . I back steadily away until the house is out of sight, then spin round, horrified at the thought that maybe someone is behind me, watching this not-at-all-suspicious behavior.

The street is empty.

I scurry around the corner and along the next block before crossing the street and turning again. I've established that I can escape out the back at night without being spotted now the gate has been oiled, but where does it leave me? I've still nowhere to dispose of Jim. And not even the glimmer of an explanation for his disappearance as Day 4 slips into Day 5.

Tipping my head back, I stare hopelessly up at the sky.

There isn't a trace of cloud. The stars swim in the darkness, fractured by the threat of hopeless tears. Sniffing, I distract myself by looking for Orion and the Plough. I wish I knew the other constellations, but what's the point of learning if I end up in prison? I doubt you can see much of the stars from a window you can't open.

A dull thump makes me turn. Suddenly I'm all too aware that I'm alone in the darkness, in the middle of the night. The houses on this side of the street are set back behind narrow gardens, screened by tall fencing. A footpath runs along the block, with a scruffy strip of grass bracketing the curb. The streetlights are all on the other side, edging a series of playing fields leading to the park. The orange glow is enough for me to see by, but I doubt anyone in the houses could make me out. Earlier that was a comfort, but now I register how isolated I am, with no one to see or hear if the wrong person comes around the corner . . .

Something slithers along the ground nearby. I wheel round, trying to pinpoint the source of the sound.

I strain my ears . . .

And there it is again . . . and again . . . and again.

I follow it to a fence. Glancing over my shoulder, I see a bench facing across the street toward the playing fields. To one side is a thin, listing tree.

This is the place I sat with the green-eyed cat the other night. The fence in front of me leads to the garden where I saw the woman with the bruised face.

I search for the knothole and press my eye to it, but this time all I see is the end of the garden. No woman. And no explanation for the noise.

But now there's a new sound: a rustling, like someone crumpling paper. Then something like a bin being toppled over and the contents tipped out. There are grunts and heaves and thumps. Then a sound like sticks clattering onto the ground and . . . someone striking a match? A sigh. Another match flare.

"Come on, come on," a woman's voice whispers, tense and full of dread. "Just a little more . . ." Then it sharpens with panic. "No, don't do that. Please don't."

I remember the sob that drew me to the fence the other

day. And the threatening voice from the house that sent the woman running back up the garden path . . .

I won't stand by. Not now I finally understand how to fight back.

Baking for Edwina and sparing some kind words for Nawar is nice, but here's a chance to really help someone in need.

I claw my way up the fence, swinging a leg over the top then turning to face what lies beyond.

17

Frying Pan Meets Fire

Below, in the garden, the woman—tall, broad-shouldered, probably in her fifties—stares up at me in horror, a burned-out match in one hand. She is alone—no man looms over her, fist raised. She wasn't pleading to a violent husband or boyfriend but rather to the match as she failed to light the hopeless bonfire heaped at her feet. There's some kindling on top, gleaming with damp, then a bunch of obviously wet leaves, then some soggy garden waste, a bunch of balls of crumpled-up newspaper, and an arm.

Yes, that is definitely an arm.

It takes me a moment, but then I realize what lies at the center of the lopsided bonfire.

I wait for surprise to hit me. Shock. Horror. Fear.

But when I turn back to the woman, who is staring at me as if her brain has stopped sending commands to her body, all I feel is recognition. Not just for the bruises I saw the other night and the body in the bonfire, but because I recognize her and remember how she moved out of the way of the teenage boys, despite how laden with shopping she was: I remember how she stopped and picked their litter from the hedge before I could do it myself.

"Does that arm belong to whoever gave you the bruises the other day?" My voice comes out so normal it startles me.

The woman continues staring at me. Finally, she turns to the bonfire and stares at that for a change. "I'm a monster," she whispers. "What am I doing? I don't . . . I can't . . ."

She shakes her head helplessly, her breathing picking up as she presses her hands over her face. "Why didn't I leave?" she gasps. "Why didn't I just leave?"

If someone had told me this would happen and asked me to guess what I'd do next, I'd have said, "Cry as all the guilt and shame and horror I'd been repressing suddenly bubbled up, sending me to the ground under the weight of what I'd done."

But that's not what happens at all. Instead, I swing my other leg over the fence and drop down onto the grass.

The woman looks up, face crumpling with relief. "I won't hurt you," she whispers, reaching out a hand. "I'm not . . . Please just call the police. I want you to call the police. I won't fight. I promise I'll just stand here till they come, but . . ." She gulps out a sob, fresh tears spilling down her cheeks. "But please will you stay with me? Just till they come."

"If that's what you want, then I will." She opens her mouth, but I speak over her. "Or we could go inside and have a little chat first. If you sit one end of the kitchen and I sit at the other, and we keep the door and windows open, it should be OK Covid-wise."

She dashes the tears off her cheeks, though new ones replace them instantly. "They'll believe me, won't they?" she gulps. "That it was an accident. I never intended . . . He was chasing me. He was going to . . . going to . . ."

I look pointedly at the bonfire and, a moment later, the woman does too.

"Oh," she says softly.

"This doesn't look very accidental," I point out.

"Why did I do this?" she asks, voice rising in panic. "Why didn't I just call them? They'll never believe me now. They'll think I meant to do it. They—"

"This is why we need to go inside and talk," I interrupt as loudly as I dare.

So far no lights have gone on in the surrounding houses, but it won't be long if she carries on like this, and there's no way I'm sticking around if that happens when I've my own corpse to worry about.

"Why would you do that? Why didn't you run away and call the police? I've just . . ." She gestures at the arm sticking out of the bonfire.

I know the sensible response would be to say that I understand she was just acting in self-defense. I could even make up a story about a friend in an abusive marriage, or tell the truth about my parents. But instead I do the stupid thing. The reckless thing. And all because she picked a piece of litter out of a hedge.

"Well, you see, *I* bashed my husband's brains in with my granny's skillet four"—I glance at my watch, "five days ago, so I can hardly criticize, can I?"

I'm no closer to solving my Jim situation than when I started, but maybe, just maybe, the missing ingredient isn't an ingenious idea.

It's a partner.

18

Partners in Crime

You bashed your husband's brains in . . ." the woman echoes blankly. "On purpose?" she gasps, stumbling backward.

"Of course not!" I snap. "Well, no more on purpose than . . ." I gesture at the arm in the bonfire. "I'm desiccating him in cat litter in a tarpaulin parcel on the kitchen floor," says my big, stupid mouth. "You might want to try it, because that fire is just not going to work with everything so wet. Anyway the bones and teeth aren't likely to burn properly. Not to mention the smell will definitely raise questions. Look, we need to go inside for this conversation, but we should take him"—I gesture at the arm—"with us. Imagine if a fox got in the garden while we're in the kitchen."

The woman sways on her feet. "I can't. You don't know what it was like dragging him down here."

"Oh, I've a fair notion."

She blinks, eyes glazed. "This is madness."

"Probably. But at least now we can be mad together. Please can we do it inside, though, before someone overhears us?" As I say it, a horrible thought strikes me. "It *is* just you here, right? No one else in the house?"

"Just me and"—she gestures at the bonfire—"Lionel."

"Well, that's something." I crouch down to get a good grip on the arm, then pull. The bonfire collapses as I drag the corpse out. Tilting my head, I survey him while the woman wraps her arms about herself.

"What have I done? What have I done? WhathaveI—"

"He's about six foot, right?"

"What? Why—"

"Six foot's basically two meters." I crouch by Lionel's shoulders. "If you get his feet, we can carry him together and still be socially distanced. Not from him, obviously, but I don't think people who aren't breathing count. Come on."

The woman crouches, hands around his ankles, then freezes again, her face a rictus of horror and indecision.

I start walking, making her stagger forward. Momentum and despair bring her with me up the garden path and into the kitchen. "I'm Sally, by the way," I huff as I struggle under the dead weight.

"Ruth," comes the equally breathless response.

Together, we back over to the counter. I lower the corpse's shoulders with a weary groan. Ruth moves to follow, grimacing with pain—and drops the feet.

"I'm sorry!" she gasps, clapping a hand to her mouth.

"I don't think he felt it," I tell her wryly as she totters to a chair.

"Shall I put the kettle on?" I cross to the sink and happy-birthday myself through a government-approved handwash routine with the antibacterial soap. "Trust me, if you're going down the police and prison route, you might as well eat all the cake in the house first."

"Won't delaying mean a longer sentence? They're already going to know I tried to destroy evidence."

"Only if you decide to go ahead with calling the police."

"*If . . .*"

"You're the one who was attempting an informal cremation, so don't pretend at least some part of you wasn't thinking it."

"It's wrong," she whispers. "I have to tell them what I've done and accept my punishment."

With a dry, hopeless little sob, she staggers to her feet and over to the phone. I watch her take it out of the charging station then stand staring at it, swaying slightly as if the ground is no longer firm beneath her feet.

Slowly the kettle roars to a boil, and still she doesn't dial. I fish clean mugs off the drying rack then open cupboards until I find a box of tea bags. Once the tea is made, I put a steaming mug down at the near end of the table and push the other toward Ruth. After a moment, she sets the phone back in the cradle.

As I fetch milk and locate sugar, she takes out plates and a packet of Mr. Kipling's.

"In for a murder, in for a Bakewell tart," I say as she tears open the box.

Ruth freezes, the plastic wrapping crackling as her hands clench, then she rips the packet open so violently one of the tarts tumbles onto the counter. Stuffing the rubbish into the bin, she puts a tart on each plate, then pauses, staring blankly at the toaster. I am so familiar with that look of wear and resignation that a double blow of pain and sympathy bows my shoulders forward. She's a stranger and yet I *know* her and she knows me. Right now I feel closer to her than anyone in the world.

With a blink she comes back to herself, gaze focusing again. She dishes out the remaining four tarts between us, putting a plate at my end of the table before sinking into the chair at the other, pulling her chunky-knit cardigan tight across her shirt. The delicate blue flowers on the white cotton peeking from below the wool are smudged at the collar with mud, or blood.

"I thought he was going to kill me," she says.

I watch her shoulders heave as she breathes in raggedly, then exhales in a long, shuddering whoosh.

"But you can't go around killing people just to make sure they don't kill you first. It's wrong and bad and—"

"Sounds like self-defense to me, and that's not wrong *or* bad. I'm not sorry to be alive—or that my husband can't hurt me ever again. And as for punishment," I say, voice suddenly bleak, "I've had twenty-three years of it. His name was Jim."

"Sixteen," Ruth whispers, eyes darting to mine then away. "I don't want to go to prison. How can I deserve that, even after . . ." She steeples her hands in front of her mouth as if about to pray.

"Do you have kids?"

"A son. He's twenty-six now." A smile softens her face. "He was only ten when Lionel came into our lives. I thought we'd won the lottery when I realized we could be a family. And it was good, to begin with. We were so happy." Her tone speaks of heartbreak instead of joy. "Then he injured himself on a job—fell off a ladder and busted his knee. Couldn't work for a while so money got tight, then he started drinking, started pestering me to get him a prescription for stronger painkillers—I'm a nurse, so he thought I could get a doctor friend to do me a favor, but it doesn't work like that."

Tears coat her lashes.

"That was the first time it happened. I thought it was just the situation—the stress—because he was sorry. So full of regret." She swallows hard. "But then it happened again . . . and again, and I just . . . I couldn't let go of the idea that it could go back to how it was."

"And your son?"

She shakes her head. "He doesn't know. I made sure . . ." Her eyes move to Lionel's feet, peeking out from the far side of the table. "I'd give anything to stop him finding out. Not just what I've done, but why I . . ." She trails off, pressing a shaking hand across her mouth.

I let her sit with that train of thought because I already know the slow realization that follows, with determination on its heels: there is no amount of guilt, shame, or horror she won't shoulder for the rest of her life if it means her son doesn't have to be caught up in it. And the only way to ensure that is for him never to find out, because if he finds out about the body lying a few feet away, he'll have to know about the rest too, and he'll never to be able to stop second-guessing what he knew all along, and what he resolutely chose not to see.

Ruth can't want that for her son any more than I do for Amy and Charlie.

"When it came right down to it, the only real question for me was whether there was a way to make sure no one ever finds out," I say, forcing myself to meet Ruth's eyes. "And before you say it'll be even worse to try and fail, I can't see how that's true as far as the kids are concerned."

Ruth shakes her head helplessly. "It'll never work. How could we get away with it, even if we wanted to?"

I shrug. "I don't know yet because I haven't figured it out. I'm failing on my own, but maybe . . ." I suck in a breath then press on, because from the moment I told Ruth about Jim there's been no point holding back. "Maybe it's the type of problem that can't be solved alone."

Ruth squeezes her eyes shut. "But that's criminal conspiracy, that's . . ."

"A partnership."

I wait. After a moment, Ruth's eyes focus on me again.

"I know you don't know me from Adam, but we're not strangers or we wouldn't be sitting here like this. Ruth, you're the only person in the world I'll ever want to tell about this . . . this thing that happened to me—this thing I've done. I told you because I *knew* you'd understand."

A shuddery breath overtakes me and suddenly I'm the one struggling to swallow the sudden rise of tears.

"Please, Ruth. I've been trying and trying, but I can't figure it out and I need someone to help me. I can't do it alone. I'm so tired of being alone."

I startle when something nudges my fingers. Looking down, I see Ruth has slid a box of tissues along the table. With a shaky laugh, I blot myself. By the time I look up again, she's watching me steadily.

"I don't want to call the police," she tells me quietly, and the look on her face . . . It's everything I can do to hold back a sob at the compassion, the understanding, the *knowledge*. However different we are, we're the same too. We've suffered the same things. Been driven to the same brink—and over it. I don't have to say a word for her to know everything that really matters.

"I won't do that to my son," she continues, slow and steady

and gentle, because she understands that anything more will shatter me. "I've no idea how we can help each other, but maybe together we can find a way to protect our children. Whether or not we deserve to go to prison, they don't deserve to have us taken from them too." Her hand goes to a locket at her throat, clutching it tightly. "Evil is a moral problem, not a police matter. We can find a way to show our remorse and still be good people . . . can't we?"

"Of course we can. We are. This isn't our fault."

Ruth shakes her head, still clutching the locket. "When this is over—if we come through it—we have to find a way to put some good out into the world to set against the bad: have to make sure we don't just slide into—"

"We're not going to become serial killers, OK?" I tell her tartly. "Get a grip."

It surprises a laugh out of her. Then her face goes serious again. "We will hold each other to account if we must," she says quietly but firmly.

I nod.

I suppose I could have seen it as a threat, or at least a warning, but I didn't. I was far too grateful that I was no longer alone.

19

Ticking Clocks

Every time I think about Ruth, the world seems bigger and brighter. It's Day 5 and the clock is ticking—but hope is enough for now. Hope and company.

We decided it was too suspicious to start texting madly out of the blue, so although we've exchanged numbers, we won't talk again until we "bump into each other" while out for our exercise tomorrow night.

Still, it's enough to see me humming as I water Edwina's newly planted iris bulbs and seedlings (the name of which I've already forgotten).

When the doorbell heralds a pile of packages that sets Edwina's curtains flurrying, I wave across at her, managing a mostly sincere smile when her door opens.

"My gardening supplies!" I call, gesturing at the parcels. "Oh, and I'll be popping some banana bread on your mat this afternoon when I go for my hour's exercise, so look out for that."

Edwina inclines her head. "I will bring over a sweet pea when I go out to do my shopping *for the week.*"

I just grin. "I've started a shopping list so I can try to avoid going so often in future. Maybe. Well, when I get the hang of planning."

Edwina purses her lips. "At least there is the promise of progress," she says, and closes her door.

Laughing, I gather up my parcels and take everything back to the kitchen, where I play Charlie's daily song, promising myself that as soon as I can think of an excuse that won't seem suspicious when Jim "disappears," I'll start calling my son again. It's been too long since I've heard his voice, but I can't risk it yet.

The Beatles' "Blackbird" provides a melancholy soundtrack as I unpack gardening gloves, a kneeler, a trowel, and some cheap secateurs. The final box contains my new dress. I bought it with a smile of anticipation, but as I let the silky fabric spill across my hands, my stomach lurches with nausea.

Last time I bought a new dress Jim gave me a bruise to match the color.

I tried to avoid buying new clothes after that, but then my favorite cardigan sprouted holes and Jim slapped me for "looking like a bag lady, as if I don't work every goddamn day to provide for you, provide for our ungrateful brats."

My fingers flick the edge of a sequin. What was I thinking? Jim will . . .

But Jim won't. He can't anymore.

Slowly I get to my feet and, turning to the corpse-parcel on the floor, I let the dress unfold down my front. The reflection in the oven door is dark and dim, but here and there light catches off the sequins, little flashes of brightness in the shadow world of the glass.

I strip off my trousers and top right there in the kitchen—let the robins peek if they want—and pull on the dress, letting it shimmy down my hips then fall free. Reflection-Sally is smiling when I glance her way—tentatively at first, but then she twists and the sequins flash and the skirt flares and the Sally in the glass beams.

"You look just fine," I tell her. "It's a lovely color on you. Granny always said so."

It gives me the confidence to crouch and poke the Jim-parcel. Then, taking a deep breath, I put my hand against the rough surface and press down. Trying to analyze the sensation makes me gag, but still I do it again. Is it just the cat litter and rice and salt or does he feel less solid and more like thick soup with bones in?

I have to go out into the garden then and breathe deeply. There is no way I am opening the parcel, even to be able to report back to Ruth on how the desiccation is progressing. The nostril-scorching stench of vinegar, coupled with the cat litter and bicarb of soda, are keeping any whiff of rotting corpse at bay, but who knows how long that will last. Yet another thing I'd better not google.

I'm about to change into gardening clothes when the phone rings. I stare at it for several long moments. Talking to Nawar through the fence, and Edwina about gardening, are the only conversations I've had with anyone other than Jim (and now Ruth) in months.

Another blast of the ringer sends me across the kitchen. "Hello?" I whisper.

"Sally! You sound a little hoarse. Everything OK?"

Who is he? I know I know his voice, but I can't place it.

"Mm," I say. "Just swallowed my tea the wrong way."

"Ah, sorry about that, but glad you're well. Is Jim OK?"

This time my "Mm" comes out at a substantially higher pitch.

"Don't suppose I could have a quick word?"

"Oh, um . . . He's . . . Can I take a message?"

"I just wanted to check in. Was a bit worried when he didn't reply to my email last week about this new system we're instituting."

Shit! ShitshitshitshitSHIT! I didn't even think about his email. Just assumed that, because he was on furlough, they'd phone if they needed him.

"I just tried his mobile, but it rang out, so I thought I'd check that the two of you hadn't been felled by the dreaded lurgy," he says with a chuckle that sets my teeth on edge. "Anyway, in case the message went astray, bottom line is that we're setting up a rota for a different member of the team to go into the office each week—only for an hour or so first thing—to keep on top of the post, let in any maintenance staff . . . I just need to confirm Jim's happy to take his turn."

My vision has gone gray. I've heard people say that before, but I always thought it was just a saying. And yet all the color has suddenly disappeared from the world. My chest pinches with pain as if the air is thin.

"Wh—when's Jim's week? So I can write it on the calendar for him?" I squeak.

"It's in the email. If he can't find it, tell him to drop me a note and I'll forward it. Can't quite remember off the top of my head."

What if I can't figure out how to get into his laptop? What

if his email is password protected and he's not written it down somewhere obvious?

"Well, cheerio," Jim's boss says, then the phone blares the disconnect tone.

For a moment I stand holding the phone out as if offering it to the air, then I fumble it into the charger. Running upstairs to the study, I sink down in front of Jim's laptop. The motor whirs softly to life as I wiggle the mouse. A moment later the lock-screen flashes up—a coastline with cliffs and gulls wheeling overheard and a box in the middle for the PIN.

So scared my ears ring, I carefully type in the PIN from our phones, hoping against hope he used the same one. I've no idea what I'll do if not—what if I only have a few tries before it locks me out?

"Please work. Please work. Please, please work," I whisper as I hit enter.

The screen goes black.

My throat closes as if under Jim's hands.

The desktop flashes up, quickly overtaken by an email window, and there it is: Jim's inbox, automatically logged in for me. My breath whooshes out and for a moment I go limp with relief, then I straighten and focus on the laptop.

Scrolling down to find the message about the rota, I click it open and scan the text, searching for the date then leaning over to flick frantically through the wall calendar to check how long I have.

Not next week. *Thank God.*

Today's Friday and I've got a fortnight from Monday—over two full weeks—though there will be no leeway on the deadline.

"I can figure it out in a fortnight. No problem."

After all, I've got over two weeks *and Ruth*.

I fire off a brief email confirming Jim's stint on the rota.

Then, impressed at my own cunning, I change his password just in case the system logs me out.

"Look at you checking your email even post-mortem!" I tell the Jim-parcel as I cross the kitchen to scrawl an addition to the *Get Rid of Jim List*: **Check email and phone every day and ensure both look active.** I make a mental note to ensure Ruth's doing the same, preening at all the brilliant tips I've got to offer my new partner, even though she's a nurse with a career and qualifications and a decade of extra life experience and I'm just silly little me.

My phone blares into song, making me jump as "Mamma Mia" fills the kitchen—the ringtone Amy set for herself last time she was here.

"Amy darling! How are you? It's so good to hear your voice."

"Jeez, Mum. You don't get on Charlie for never ringing. Why do I have to be the dutiful one? How's Dad?" she asks, with no indication of interest.

Still, my heart lurches. Charlie and Jim have never got on, but Amy's always understood the value of playing Daddy's Little Darling when she wanted something and being quiet enough to avoid trouble the rest of the time. Where Charlie was too straight-talking to avoid shouting matches and being sent to his room, Amy went babyish when she was stressed. Then Jim would pass her off on me while he took himself off to watch sports. She's never been close to her father, and most of her calls since she went to uni have been about money, but she must love him in her own way. Yes, he was grumpy and bossy, often sullenly angry and rarely affectionate, but he never laid a violent hand on her or Charlie—or on me when they were there to see.

"Mum? You still there?"

"Sorry, darling. Was just watching the robin. I've started gardening and he's very happy about all the worms I'm digging up."

"Good for you. What's Dad been up to?"

"Not much. Barely moved in days."

I'm an actual monster. Only a monster would make jokes about this. I want to be horrified at myself, but it doesn't seem to be in me. All I feel is sad and tired. So very, very tired.

"I thought he was doing all the shopping?" Amy says, jolting me back to the present.

"He was getting so cross about having to wear a mask it wasn't worth the aggro. You know how he can be." I throw in a breathless little laugh.

"Want to pass me over to say hi?"

My whole body warms at how reluctant she sounds. Then shame turns me cold. "He can't come to the phone right now. Not feeling very talkative. Little bit down and out."

There's a little pause then. "Do you need me to come over?"

I want to believe, as I've always made myself believe, that all Amy knows is that her parents' marriage is unhappy. This cannot be the moment she finally stops being oblivious.

"It would be so lovely to see you, darling, but please don't tempt me. You know Edwina opposite? Well, she's being a right sergeant major about the Covid rules, and your father is ready to blow his top. Better not give her an excuse to send him over the edge. But how about you? Everything OK?"

"Mm," she says. "Just wanted to check in like a good daughter and all that. Love you."

"I love you too," I say as the call disconnects. I turn to Rosemary and Petunia. "She chickened out of asking for money, right? She wasn't . . . You don't think she was just being considerate, do you?"

The words sound thin and unconvincing, instead of dry and sarcastic, but the very last thing I need right now is for my rather self-centered daughter to develop a sudden concern for her parents' well-being.

"Oh, they won't miss you, dear," I tell Jim. "I mean, they'll notice you're not there. Eventually. But miss you—not so much. It's me they'd miss."

But would they miss me if I wound up in prison for killing their father, or is that just another lie? Maybe they'd hate me.

I can't let that happen.

Pulling over the *Get Rid of Jim List*, I add the date he's due in the office then write **DEADLINE** above it and circle the lot in red.

20

Experiments in Failure

A mile away, Samira and Leila were just as stumped about how to dispose of Yafir's body, let alone explain his disappearance.

"A pond or a lake?" Leila proposed. "A river, if we weigh him down?"

Samira shook her head. "With climate change and regular droughts, the body might not stay hidden."

"Abandoned mines, wells, bunkers?" Leila scribbled each down. "Could we dissolve him in acid?"

"But where would we do it?"

"In the bathtub?" Leila asked.

"We might kill ourselves with the fumes. And it would ruin the finish, which means an evidence trail."

The doorbell rang, followed swiftly by the phone. Samira hurried down the hall, while Leila picked up the handset. Ever since they'd put out word that Yafir was "self-isolating in the garage," everyone in the extended family network had been in touch to offer sympathies and support. She wanted to be grateful to be part of community and culture, where, if anything, there were too many offers of help, but the situation made it impossible.

"No, please don't send my cousins round, Auntie," came Leila's voice from the kitchen. "It's very kind, but with you and the others stuck in Pakistan, everyone here needs to stay well."

Samira hooked the loops of her mask over her ears, secured her hijab, then took a deep breath and opened the front door. Her husband's cousin twice removed was standing on the drive, smoothing a hand over her abaya.

"Ah, you look so tired. I knew it would be like this with so many worries, so I said to myself, 'I must think of some way to help,' and then Yafir's aunt called and she said to me, 'Samira is a good wife, a good cook, but her aloo gosht, this is not good,' so then I had my purpose." She pointed to a pot beside the door. "I know it is the smallest thing, but with your husband ill"— here the cousin leaned to the side to peer down the hall—"and all his brothers with their poor father in Pakistan, I said to myself that a good meal—a healing meal—this can only help, and then I can say to myself that I have not neglected you in your time of need. Also I brought some paracetamol"—she gestured at a small paper bag beside the pot—"as there is none to be found in the shops now."

"That's so thoughtful—"

"Poor Yafir. His father so ill, and now ill himself. So many worries when there is so little any of us can do. You must tell us if there is something you need—shopping or someone to help nurse Yafir."

"You must excuse me for not staying to thank you properly. I don't have any symptoms yet"—at this Yafir's cousin took a step back—"but I cannot bear the thought of answering your kindness with even the smallest risk." Inclining her head in gratitude, Samira spoke the parting words and eased the door shut.

She hurried to the kitchen to find Leila pacing back and forth, making the occasional noise of assent or concern as the phone in her hand spewed fury about the current travel restrictions and admonishments to be obedient to her father and uncles' guidance, in between buzzing to signal at least one call waiting.

"Leila? Leila, come help me with your sister," Samira called just loud enough for the voice at the end of the phone to go quiet.

"So sorry. My mother needs me," Leila told the phone. "Thank you so much for calling." She hit the end button even as a new voice came over the answering machine. Reaching over, she turned the volume down till the message was a mere murmur. "Well, that's the full complement of aunts." She flopped down in front of their list of possible body-disposal sites.

Samira sank into the chair beside her, taking the pen from her hand. "You shouldn't be doing this. You should go and—"

"Mum." Leila smiled gently. "We're in this together." She cocked her head to one side. "But if the guilt is too much and you've just *got* to make it up to me somehow, my life would be immeasurably better with some paneer paratha and a side order of cardamom and strawberry lassi."

"I'm sorry," Samira whispered, burying her face in her hands. "I'm so sorry. I should never have let you find out what I'd done. What sort of mother—"

"I'm the one who came downstairs when you told me not to."

"You didn't know what you'd find. I didn't think it would be so quick." Samira pressed her fingers into her eyes, wishing it would banish the vision of her daughter in the kitchen doorway watching her father convulse on the floor.

"Well, we're never going to complain about Maryam scarfing her food down again because at least she was out of the way for it." The brightness of Leila's voice was like light catching off broken glass.

"Why *did* you come down? You knew something was wrong."

"I thought the bashing sound was him hitting you."

It had been Yafir's feet knocking against the bottom of the counter as he'd seized and seized until the poison stopped his breathing.

"I wasn't going to leave you down there alone. Not anymore. I thought it was time to start being brave too."

Samira pulled her daughter into her arms. As Leila's tears seeped into the fabric of her shirt, she wished she could pray for forgiveness, but it felt impossible when she intended to do everything in her power to get away with her crime. Perhaps later there would be time for reflection and repentance. For now, all her focus had to be on keeping herself out of prison so she could secure her children's safety.

As she'd stared at the rat poison in the garage it hadn't felt as if she'd come to a decision; she'd simply accepted that there was no other option if her daughter was to live. As that knowledge had sunk through her, everything had become very bright and sharp, as if she were looking at the world through crystal. She remembered thinking that surely it was the breeze, not her own will, that had wafted her from the garage back to the kitchen like one of those little dandelion seeds she'd taught her children to make wishes on, because how else could she have felt so light and airy instead of leaden with dread?

The act of lacing Yafir's food had seemed like a prank. After all, how could gentle, quiet little Samira be doing such a thing even as her girls moved around her, setting the table. She wouldn't poison their father right in front of them. Wouldn't let him die there in the house. Wouldn't . . .

"Mum, you need to breathe."

Leila was rubbing soothing circles on her back.

"I'm fine, I'm fine. You shouldn't be comforting me—"

"Yes, I should," said her defiant child, eyes flashing, then she grinned. "Isn't it about time that my tendency to be a bolshy little shit actually did some good?"

"Leila." Samira sighed scoldingly. "That language."

"Given everything else, I doubt anyone's going to care if I swear too." The words were light but the tone tight with misery. She twisted her hands in her lap. "I . . . You still love me, don't you? Even now you know that I . . . I won't be marrying. At least not . . . not anyone the family would accept, because it's not just . . . It's how I am. It's not going to change and I—"

Reaching out, Samira placed her hand on Leila's cheek, bringing her face round till their eyes met. "You are my beloved daughter."

Leila leaned into her touch. "Were you ever happy with Dad?" she asked, voice all but a whisper.

Samira's eyes went to the door to the garage where Yafir's body was now packed in cat litter in a tarpaulin package stuffed into a hastily emptied shipping crate. "I hoped I would be. Our families said it was a good match and I trusted that they knew what was best for me." She fiddled with her favorite bracelet— the one Maryam had made for her in a Mother's-Day-themed art class the previous year. "I wonder if anyone really knows the person they're marrying. If it were as simple as choosing for yourself, then why are there so many divorced parents among the white families at your school? When older, wiser people who love you—"

"How could they have loved you and made you marry Dad?"

"They didn't make me. They only asked. I was willing. I said yes."

"But why? I don't understand." Leila raked her hands through her long hair, snapping on a band then tossing the ponytail angrily over her shoulder. "Why didn't you leave? If they picked for you, wasn't it their responsibility when it all went wrong and you realized how awful he is? Was."

She would never tell her daughter about the one time she had sought aid. With her parents and brother dead, Yafir had isolated her from the rest of her own family, so she had turned instead to the sister-in-law who lived closest and who had always been kind to her. There were no words in their shared language for the things that were happening in the darkness of her marital bedroom—perhaps that was to stop them being spoken. And yet, in desperation, she had tried to explain all the same.

In response, Kiran had shaken Samira's hand from her arm as if it dripped with filth. The look of revulsion on her face branded itself through every layer of Samira's skin until shame was burned across her heart, trailing her like a second shadow; every time the idea of seeking help had raised its head, she'd looked down and seen that shame lying at her feet.

"It is a wife's duty to be pleasant and pleasing," Kiran had said. "A wife who cannot hold her husband's secrets brings shame on him. What right does she have to expect kindness and good treatment when she gives him none?"

Samira had wanted to cry out that Islam demanded no such thing—that these were the prescriptions of men, not God. Scripture told her that God would not try her beyond her capacity, and yet she could see no way to make her husband treat her with the goodness their faith commanded. So she never spoke of her husband's cruelty again. What was the point in doing it now, after all those years of pain, when it was finally over?

"My brother had just died and my parents were . . . we were all heartbroken," she told Leila instead. "A marriage—the start of a new family—was a promise of hope that soon there would be happiness again." Her face softened as she looked at her daughter. "And you are my happiness. You and your sister. You were your grandparents' joy."

"Why wasn't Dad happy? Was it because Maryam and I are both girls?" Leila shook her head. "I don't understand how he could treat you like that. I don't understand how he could even consider . . ." She trailed off, swallowing. "I keep thinking about when we all used to play Monopoly together and we'd all be laughing and laughing because he'd try to sneak money out of the bank, but really obviously, so Maryam always spotted him and . . . How can someone be like that and then do things like this?" Her fingers trailed the edge of a bruise on her mother's arm.

Samira pulled her sleeve down.

"I know I should feel bad about plotting ways to get rid of his body, but I don't really feel anything." Leila turned her solemn, dark eyes on her mother. "Is there something wrong with me? Is that why he—"

Samira's hand closed about her daughter's. "No," she said. "There will be time for sorrow and guilt later. For now, we are doing as we must. I am just sorry that you are a part of this." For a second, despair rushed through her, but she forced it away.

There was nothing she could do about Leila's involvement now, but at least her daughter's hands were clean of the killing itself. All she'd done was help move her father from the kitchen, then she'd taken Maryam out to fetch supplies to parcel him up, leaving Samira to scrub and scrub and scrub the floor as if she could bleach the sin from her hands like the evidence from the tiles.

Leila shook herself. "Well, we are where we are, right? You're safe and I'm safe, and we're going to keep it that way, so Dad'll just have to go." She tapped her pen against the list. "If we backed the car up to the garage, we could move the crate to the boot then . . . No, the satnav would record the journey and the exact GPS coordinates of wherever we put him. It'd practically be a signed confession if the body were found."

Samira took a deep breath, hands clenching on her knees. "We'll have to cut him up. Then we can get rid of him." She forced the words out in a rush, hurrying on before she could hear the echo of them hanging there in the air. "It'll be easier when it's . . . when it's bit by bit." Her eyes fixed on the scuff mark Maryam had made on the wall the other week with her muddy gym kit. She'd scrubbed with soap, with spray, and even resorted to bleach, and there it still was, though the only trace of Yafir was sitting in the shipping crate in the garage.

"The difficulty," she heard herself say in the calmest, coolest tone, as if talking about her favorite brand of disinfectant, "is that if we put the bits in different places it maximizes the chances of parts being found, but if it's one place it needs to be big enough *and* it'll mean at least several trips if we're on foot, unless . . . What if we used one of the . . ." She snapped her fingers in frustration. "Oh, what are they called again? You know—those roll-y suitcases?"

Leila swallowed hard, her face pinched and sick. "Wouldn't it seem suspicious to be out with a suitcase in Lockdown?" She shrugged helplessly. "But I guess, under the circumstances, it would make sense to find out."

21

Old Friends and New Enemies

Two hours later, with no progress on the *Get Rid of Jim List*, I turn to the *Be Happy* one. My eyes land on **RECONNECT WITH OLD FRIENDS** and refuse to move on.

Janey. That's what that line means. Not the cousins I've fallen out of touch with. Not the members of my old book group or the mums from Amy and Charlie's school. I could call any of them right now and, though I'd be sorry if they made excuses to get off the phone, it wouldn't break my heart. If Janey hung up on me or I left a message and she never called back . . .

Picking up my phone, I scroll my contacts list to the Js and click into Janey's entry.

"God, I want to hear your voice." I lower my finger, but it freezes above the screen. "You've just parcel-wrapped your husband's corpse. You can phone your oldest friend," I tell myself.

Instead, I take a sip of lukewarm tea. Then I fetch myself a biscuit. Rosemary and Petunia eye me disapprovingly.

I drop back into my chair, pick up the phone again—and sit there, failing and failing and failing to hit the call button.

What am I going to say? "Hey, Courage. It's Courage!" as if we'd talked yesterday and nothing had changed between us instead of everything?

Will it matter to Janey that I want to talk? Will it matter that I'm sorry?

I miss her voice and her ghost stories. I miss our in-jokes. I miss our memories.

I miss her as if I've lost part of myself.

My phone switches itself to sleep mode. Reflected on the black screen, my eyes are hollow with misery.

Suddenly the kitchen is too quiet, the house too big and too small, too empty and too full with the parcel, the parcel that is Jim, Jim who is dead and . . .

I grab Jim's phone, my bag, and keys and rush out on to the front path, closing the door on the horror, the grief.

The sky is flecked with blue and gray like a bird's egg. It looks oddly delicate, as if the trees could tear it. My heart is beating too fast, but I feel it settle as a warm breeze brushes my face like a gentle hand. The air smells of cut grass and . . . Ribena?

I close my eyes and I'm in Granny's tiny garden, burying my nose in a trailing frond of magenta flowers.

"Ribes," I whisper, the word floating up from my memory. "Flowering currant."

I can almost feel the texture of the leaves. Opening my eyes, I look across the street and there it is, flowering in a sheltered spot in the corner of Edwina's front garden. As I stand smiling across the street, the curtains in her front room quiver. I wave before I can stop myself, then feel my heart sink as her door opens.

"Good morning," she says in a voice that makes my insides shrivel. "Everything all right? Only I noticed you were out earlier too."

"That was food shopping." I think about adding, Since cheese and cake are about all that's stopping me from screaming in the street, I figured it was the lesser of two evils, but would you rather I did that instead? but manage to stop myself.

Edwina's eyes narrow. "If this is your daily exercise, I trust you'll not be joining Jim if he decides to take another midnight stroll," she says in that mild but terrifying way she has. "Rules are rules. If being a true-crime buff for fifty years has taught me anything, it's that people who sneak about at night are usually up to no good."

"What would we be up to?" I ask, intending to make a joke of it, but the words come out sharp and biting.

"That tone is uncalled for."

"The other one on offer is primal scream, so take your pick," I say before I can stop myself.

Then I turn and stomp off down the street, furious with myself, because it was pure stupidity to let my frustrations and stresses boil over just when Edwina was actually, if unintentionally, being so useful.

I march up the street and round the corner. My thoughts are so flooded with anger and misery that I pay no attention to my route, which is how I find myself approaching the house from the opposite direction only ten minutes later. When Edwina's curtains promptly seethe, I give up, storming up the front path, through the door, then on down the hall and out of the kitchen into the garden, where I glare at the sky, hands raised into claws.

Edwina turning out to be a budding Miss Marple is the one thing that could possibly make her even more of a danger to my staying-out-of-prison plans than she already is.

"Why did she have to be into true crime?" I ask the sky. "Why couldn't it be carpentry? Or chess? Or taxidermy?"

If only I could ask her all my questions about the forensic mistakes I'm doubtless making. I bet she'd know the answers . . .

With a blink, I realize she's inadvertently given me the perfect way to carry out some entirely innocuous research. A wide smile breaks across my face.

Five minutes later, I've ordered myself a stack of forensic-heavy murder mysteries: finally, I have a way to solve some of my body-disposal problems without the aid of dodgy Google searches.

With a true-crime podcast playing in the background, I set about making a batch of Granny's beef stew by way of a reward. When I bought the ingredients, I thought it would bring back a wave of happy memories of teaching Amy and Charlie the recipe. Instead, I drift into misery again. What will they remember from their childhood? How common laughter was when we were three but how rare when we were four; how we all spoke more softly, moved more quietly, when Jim was home?

I refocus on the cooking to find raw beef bleeding across the chopping board even as the podcast presenter describes a particularly gory murder. I move on to chopping carrots, but the knife is too blunt. I lean my weight into it and the carrot cracks with a sound like bone breaking.

BY THE TIME I'VE pulled on Jim's hat and coat for my midnight rendezvous with Ruth, I'm half convinced she'll have thought better of it, but there she is, waiting in the shadow of the first cluster of trees at the edge of the wood. I thought we'd launch straight into a discussion of possible body-disposal sites, but instead I tell her about Amy and Charlie, and she tells me about her son. It still feels like progress—in more ways than one.

After years of struggling to keep my texts and emails secret from Jim, it is the oddest thing to find myself eagerly reading aloud Amy's latest message to a stranger, but maybe that's the point. I'm choosing to read it to Ruth—just as she chooses to read the email her son sent that morning in exchange.

Charlie's song of the day is "Somewhere over the Rainbow." We listen to it sitting at opposite ends of a fallen tree trunk in the moonlit woods, our faces wet with tears but bright with smiles.

"I keep telling myself the main thing is that Jim never hit the kids—he knew that was the one line he couldn't cross—but he didn't have to hit them to hurt them." I take a shuddering breath. "I promised myself I wouldn't live a life like my mother's—that if I ever had kids, it would all be different. But is it enough that they never saw what he did? Charlie knows *something* is wrong. Last time he was home he was going on about how unhealthy our relationship is—hence the big blowup and not seeing him for months even before the Lockdown."

"I don't know them, but a son who sends you songs and a daughter who calls to check in are children who've been raised well and given all the love they need. You're not to blame for their father not doing the same." Ruth looks down at her phone. "My son has grown into such a good man. He's my mother all over again." Her fond smile dissolves suddenly into bleakness. "If he knew what I've done . . ."

"We'll make sure they never find out," I promise. "And maybe one day, after this is over, we can all have dinner together. If you want," I add shyly.

Ruth smiled. "I'd like that." She shakes her head. "What will you do after, if we find a way through?"

Technically, it's now Day 6 since Jim died—another day closer to his stint on the rota. There's time, of course, to sort it all out, but how long can I afford to keep telling myself that when I've no solutions? When does it stop being optimism and turn into stupidity?

I hunch my shoulders. "I've always wanted to have a job, but Jim . . ." I shake my head. "What have I been *doing* these last years with the kids off at uni?"

"It takes a lot of time to second-guess everything you do and say, trying to spot the next thing that'll be a problem before he notices. It's been my full-time job for years too."

For a while neither of us speaks.

"I'm doing some gardening," I say eventually. "And I've got this list. I call it my 'Be Happy List' and it's all the things I'm going to do to make my life better, bigger, fuller. I'll never be clever enough or qualified enough to do something important like being a nurse, but I'd still like to help people somehow. Do you ever think about going back to work, or would you have to retrain?" I hurry on, before Ruth can say anything that would cut me with kindness. "Not that it can be any fun as a nurse right now, but—"

"I'd love to go back to the hospital," Ruth says, her voice aching with longing. "I thought I was only stopping temporarily, but Lionel was so happy when I was home more, and things between us were so good, and . . ." She grips the battered old locket that hangs at her throat on a thin gold chain. "When our situation is sorted, I'm going back. It's the first thing I'll do."

"Nursing during a pandemic has got to be worth excellent penance points." I wince as the words come out of my mouth. "That was meant to be encouraging."

Ruth just laughs. "It wouldn't be penance. It would be a joy. A gift. And nurses are so needed right now I wouldn't feel as if I was being rewarded for . . ." She gestures vaguely, then suddenly her expression shifts. "What if we drove the bodies to the coast? Isn't that what gangsters do: put bodies in the sea tied down with weights?"

I blink at her, wrong-footed by the change of topic. Then I remember how often my own mind has jumped from terror to something entirely ordinary: there's an odd comfort in discovering that this too is normal for our situation.

"The trouble is what we'd say if we got stopped by the police to ask where we were going in Lockdown. Not to mention that it won't help to explain their disappearance. Maybe there's a river that's not too far away where we could set up a fishing accident?"

"My husband never fished in his life."

I pick at a loose bit of bark on our impromptu bench, shaking my head. "It's no good anyway. Rivers can be dragged and that won't end well, since people don't tend to accidentally parcel themselves up in cat-litter-filled tarpaulins."

"What if that's where we say they've gone, but we hide the bodies somewhere else? Surely two of us telling the same story would have to count for something."

"Except that sooner or later the police will try tracking their phones. Even if we drop them on the riverbank, it begs the question why the phones are there but not the bodies. Given it's usually the spouse when someone vanishes or dies, they'll get crime-scene investigators to examine our homes, and they're bound to find something, no matter how carefully we clean."

I lapse into silence, doing my best to Think Great Thoughts. When I glance over at Ruth, I find her stroking her locket, a sick look on her face.

"Do we need to go through it again?" I ask gently.

Ruth shakes her head, but her free arm wraps around her middle.

"It's too late to go to the police," I remind her, trying to keep my voice soft and reassuring. "They won't believe it was self-defense at this point. And it is not going to make the world a better place—certainly not for our kids—if we spend the next two decades in prison when we could be living our lives and doing good and helping our children cope with their fathers disappearing."

It's the third time we've gone through this, but instead of it being irritating I find it soothing. Every time I put her mind at ease, it cements my own determination.

Ruth checks her watch. "We should sleep," she says dully, standing and brushing off her trousers. "Maybe I could call you in the morning?" she asks as we make our way back through the woods to the street. "It feels like such a long time until tomorrow night—"

"I'd love that."

We exchange a shy smile as we step from under the shadow of the trees into the orange glow of the empty street.

"Actually, you shouldn't call me—you should use Lionel's phone to call Jim's. That way we can build up a picture that our husbands knew each other first. It'll be a whole lot less suspicious for giving each other alibis."

Ruth nods solemnly. "Thank goodness one of us can be clever about the details. I did everything you said about the tarpaulin and the cat litter, and it was awful, but at least I've got the comfort that he won't start to smell. I wish I could come up with something useful in return. My best thought is that my cousin has a big van." She pauses, frowning. "He's also got a wood-chipper."

A moment later her eyes widen in horror as she registers her own words. "I'm going to hell," she says—to me, the street, the universe. "I am definitely, one hundred percent, going to hell. If there *is* a hell. And if there isn't, I'm going to get reincarnated as something awful—a poodle, maybe. Or one of those cats without fur. Or a bluebottle. I probably deserve to be a bluebottle. 'Be a good person,' my mother told me, and now I'm not just a killer, I'm trying to get away with it."

"We'll sort ourselves out, then you can rebalance the cosmic scales caring for the plague-ridden."

I expect a gentle chiding when she stops to stare at me, but instead her face is soft with kindness.

"I may change my mind about going to the police, but I will never tell a soul your secrets," she says solemnly. "My mother was the best person I've ever known and, though she'd despair of what I've become—what I've done—she'd forgive me. 'If you can't have faith, show conscience'—that was the last thing she told me."

I'm still fumbling after a reply when a strange noise—a gathering roar punctuated by sharp clacks—makes us both look around.

"How loud were we being?" I hiss as the noise grows closer.

A tall, slim figure rounds the corner.

22

Merrily We Roll Along

The figure marches resolutely down the middle of the road in high-heeled boots, dragging a wheeled suitcase. Although her head is down, below her carefully pinned hijab I can just make out that her lips are pursed in a determined line. As she passes under a streetlight, I realize she's a teenager.

The girl looks up, eyes widening in fear when she sees us, her pace faltering. Taking a deep breath, she steels herself to carry on, but as she steps forward her heel catches in a pothole, sending her lurching to the side, the suitcase careening away. One of the wheels catches in a grate, the jerk wrenching the handle from the girl's fingers as she sprawls onto the tarmac.

Ruth and I hurry forward.

"Are you all right?" Ruth calls, slowing her rush when the girl sits up with a frustrated rather than pained groan.

"Peachy," comes the dour reply as she inspects her palms.

"I have hand gel," Ruth offers, fishing in her pockets.

"I've got some too, but do you think I have to? It's going to sting something fierce."

"But you won't get an infection. Nurse's orders," Ruth says, gentle but firm.

The girl heaves a sigh but complies. I crouch to examine the suitcase, but when I try to jiggle the wheel loose, the girl bounds up, fear on her face.

"That's OK," she says, hurrying to take the handle again. "I'll figure it out. Don't want to break social distancing over a silly old suitcase."

I raise my hands, backing away. "If you're worried about the Covid restrictions, why are you out with a suitcase in the middle of the night? You can't be traveling, and it's illegal to stay overnight somewhere unless . . . Are you in trouble?"

The girl's eyes fly wide. "I'm fine!" she says, voice suddenly tight and high. "I'm just . . ." She blinks rapidly. "Collecting books," she says. "My aunt put some books at the bottom of her garden for me and I was just picking them up so we had something new to read. I'm allowed an hour to exercise, so it's all fine, totally aboveboard, nothing to see here so . . . yeah."

We stare at each other.

"Gotta go. My exercise hour's nearly up," the girl says brightly, "and I promised my sister—"

Suddenly I recognize her: the girl with the purple boots and hijab from the DIY store. The one with the little sister—and the trolley of items disconcertingly similar to mine.

"How's your cat?" I blurt out, sensing that I need to delay her, but not quite understanding why.

"What cat?" the girl asks, face completely blank.

"We bumped into each other at the DIY shop. You were buying a ton of cat litter."

The girl does the rapid-blinking thing again, like a computer taking its time to process a command. She swallows thickly.

My eyes drift to the suitcase.

The girl tenses as if readying herself to run, and something flashes through me: some sense that here is the missing piece of my getting-rid-of-Jim puzzle. What Ruth and I can accomplish together, using each other as alibis, is still risky. But as a trio—three unrelated women who've only met recently—the police will never suspect a thing.

Plus, if we have to dig a grave, it'll go far faster and easier with another pair of hands.

"Do you have actual body parts in there, or is this a trial run?"

Ruth gapes at me.

"Wha—Why . . . That's not . . . That's a really strange thing to say," the girl blusters. "I'm just . . . No," she says, backing up. "No, I'm not talking to you, you weirdo. As if I'd have body parts in here."

When she attempts a laugh, I want to crow. I *knew* it.

Tilting my head, I squint at the suitcase again. "I can't see any blood, so either you've wrapped the parts really well or you're wheeling around some rocks to see if anyone stops you."

Her face tightens. "I'm going to see my auntie."

"I thought that's where you were coming from."

"You're confusing me!" the girl snaps, wrenching at the suitcase. A particularly vicious twist sets it free, making her stagger backward. "I've got to get home. Leave me alone or I'll scream."

I raise an eyebrow. "If you don't like my questions about cats and what's in the suitcase, I doubt you'll want to summon the police down on yourself."

"Well, what are *you* doing out here?" She eyes Ruth. "And what does your friend think about you accusing teenagers of carting about bits of dead body?"

"I think we're probably going to end up in prison, given we've got a rather similar problem," Ruth says, "but that at least it'll be together."

The girl goggles at us. "What even is this conversation? What is happening here?" She throws her hands in the air.

"Why *do* you think she has a body in the suitcase?" Ruth asks me.

"We had the same odd stuff in our trolleys at the DIY shop," I explain.

"Do you *really* have body parts in there?" Ruth asks the girl.

"No!" she snaps. Then she deflates. "It really *is* a bunch of books. I wanted to see if I could get away with going out with a suitcase without getting stopped. Clearly not, though I never figured the questions I got would be this sort." She glances around warily. "We should *not* be having this conversation in the street."

"I know," Ruth says, "but before you go, *do* you have any tips about disposal methods? We could really use some."

23

Two Plus Two = Hope

Twenty minutes later I am part of the oddest tea party I've ever heard of.

We're in a garage with the door to the street wide open. Ruth and I sit on the street side in folding picnic chairs, one on either side of the space, both to socially distance and to ensure no one can approach and overhear without us realizing. On a crate next to the door to the house sit Leila and her mother, Samira, who I'd guess to be in her mid-thirties. She's slim like her daughter, but short where Leila is tall, and shy where Leila is—or at least seems—confident. There's a brittleness to Leila's spark, though whether that's the product of the current situation or just because she's seventeen I can't yet tell. After all, anyone would be a little brittle when sitting in front of a large plastic crate that's surrounded by mousetraps, topped with bowls of vinegar and bicarb of soda and filled with a dead dad.

"Did you just use cat litter or something else too?" Leila asks, as I examine her setup. "I ordered a bunch of those little desiccant pouches they put in new handbags, though I've no idea if they're useful with something so large. At least the salt should prevent any bugs hatching."

Samira turns anxiously toward the door into the house. "Should I—"

"You'll just wake her up, Mum," Leila says. "My little sister," she explains to Ruth. "She's seven."

"Does she know about . . ." I gesture at the crate.

"She's seven," Leila says pointedly.

"She believes her father is self-isolating in here to keep us safe," Samira whispers.

Leila snorts. "First time for everything, I suppose."

"Leila!" Samira sighs.

Leila rolls her eyes nonchalantly enough, but the way her arms cross over her chest speaks volumes. "It's OK, Mum. They understand. Literally."

"If you speak with such callousness, how are they to know we aren't bad people? How are they to believe we had no other choice?"

I raise a hand. "I believe you." I gesture at Ruth. "And I believed her before she'd said a word."

"The fact that we all recognize ourselves in each other tells us that we are in the same boat," Ruth says in her gentle way.

Leila gives us a doubtful stare. "You offed your husbands because they were planning to commit some nice patriarchal violence by way of marrying your daughter to a stranger just to avoid a bit of gossip?"

I stare at Samira, who presses the flat of one palm to her forehead. "Good for you," I tell her. "Why on earth would he do that?"

"My cousin—we're at the same school—was going through photos for the yearbook, and in the background of one of the Valentine's Day ones you can just make out that I'm holding hands with my girlfriend and she's giving me a rose." She shakes her head. "I was always so careful, but she just surprised me." She shrugs helplessly. "I didn't even know about the bloody photo. One step to the left and I'd have been out of the frame. I tried to tell Dad that it was nothing—just a joke with a friend— but he didn't care. Said that the rumor was as bad as the truth. That for our family to be associated with . . ." She looks away. "He beat Mum up when she tried to stop him laying into me. Then it all went quiet and . . ."

Samira's hand goes to her throat, splayed there protectively. "I heard my husband on a video call with his brothers and uncles—they're all together in Pakistan because their father is ill. We were meant to go with them, but Maryam's passport was out of date and by the time we renewed it and rebooked our flight it was Lockdown, so we were stuck here, and they're stuck there—"

"They don't need the epic version, Mum," Leila cuts in, rolling her eyes. "The important bit is that they had a charming family conference about how to salvage the family's reputation and give me a chance of a 'normal life' by making me marry a total stranger whose main interest in me is that I'm a British citizen. I mean, I'm sorry for anyone who'd be so desperate for a better life that he'd tie himself to me just for a visa, but—"

When she breaks off, nostrils flaring, Samira finishes the explanation. "The plan was for us to go over as soon as the restrictions lifted on the premise of seeing my father-in-law, only we'd get off the plane and step straight into a marriage ceremony."

Leila tosses her head. "You probably think there were about a million ways for me to get out of it, but if your whole extended family is conspiring to make it happen, sooner or later it will. Even if you go along with it then leave the marriage afterward, they come for you, and you can't get away because they're all in on it and you have to go back to him, and if you don't 'behave' and let him do whatever he wants to you, then they . . ." She looks away. "The papers don't always make the same fuss as when white teenagers are murdered, but I've read too many stories about girls like me, and if anyone is going to end up in pieces in a suitcase, then better it's my father."

She tosses her head defiantly. Then bursts into tears, burying her face in her hands while Ruth and I look on in misery. Where is the triumph in having to do awful things to escape worse?

Samira puts an arm around her. My body aches with the need for my own children. To hold them so tight you feel you can almost press them back into your own body, where they'll be safe.

"It is not all of the family, Leila," Samira says quietly. "Only some of them believe such things are right. The others . . . they're as trapped as we are. They know this is not part of Islam. But they don't have the power or the will to stand in the way when it comes to other men wanting to control women." Her face goes bleak. "Your father will never hurt you again. That, at least, is over now."

"But it was fine all those years he hurt you?" Leila bites out, dashing her hand across her cheek. "I should have said something at school. The teachers are nice. They'd have helped us."

"Helped us do what?" Samira asks, with a patient sigh—this is clearly an argument they've had before. "Run away and change our names and never, ever come home again? Never speak to anyone in the family? Never . . ." She trails off, raising her hands helplessly, then turns to me and Ruth. "Everywhere I turn, there is no solution. What are we going to do?"

"We're four smart, capable women—together we're going to take control of our lives and figure it out," I tell her with all the confidence I can muster, which isn't very much, but then beggars can't be choosers.

"We should cross-stitch that. Very moving," Leila says, biting her lip.

"Leila!" hisses her mother.

But I just laugh. "It *was* good, wasn't it? Inspiring, motivational, authoritative . . ."

Leila grins. "Very suffragettes meets Wonder Woman."

For a moment my heart pinches with longing for Janey as a memory floats up of the lesson where our stupid, beloved in-joke started. If I close my eyes, I can see the classroom and our gray-faced, gray-clad teacher: see the way she snapped her textbook closed, a fierce look transforming her face. "The suffragettes may mean nothing to you now, but even if you don't remember their names, remember this—five of the strongest words in our history: a pledge from each woman to her sisters, and a call for their pledge in return. 'Courage calls to courage everywhere.'"

How I wish Janey were here to say, "We need some courage now, hey, Courage?"

I push the need for Janey away. Instead, I focus on the new friends around me.

24

Tag, You're It

The next day, Leila stays home with Maryam while Samira joins me and Ruth on our first daytime walk. Despite the welcome distraction of my new partners in crime, longing for Janey twinges at the back of my mind like a raw nerve.

I can't imagine a life where I never talk to her again, but I still haven't summoned the courage to call, though I know that if she were the one who'd cut herself off I'd want to fix things. But Janey has always been prone to strops, so if I called and she didn't pick up, a day might become a week, might become a month, before I knew for sure if there was any hope or not. I couldn't bear that. Not with Jim still lying along the washing machine. Not with four new friends counting on me to do my fair share to get us out of our mutual mess.

"We should agree to some ground rules about how to reach each other," I say, before I disappear down a Janey-shaped hole of despair. "It's going to be impossible to pretend we don't know each other at all, but if everyone thinks we know each other through our husbands that makes everything much less suspicious. We should use their phones for calls, then it'll create a digital trail that they're still alive, while cementing the idea that they got to know each other pretty well during Lockdown."

Samira nods. "What's the explanation for how they met?"

"For us, it's that Lionel did some minor decorating work at Sally and Jim's house." Ruth can't help a proud little smile as she adds, "I even wrote up an invoice with 'payment in cash' to create a paper trail."

Samira tils her head thoughtfully. "Has Lionel's van ever broken down? Could he have hired Yafir to taxi him around for a day?"

Ruth shakes her head. "No go on the van. He'd find a way round paying for something like that. But"—her face brightens—"before the pandemic a friend of his with Man United season tickets used to invite him to the odd match and he'd come home so late he'd spring for a cab from the station."

"I'll write you a receipt," Samira says. "We just need to think of an excuse for why they got back in touch."

"Lionel and Jim have been WhatsApping about sports, so let's give it a day to find something credible, then Lionel can add Yafir to the group."

"Maybe Lionel can say something about Yafir sharing some strong political views during the post-football taxi ride when they met. That'll seems natural enough." Ruth grimaces. "Well, natural in Lockdown terms at least."

"I'd never believe it usually," Samira says, fretting with her bracelet, "but with the world upside down . . ."

"Exactly," I say. "Anyway, Ruth and I have made it look like Jim and Lionel are going on the odd walk together, but obviously, with Yafir self-isolating, he couldn't join even if he wanted to."

Samira looks relieved. "If we're going to create a story about them all disappearing together, we need to take it step by step: focus on making it seem believable that they finally got together in person."

"Right now, though, we need some code words for getting hold of each other in emergencies—something in case we need to meet asap at an agreed place, and another code word to call each other." I flash a glance at Ruth. "How about 'Bakewell Tarts' for a meeting, and 'bonfire' for a phone call?"

Ruth shakes her head, suppressing a grin, then her eyes move beyond me and she hurries forward. "How about this?" She crouches to look closer at the manhole cover by her feet. "There's no lock, so we'd just need a claw hammer or something to get it open, but it's big enough and we could drive right up."

Samira looks around at the houses that line the road. "Lots of upper-story rooms with a view of the street. It's too much of a risk. And it would be bad enough if one of the bodies washed out, but if it were all three . . ."

Ruth sighs but walks on. "I found a website about abandoned properties. Don't worry," she adds quickly. "I made sure it was part of a bunch of research on archaeology courses, then a series of googles about whether there are old coal mines or wartime bunkers nearby."

I give her an admiring look.

"Don't smile at me like that. It makes me feel like I'm giving into—"

"Corrupting influences?"

"You and Leila have the same sense of humor," Samira tells me, a little smile at the corner of her mouth. Then it fades. "There is something I must tell you." She gulps in an uneven breath. "Lionel's death was an accident. And, Sally, you only hit out in the moment, but I . . . I used poison. Please," she rushes on, "you have to know it wasn't planned. At least I overheard the conversation, just like we told you, then I . . . I don't know how to describe it. It was like the world moved itself a step to the side and it just . . . It stopped feeling real."

"It was spur of the moment," I say. "We get it. You just grabbed it—"

"But I didn't! First, I tried the doors, but they were all locked and the keys were gone, and the last one was the door into the garage, only that was locked too so I couldn't even get Leila out of the house. I don't know what I thought would happen if I didn't do something immediately—maybe nothing would have happened, but maybe they'd have fought and he'd have killed me when I tried to stop him hurting her, then there would have been no one between him and Leila . . ."

She shakes her head. "I was just standing there, and I saw the poison, and I don't know if I meant to kill him. Part of me wants to believe I thought it would just make him ill—ill enough I could get the keys while he was being sick, but . . ." She lets her breath out slowly as acceptance steals across her face. "But I knew it might be worse than that. And, when it happened, I didn't call an ambulance. Perhaps I might have, but it was so fast."

"You did it to save Leila." Ruth's smile is pained, but there is no conflict in her eyes. "What else were you to do when you'd already tried and failed to fight him, and there was no way out? Self-defense has to include fighting in a way that might actually let you win."

"But will we win?" Samira asks, voice quavering. "Or will we all end up in prison instead of the ground?"

"Look," I say when Ruth and Samira's shoulders slump in unison, "we're going to have to go through lots of ideas before we figure it out. We've got time." I don't mention my little ticking-clock situation. I'm trying not to think about the fact that there's only a little over a fortnight till Jim's stint on the office rota.

"That may be true for you, but not for me," Samira says grimly. "But I have an idea. One that will work." She takes a deep breath. "We will say that your husbands developed symptoms, so they agreed to self-isolate with my husband, and then I killed them all. I fetched the poison into the kitchen more than an hour before I put it in his food. Under the law, that's premeditation. I'm the one who should pay the price." Ruth and I stare at her, then at each other, then at Samira again.

"Leaving aside the fact that we've just agreed we don't see you had any more choice than we did, I'm not following how this is going to help," I say, baffled.

"We'll say that I did it. That you didn't know because I took their phones and texted regularly to pretend all was well. Then, after the fourteen days, when they didn't return home, you came to find out and . . ." She spreads her hands wide.

"I still don't get it." I look over at Ruth, who just shrugs. "And then . . . what?"

"Then I go to prison, and you make sure Leila and Maryam are safe. If I tell the police that I killed Yafir to stop him forcing Leila into marriage—and that Jim and Lionel were collateral damage—the family will know they can't touch Leila. If anything happened to her after that, the police would know exactly why and who was involved. They wouldn't risk it. She'd be untouchable till she was old enough to get away and make a life of her own, but you would have to promise me that you'd watch over her. Maryam will be fine while she's so young." She says it confidently, but the expression in her eyes tells a different story. "One of the best things about our culture is that family will always step in for children who lose their parents. Her aunts might try to teach her things I don't agree with, but she'd have her sister, and school, and the two of you to ensure she gets to live the life she deserves."

"Your kids are still children: ours are grown up. If someone needs to take one for the team, it's going to be me," I say tightly.

"Or me," adds Ruth staunchly.

"If it comes down to it, there's no way we would let you take the fall," I promise.

"As if we could live with that," breathes Ruth, clutching her locket. "Whatever happens to you happens to us too. We get through this together or not at all."

Samira turns away, shuddering, and I realize she's crying. I want to offer a hug or at least press her hand. In the end, I just stare helplessly at Ruth while we wait for Samira's shoulders to stop heaving.

"If only we had all been friends before this," she says softly as she wipes the tears from her cheeks.

"Well, we're friends now."

Samira's face goes impossibly gentle but sad. "And I am so grateful for that—even to have people to talk to as I try to figure out what to do . . ." She sighs. "The thing is, you may be able to persuade your family, your friends, your community that your husbands have gone out with friends and met some terrible accident, but that is not a possibility for me. It would take something catastrophic—a mental breakdown, the family being wiped out in an earthquake . . . Even now it's hard enough to find excuses for my husband not making phone calls while he's ill, but soon—a fortnight at most—his brothers will expect either to talk to him or hear that he's in the hospital. And it's not just one person or two who will know there's something wrong: it's a dozen in the close family alone."

"So, it's going to be complicated, but most of the close family is stuck in Pakistan, right? It'll be a while before they can get back, and that buys us some time."

"I can tell you about various symptoms that would mean Yafir can't talk," Ruth adds.

But Samira shakes her head, hands clenching with frustration. "You don't understand how it is in our community. Everyone knows everyone—everyone *talks* to everyone."

"But the regulations," I say. "Surely—"

"I don't know how to explain so you will understand." She flings her hands up in frustration. "They had a family meeting: they decided about Leila together. If Yafir cannot make the arrangements, one of his brothers will step in. In their way of thinking, if we—their wives, daughters, nieces—misbehave, then, because the men in the family are responsible for us, they are to blame and must make sure everyone knows they have corrected us. If they don't, they are seen as condoning our behavior instead of doing their duty to set us on the right path. It's . . ." She shakes her head. "It's too much to explain."

"But to force your child into lifelong misery . . ." Ruth says, aghast. "Was your family like that too?"

"No!" She sighs. "No, my parents were different. At least until my brother died." She looks away, face lined with misery. "He was in a car with three friends from university. They'd all been drinking, and somehow the car came off the road and went into a tree. My brother and one of the others died. It broke my parents' hearts. Broke all our hearts. He was . . ." A tear slips onto her cheek. "The shame that he'd been drinking when he died—that he'd been in a car with a drunk driver . . ." She shakes her head. "The things people said to my parents. That they had failed my brother by letting him become westernized, instead of guiding him as they should. How irresponsible it was to even consider letting me go off to university when they owed it to me to be there to protect me from making similar choices . . . They couldn't bear it on top of the grief. None of us could. I would have agreed to anything that . . ." She trails off wearily. "Please. It's too much to talk of old griefs now. We have to focus on what to do to keep ourselves safe, because there's only so long I can keep making excuses, and then . . ."

"Maybe there is no other solution than one of us fessing up," I say, "but we've got four good brains between us. Let's see what we can do with them before we go down that path."

Samira clearly thinks it's hopeless, but she does her best to smile. "It will bring Leila comfort to know we tried," she says.

We walk on in silence.

25

Midnight Monsters

Silence was in great demand but short supply across town that night in the house of the very, very tired new mother.

"GET YOUR FAT ARSE OUT OF THE HALL!" bellowed her husband as she wandered the house trying to comfort their wailing baby.

Gulping down her sobs, the very, very tired new mother stumbled into the nursery, where she sank onto the laundry chest in the corner, clicking on the night light—Titania, the fairy queen, with wand raised aloft in a pose more like a Valkyrie with a spear. Keith said it looked violent, but to her Titania's face spoke only of a resolve to protect those who fell within the sphere of the golden light spilling from the bulb at the end of her wand.

Now it felt like a safe little island as she nestled with her daughter while her favorite children's book characters romped around the encircling walls.

"Look, darling," she whispered, just to hear another voice that wasn't wailing or shouting. "There's Winnie-the-Pooh and Tigger and Eeyore."

As her eyes blurred with exhaustion, she jerked upright.

For a second, Eeyore had seemed to turn and snarl at her, revealing a set of extremely sharp teeth.

As she looked to the side, the Mad Hatter doffed his cap, while the White Rabbit gave her the finger.

Curling over the baby, her long red hair spilling around them, the very, very tired new mother pressed a kiss to her daughter's hot little head. "I love you," she whispered. "I love you and I want you." She squeezed her eyes shut. "Daddy wants you too. He's just so tired. We're old, you see—over forty! And it's hard, not sleeping, and all the cleaning . . ."

The baby promptly sneezed, spraying snot into her mother's face.

"Yes, my love—exactly. It's a lot of spit and it's everywhere, and then there's all the wee and the poo and the puke, and that may be par for the course for you, but your mummy isn't a very good mummy yet. She's trying her very best—and she's going to get better, I promise—but she keeps forgetting to cook dinner and she's too sore to do the cleaning properly, and she keeps eating and eating, even though she's already made herself so fat and ugly . . ."

Taking a shuddering breath, she forced the tears down, then opened her dressing gown, proffering her breast. After a few attempts, the baby latched on and settled.

Reaching out, she turned off the night light and set the music box going. The top lit up, sending a procession of blue witches and green sea-dragons dancing across the ceiling.

"Everything is going to be like it was before, only better, because you'll be there too."

Rocking gently, she let her eyes follow the bright figures swimming across the walls. "When the pandemic is over, we'll take you to the seaside to visit your grandmother—she lives in *my* granny's old house up on the cliffs—and we'll play on the beach and, maybe, if we're feeling very brave, we'll visit the hidden cove on the far side of the caves. You remember, don't you, darling? How the brave and clever girl faced the darkness and, with the moon's help, made it safely to the cove beyond the caves, only to find someone waiting. Do you know who it was?"

The baby blinked sleepily.

"Waiting for the girl was a woman with hair as blue-black as night and eyes like the moon. 'Come with me and I will take you as my apprentice,' she said, offering her hand. 'I will teach you to become a bird and soar with the wind, calm the waves or whip them into a frenzied storm.'"

The baby's eyes slid to half-mast. Her very, very tired mother smiled, her voice growing quieter and quieter with every word.

"'But what is the price?' asked the girl, for she knew such learning was not without cost. The witch smiled, pleased by the girl's cleverness. 'You must make good on the lies of the men who condemned you by becoming all that they claimed you to be,' she said. For a moment, the girl was silent. Then she smiled too, and took the witch's hand, for she knew that, against the odds, she would live happily ever after."

Story finished, the very, very tired new mother let sleep wrap around her aching limbs, drawing her gently down into nothingness . . .

The baby broke free from her breast and, winding up like an air-raid siren, launched into a fresh fit of screaming, jolting her very, very tired mother back to wakefulness.

An enraged bellow erupted from nearby. It thrummed through the house, shaking the walls as if they were water. The blue witches and green sea-dragons tumbled through the air as if tossed by a gale.

Desperately, the very, very tired mother set her screaming baby safely into her cot as the monster charged from the deep with a sound like a hurricane descending, reality, story and dream warping into one in her exhaustion and fear.

A monster or the villagers come to destroy the witch-woman and the girl-child she had sworn to protect?

The door burst open, casting the witches and dragons into shadow, darkening the world. A moment later claws wound into her hair, dragging her to her feet. Another set clamped around her arm, shaking her as the monster breathed its hot, rancid breath into her face, opening its mouth wide to show its sharp, sharp teeth.

But though the witch was very, very tired—so tired she longed to give in and just let the monster eat her—she knew that then it would eat the baby too.

Her hand reached out and, summoned by desperation and love, a weapon appeared in her grasp. A spear worthy of a shield-maiden from legend, as if it had been gifted by fairy-folk. Gathering the last of her strength, she drove it into the monster's throat.

There was a tinkling, shattering, crumpling sound. A strangled shriek. Then a *BANG* that rocked the world like a tidal wave. Everything went black.

The witch stood trembling in the darkness. Then the baby began to cry again.

Throwing her weapon aside, the witch scooped the baby up, cradling her close as she stepped carefully between the sprawling limbs of the fallen monster.

Far off, a cloud pulled itself from the face of the moon, send-ing light streaming across the beach. Obediently the witch fol-lowed it, bearing her child to the safety of a warm bed where she crawled between the sheets, sinking into the softness of pil-lows and quilt and mattress.

She was so very, very tired, but now she could rest.

26

World Gone Mad

After a restless night searching fruitlessly for a solution to our three-corpse problem, I pad downstairs to find the house cold and lonely. Borrowing an idea from one of my new forensics programs, I set to bleaching the entire kitchen floor to ensure there's no suspicious body-sized clean patch if the police ever examine the house. After all, no one is going to think excessive cleaning odd in the middle of a plague.

A knock summons me mid-elevenses to find an envelope on the doorstep. The instructions on the back brusquely inform me that the seeds inside are from Edwina's garden and should be scattered on newly turned earth in the next day or two, with potting soil sprinkled on top. I try to see it as a good sign that I'm getting Edwina on my side, but my brain chanting *A fortnight tomorrow Jim's due at work!* on loop puts rather a dampener on things.

Charlie's song of the day raises a momentary smile but being "Happy" doesn't seem to be in me today, even with Pharrell Williams' help. A cute cat video from Amy barely distracts me for the ten seconds it plays.

My warmest cardigan—the big, floppy, holey one that Jim

hated but I refused to throw away, secreting it at the back of the cupboard under the stairs—is calling my name, so soon I am waist deep in buckets and mops and boxes of rubbish I've been meaning to sort through for years.

I'm so busy crashing around that I don't register the phone ringing till I back out of the cupboard, swiping cobwebs out of my hair. When I realize that I've been hearing it for a while, I scramble to my feet and dash into the kitchen, wrenching the receiver out of the charging unit, expecting it to be Ruth or Samira.

"What's happened?" I pant, only then considering that it must be someone else, since we'd agreed to contact each other on our husbands' mobiles. Given that no one else will think this greeting remotely normal, I quickly add, "I mean, hello, who is—"

"Sally?"

The voice on the other end is so distorted by tears that for a moment I don't recognize it.

"Sally? Are you there?"

"Janey?" I gasp, bracing myself against the counter. Fear over the sound of her voice collides with the sheer relief that she's calling.

"I need you. Please. I'm so very, very tired, and . . ."

I haven't heard her sound like that since the day her dad died.

She wrenches in a breath as if the air around her has turned to water. "Keith's dead," she says. "Last night he was . . . and now he's dead. And I . . . I don't know what to do."

I can barely breathe. Twined around the soul-deep joy of hearing her voice is a barbed-wire thread of anger and grief. I've missed her like a cut to the heart, but how can she just call me up as if nothing had happened between us? As if the only possible outcome is that I'll be utterly and always in her corner, though she refused to stand in mine? She walked away, and in the wake of that Jim's control and violence obliterated the last few normal parts of my life. She left me with him. To him.

"Sally?" Janey sobs. "Sally, please . . ."

I want to scream at her. I want to turn my back. I want to blink and be beside her.

It's still there, our friendship. All those years. All those memories. It's still there, waiting for us. Dented and fractured and bent, but not shattered—not if I reach back now.

I've had so much taken from me. To get back any part of the life I lost is a gift too great to squander on a moment of fury. If we are to repair the wreck of our relationship, there will be a reckoning. But not today.

"Are you sick too?" I ask. "Where is he—where are you?"

"We're at home."

Oh God, he's died in the house, just like her father.

"I'm coming, Janey. I'm coming right now. I'll take care of everything, I promise, but you need to tell me if you're sick. Do you need a doctor?"

"No," she gasps around another sob. "No, it's not . . . That's not . . ."

"Did he fall? What happened?"

"I killed him." The words come out jagged, then she takes a breath and says again, quite calmly, "I killed him, Sally."

My first thought is, *This is it—I've finally lost it.*

Then I realize that it must be a frighteningly vivid dream.

You just need to wake up, I tell myself. But I don't, because I'm not asleep. And I don't crumple because, after twenty-three years of making myself passive in the vain hope it would protect me, these last few days I've been learning how to think, how to act, how to be brave. Now, for the first time, it's not just necessity driving me. It's courage.

"Stop exaggerating, Janey. In fact, *stop talking at all*," I tell her curtly, making the words slow and distinct. "You've always been a drama queen, turning every little argument into a whole saga of death and disaster, but you *shouldn't talk like this. Imagine if someone heard you.*"

There's a sharp intake of breath on the other end of the line.

"Now stop being so silly—and definitely don't go calling anyone else and making a fool of yourself, right, Courage?" Then a thought strikes me. "You haven't moved house, have you?"

"No," Janey whispers. "Sal—"

"I'm on my way."

27

Friends Reunited

clutch the steering wheel, ignoring the flutter of Edwina's curtains as I pull out into the street, making sure not to speed.

It's less than four miles to Janey's, but everything seems suddenly unfamiliar, the streets tunneling into the distance, as if space and time have stretched.

There are only a few blocks to go when I hear the sirens. I tell myself it's nothing—at least nothing to do with me. No reason it should be.

They get louder and closer.

So then I tell myself that it doesn't mean anything except that they're heading in the same direction.

But they get louder still.

Then I see the car crest the hill behind me, lights flashing. I force my breath in and out, hands white-knuckled on the wheel as I fix my eyes on the speedometer, making sure I'm not accelerating in alarm.

"They're going to pass," I whisper. "Don't be stupid. Don't panic."

They get closer . . . closer. I pull in tight to the curb, hands aching with how hard I'm grasping the wheel. I squeeze my eyes shut and will them to pass: to just keep going, not pull in ahead of me and . . .

Louder, closer. Louder, closer. A whoosh as they pass.

Then a crunch of gravel by the curb just in front of me. My heart kicks in my chest.

They're pulling in. They *are* here for me.

Is this about Janey or Jim? Has Ruth let the guilt get to her and dobbed me in?

The sirens are softer than they were a moment before. Now softer still.

I open my eyes in time to see the police car disappear down a street to the right. My breath rushes out in relief.

An angry beep makes me jump, eyes flying to the rearview mirror as the driver behind pulls round me and swerves off with another blast of the horn.

I give him the finger as I shakily pull out again. A minute later, I turn into Janey's street and park across the top of her driveway.

Grabbing my bag, I hurry down the side of the house. Letting myself into the garden, I rush up the steps into the kitchen, calling her name.

A movement in the doorway, and there she is, frizzy red hair sticking out in all directions, face gleaming with tears and snot, one cheek and brow reddened and grazed.

A moment later we're wrapped in a hug. Janey howls into my shoulder as my own tears dampen the collar of her dress. I thread my hand under her hair and grip the back of her neck as we press into each other as if we can squeeze the pain away.

28

Terrible Taste in Men

A piercing wail makes me jump. Janey draws back with a sigh and hurries away through the archway into the living room. I follow her in a daze because I already know what I'm going to see when I get there, but I can't believe it. And yet Janey is cooing comforting noises in a tone that can only mean . . .

She had a baby. My best friend had a baby and I didn't know.

I stare across the room, hollowed out by the blow.

She didn't tell me. Didn't send a picture. Didn't ask for advice or reassurance for any of the million fears that a newborn brings.

My life might as well have been in limbo while Janey's world shifted. Without me.

She looks back across the room over the baby's head, and for a second I think of turning and leaving. Just walking away from the pain. But the look in her eyes as she meets mine is longing and emptiness and loneliness and love, tender and unsure.

"This is Ava," she whispers. As she turns to the baby, a tear curves down her cheek. "Look, my love, your . . . your Auntie Sally's here."

We meet in the middle of the floor, Ava burbling, her tiny hand flailing in excitement. I take it in mine.

"She's . . ." There are tears on my face too. "Hello, Ava," I say.

She shrieks in delight, and I find myself smiling, despite everything, as her tiny fingers flex in mine, then Janey is passing her over and I'm bouncing her as she steadies herself in my arms. Janey presses a shaking hand over her mouth.

My heart is too full. I squash down everything but the present. The implications of Janey having a daughter can wait. The dead husband can't.

Gently, I settle Ava down in her playpen.

"I'm so sorry," Janey says when I turn back. "I'm so sorry, Sally. For everything. I always hated Jim, but I should never have—" She looks away into the light spilling through the big bay windows, wrapping her arms tight around herself. "I wanted to help, but I was so cross with you and so stupid that all I did is hurt us both, and I . . ."

I pull her in for another hug. "Later," I say.

A curl of her mad ginger hair flicks itself into my eye as she clings to me. It feels like coming home.

"I should have told you about Ava," she gasps. "Even if I wasn't sure you wanted to hear from me, I should have called."

"Of *course* I wanted to hear from you." My voice is rough with all the things I can't say. I cling to her and try to think only of how much I missed her. A sob of laughter forces itself out of me. "I'd forgotten how tall you are. How did I forget that you're a bloody giant?" I step back, wiping my sleeve over my face as I look around. "Where's Keith?"

"Upstairs," she whispers with a shudder. "All this time I never understood why you didn't leave Jim. It didn't make sense to me that you'd let him ruin your life like that, and then Keith . . . He started . . ." She shakes her head helplessly. "He hurt me and I *stayed*. I stayed, and I don't understand why. Did I think it would get better? Did I think it would be easier when Ava was older?"

"I thought you and Keith were happy," I say softly.

Despair floods her face. "We *were*. Everything was fine till I got pregnant, and I was just so surprised because we both wanted it, but he hated how my body was changing and how I didn't want as much sex as before. I thought it would be better when the baby came, only then there was no sleep and so much mess and he realized it was never going to go back to how it was before—that the baby would always get most of my time and energy. I just couldn't believe it was happening to me—thought it was my fault for being stupid enough to have a baby at forty-two and . . ." The flow of words fades into a sad little gulp. "Why did I do it, Sal? Why the hell did I let that happen to me?"

I squeeze her hands in mine. "We didn't *let* it. They did it. And we didn't know how to make it stop."

Her gaze snaps up to mine, questioning, then finding the answer. "Oh, Sally." Her face crumples. "I wanted to be wrong."

I shake my head. "You said Keith's upstairs. How did—"

"I thought he was a monster." She gasps out a quavering little laugh. "An actual monster from one of my stupid stories. I didn't even know what I was doing. I was just so very, very tired and I must have been half-asleep and . . . God, you're going to think I'm mad. You're going to think it's right that they come and lock me up forever."

"You're not mad. The number of times when Charlie and Amy were tiny that I dreamed the toaster had come to life or hallucinated them transforming into animals or . . ." I shrug, wiping her cheeks gently with my sleeve as she stares at me in stunned hope.

"Really? It's really happened to you too?"

"You can't be that sleep deprived and not have a couple of moments when you lose track of reality."

She stares across the room at Ava. "This morning, when I woke up and found him, I couldn't even work out what had happened. Then I remembered my dream—a monster attacked us and I hit out with the first thing to hand . . . Turns out it was Ava's night light and the whole thing shattered and somehow the wire must have met his skin . . . I remember this massive bang—it fused half the house—but I was so far gone I didn't even twig. Just grabbed Ava and hid in the bedroom, but then I was so tired I went back to sleep . . ."

She shivers, pulling her cardigan tight across her chest. "They'll let me keep Ava with me in prison while she's so little, but after . . ." Her face grows bleak. "If it's not me with her, loving her, I'd want it to be you, but Jim—"

"Is not a problem anymore."

Her head jerks up, eyes blown wide with shock. "You left him? When? Why didn't you tell me?"

I sink onto the sofa and take her hand in mine. "Ava's not going to lose you, and you're not going to lose her, because I'm going to fix this."

Janey wrenches her hand away. "You can't fix this, Sally! What are you going to do? Help me bury him in the garden?" She pushes herself up, pacing toward the window, then stopping at the sight of her daughter. "At least if I turn myself in, I might get out while Ava's still—"

"You're right." I wait till she turns, then get slowly to my feet and join her by the cot. "The two of us would never manage it alone. But the world is a surprisingly small place and I've been busy accidentally setting up a self-help group."

"Your Lockdown social club isn't going to help me get away with murder! Christ, Sally."

"Self-defense isn't murder."

"It doesn't matter! They're still not going to help me get away with killing my husband."

I purse my lips. "See, that's where you're wrong. They've no issue helping me get away with killing Jim."

Janey's face goes blank and for a second she sways where she stands.

"I know my little self-help group *is* going to get me through this and not dob me into the police for one simple reason—they're all in the same boat."

I stand beside her, hand curled around the railing of the cot.

"We're none of us murderers. And we all have children to protect. If I can trust them when it's only been a few days, then you should be able to trust me. I'm going to fix this, Janey. For you, for me, for all of us."

"We can't do this," she gasps. "It won't work." She presses a shaking hand to her temple.

"If it goes wrong, I'll say I killed Keith."

Her eyes widen with shock, and desperate hope.

"The rest of us have already made a pact. Ruth and I are the ones with grown-up kids. If it all goes wrong, we'll take the blame. Better one or two of us in prison than the whole group, so you can join us and try to make sure we all come through it, or you can turn yourself in. Only one of those options means you get to raise your child."

I meet her eyes with all the love and determination and courage that seeing her again, being able to have her at my back as we navigate this crisis, has given me.

"Which is it going to be?"

29

Getting to Know
All About You . . .

I hereby declare this meeting of the Lockdown Ladies' Burial Club called to order," I tell the group assembled in a socially distanced circle the next day.

We're in the park by the duck pond so that Maryam can run around, looking for feathers, while we talk.

"First item on the agenda, I propose that we close to new members. All in favor." I look around the circle as the others eye each other—warily in Samira's case, suspiciously in Janey's, curiously in Leila's, and sympathetically in Ruth's.

Leila raises her hand. "Five is enough to do whatever we have to, but more increases the risk of someone doing something stupid and getting caught, then dobbing the rest of us in for a deal—or just by accident. I vote no more new members—and definitely no new corpses."

"I second the vote for no new members, but we mustn't joke about it," says Ruth, though gently. "We are talking about people's lives—"

"Deaths," corrects Leila.

"Leila," Samira sighs, then turns to the rest of us, raising her hand. "I agree."

"Who's an urble, burble bundle?" says Janey, as Ava gives a little shout from her carrier. "Yes, Mummy agrees, doesn't she, darling? She really does. Five is sufficient. In fact, it might be more than sufficient." She gives me an apologetic shrug, then casts a rueful grin at the others. "Not to dunk on anyone, but is this really a good idea? Four is a lot of people to trust."

"The greater our number, the more chances that anyone's smallest slip could see it all unravel," Samira puts in quietly.

Janey makes a "there we are" gesture at Samira. "That. What she said."

"But surely, if we all vouch for each other, that's practically ironclad in police terms?" Ruth wrings her hands, biting at her lip.

"Not to mention that we've got four bodies now," I remind them. "Getting rid of them is going to be a lot of physical labor."

Janey shudders. "Can we please leave that discussion till later?"

"Excuse me? Who packaged up your body? Who cleaned up afterward?"

"You are a goddess among women," Janey tells me in heartfelt tones.

I sniff, trying to keep a straight face. Then we're laughing. "God, I've missed you," I tell her. Then I pull myself together, because the inaugural club meeting is not the time to deal with our fractured friendship.

"Look, I know it's scary. And I know we're all asking a lot of each other—and ourselves. But let's see where some group plotting takes us. If it's nowhere, we go our separate ways."

Janey pulls a face. "How about that plea-deal stuff? One of us could tell on the others to stay out of prison."

Samira shakes her head. "That's the American system. It's

terrible, because innocent people confess to crimes they didn't commit to be assured of a lesser charge rather than risk things going against them in court, while guilty people bargain themselves down to a sentence that doesn't fit their crime. In the UK, the charges are almost never changed. Any information given on another crime is just taken into consideration at sentencing."

We all stare at her, even Leila.

Samira flushes, reaching down to pick a daisy from the grass and start building a chain. "I wanted to study law when I was young." There's sadness there that I promise myself I'll ask about one day.

"Back to the agenda," I say. "Item two, extended family. I'm OK—my kids have their own places, my parents and Jim's are dead, and he hasn't talked to his brother in about four years. Ruth?"

"Most of my family is in St. Lucia, and his brothers and sisters are all back in Dominica—well, apart from the brother who just died. I've been emailing them from Lionel's phone, trying to copy his style. If the messages sound odd, hopefully they'll just think it's the grief talking."

Janey looks impressed. "Glad I don't have to worry about that, since I'm always the one talking to Keith's parents anyway. I can just send them the occasional text—and photos of Ava— on his phone, and they'll never know the difference. As soon as restrictions ease it'll be a problem because they're dying to see their granddaughter, but we're good for now on his side, and mine's not an issue."

She flashes me a look that says she knows our thoughts have instantly sprung to the same memory. A rainy afternoon two days before Janey's fourteenth birthday. The phone going just as I was trying out different ways to do my makeup for the party then wiping it all off because no way would Dad let me leave the house "looking fully like the little slag you are." He was out at the pub, so I hummed as I clattered downstairs and grabbed the phone off the hook.

The sound of gasping sobs made my cheerful greeting dry in the back of my throat.

"Sally. Sally, I think . . . I think my dad's dead."

I got a belting for rushing out without locking the garden door, but I didn't regret a thing. It meant I could sit with Janey beside her father's body until the ambulance arrived to take him.

Then we sat together on the sofa while her mother went from work to the hospital before she finally came home, hollowed out by the shock of starting the day a wife and ending it a widow.

I hadn't heard Janey's voice sound like that again until yesterday. Surely those memories mean we can get our friendship back on track. Whatever time we've lost can't matter half as much as the lifetime between us, can it?

"Anyway," she says, turning briskly back to the others, "it's just my mum, but she's down on the coast, and she's a bit . . ." She takes a deep breath. "They think it's vascular dementia. I got her on some pills, but then the Lockdown—" She cuts herself off. "It's not a problem as far as we're concerned." She turns to Samira. "Last but not least?"

Samira's face goes bleak. "As soon as the restrictions ease, they'll all be round to help nurse him back to health, and we're expected in Pakistan—"

"Mum!"

We all jump, looking up to find Maryam jiggling about beside Samira.

"My zip's stuck, and I'm hot."

Samira pushes up to her knees and works the zip free. The second she does, Maryam wriggles out of the coat, flinging it in her mother's face, and sprints off again.

I clap my hands to draw their attention back to the meeting. "If they announce changes to the restrictions, we'll just have to put our heads together to make sure Samira and anyone else with a deadline has a solution. On to item three. How's everyone fixed for money? Are there going to be issues with bosses or colleagues asking where your husband is? There's no point coming up with a brilliant plan only to have someone's house repossessed with a corpse in it, or to have questions raised about why they're not turning up for work."

"Keith's a freelance surveyor, so there's no work to worry about during Lockdown. I can probably put his clients off for a bit even after, so we're OK, aren't we, darling?" Janey coos as she wiggles Ava's toes. "Mummy's got maternity pay—plus my mum said that if I sell her car, now she can't drive anymore, I can keep the money."

I smile at Ruth. "I know you won't have any trouble getting back to work, but are you OK until everything's sorted?"

She nods. "All of Lionel's decorating jobs have been postponed for now."

"Well, Dad's a taxi driver so he has been working," Leila says, "but of course no one's expecting him to be out and about when he's supposedly self-isolating with Covid. Anyway, for once his worse tendencies are playing in our favor."

"Leila, please," Samira scolds, though she doesn't correct the sentiment.

Leila rolls her eyes. "My father liked to stash envelopes of cash around the house to avoid having to declare all his income for tax. He even buried some in an old picnic cooler by the shed."

"Really?" Janey looks awed. "Wow. That's . . . I did not know people actually did that."

"There's also a certain amount of gold—jewelry, not bars," Leila says. "Mum and I did the sums last night, and it's enough until one or both of us can get a job."

"But how about you, Sally?" Samira asks.

Time to fess up: it wouldn't be fair to keep them in the dark.

"Money-wise, I'm fine for now. I've got Jim's furlough pay, and I'll try to get a job as soon as I can, but . . ."

"But what?" Janey demands.

They all stare at me.

"But Jim's expected at the office in a fortnight."

30

Deadlines and Dismemberment

T hey stir uneasily, smiles fading into worried frowns.

"They've got a rota for one person to go in each week. If I have to, I can try to make out Jim is ill—see if I can push it back a little—but later on that might seem suspicious, so . . ."

"So we've got a looming deadline," Janey says darkly.

"Unless something happens to shift our family's attention, I doubt we can keep them off our backs any longer, so at least it's a shared deadline," Samira says, voice faltering on the final word.

"Uncle Ayaan dropping dead would be a nice start. And before you think I'm being a total cow," Leila hurries on, "I should point out that he was the ringleader at the family meeting at the Pakistan end of the call where they . . ." Her jaw works. "I hope one of them had Covid and the rest of them caught it too—it'd be a neat piece of karma if meeting to decide my fate actually decided theirs and the whole bloody lot of them drop dead one by one."

Samira closes her eyes, even as she reaches out and tucks Leila's hand into hers. "Your aunts by marriage and girl cousins did not take part. It is not the whole family."

"Whoopee! Only all my male relatives. And the aunt I'm related to by blood."

"Some of your younger uncles and male cousins will have had little choice but to go along with the rest. To resist would have put them in danger—and risk trouble for those around them."

I clear my throat. "While we're doing hard truths, let's get item four out of the way . . . Whatever the eventual plan, it is almost certainly going to involve at least some degree of dismemberment, so we'd better resign ourselves now."

Samira laces another link into her daisy chain while Ruth goes back to fussing at her locket and Janey bends over Ava. Only Leila refuses to look away.

She heaves out a huge puff of air then nods. "Here's hoping the cat litter has done its work by then—or at least enough to help."

Janey claps a hand over her mouth. "Stop talking," she pleads. "I'll figure it out if I have to, but I don't want to talk about it in advance. Jeez, Sally. Nothing like jumping in at the deep end and seeing if we sink, swim, or just vomit."

I ignore her and turn to Ruth, Leila, and Samira. "I'll google butchery skills on cooking blogs so I can get some tips without raising suspicions. The main thing we should bear in mind is that joints are the natural division points. Ruth can help with advice on the details."

On Janey's lap, Ava stirs, blowing a spit bubble in her sleep. "Lovely, darling," says her mother, wiping it away with her sleeve. "Anyway, what's the point of chopping anyone up if we don't know where we're going to put them? Talk about chicken and egg, only the horror-movie, stuff-of-nightmares version."

So we move on to item five—possible disposal sites. All progress promptly grinds to a halt. When everyone looks off in different directions, clearly not a usable idea between us, I try not to let the disappointment show on my face.

"That's probably the hardest thing, so let's skip to our final item—the men's WhatsApp group."

"Won't that effectively be an evidence trail?" Janey asks warily.

"Of course—but it's an evidence trail in our favor. We need a way to show they all knew each other to explain them going off together to meet their fate, but it's also a way for us to have got to know each other. If their group is going strong first and there's just the odd text between us—Samira to Ruth, Ruth to me, me to Janey—then it all seems a bit more normal. Or at least normal for Lockdown. We can even use our texts to support the story that our husbands have started going for walks together—well, apart from Yafir—"

"Actually"—Janey shifts onto her knees, suddenly intent—"that could work. Keith's always loved hiking. If he heard about Jim and some mate going on walks, he'd be well up for that. In fact, he'd probably be pushing to go off on some full route-march adventure—as far as he's concerned, that's blissful stress relief. Anyway, if we could make it seem they were all a bit depressed, or at least stir crazy, then that's a great setup for wherever they're meant to have disappeared off to when we figure out that bit of the plan."

I take out my phone. "Jim's going to text Keith right now about his new walking pal—"

"Wait!"

We all stare at Samira.

"From now on, we should make sure to either leave our

own phones behind or keep them off when we meet. We want our husbands' phones to have been wandering around and sometimes coinciding, as that's part of the story. But unless any of you know for sure that the police can't retrospectively pinpoint where two phones were in relation to each other, we shouldn't take any chances."

I summon a bright smile, but the mood has soured as, silently, we all click our phones off. "When I get home, 'Jim' can text 'Keith'—I'll make out that he and Lionel bumped into Keith on their walk and they agreed to make a trio in future, so then all the men know each other and Keith can get added to the WhatsApp group. And once *that's* done, I can text Janey about it, and she can say how nice it is because Keith's been so low, et cetera, et cetera, and we're halfway to an explanation already."

"It's still a bit weird that Dad would get involved," Leila says warily. "He'd hate the whole thing."

"Maybe he usually would, but we just have to lean into the idea of it all being different in the pandemic and build up how difficult he's finding the whole self-isolation thing, especially with his father so ill," I point out.

"We could make something of the idea that he feels guilty for being stuck here in the UK while his father is dying," Samira muses. "Perhaps I—pretending to be Yafir—could say a few things in the chat about the fact that self-isolating means he can't work so he's stressed because he has a big expense coming up." She smooths a hand down Leila's arm.

Leila swallows, eyes growing bright, but nods. "Worries about how to pay for the wedding would actually make sense of why he'd be ducking messages from the family while being active in this random WhatsApp group."

"It won't be the strangest set of friendships to come out of the pandemic—look at me baking for Edwina in exchange for gardening lessons!"

"Not to mention the five of us and our new routine of daily plotting," Janey adds ruefully.

"Exactly!" I say. "The important thing is that instead of four stories about how our husbands have disappeared, we just need one. Whatever we end up telling people, the simpler the plan is, the fewer things can go wrong."

I don't add that we can only hope the coming fortnight doesn't bring our careful plans crashing down around us. The fear is on all our faces anyway.

31

The Seed of a Plan

'm just slotting my key into the front door when there's a furious scurrying in the lilac on Nawar's side of the low front wall. The branches part and her face appears.

I blink at her, then follow her gaze to the other side of the street, but Edwina's curtains are still.

"Are we really not allowed to talk from the end of the drive?" I ask, though my voice is little more than a furtive whisper. "Surely she can't report us for that. In any case it turns out she's more lonely than mean—she's been teaching me how to garden!"

"You're a saint, Sally. But everyone's got their limits. If you end up caving her head in with a spade and need an emergency grave-digging buddy, you know who to call!"

"I appreciate the offer, but I'm all set with volunteers, thanks," I tell her truthfully.

"Well, you can always change your mind," the lilac hisses back, "especially since I'm about to ask you a huge favor and if you say yes, it'll be the least I owe you."

"How can I help?" The eagerness in my voice is instant and

sincere. I like Nawar and I want to help if I can, but the leap of delight takes me by surprise.

"Bless your socks," says Nawar, her relief equally sincere. "You know I said my dad's sick—underlying condition, not Covid," she adds quickly. "Well, it's all going pear-shaped and there are no carers available, so we're going to have to relocate up there for the rest of the Lockdown."

"You want me to do the thing where I creep in a few times a day and turn the lights on and off so Edwina doesn't report you for being away?"

Nawar laughs. "I love the way you think, but it's within the rules because my dad's so ill. It's really just the plants and the fish. If I left you a key, could you possibly—"

"No problem!" Not only am I happy to help, without Nawar's lot next door it'll be much easier to get in and out the back of the house—with or without bits of Jim. Not to mention that it'll take some of the stress out of the possibility of being overheard during the dismemberment process.

"Thank you," she says, gratitude making her voice almost gruff. "I know I've probably forgotten half the things we need to take, but so long as no one in the family has the plague or gets murdered, I figure we'll manage."

My breath catches.

"How's Jim? He managing to keep his head up on furlough?" she continues, blissfully unaware of the heart attack she's just gifted me.

"He's been taking the chance to lie around all day. Look, don't worry about Edwina," I say, eager to change the subject. "I'll let her know, so that's another thing off your list."

My brain is already churning over all the possibilities of

Nawar being gone. If I can get whatever things we need to disappear Jim and the others delivered to Nawar's house, I can toss them over the fence to mine so there's no paper trail. More than that, perhaps she has a desktop computer I can use to google all the things I need to look up but don't dare search from Jim's laptop.

I'd be delighted to do Nawar a favor, but the reality is that she's probably doing me a bigger one.

WHEN I LET MYSELF back into the house, I seek inspiration from a true-crime podcast, but it utterly fails to present me with the magic seed of a plan to dispose of one corpse, let alone four.

It's a fortnight to the day until Jim is due in the office. Even the thought sends a lurch of panic through me—a fortnight to figure it all out and put the plan into action. Already he's been dead a week and, for all my progress, I'm no closer to a true solution than when I started.

Thankfully, my latest round of *Be Happy* shopping arrives mid-afternoon—the perfect distraction from the temptation to mope.

Soon I'm ripping the packaging off a series of tiny "plant plugs" ordered on Edwina's instructions. Throwing my padded kneeler onto the grass, I settle in front of a "flower bed" (i.e. four dead shrubs and some unattractive weeds) and set to work clearing the ground. When that's done, I dig a neat set of holes for the baby plants. I press the soil down comfortingly around each stem as if tucking them in. Finally, I water the lot and stand back to survey the result.

Two lines of tiny plants droop over the bare, newly turned earth. A chill breeze shakes their leaves as the sun breaks through the clouds for a moment then retreats.

"Guess we'll see if Edwina's the gardening guru she thinks she is or whether everything I put in the ground might as well be dead to start off with," I tell the plants.

My eyes drift to the kitchen door, where the foot of the Jim-parcel is just visible.

As I step back inside, I hear the clatter of the letter box, but instead of junk mail I find a gardening book sitting on the mat. A surprisingly purple Post-it Note instructs me to **Wipe with disinfectant immediately. If you find this useful, you may keep it.**

I stare at the note, then at the book. Edwina's obviously had it for a while. There's something about the well-thumbed soft-ness of the pages that reminds me of Granny's skillet. Which is nonsense of course. Edwina doesn't have a sentimental bone in her body. Maybe she feels she owes me for the strawberry tart I delivered yesterday? But even if she's just settling a debt, the book has to count for something.

Wanting to be able to report on how useful it is, I take it out-side and attempt to prune the rosebush that hasn't flowered for years. Pulling up a dandelion choking its roots, I snap off the clock and blow the seeds across the garden, watching as some spiral up and away while others come to rest here and there, ready to blossom into new flowers—probably exactly where I don't want them.

The sudden crawling sensation of being watched makes me spin round—*Has Edwina come to peer over the fence at my efforts? Will she spot the Jim-parcel in the kitchen?*—but it's a fox, not a per-son, who is standing behind me.

It ducks into the grass, eyeing me warily.

"Shoo!" I tell it.

The fox slinks toward the kitchen door.

"Oi!" I hurry up the path, cutting it off. "Get lost. Piss off."

It pauses, looking irritated, then turns tail and pads off, wriggling through a gap in the back fence.

Unnerved, I gather my book and tools up and go back inside, dumping everything hurriedly across the table when I realize my phone is ringing.

"BORED. TIRED. BORED," Janey snarls at me. "How can I be so bored when I'm simultaneously so tired but also scared out of my mind? How does that even work?"

"If I can find anywhere that has flour, I'll bring you some melting moments tomorrow."

"I love you," comes the heartfelt reply. "You don't know how much I've missed your baking. Well, and you, but mostly the baking."

Picking up Jim's phone, I scan the array of texts on the men's WhatsApp group with a grimace. "Do you know anywhere that has bog roll? Ruth just texted about tinned tomatoes, but she says Samira's desperate for loo paper. Doesn't care what sort so long as there's enough that she doesn't have to panic every time one of the girls goes to the loo."

"This is not improving my boredom levels," Janey grouses as I scribble the items onto my shopping list. "Though, to be fair, any ideas of where might have pasta would be welcome. Can't believe that's my current wish-list item. Some people must have a cupboard of it. Bet that Edwina woman is sitting on a mountain. Probably how she sees out of the window to watch you. Maybe that's why she's always there—can't move for loo roll and spaghetti."

"She's helping with my garden—gave me one of her own books today—so I think she's mellowing. Maybe I could offer to lend a hand with her little gardening project at the end of the street," I muse. "She said she'd never manage to clear the whole area by herself. Maybe it was a hint that . . ." I trail off, thoughts whirling.

The first seed of a solution starts to germinate.

32

A Spot of Gardening

The others are equally excited about the possibilities of Nawar going away when I tell them at the duck pond the next day.

"Does anyone have a spare device?" Leila asks eagerly.

"Would Lionel's tablet do?" Ruth offers.

Leila grins. "Perfect! I'll wipe it then set it up with accounts under Nawar's name. Sally can take it next door, log in on Nawar's wifi, then there's no digital trail via her IP address."

"Good thinking," I say, relieved I won't have to rely on whether Nawar has a desktop. "Can I really search all sorts of suspicious stuff and be sure it won't trace back to me?"

Leila nods. "Unless you log into your email or buy something on a credit card, you're fine."

"Great. And that wasn't my only good news—I have the start of a plan."

Relief paints matching smiles across their faces.

"My first good thought for getting rid of Jim was going to a churchyard, finding an empty grave and digging it down deeper, then popping him in and covering him over to the normal level so someone else could be planted on top. The trouble is there's too much opportunity to be spotted. So what we need is a reason to be digging a really big hole. Now, there's a patch of scrubland at the end of my street and my neighbor, Edwina, has turned a corner of it into a little garden, so we're going to take a leaf out of her book."

The others stare at me, clearly not getting it.

"We're going to turn the whole area into a community garden. That means clearing the ground. It's basically flat, but there are small trees and a bunch of overgrown bushes, so we'll need to dig out the whole area to get rid of enough of the roots that the shrubs won't grow straight back and ruin everything. At least that's what we'll say if anyone asks. It'll be a hell of a job, but it'll justify the depth of hole we need for the bodies." I pause. "Probably. Maybe. I don't actually know how deep it needs to be exactly, but in a few days I can look it up at Nawar's. The point is that if we're creating a garden in that spot, we can get away with digging a hole that's at least seven foot by nine across and three deep."

The others look appalled.

"Is that possible without a digger?" Leila asks in a small voice. "How big even is that?"

"It'll be a slog, but there are five of us and we've got nearly two weeks. It's doable."

"And people will buy the idea that we need to go down several feet for the whole area?" Janey asks dubiously.

I nod, schooling my face into a look of confidence. "Definitely. I talked to Edwina about digging up this scrubby bush in the corner of my garden, and she said I'd have to dig the root ball out if I wanted to plant seeds on top. So we do the same, only these bushes are even bigger, so the roots will go deeper and, hey presto, perfect excuse—especially if we tell anyone who asks that we want to put in a layer of topsoil before we add any seedlings. We'll just plant a few bodies down the bottom first."

"Won't someone see us?" Ruth asks, looking around as if already feeling eyes on her.

"So what if they do?" Leila answers for me. "They'll just see us gardening. If it's a big enough space, we can be socially distanced; there shouldn't be a problem. After a few days, everyone will be used to us and they'll stop watching too closely."

"Plus the topsoil bags will be so big they'll help disguise what we're up to when we get to the bit where we bury the bodies," Ruth adds.

"Actually, we'll need a whole load of heavy bags—Edwina's instructions involved a layer of gravel and fish, blood, and bone."

"Flesh, blood and bone more like," Leila mumbles.

Janey groans. "Nope. Shh. We don't need a picture, thank you."

Leila grins, unrepentant, until Janey, despite herself, grins back. I catch Samira's eye, relieved to see that she looks a shade less drained, the lines of misery around her eyes softer today.

"Can we really do it under everyone's noses?" she asks.

"Especially Edwina's?" Ruth adds. "Because from what you've told me—"

"She's the best alibi we could possibly have. We should get her *involved*."

"Isn't that playing with fire?" Janey moans.

"We can ask for her expertise. It'll help distract her. She's going to be watching anyway—checking we're not going near her precious cherry tree." I sigh. "I feel bad about desecrating her special spot, but her tree is just one corner of the area and we'll make sure to cordon it off safely first."

"I suppose if we're buying big bags of soil and gravel and bringing them in our cars, it will be easy enough to include a few body bags," Samira says. "And it'll make sense of why we'll have to work together to lift them out. Even so we'll need to"— her face twists into a mask of disgust—"reduce our problems to manageable amounts first."

I grimace. "At least we won't have bought all those saws for nothing."

33

Repairs Underway

The meeting lasts far longer than it should, so when I arrive home to frenetic movement on the part of Edwina's curtains, I accept the inevitable and simply wait by my front wall until she steps outside.

"I'm sorry I'm late," I call, before she can start lecturing me on the rules. "I got myself turned around in the woods like a muppet. Truth be told, I was distracted—I've been wondering how you'd feel if I did a little work on the green area along from your cherry tree."

Edwina's eyes widen, her jawline tightening.

"I promise I won't touch your patch," I hurry on, "but I remember you saying you'd never get around to clearing it all and I thought maybe that was something I could do now you're teaching me about gardening."

Cheeks pinching as if she's tasted something sour, Edwina shakes a finger at me. "You have to remember that trees have large roots, so you'll need to leave a good six feet on all sides—and no encroaching. I planted that cherry as a memorial for my husband and I . . . I couldn't bear it to be disturbed." There's real anguish on her face as she trips over the words.

"I promise we'll keep a wide berth," I say solemnly, feeling guiltier than ever.

"We?" Edwina snaps suspiciously.

"A few friends were talking about making it into a community project—socially distanced, of course. But it's quite a big area and, if we're going to plant it properly, I figure we'll have to dig out the brambles and all those scrubby little saplings, then put in some better soil and fertilizer." I give her a hopeful look. "Do you think you could do some socially distanced supervising when we're at critical points?"

Edwina sniffs. "You'll have to email the council about it, but if they know I'm on board to give expert advice I doubt they'll have an issue with it. And at least that way I can be sure my husband's tree remains unmolested," she says stiffly. Then she sighs. "It's a good thought about the garden: a productive use for your need to be outside the house so much."

I beam at her. "That's exactly what I thought!"

"We'll need to talk about the plants. They have to be things that won't take over and ruin my work, mind." Her eyes move to the dog rose rambling over her front wall, her expression turning melancholy. It smooths the usual harshness of her features, making her look suddenly beautiful—and kind.

I blink, but the mirage doesn't vanish. "Did you and your husband like to garden together?" I ask gently.

She starts, gaze snapping over to me. "No," she says, voice gruff again. "My mother was a horticulturist. Created new types of rose. And my aunt worked at Kew in the orchid house. They learned it from their mother. Wonderful woman. Too clever for the life she led."

"My grandmother was like that," I say before I quite realize I'm going to. "I wish I was more like her."

Edwina tilts her head. "Sometimes these things come to us later in life." She straightens, face going hard once more. "Now, we've been rambling—and bending the rules—quite long enough."

"Thank you so much for the book—and your support with my little gardening idea!" I call as she turns to go back inside.

Edwina pauses to look down her nose at me. "I've conceded your point, now stop buttering me up. I'm not a crumpet."

Her front door snaps shut while I'm still gaping in astonishment. *Where did the sense of humor come from?*

Hurrying down my front path, I let myself inside, then call Janey to tell her the news.

"Put in a photo when you email the council," she advises. "Once they see what a mess it is, they'll be begging you to go ahead. Do people tend to drop litter there?"

"With Edwina on the prowl?" I shudder at the very thought.

"Well, take some out of your bin for the photo. Crouch down so you're blocking the view while you snap the pic, then pick it straight up again and even Edwina need be none the wiser."

"Why on earth did you go into marketing, Janey? You should have been a criminal mastermind."

"Think you'll find you're the leader—or at least head planner—of this little gang, Courage," she says with a laugh, though it's thin and ends in an anxious huff. "I couldn't bear to let you down, but I don't know how I'm going to cope with all this . . . stuff with Keith, and Ava being so all-consuming, and Mum's dementia on top," she whispers, voice cracking. "Somehow I've got to get down to the coast to pick up her car before she forgets they've taken her license and drives it again."

"I'm sure it'll be fine—"

"It's *not* fine, Sally," she growls. "She took the car into town last week, then forgot how to start it. The police had to take her home and call me to figure out where to hide the keys so I could find them, but she couldn't."

"Well, there you go—if she can't find the keys, she can't do it again. As for the rest, we'll figure it out. Once the restrictions ease, I can help with Ava. Hell, with Jim gone you can move in with me if you want." I say it flippantly, without thinking, but Janey's sharp intake of breath brings me up short.

"Do you mean that?" she whispers.

The ache in her words strikes straight into my chest.

It was just a joke. After everything between us, how could it possibly work? Would I even want it to when I'm still so angry, so hurt, so—

"Sally?"

"Move in with me," I breathe, my own voice suddenly rough with tears.

"For how long?" Janey whispers back, softer than ever.

Something in her tone goes straight to my bones, filling them with warmth in place of the cold, hard anger. I hear myself laugh, light and airy, as if some great weight has lifted off my shoulders. "How long are you planning to live?"

Janey gives a wet little sniff. "You don't know how much I've missed you."

"You'll probably be bloody sick of me in a week," I warn her. "Just don't think it's all about me helping you, because I'm expecting a partner in paying the bills. Plus, as the career woman in this friendship, you're going to have a lot of coaching and mentoring to do to get me up to scratch when I start on this getting-a-job business."

"Help me keep my kid alive and well and I'll mentor the shit out of you," my best friend promises.

I clear my throat. "Thank you for everything you've done for the kids."

"You're welcome?" Janey says, the upturn at the end turning it into a question. "But, um, what are we talking about here, because I am not following the leap?"

"You didn't stop sending presents and cards to the kids." I take a deep breath, then force myself to go on. "Even when we weren't . . . after our . . . fight. You carried on as normal with the kids, and I . . . I didn't know at first, then Amy let it slip and I . . . I was angry, but so relieved you were still in their lives. That they weren't being punished because you . . . because I . . ."

"Charlie yelled at me, you know. Said that whatever Jim had done to insult me, I shouldn't take it out on you, because you were isolated enough and without me . . ." She heaves in an unsteady breath. "Sally, I . . . We should . . . talk. I need to apologize—properly I mean. Because I am sorry." She sniffs again. "You don't know how much. I thought I was doing the right thing. At least I convinced myself it was the only thing I could do. And I know you think it was just stupid and cruel and awful and a little bit of you hates me for it . . ."

She pauses then, and I know she's hoping I'll say that's not true. When I stay silent, she gives a quavering little sigh.

"I'd probably hate me a bit too, but I just couldn't bear seeing what he was doing to you. And I . . . I really did hope that if

I could somehow give you a big enough wake-up call, you'd see what I saw . . . Or that maybe you'd decide I mattered more than he did, or . . ."

I imagine her tugging on one of her curls, the way she's done her whole life when she's trying not to cry. Part of me longs to make it better, but I don't. Because she cut me out of her life when I needed her the most. She made me go through it all alone.

"You were one of the few things that made my life bearable, and then you—" I cut myself off.

"I couldn't watch," she says so quietly I have to strain to hear. "I just couldn't watch it anymore. It felt . . . it felt like I was being part of it somehow. I didn't know what else I could do to get you to leave him."

I can hear the wretchedness in her voice, and for a moment I relish it because I want to scream that how *dare* she say that. How dare she say she couldn't stand it when she wasn't the one suffering. Jim wasn't doing anything to her. And if she felt bad about it, what was that tiny sliver of pain compared with what I was going through . . .

"I kept meaning to call you, but the longer it got, the less I knew what to say. And then suddenly I was pregnant and my life was in tatters and I finally understood why you didn't leave, because there I was, in exactly the same position."

"Then why didn't you call me!" It's not a shout, but it wants to be.

"I was too ashamed," comes the tiny reply.

I cut my teeth into my lip.

"I knew what I'd done to you. I didn't deserve to call you."

"But on the day that Keith . . . why did you call me then?"

"I didn't have anything left to lose." The words are a plea, her voice a sob. "I thought I was going to prison for life, and all I wanted was to see you again. I wanted to see you meet Ava."

I open my mouth, then swallow the words on my tongue. They'll only open old wounds, not heal them.

"I'm glad you called me," I say when I can speak again.

"Will we be OK one day?" Janey whispers. "When this is all over, if we manage to come through it, do you think we can . . ."

It's not forgiveness I feel—it's more complicated than that. I just wish the new understanding between us wasn't tinged with despair over all we've had to go through to come back together.

I'm saved from answering by a wail on her end of the phone. "You should feed Ava," I say. "I'll see you tomorrow."

Then I hang up because there's nothing else I'm ready to say yet. Nothing else I'm ready to hear.

And yet it doesn't feel as if I'm having to push down a wave of fury as I pick up the watering can and tend to Rosemary and Petunia. The hurt will need healing before we can move on, but it's funny how anger just seems small when set next to a lifetime of love and the fresh hope that one day soon I could be happy again.

34

Catastrophe

The following day starts with a flurry of progress. I wake to find a thank-you note with the keys to Nawar's back gate and kitchen door on the mat when I come downstairs. Setting them aside, I hurry to follow Janey's instructions about the litter and the photo.

Next, over breakfast, I send off the email to the council with a disproportionate sense of accomplishment, which I promptly enhance by baking a batch of exceptional snickerdoodles. I deliver a portion to Edwina's doorstep, finding a paper bag with my name scrawled across it waiting for me. Inside are several muddy lumps. I tear into the note tucked down the side.

More irises—black ones this time. Follow the same planting instructions. E

Grinning, I take the bulbs home, planting them behind my little seedlings, then I settle at the kitchen table. Despite my determination that today I *will* figure out how to explain the disappearance of our husbands, every idea brings its own stumbling block.

"What's that creature where, if you cut one head off, extras grow back?" I ask Rosemary and Petunia. They either don't know or won't tell me. "Where *can* a bunch of people go, then just disappear—without their phones with them?"

Skydiving? Bungee jumping? No, those would involve other people. *Boating?*

"But where would the boat come from?" I ask the Jim-parcel. "And why would everyone on board disappear simultaneously, unless it sank?"

While I'm sure we could arrange that, ensuring the damage to the boat is plausible for an accident is another matter. Determined not to let my progress stall, I take Nawar's keys and let myself through her back gate, then into the kitchen. With the plants watered and the fish dining happily, I check the wifi code is on the back of the router so I can log in on Lionel's old tablet next time.

The buzz of a phone makes me smile in anticipation—Charlie's song of the day is due—but it's Jim's mobile ringing, not mine. With a jolt of panic, I see the call is from "Yafir." I've barely tapped the button when Samira's speaking.

"Sally, there's a man outside. I think he's one of Yafir's cousin's sons. I've put the TV on really loud to pretend we can't hear the door if he rings the bell, but he keeps moving over to the garage as if he's trying to listen for someone moving about inside. He's on the phone now, pacing the street, but I think he might try knocking at the garage or calling through the door and I don't know what to do!"

Before clobbering Jim with Granny's skillet, I'd have frozen in panic. Now, I barely pause before grabbing my keys.

Locking up the house, then the gate, I rush back home.

"I'm on my way," I pant as I pound upstairs. "See if Leila can put some music on in the garage. I'll be there soon."

The second I hit disconnect, I snatch up a large hair clip, twist my unbrushed mop into a messy bun, then pull on my smartest cardigan. In the study, I hang the lanyard with Jim's key-card from work around my neck, hoping it'll look like official ID of some sort from a distance. Then, snatching up the leather folder I got Jim for his fortieth, I stuff a notepad and a handful of random papers inside before tearing downstairs and out the back. Slipping into the alley, I sprint along to the street, hoping that I'm fast enough that Edwina won't spot me. Even she has to blink, after all.

Once I'm safely round the corner I drop into a brisk march as I fish my reading glasses out of my bag, doing my best to apply lipstick without breaking stride.

As I turn into Samira's street I slow, forcing my breath under control. With my folder open and pen tracking down the blank page inside, I pause, channeling Edwina as I look thoughtfully around then tap my pen artfully against my chin before making the following important note: **The cat sat on the mat.**

Giving a satisfied nod, I set off again, only for my stride to falter dramatically as I fix my eyes on a large man looming in front of a house halfway down the block. Tilting my head as if in surprised concern, I watch as the man moves toward Samira's garage then stops, spotting me.

For a moment we stare at each other. I take a nervous step back, then raise my phone and snap a picture before tapping into my voicemail.

"Hello, I'm on the street team checking for Covid breaches in quadrant four," I say in anxious tones as the recorded voice reports that I have no new messages. "There's a suspicious man lurking by a house—looks like he's trying to find out if anyone's home so he can break in."

I hurry back toward the corner as I speak, glancing worriedly over my shoulder as if concerned about being followed. The man is legging it in the other direction.

With a grin, I tap out of my voicemail then slip my phone back into my bag as I stride away.

A few minutes later, Jim's phone pings with a WhatsApp message from "Yafir."

What's it take for people to believe I've lost my voice? One of my dafter cousins has been round now, trying to see me. Hassling Samira. What bit of "self-isolation" don't they understand?

Just be glad they're all healthy, comes the tart reply from "Lionel."

I hesitate, then put the phone away. It's more believable with Jim staying out of it.

Turning the corner into my own street, my eyes move warily to Edwina's house.

Her curtains ripple and I brace for the inevitable ambush from her side of the street.

Instead, it's waiting on my own doorstep.

Amy. With a massive suitcase.

35

Family Reunion

The only thing that could have made the situation worse is if Amy had managed to let herself in and found her father in the kitchen. I know I should be terrified, but I just feel numb.

"Where's Dad?" Amy demands, jutting out her chin in that faux-belligerent way she has when her father is safely out of the way. "I forgot my key, so I've been knocking for ages!"

"Upstairs. Having a nap." It's the first lie that comes into my head.

Amy casts the house a skeptical look. "Since when is he deaf?" She heaves a sigh. "My whole life we've always had to creep around whenever he wanted a rest, and the moment I leave home he starts sleeping like the dead."

I force myself not to wince at the words. "I got him some noise-canceling headphones," I say weakly. Then I pull myself together and stride past to open the door. Whatever is going on here will not be improved by Edwina turning up to tell us off.

Amy sets her suitcase down by the hall table, piling a huge holdall and a bulging tote bag onto the staircase. Flicking a look upstairs, she eases the front door shut before marching into the living room. When I follow, she closes that door too—carefully, slowly—and for the first time I see how wrong it all is. None of this is a normal way to behave. How did I ever fool myself that I was giving my kids a happy, healthy childhood?

I'm saved from dissolving into despair by Amy throwing herself on me.

At least she chose the living room, not the kitchen, I think as I raise my arms to hug her back.

"Men are scum," Amy sniffles in my ear. "I hate them all." Then she bursts into tears.

"Darling, what are you doing here? You know the rules don't allow—"

"Sod the rules!" wails Amy. "Or do you care more about some stupid regulations than your own daughter?"

"We are talking about worldwide plague, not overstaying in the supermarket car park."

Amy pulls back, face red and tear-stained. "So that's what I get after two months of separation? Not 'I'm so happy to see you.' Or 'I've missed you so much.'"

"Well, of course I have, but I'm just so surprised, darling. What's this about men being scum, and why do you have a suitcase?"

"I've left him!" Amy declares, throwing herself on me again. "I couldn't stand it there another day. And that nosy old bag glaring at me from over the road will just have to deal, because I will *not* stay with a man who's mean to me, whatever the bloody government says about it."

"What did he do?" I whisper, pressing her close. "Did he hurt you?"

Amy pulls back, scowling. "Of course he hurt me! Why do you think I'm here?"

The pain is like swallowed glass. Amy never saw Jim hit me—never saw any bruises or marks that couldn't be explained away as everyday accidents. The violence didn't escalate until the kids were older, so it was easy enough. As teens, they were so busy out of the house, all Jim had to do was make sure he didn't hurt me in a way that was readily visible. In any case, he used words more often than not. But words land differently when there's always the chance they'll be followed by a punch. Through it all I told myself that at least I wasn't allowing history to repeat itself by letting my kids think violence and abuse are normal. What was the point if it's come to this anyway?

"Well, he won't do it again." I draw in a deep breath. "Now, let's sort out the physical troubles at least. Do you need antiseptic? Some arnica?" I force down the acid rising in my throat. "Do you need a doctor?"

"A doctor? Why would I need a doctor? Are you seriously making a joke about the fact that my *heart* is *broken*?" Amy wrenches away from me and storms over to the sofa.

"You said he hurt you—"

"We broke up, Mum! I've had to come back home and move in with my parents, in the back end of beyond, like some loser. Of course I'm hurting!"

As I look into her blotchy face, I simultaneously want to explode with anger at her stupidity and rejoice that *my* daughter has got to this age so unused to pain and ill treatment that she thinks a breakup is the same as cruelty.

Relief wins out. So long as she is safe—so long as she hasn't been hurt as I've been hurt—the rest can be fixed.

AMY GOES THROUGH A mound of tissues as she explains why she had to leave her boyfriend. The reasons are many and varied. Together, they add up to a mountain of nothing.

"So," I say cautiously, "it sounds like you both realized you're not suited. I know that's sad, but why leave him in the middle of a national Lockdown? Couldn't it wait a few weeks?"

"We were going to kill each other, locked up like that!" Amy snivels.

"Don't you dare make light of people who are actually in that position."

Amy fixes her eyes on me. For a moment she just stares, while panic blooms through me at my own loose tongue. I feel exposed, all my secrets written across my face.

Then Amy flushes, looking away. "Sorry." She gulps in a breath, squeezing her hands into fists around her soggy tissues. "It's just . . . I was so lonely. It's horrible living with someone you thought loved you but now doesn't even like you."

I look away, forcing aside the rush of grief at her words— I've spent the last twenty-three years with that loneliness: it can wait a bit longer. "Well, I love you, and I'm glad you know you deserve better, darling."

Amy sniffs, wiping her nose on the back of her hand, then laughs as I press a new tissue—and bottle of hand gel—on her. "So that's the sob story. Does it at least earn me a cup of tea and a biscuit?"

I am all too glad to flee to the kitchen, but there my sense of purpose stalls.

If Amy stays, even if I manage to hide Jim, she's going to figure out *something* is up. I can tell her he's self-isolating in the bedroom—I can even pretend this means her staying will displace me from her room to the couch, but she'll just offer to help clear the study. And how am I to make her believe there's nothing strange about not hearing her father moving around upstairs, even to use the loo?

She's going to work it out.

Should I induct her into the club, despite the "no new members" rule? It floats through my head like a waft of hope . . . then reality snuffs it out.

"They'll muddle through if Amy calls the police on me, won't they?" I ask Rosemary and Petunia. "It's not as if I'm indispensable."

I want to believe the others will be fine without me, but I know it isn't true: the plan will take all of us—me to come up with ideas, Samira to turn them into a workable plan, Ruth to ensure we're minimizing harm and hurt, Janey to spot all the ways things could go wrong so Samira can problem-solve those too, and Leila to keep us full of hope that, somehow, we really can pull this off.

For too long I let a small man steal my joy and potential. But the type of person worthy of friends like Janey and Ruth, Samira and Leila has got to be someone special, even if I'm still learning to believe it. I know it's partly just the situation, but they've put their trust in me as much as I've put mine in them. If I can live up to them, I'll be on the path to becoming someone I can be proud of.

"Any biscuits?" comes Amy's plaintive moan.

"Coming, darling!" I call, though I don't move. "How the fuck do I get rid of her?" My eyes fall on Jim. "And where the fuckity fuck do I store you?"

I can't thump him upstairs without drawing Amy's attention, but she's bound to come into the kitchen sooner or later. Probably later, since Amy's never been one to set the table or help make dinner if she can busy herself elsewhere. I always let her get away with it, at least when there was no chance Jim would notice, because I loved that she wasn't afraid to be less than dutiful every second of every moment of every day. Still, she'll deign to make her own tea at some point, even if she never puts the washing-up back in the cupboards after—

And just like that the fog of panic clears and the obvious answer presents itself.

First, I make tea, then take the mugs and a packet of M&S chocolate-coated shortbread rings through to the living room.

"Ooooo, fancy!" Amy says, perking right up. "What did Dad say about these?"

"Absolutely nothing." I grin conspiratorially. "There's got to be some upside to him self-isolating, texting me for tea and meals like bloody room service."

"He's got Covid?" Amy edges away from the living-room door.

For a minute, I wonder if this is the solution, but if Amy lets it slip to Edwina . . . No, it's not worth the risk.

"I doubt it, but he definitely hasn't been himself. First, he didn't want me going out at all. Then *he* wouldn't go out. Stopped doing much of anything."

Amy groans, then drags herself to her feet.

I snap out a hand, grabbing her wrist. "Darling, where are you going?"

"Better say hi."

I tug on her hand. "I think he's sleeping right now, and in any case . . ."

In any case, what? Why won't her father even say hi through the door? Can I set up a recording of a male voice and figure out some way to trigger it at the right moment?

"In any case . . ." Amy prompts impatiently.

"Your father's lost his voice."

Amy's forehead wrinkles in confusion. "I thought you said he wasn't sick."

"I'm not sure he is. The thing is . . ." My brain sticks there. *What is the thing?*

"The thing is . . ." Amy prompts even more impatiently.

I throw up my hands. "Actually, you know what, I have no idea. I really don't."

"Guess Dad's not the only one who's gone a bit cuckoo during Lockdown," says Amy helpfully.

Thank you, darling. That makes me feel so comforted, says the voice in my head.

"But why's Dad lost his voice if he's not sick? Just tell me the truth," she demands, fixing a determined look on me. "Do you think he's lost the plot? If it's that bad, we should call someone."

"If he doesn't come out of it, we can do that. But let's see if a few quiet days does the trick first."

"Ah," says Amy. "So it's less 'mental health crisis' and more 'man-child strop.' In that case, I suppose I should at least try saying hello so he doesn't think I'm ignoring him. He won't like that." She casts the ceiling a nervous look, worrying at her lip.

"He might be listening to the radio with his headphones on, so don't be upset if he doesn't answer," I warn her.

Amy nods, snaffling a second biscuit. "Might as well, while he's not here to see!" she whispers, as if he'll somehow overhear.

The second she starts up the steps, I'm down the hall, flicking open the door to the cupboard under the stairs to block the view.

Hurrying to the kitchen, I grab the feet of the Jim-parcel and start dragging. At least I know about the slaloming technique now, so I get some momentum going fairly quickly.

I'm almost into the hall when the other end of the parcel snags on something. As I give a sharp tug, the parcel makes an ominous noise. Cold sweat breaks out across my skin.

Blank with horror, I picture the tarp tearing open, cat litter and salt and rice—and wriggling worms and globs of red-black mess—spilling out. I imagine myself dropping to my knees, frantically trying to shovel it all back in, but it's too late because I can hear Amy's feet on the stairs again, and I call out that she should "Go back to the living room, everything's fine," but my voice is high and squeaky, and she's peering over the cupboard door, and . . .

The tarp slides free and glides on, nearly tipping me on to my bum. I sink to my knees. Something is going to go wrong, and it'll end with Amy finding her father's body and—

I squeeze my eyes shut, forcing the panic down.

Grasping the end of the parcel, I slide Jim the last few feet to the cupboard, ducking inside to pull him to the back of the space. The way the parcel sags when I wedge one end up against the wall makes my stomach swoop.

I slam the door shut and slide the bolt home just as Amy clatters downstairs.

36

Ducks in a Row

Two hours later, Amy is still producing copious amounts of tears and snot—*where is it all coming from?* I'm getting rather worried about dehydration, but if I don't leave soon for the club's daily planning session the others are going to start calling in a panic.

"I'm just going to nip out for a walk, darling, but we can talk some more later." Cupping her face, I press a kiss to her forehead. "Back in an hour."

"Mum!" she squawks, outraged. "You can't go when I'm like this! Anyway, I'm hungry. I thought we'd have cheesy scrambled eggs together."

"I don't have time, and anyway there's only two eggs and I need those for baking. But there's about ten types of cheese in the fridge and plenty of bread, so why don't you make yourself a nice sandwich? I'll take Dad's lunch up, so all you need to do is fix something for yourself."

"You're really going?" Amy says in a tiny voice.

"Yes, dear. Your mother is really leaving the house for an

entire hour of fresh air and exercise. I'll even get eggs on the way back, provided the shop's not out again."

I hurry upstairs, nominally for a wee, though mostly to stuff some pillows under the sheets so it looks like there's someone in the bed, should Amy peek through the keyhole; I doubt she would risk disturbing Jim, but better safe than sorry. I pocket the key with my mind fixed firmly on the list of things the club needs to collect or buy for step one of the plan—another tarp, bamboo sticks, and some rope. It's better than letting my thoughts dwell on all the misery that bedroom lock has represented, despite its usefulness now.

Amy gives me a wounded look as I collect my handbag. After a lifetime pandering to her out of guilt for giving her a man like Jim as a father, perhaps it is a little harsh to just stop.

Or maybe it's well past time, I tell myself as I march out onto the street, turning off my mobile.

The relief on the others' faces when they see me hurrying across the grass to join them by the pond warms me from the inside out, even as I call apologies for my lateness.

"But what are you going to do?" Janey asks when I've explained the situation. "Even Amy is bound to work out that Jim's not just a little off. How long can you possibly string it out?"

I groan. "Maybe the boyfriend will call and they'll make up . . ." I shrug. "I've only got until Jim's stint on the rota anyway, and that's just twelve days now. Speaking of ticking clocks," I say, turning to Samira, "how are things with the family?"

"Actually," says Leila, biting her lip to suppress a smile, "the clock may not be ticking quite the same way for us anymore. Apparently having the whole family on devices all the time to argue and gossip overloaded the electrics in my grandfather's house and it blew up the fuse box."

"Now they only have their mobiles, and the network is patchy at best where they are, plus it's expensive, so communication is going to be limited for a while," Samira adds, trying but not entirely succeeding in hiding her delight.

"Also, my grandfather needs oxygen, but it's really hard to get now, so they're all busy with that," Leila says.

My handbag beeps. As the others carry on chatting, I reach for my mobile, then remember it's off. Frowning, I grope around until I find Jim's.

Amy: Mum's looking totally frazzled. Are you coming out soon?

"Sorry. Amy's texting Jim," I tell the others as I tap out a reply: Sore throat. Can't chance it.

Amy's reply pings in a moment later: Feel better x

I wait to see if there's more, but Jim's phone stays silent. I'm not sure I trust the quiet, but before I can decide whether I should just head home or ignore Amy for a bit, there's a shriek and an almighty splash as Maryam falls spectacularly face-first into the pond.

We spring to our feet as one, pelting down the grass. Leila gets there first, plunging straight into the water. Samira splashes in beside her and together they lift Maryam to her feet, leading her tenderly back to dry land. Leila pats her sister's back as she spits up muddy water, while Samira smooths filthy hair out of her face.

"I just slipped," Maryam sobs. "I didn't mean to."

"We told you not to go up to the edge," snaps Leila, but the waver in her voice speaks of fear rather than anger. "Look, you're fine now. Stop crying."

Maryam gives her a wounded look. "I've got a muddy tongue," she whimpers.

Ruth produces a tissue. Maryam spits a gob of gritty saliva into it, then offers it back to Ruth.

Her mother snatches it away with an apologetic grimace. "After all this is over—the pandemic, I mean," she adds quickly, "you're both learning to swim."

"Can we go to the beach?" asks Maryam, brightening. "Can I swim in the sea?"

Leila rolls her eyes. "She wasn't going to drown, Mum."

"Actually, people can—and do—drown in just a few inches sometimes," says Ruth. "Everyone should learn how to swim."

Leila snorts. "In case of marauding puddles and tripping into duck ponds?" Then her eyes fly wide and she reaches for her pocket. "Thought I'd dropped my phone. Next time I'm taking it out before coming in for you," she warns her sister.

"You'd let me drown to save your phone?" Maryam asks mournfully. "Guess I'll *have* to learn to swim."

"It's one of those basic skills you never know you're going to need until it's too late," I say encouragingly. "But why not make it something fun? You, Leila, and Ava can learn together and, as a reward, we'll all go on a group holiday to the seaside, and those who want to swim will be able to, and the rest of us can sit on the sand and stuff ourselves silly with fish and chips and ice cream."

"Well, in that case I'm in," says Leila as we start the trek back to the street, Maryam and Leila squelching with every step while Ruth does her best to distract them with tales of the trips she and her mother had made to St. Lucia so Ruth could know her homeland.

"One weekend when we were there in June, we went to the Fish Fry—a festival in the fishing village of Dennery. Everyone spends the evening eating lobster and crab and tuna roasted over grills, then a DJ plays zouk and calypso and reggae music until two in the morning and we dance into the night. My aunties had given me my very own *wob dwiyet*—our national dress—and I felt . . ." She closes her eyes, joy painted across her face.

"I'm not sure we can afford St. Lucia for a while," I say cautiously, when she doesn't go on, "but perhaps one day . . ."

Ruth smiles gently. "One day," she echoes.

Yet, when we head off in separate directions, it's not Ruth's stories I find myself replaying but Leila's worry about her phone falling into the water. If our husbands are going to vanish without it being weird that their phones aren't with them, then water *is* the most logical reason that they'd *all* leave their devices behind.

The thought occupies me through the faff of checking three shops before I find eggs. It means I'm nearly running as I turn down the block a sinful seventy minutes after leaving. *Please let Edwina be in the loo.*

But, no, as I approach the house, the curtains flutter, then the front door opens and . . .

"Good afternoon, Sally."

"I know, I know. I'm ten minutes over," I pant.

Edwina heaves a sigh. "You really do need to keep better track of changes in the regulations, Sally. As of today, we're allowed to leave the house to exercise as much as we like—and meet one other person, provided we remain socially distanced. But," she adds forcefully, when I practically glow with relief at how much easier that will make things with the club, "there has been no alteration with regard to the rules about socializing with family inside—and overnight stays are still strictly prohibited."

I do my best to look put upon, which is hardly a reach. "I've tried telling Amy, but she's broken up with her boyfriend and didn't have anywhere else to go. Surely there's an exemption for relationship breakups."

"There are exceptions for domestic violence. I hope for both your sakes that is not the case, but otherwise—"

I heave a sigh. "I did try to tell her that so long as she's safe she should wait out the Lockdown, but I can hardly throw her out. It's all I need right now, with Jim taken to his bed—no, he's not sick," I add quickly. "It's just . . ." I gesture vaguely. "Lockdown blues."

"I wondered why I hadn't seen him lately," Edwina says, eyes narrowing.

"I'm worried Amy being here will be the last straw." I don't have to fake looking overwhelmed. "She insisted we have eggs for dinner so . . ." I heft the bag. "I know I shouldn't indulge her, but I can't bear to be arguing with her as well."

Edwina shakes her head. "She'll have to learn. Cossetting them isn't the answer." Then she softens. "But we all have to pick our battles. Just remember that breaking eggs is only the solution to *some* of life's problems," she tells me. "The others mostly involve alcohol."

It jolts a laugh out of me. There really is a sense of humor lurking under all that sternness and glaring.

Turning on to the front path, I carefully flick Jim's phone to silent in case Amy texts him again then wonders why his mobile is in my handbag. I expect to hear her voice sounding plaintively from the living room when I let myself in, but all is quiet—suspiciously quiet.

"How are you feeling, darling? Did lunch help?" I call.

No one answers. Cautiously, I creep halfway upstairs: the bathroom door is wide open. Frowning, I hurry to the kitchen and look out into the garden: empty. Anxiously, I turn on my phone; the last message just says cheezy eggs pleeeeeeeeeeease, with a begging-face emoji.

Where is she? Has she found Jim and run off?

I whirl round, but the cupboard under the stairs is still closed and bolted. When I peer inside, nothing looks disturbed.

I fling open the door to the living room and look around. There's no Amy. But there *is* an igloo.

In my living room.

It seems to be wearing a forest-print quilt.

"Amy?" I whisper.

Nothing.

"AMY!"

The igloo shivers and squirms. The quilt tips off onto the floor, revealing a sleeping bag beneath, which slips in the opposite direction. An opening unzips and Amy's head pokes out, hair standing up every which way around a pair of padded headphones.

"What?" she snaps as she drags them down around her neck.

I gape at her, gesturing at the igloo.

Amy rolls her eyes but takes off the headphones and scrambles out. "I *told* you about this weeks ago. They wouldn't let us come into work, so we all had to set up our own home studios. I mean, we're doing automated corporate voice-overs—it's not like the quality has to be perfect, so long as we minimize background noise. Some of my mates have padded their closets, but I figured why not get a little tent and cover it in quilts and sleeping bags, then it's, like, fun to work in."

"I just didn't expect an igloo. In the living room."

Amy rolls her eyes. "I was *trying* to get some work done, since Dad's playing dead. Has it been like this the whole time?" She casts a look at the ceiling, face bleak. "Probably came out while I was in the tent and I've missed him."

Guilt stabs me between the ribs, cold as a knife.

Amy sees the pain on my face and tightens her lips into a smile, though it takes an extra moment to reach her eyes. "Can we eat now, or do you have some urgent washing-up that needs doing, even though I'm literally starving here?"

And there she is—back to normal: all snark and sass and bloody cheek.

At least she's not afraid of me, the voice in my head says sadly.

"I've canceled Zoom karaoke, so I'm all yours for the afternoon," I promise.

Amy brightens further. "Can you make hot chocolate too? Like old times?"

Revisiting the past is the last thing I feel like doing, but if that's what it takes to keep her happy while I deal with the local corpse infestation, it's a small price to pay.

37

Milk, One Sugar, and a Minor Heart Attack

Leaving Amy to eat, I make a cup of tea to Jim's specifications. My hands tremble as I find my mind going to that last morning together and how the tea was one shade too light, which led to the kettle, which led to the skillet, which led to the parcel in the cupboard under the stairs . . . and suddenly I find myself remembering the first time I let myself wonder, just for a moment, if marrying Jim wasn't "happily ever after" but a plunge from the proverbial frying pan.

We'd been married just a few months, and the only rooms we'd managed to furnish were the living room and our bedroom. Still, Jim had insisted "we" host a party for his colleagues that included none of my friends, not even Janey. I spent it presenting people with homemade canapés while they barely glanced at me.

"How else am I to get promoted?" he'd demanded, running his hands through his thinning hair, then smoothing it carefully back into place. "It's a family business, so if I show them I'm a settled, married man, that has to count for more than being good at chucking darts about in the pub."

Not a single one of Jim's family-oriented colleagues stopped to talk to me, though several asked if there was anything stronger on offer than the wine Jim hadn't stopped gushing about to everyone who could be trapped into listening.

"Nothing like the fresh citrus and grass tones of a Chilean Chardonnay," he told his boss airily, only for the other man to roll his eyes.

"Not exactly their number-one grape variety, though, is it?"

The look on Jim's face when he saw I'd overheard left me cold all over.

When Jim's smarmy easy-listening jazz came to a stop, I hurried over to change the CD to something fun, but the fury in Jim's eyes when I turned . . . I smashed the eject button only to drop the disc and fumble two attempts to pick it up, by which point Jim was there, grabbing it from me. His fingers bit white marks into my arm as he shoved me aside.

I don't know why that's the memory I always think of as *the* moment. It wasn't as if there weren't other times I pushed aside unease or pretended that Jim's anger at some minor irritation wasn't just a little too hot and sudden and dangerous. He'd started in with those quiet little digs less than a month after the wedding, always presented so dispassionately it made them seem less like insults and more just statements of fact. But that was the first time he got physical, and he did it in front of people. Not one of them batted an eye.

I was pregnant by then, and still even more afraid of my father than my husband. So I put on a smile and pretended it was no big deal, because it wasn't as if he'd punched me, right? He'd just grabbed a little too tight in his stress over wanting the party to go well, no need to blow it out of proportion . . .

"How much stirring does one cup of tea need?"

Amy's voice jolts me back to the present. I shake my head, manufacturing a laugh. "Best take this to your father." I hurry out before she can notice the flush of misery burning my cheeks.

Knocking loudly on the bedroom door, I unlock it and slip inside, leaving the tea on the chest of drawers before locking up once more.

Amy's face is anxious when I get back, but her phone buzzes before she can ask any awkward questions. She glances at the name, smirks, then hits the decline button. "Third time he's rung."

"Well, you'd better pick up next time. What if he's found out he had contact with a Covid case and is trying to tell you to self-isolate?"

When the phone goes again five minutes later, I give Amy a pointed look. She huffs irritably but swipes her phone off the table and stomps away to the living room. I have a peaceful ten minutes to admire the garden before I hear her voice rising. It drops quickly again, before rising once more—a lifetime of keeping the volume lowered when her father is home clashing with more recent habits formed at uni, then the flat with her boyfriend.

When a burst of shouting ends in sudden silence, I peek into the living room in time to see Amy throw her phone at the sofa, where it bounces harmlessly off a cushion.

"He says I've still got to pay my half of the rent!"

I lean against the doorway. "Unfortunately, he has a point."

"Why should I pay when he's getting the whole flat to himself?" Glaring, she zips herself up inside her igloo.

Leaving her to it, I perform my daily check of Jim's email in the study, then turn to my own. To my delight there's a reply from the council confirming that our community gardening project doesn't need further approval. My triumph is followed by resignation. We really are going to have to dismember the bodies.

Unable to bear the flood of images, I pick up my latest forensics-heavy mystery novel, only to remember that I abandoned it yesterday when the clever murderess was uncovered by the detective, despite an extremely good plan and entirely reasonable motive.

My attempts to advance the plan for how we'll explain our husbands' absence are equally unproductive.

"Something will come to me," I tell myself encouragingly.

My mind remains blank.

"Something will come to one of the others then," I snap as I head downstairs, humming Charlie's song of the day, "Don't Rain on My Parade."

Amy is sitting at the kitchen table with a flapjack, a cup of tea . . . and my notebook.

38

Never a Dull Moment

stare in horror, my mind filled with a roaring, rushing sound like screaming.

Amy's head comes up, her eyes wide and bewildered. "I get the cheese and chocolate and cake, but you really think karaoke's the key to happiness?"

Breath rushing out in a gasp of relief, I dive forward, snatching the notebook out of reach.

"Uh . . . Little overreaction maybe?" Amy's face twists into a sly grin. "Or is there something embarrassing further down the list, 'cos, you know, there's nothing wrong with having a vibrator, Mum."

"Oh my God, we are not having this conversation." Too afraid to put the notebook into my handbag in case Amy decides to pry, I stuff it down my top.

"What are you doing?" she asks. "Jeez, what else is on that list?"

"None of your business." It comes out harsher than intended. With a sigh, I bend and kiss her forehead, then tap her nose. "This cute little schnoz stays out of my notebook."

Amy frowns. "What's the big secret? You know I'm grown up now, right? You don't need to protect me." She casts an eye at the ceiling. "Is there something you're not telling me about Dad? I barely heard him last night."

Fed up of lying, I settle for a partial truth. "I'm worried about a friend of mine. Her husband has reacted badly to finding out that their daughter's a lesbian."

Amy pulls a face. "Yikes. I'd need moral support too if I realized I was married to a homophobic moron."

"Well, they're going to separate once restrictions lift."

"Why doesn't she go now?" There's a sudden sharper note in her voice.

"There's a lot to sort out. You can't just unravel a whole life overnight."

Amy snorts, but there's no humor in the sound. "I did, didn't I?"

"It's different when there are children involved," I say quietly.

Then neither of us says anything at all.

It's a relief when my phone buzzes. Then I see the message.

Ruth: SOS! Burst pipe. Plumber on way. Need help moving THE LARGE PACKAGE somewhere safe!

"Friend's having a crisis," I say, grabbing my handbag and a cardigan as I clumsily text back that I'm own my wahey.

I'm out the door before Amy can speak.

I only manage to jog for half a block before I have to stumble back to a walk. It feels as if I'm taking forever, but it can't be more than five minutes before I let myself in through Ruth's back gate with the key she gave me for emergencies.

I pull on my mask as I open the kitchen door, closing it behind me before calling her name.

"Up here!" comes the exhausted reply.

I squelch up the staircase, past a glorious print of a palm-tree-lined beach between two cones of towering rock, to find a frazzled Ruth on her knees in a mess of sodden towels, frantically swapping between a pair of buckets. Even though she's darting back and forth as fast as she can go, by the time she's emptied one into the bath the other is already overflowing.

I kneel beside her and take over the emptying.

Ruth sags in exhaustion. "The plumber should be here soon. I tried to get the water off, but the stopcock's too tight for me to turn." She pauses to swipe her hair away from her forehead. "If you can keep the flood under control for a few minutes, I'll move Lionel to the living room."

"Happy to go the other way round," I offer. "You look done in."

She flashes me a wan smile. "I couldn't ask—"

"You don't have to." I squeeze her shoulder.

Ruth puts her hand over mine. "This has been the worst week of my life, but it has brought me the best friends."

"It's a hell of an upside," I agree as I stagger to my feet and head downstairs again.

I've just seized the corpse-parcel's feet when a hammering at the front door makes me reel back into the kitchen counter.

Ruth comes stumbling down the steps. For a second her panicked eyes meet mine, then I dart forward and close the kitchen door.

A moment later, I hear the front door open.

39

Hide and Sneak

"O h, thank goodness," says Ruth from the hall, her voice liquid with relief.

Creeping to the kitchen door so I can hear, I make out a man's voice saying, "I'll put in a valve so it can't happen again, but first we've got to get the water off. Main stopcock in the kitchen? It's usually under the sink . . ."

I don't stop to think, just throw open the back door, grab the parcel's feet, and start slaloming frantically across the floor.

"Wait!" comes Ruth's panicked gasp from the hall. I imagine her trying to block the way as the plumber pushes past, just like me and the meter man.

"Best get that water off immediately," says the plumber, closer now.

"Just give me a sec. Bit of a mess—"

"Don't worry about that, love. It'll be much more of a mess if this water keeps on and gets in the electrics."

All the corpse-maneuvering practice must be working, because I thump the body's head and shoulders down the step into the garden in a burst of desperation.

"I should get the cat out the way," Ruth says loudly, backing into the kitchen. "Don't want her biting you."

"You take care of the cat and I'll get the water off and it'll be a grand piece of teamwork," says the plumber.

Wrenching the body to the left so it lies flush against the outer wall, I duck below the level of the kitchen window and freeze, trying my best not to breathe, despite the fact that my lungs are burning with exertion.

I flinch at a bang close to my head, followed by a volley of curses, a series of scrambling noises, and a loud grunt.

"That slowing down yet?" the plumber shouts, voice growing quieter as he presumably heads back up the corridor to the stairs.

I collapse against the wall, legs outstretched in front, just as a bright pink football comes sailing over Ruth's fence from the neighbor's garden.

"Noooooooo!" shouts a girl's voice. "I told you to watch it! Where are you going? We need to get our ball back!"

"I'm going to get it!" snarls a boy.

"You can't go and knock on her door in a pandemic! You're so useless," snaps the girl.

By the time I realize what the strange slithering sound coming from right behind the fence is, it's too late. A head of close-cropped hair crests the top and a second later the girl throws her leg over and jumps down onto the grass.

She turns, locks eyes with me, and we both freeze.

The girl recovers first. "Sorry, miss. Thought it was better to come and get it. I didn't think anyone was out here."

"It's fine," I squeak.

The girl picks up the ball then pauses, frowning at me. "Visitors aren't allowed, you know."

"I'm with the plumber. There's a leak."

The girl gives me a dubious look.

"Just taking a little break. Hard work, you know, plumbing."

"You were smoking, weren't you?" the girl says accusingly.

I raise my hands. "Don't tell on me, and I won't tell on you climbing over the fence."

The girl purses her lips but nods. She throws the ball back over the fence then scrambles up, pausing as she straddles the top. "Smoking's bad for you. If you get Covid you'll probably die."

"You're right. Going to quit. Tomorrow."

The girl shakes her head. "Lying's bad too," she says, then disappears into the other garden.

I look to my left and heave a sigh of relief that from her position the body would have been mostly hidden behind a trough of herbs.

For a moment, I let my head fall back against the brickwork. Then I crawl to the kitchen door and peer cautiously inside. There's no one there, but I catch the creak of footsteps on the stairs and quickly flatten myself against the wall again.

"Sally?" Ruth calls softly a moment later.

I scramble up, beckoning her out onto the patio. "It was the only thing I could think of so the plumber wouldn't see, but your neighbor's kids came over the fence to get their ball, and they'll probably be back, so we can't leave him here."

We heft the body up and stagger into the kitchen, the middle of the corpse-parcel dragging along the ground as we falter under the weight. Huffing and puffing and ready to fall down and never get up again, we're stumbling through the living-room door when we hear rapid footsteps crossing the landing over-head.

Ruth, still in the hall, freezes, the feet of the corpse-parcel tumbling to the floor.

For a second, I contemplate a heroic effort to get the body out of sight on my own, but I'm out of time and strength. As the plumber comes pounding downstairs, Ruth braces herself in the doorway. I stand tall, determined to face my fate head on.

"Left the bloody washers in the van," the plumber says, and breezes out of the front door without even glancing at us.

THE PIPE IS FIXED and the plumber gone.

Ruth and I are slumped on the sofa, drinking strong coffee laced liberally with rum and cream.

I rub wearily at one shoulder, then the other. "It was like a bloody Victorian farce, but with more corpses."

"We can't go on like this. Someone is going to find out, and then . . ." She takes a deep breath, steeling herself. "If it comes to it . . ."

"It won't. But if it does, we're in it together. You and me. The founding members."

We manage a wan smile for each other, then apply ourselves to our drinks.

Ruth groans, rolling her head stiffly from side to side. "I haven't ached like this since . . ."

I don't have to ask to know it's not a long day at the hospital she's thinking of, but the last time Lionel went for her.

"How often was it bad?" I whisper. Because we don't ask. Or at least we haven't so far. There are things I need to tell someone but don't ever want to hear myself say: things I don't think *will* be better shared. I guess that's the point, really—to finally be able to choose.

I'm about to take the words back when Ruth sinks a little deeper into the cushions, as if something that was keeping her taut has released and she can breathe fully again.

"Not often," she says softly. "Sometimes it would be fine for weeks, months, and I'd think, 'It was just a blip. We all make mistakes. He's always sorry.'"

"Jim was never sorry," I say, though I'd intended just to listen.

Ruth's face is gentle. "I don't know if it's better or worse that Lionel was and yet he just kept . . ." She lets out a breath in slow stages, as if measuring the weight of the air. "When it started being difficult between us, I told myself, 'At least he'll never hit you.' Then, when he did, I pretended it was just a one-off. And then . . ."

She shakes her head. "My aunt suffered with her husband, and I thought it was so simple from the outside—just leave him, you stupid woman. But it looks different from the inside: sometimes I could barely keep track of what was real and the lies he'd spin that he hadn't said this, hadn't done that and I was remembering it wrong."

"Sometimes the way he acted made me feel as if I'd imagined half of it," I echo quietly. "Or at least exaggerated it all in my head."

Our lips quirk into smiles while our eyes speak of heartbreak.

"I thought Jim was different from my father. Then, when

he turned out to be the same, I told myself that so long as he never touched the kids it was different *enough*. Because I thought I'd kept it from them, but now . . ."

The tears spill out then. Beside me I hear Ruth's breathing change and, for a while, we cry silently beside one another. Eventually I swipe my tears away.

Ruth sighs sadly. "We broke social distancing today."

"Your house was flooding. We're being as careful as possible, but between us we've four rather large complications that other people don't have to deal with."

We glance over the back of the sofa.

"At least he's out of the way there. I kept tripping over him in the kitchen." Ruth purses her lips then, and I see guilt flash across her face.

"Much like when he was alive?" I suggest.

She gives me a look.

"Don't turn that on me when you were thinking it every bit as much as I was," I tease.

"Yes, but at least I felt guilty about it."

My phone erupts in my handbag. I fumble through the contents, praying it really is my phone ringing and not Jim's.

It's mine—with Amy's name flashing on the display.

"Mum, you've got to come!" Amy shrieks, the minute I tap accept. "Hurry! There's . . . I saw . . . Oh my God."

"What's happened?" I ask, already throwing my handbag over my shoulder. "Where are you?"

"In the living room," Amy whispers. "I can't get out with *that thing* in the hall!"

Despair floods through me. She's opened the cupboard under the stairs and Jim's fallen out.

Well, it was good while it lasted, the little voice in my head says. *This is your punishment for all those years lying to your children, making them lie to you, all so you could lie to yourself.*

"Hurry! Please, Mum! Please!" Amy gasps, then hangs up.

I turn to Ruth, my whole body aching with dread. "Amy found Jim."

40

My Family and Other
Rabid Animals

t's over. I'm going to prison. And Amy will hate me, both for what I've done to her father and what I've done to her, letting her be the one to find him. What will she do when she realizes we've been talking and laughing and eating together with his body a few feet away? Surely only a psychopath could do such a thing. Is that what I am? Did Jim's violence awaken it in me, or was it always there underneath?

"I have to go," I hear myself say.

Ruth stands so quickly she shoves the sofa backward. There's an unpleasant scrunch as the tarpaulin-package is squished against the wall.

I smooth my hands down my skirt, straightening the hem, then hurry away before I can give in to the temptation to sink back down and wallow in despair.

There's no avoiding what comes next, and delaying will only make it worse, so I let myself through Ruth's back gate, then I run. It's messy and ungainly, and I'm sweaty—hair sticking to my forehead and clothing clinging to the backs of my knees—

before I've gone a block, but I keep going, face set in an ugly grimace.

The acrid tang of burning hits me as I hurtle through my own gate, hurrying across the lawn to the open back door, only to halt on the threshold as if some part of me is determined to run in the opposite direction.

Grabbing the doorjamb, I sway with the urge to flee.

When I step inside my life is over, says the voice in my head.

Closing my eyes, I draw my foot up, set it on the kitchen floor, and force myself forward. I can't hear any sounds from deeper inside, but when I open my eyes I realize that the kitchen looks as if it has exploded. Half the cupboards are open. Pots and pans cover the counters and hob. Next to the sink a large mixing bowl is sitting in a puddle of grayish-brownish goo. The same mixture is splattered down the counter and across the floor in various directions.

Clenching my fists, I summon all the courage in me and cross the kitchen, preparing for what lies ahead: the cupboard under the stairs open and the Jim-parcel collapsed in the hall with Amy whimpering beside it.

Grayish-brownish footprints lead down the hall, growing fainter as they approach the living room . . . but that is it. The door to the cupboard under the stairs is closed and bolted. There is no Jim-parcel on the floor.

"Amy?" I call, voice thin and quavering.

The living-room door inches open. "Mum?" She peers along the hall toward the kitchen, then, bafflingly, toward the stairs. "I don't think it went upstairs, but I'm too scared to check. Who do we call? The police? A vet?"

"Vet?" I echo faintly. "Amy, what is going on?"

"There was a fox!"

I nearly collapse as relief turns my knees to water. She doesn't know about Jim. She's fine, and I'm not going to prison.

When I tune back in, Amy is babbling on in that half-accusatory, half-apologetic way she has when she's thrown a hissy fit and wants everyone to pretend it never happened.

"I was cooking muffins and they got a little burned—OK, they were on fire—so I panicked a bit and knocked over the bowl with the extra batter. Then I calmed down and took the tray outside, but when I came back into the kitchen there was this massive fox snuffling up the spilled mixture." She flushes. "I sort of tracked it around a bit."

We both look down at the footprints.

"So I see."

"I thought the fox would run away when it saw me, but it just sat there, so I tried shouting at it, but it hunkered down and glared at me like it was about to charge, so I backed away, but it kept coming, and . . . and I threw the spatula at it and ran in here for safety." She folds her arms defensively. "You don't know what it was like! There was something wrong with it. Rabies maybe?"

I press a hand to my chest. My heart is still going so fast the beat is practically a flutter. "You don't know the fright you gave me."

"Sorry for nearly being eaten by a rabid wild animal," Amy says huffily, then she peers around again. "How can we be sure it's gone? Maybe it's lurking upstairs."

"I guess we'll have to go and find out."

Amy gives me an impressed look, then squares her shoulders. "Let me just get my ladle, and I'll be right behind you."

"Let's think this through. All the doors down here are closed. How about upstairs? Did you leave your bedroom door open, or go into the study?"

Amy shakes her head.

With a sigh, I push myself off the wall and head to the kitchen. "Then it's probably gone. Let's get the worst of this cleared up and—"

As Amy steps into the kitchen behind me, she lets out a piercing squeal. We both stagger into the counter as she points a quivering finger at the opposite side of the room.

In the shadow of the back door, wedged between the recycling box and the edge of the washing machine, is a large, mangy fox crouched low over a muffin tray.

"What do we do?" Amy squeaks.

"Nothing that's going to bring your father down on us," I say sternly. I've not swerved disaster only to let this fox situation unfold in such a way that Amy can no longer be persuaded that her father's just ignoring us.

Bending down, I scoop up the discarded ladle and pass it to Amy. "Here. Just in case." Then I slip back down the hallway and grab Jim's big umbrella from the hat stand. Stepping protectively in front of Amy, I ease the door to the hall closed so the fox's only option is the open garden door, then I step forward, umbrella outstretched.

"Go away," I tell the fox firmly.

It bares its teeth at me, then tries to clamp them around the edge of the muffin tray as if to drag it away.

I lunge the umbrella forward, expecting the fox to scarper, but it backs deeper into the gap between the recycling bin and the washing machine, eyes glinting malevolently.

I bare my teeth too, then stab the umbrella down toward the washing machine, aiming just above the fox's head. It bolts at the last second, diving out into the middle of the room.

Amy shrieks and chucks the ladle at it. It misses the fox, clattering as it lands against the recycling box. The noise sends the fox racing out of the door. With a flick of its tail, it disappears under the fence.

"Well," I gasp, brushing my hair back from my face. "We're blocking up that hole right now." I turn to find Amy staring at me.

"You were brilliant, Mum. When did you get so brave?"

All I can do is laugh.

41

Amy Has a Cunning Plan

Once the fence is secured, I pretend to check on Jim, reporting that he was asleep with his earplugs in and that's why he didn't see Amy's texts or hear her screaming. Then I set Amy to cleaning the kitchen while I make Jim a sandwich and take it up on the way to have a shower.

Leaving the sandwich on the side of the bathroom sink, I place the tray and empty plate outside Jim's door, then hurry back to the bathroom to wash away the sweat of the day's exertions. After I've cleaned myself up and scarfed down the sandwich, I feel almost human. I consider slipping into my new evening dress, then sensibly (and sadly) pick a more normal top and skirt.

Still, Amy does a double take as I walk into the kitchen. "You look nice, Mum! You going somewhere?"

"Thank you for the compliment—and the astonishment. Right now, I'm going to sit at the table."

Amy joins me. "Can we talk a minute?"

I nod, patting the chair beside me, despite the temptation to busy myself with cooking or washing or anything that would stop her asking about her father.

But instead of any of the questions I'm dreading, she says,

"I've been thinking about whether Edwina's going to report me for being here, and what Dad's going to say when he surfaces. Then there's having to pay rent on the flat even though I'm not going back . . . and I had a brain wave."

Oh God, says the voice in my head. "Mhm?" is what actually comes out.

It's obviously encouraging enough to pass muster as Amy leans forward. "My boyfriend and I are friends with this other couple that've also been finding Lockdown superhard. Anyway, she and I get on really well, so I called her and asked what she thought about the two of us moving in together in one flat, while the boys take the other. Well, she talked to her boyfriend and he was all for it, so they're going to take a break till their lease runs out . . . Anyway, the point is that now I can leave my boyfriend without moving back in here." She gives me a tentative smile. "I just wanted to check that it's OK for me to leave again while Dad is being so . . . Dad-ish. I can stay if you need me to."

I know she means it, just as she knows *I* know it's the last thing she wants.

"It sounds like a wonderful solution, darling—a clever, mature way to make everyone happy. I'm really proud of you. So don't you worry about us. We'll be just fine."

I expect her to turn sunny again, bounding off to finish the arrangements, but instead she reaches across the table to take my hand. "Are you sure? I . . ." She looks down, twisting a bracelet about her wrist. "I knew Dad would be angry about me coming home, but I wanted to see you so much and . . ."

The air feels suddenly weighted. If I'd really protected my children as fully as I told myself I had, why would my loud, confident, outgoing daughter always tiptoe around her father—

always do her best to placate him, constantly on the alert to avoid trouble? I know Amy is often babyish and selfish with me because she had to be the opposite with Jim, but I told myself that if I spoiled her enough it would make up for it, even though I knew it wouldn't. Couldn't.

I knew that they saw how Jim controlled me. I knew that through me he controlled them too. I knew it all, but I never let myself put the pieces together because if I just thought about each element separately, I couldn't see what picture they made.

Did I really think I was protecting them? That the only thing that mattered was ensuring the violence in our home was kept firmly behind closed doors with them safely on the other side? I can't have thought that was all it would have taken for my own childhood to have been OK . . . can I?

"Mum?" Amy's voice is so tiny, so full of need. "Are you sorry I'm here?"

"Never!" I push the past aside, focusing all my attention on my daughter. "I could never, ever be sorry to have you with me."

She swallows hard. "I knew Dad wouldn't like it, and I don't want to cause trouble, but I just . . . I needed to know you weren't angry with me for calling it quits on the relationship. You were younger than me when you got together with Dad and you're still—"

"I told your father I'm leaving him."

Whenever I imagined this moment, I thought my stomach would tighten with fear as I waited for Amy's reaction. Instead, I watch the briefest flash of shock pass over her face before it's replaced by a sad, tender understanding.

A moment later, she's out of her chair and hugging me, but gently, as if I'm hurt.

"I love you," she whispers. "I love you so much, Mum." When she pulls back, her eyes are bright with tears, though she's smiling.

And I can see that she knows. Whether Charlie persuaded her, or she realized on her own, I can't pretend anymore that the worst they suspect is that I've been living under Jim's thumb. They'll never know how tight his rein was—the phone calls when he was at work to check I was home, the times he'd randomly come back to ensure I was alone—but it's time to accept that all I've been doing by lying is forcing them to play along.

Yet, despite my example, Amy left her boyfriend because she was unhappy. Despite all my failings, their childhood left them strong enough to make the best choices open to them.

Now it's time I found the courage to say the things I hope would have been true even if Jim really were sulking upstairs, instead of parceled up in the cupboard underneath them.

"We're . . . we're going to wait out the Lockdown, but afterward . . . Afterward, it's over."

I can't change the past, but I am changing myself and my life for the better, and that'll have to do.

"Are you going to be OK here till then?" Amy asks, face tight with worry. "You could come with me, you know. It wouldn't be very comfortable, but we'd manage."

I reach out and squeeze her hand. "*Thank* you, my love. That's . . . You're a wonderful daughter to say that. But I'm OK." I can see she's about to argue, so I say, quite truthfully, "Your father has no plans to emerge or engage—now we've got our little system worked out, it's really quite peaceful. I just want to enjoy getting back to gardening and being the one making the choices about meals and what's on the TV."

Amy grips my hand. "Whatever happens, please don't lie to us. Charlie and I . . . we need you to be all right."

In that moment, I know that my children will be OK about Jim's disappearance. It'll hurt, but not too deeply. Not the way that me dead at Jim's hands would have.

"No more lies." *Apart from about what's under the stairs.*

Steeling myself, I take a deep breath. "I am sorry for how many there have been till now."

Amy shakes her head. "We know you were doing it for us." She gulps down a breath. "But it's time you came first, OK? We're grown up now and we'll be fine with whatever happens so long as you're all right."

This time I'm the one who lurches forward to hug her.

There's so much I want to say. How much I love them. How sorry I am. How grateful. Instead I just hold her tight and let her hold me.

"We're both going to be happy now, aren't we?" Amy whispers.

"Yes," I whisper back. "At least mostly."

And then we both laugh, even though we're crying a little, because it's the truth. It turns out that even when it hurts it's not nearly as unbearable as the false promise of lies.

Eventually Amy sighs. "I suppose I'd better tell my friend the apartment swap is a go," she says, but doesn't get up. "I really wanted him to be the right one. I really wanted to believe we'd stay happy and that would be it, forever: one good thing I could always count on." Her chin trembles. "Was that really stupid of me?"

"Of course not. We're not fools for wanting love, only for lying to ourselves about whether we've found it."

I know she'll think I'm talking about Jim, and I am, but it's only part of the picture. It wasn't just that I wanted to be in love with Jim and have him love me back—I *needed* it, because it was the only way I could escape my father. I *needed* Jim to be the promise of a happy life. And that need—that desperation—stopped me seeing any of the warning signs until it was far too late. Maybe, instead of being angry at myself that I walked straight into the same life as my mother, it's time I accepted that I was doing the best I could. There *was* no better option than Jim. And if fewer men were like him and my father, fewer women like Mum and me and the rest of the club would be faced with a set of choices that all turn out to be mistakes.

Maybe, if there's no way to win, there's no blame in losing.

Amy sniffs, wiping her nose on the back of her hand. "Well, guess I'm lucky to have an option that gets me out of your hair while you're working everything out."

My breath catches. "You can always, *always* come home if you need to," I say so seriously she looks up in surprise. "Always," I tell her again.

I've made so many stupid choices, but my life hasn't been a waste. Somehow, despite it all, I've raised two children who expect more than I did, not just for themselves but for me. That's not too shabby, as Granny would say.

It's not shabby at all.

42

The Kids Are OK

When Amy turns on the doorstep the next day to hug me tight it feels as if a year has passed, though it's been scarcely twenty-four hours since I found her waiting on the mat.

Time is moving so strangely at the moment. The thought that it's now only ten days until Jim needs to be gone and his disappearance explained is a constant thrum below my heartbeat. I keep telling myself to stay calm, that together the club and I will find a way, but can we? What if I'm just repeating the mistakes I made with Amy and Charlie—thinking that I could protect them with comforting lies when all they really needed was the truth?

"Bye, Dad!" Amy bellows up the stairs.

I reach out to squeeze her arm. "It's not about you, darling. He's just humiliated about the breakup. Doesn't want to deal with anyone until he can repair the dent in his pride."

Flattening her lips, she shrugs. "Guess the cold shoulder is better than the alternative."

I have to blink back tears, but Amy doesn't even notice as

she screeches her suitcase along the drive to a car sitting at the curb.

"Ring Charlie, OK?" Amy calls. "I already told him about the whole . . . silent-treatment thing. It'll be a relief for him to know what it's really about. It'll *all* be such a relief."

There's no chance to reply as she turns to squish her suitcase into the back of the car.

The masked young woman in the driver's seat opens the window and gives me a friendly wave as Amy climbs in beside her. I return the wave with a smile, watching the car until it's out of sight. When I finally look away, I realize Edwina is standing on her front step. She gives me a nod—a regal inclination of the head—as if she approves.

Nodding back, I close the door and make a beeline for the kitchen—I've earned rum-raisin brownies—but I've only just started fetching out the ingredients when my phone pings. Picking it up, I frown in confusion—no new notifications. I reach for Jim's, jolting when I see a new message from Amy, but all it says is Bye, Dad. x

When I first found her standing on the doorstep with that massive suitcase, I thought it was the worst thing that could possibly happen, but now I am filled with renewed determination.

With Amy safely on her way, I've another child to think of. I've wanted to ring Charlie since the morning I dispatched Jim, but I could hardly tell him why I was sure there was no possibility of his father interrupting us.

But now, finally, I can call my son.

The phone rings . . . rings . . . rings . . .

I'm just about to hang up when Charlie's voice, sharp with worry, startles me.

"Mum? Everything OK?"

"Hello, darling. Amy's probably told you that your father's holed up in his room, so I thought I'd take the chance to call. It's been too long since I heard your voice."

"If you'd pick up your own phone, you'd get a call every day." He tries to make it sound teasing, but the words come out with too much edge. "I just don't want to risk him answering and the two of us getting in a row when you're locked in the house with him," he hurries on.

"It's not going to be a problem anymore. I've put my foot down about the phone—among other things."

He gives a delighted laugh, the sound warming me all the way through.

God, I love my kids.

I take a breath. "I told your father I'm leaving him after the Lockdown."

For a moment there's silence. "Are you OK? What . . . what did he do?"

"He locked himself in our bedroom and has barely come out since, as Amy's probably told you. She just didn't know why until now. Your father and I agreed not to share the news with anyone till we could separate, but with Amy here and Jim acting so strangely . . . Well, I had to tell her last night. But it means I could finally call and tell you too."

"Are you . . . are you safe there, now he knows you're leaving?"

The air is viscous with guilt. One day, when Jim is gone for good, there are so many things we need to talk about.

"If you're not safe I'll come and get you. It's allowed, you know. The restrictions—"

"I'm fine, my darling. It's . . . it's nothing like that."

Charlie stays speakingly silent.

"This time I really *am* going to be OK," I say, putting all the sureness of the truth into the words. "We've come to an arrangement, but I promise to call you if it stops working."

I can hear Charlie's relief in the way he starts absentmindedly clicking his fingers. It's been his happy fidget since he was a child, and it makes me smile just listening to it. But then I think about the real reason we can finally talk and my mind goes to all the news stories I've read about people disappearing, never to be seen again. The families always talk about the not-knowing—how it burrows under the skin, needling at unexpected moments, refusing to be dug out or soothed. Whenever I imagined being in their shoes, my mind stuck on how, at night, the missing must appear in every dream, while daytime must see them superimposed on random faces in shops, or strangers walking away on busy train platforms—endlessly present in their absence. Not an elephant in the room but a gaping hole that everyone must navigate around: a space that sucks in everything that gets too close. That is what I'm condemning my children to. What I'm condemning myself to watching them go through.

Only not everyone who goes missing is equally missed. A missing child must be like a constant silent roar, a vibrating silence, but what of a parent to a grown child? An indifferent parent at that—one who might not have been violent, but who had few kind words. One who offered no sanctuary. Perhaps the worst thing for Amy and Charlie will be thinking that Jim might turn up again one day. I don't know if that will be a source of hope or dread.

"I'm sorry I didn't leave sooner," I say, because if I don't have the courage for this, I'll never have the courage for the rest. "I'm sorry, Charlie."

"I wasn't wrong, was I?" he asks, voice tight. "That it was worse than just him being controlling."

"No, you weren't wrong," I whisper. "But that's over now. And I know that doesn't make up for all the lies—"

"I know why you did it," he says softly. "You didn't want us to be afraid of him or hate him."

"I didn't know what he'd do if I left." The words burn like acid, but it's time for the truth. And it's to Charlie I owe the real heart of it.

While Amy never knew what to believe, Charlie did. Instead of facing up to that, I lied and manipulated and tricked him. I left him to simmer in his anger because he would never take it out on me, and he didn't dare front up to his father for fear the punishment would fall on my shoulders. So he was stuck. As trapped as I was. But instead of helping him, I did everything I could to make him think it was all in his head until all he could do was leave.

I can't take any of it back. But I can help Charlie understand why I did that to him.

"I knew I could keep you safe if we stayed. And I know it wasn't good enough. It wasn't the childhood I wanted for you, but I didn't know what would happen if we left. I just didn't know, so I . . . I chose the option that I was sure would keep you and Amy safe."

For a while we just listen to each other breathe.

"And now?" Charlie asks, voice quavering. "Amy and I, we're not going to be OK if you're not. I can come and get you, Mum. I can—"

"You're not children anymore, so now he can't control me. Turns out that he's just a pathetic little man and all the power he had over me vanished with his leverage."

"Do you promise?" Charlie asks, so softly I barely hear him. "Because you can't lie, Mum. Not about this."

"I promise, my love. I *promise*."

"OK," he whispers, voice rough with tears. "OK." He takes a shuddering breath. "I know it's going to be scary and sad, but it'll be OK. Amy and I are fine. And you're going to be so much happier."

"I already am," I tell him.

When we say goodbye, I sit in a daze of emotional exhaustion, jumping back to awareness only when a text pings in. I frown when Charlie's name flashes up, then smile to see a new song.

I click on the link and Sara Bareilles' "Brave" fills the kitchen, but instead of making me smile, it floods my eyes with tears. My son thinks I'm brave, but only because I lied to him. I've stolen his admiration, instead of earning it.

43

Memory

'm sprawled on the floor in the living room with seemingly every photo in the house spread out around me, some loose, some in frames.

Unsurprisingly, my anything-but-happy family took few pictures when I was growing up, but I linger over one of me and Mum at the beach. Closing my eyes, I wish myself there again, the waves washing around me, the fresh sea wind rushing through my hair. What I wouldn't give to be back there now. I'd tell Mum that even if it was a struggle on our own we could manage and it'd be worth it.

I press the photo to my chest, gritting my teeth against the grief. My mother was kind and gentle, but she gave me a childhood witnessing the violence she endured—when I wasn't taking my own share of pain. A little bit of me hates her for that, but mostly I hate myself.

How could I let myself end up with almost the same life as hers?

I still remember the way my dad scoffed when Mum shyly

asked whether he thought she should apply to become a teaching assistant at my school.

"Something to do with myself, now Sally's older. Maybe I could even learn a few things. See if . . . see if there's something more I could go on to," she said, strangling a tea towel between her hands.

"You?" sneered my father. "What would you teach anyone? You can't even teach our daughter to boil a bloody egg right."

At which point, he scooped up the mess of his half-eaten breakfast and threw it in her face while I cowered against the counter and hoped he wouldn't slap me on the way out. My father didn't care if the bruises were visible so long as no one saw him inflict them; all that mattered to him was that it stayed "in the family," as if then it didn't count.

Jim wasn't like that; after that first time, at the party for his workmates, he never hurt me when someone might see, and he made sure all the evidence could be easily hidden under long sleeves or a buttoned-up collar.

And yet history repeated itself time and again. Like the day when Charlie suggested I should sign up as a school governor.

"Dr. Blake said she wanted more women, and you'd be great, Mum." He beamed up at me, so proud and hopeful, not realizing how foolish he'd been to say it in front of his father.

"You could come and do reading hour," Amy added, catching her brother's enthusiasm.

"You're taking us to school anyway. Would it matter to stay for an hour or so?" Charlie wheedled.

"Just an hour or so?" Amy echoed, as Charlie offered her a rare, approving high five.

What could I do but shrug? "I suppose I could try," I said

tentatively, glancing at Jim. "That'd be OK, wouldn't it? To set a good example for the kids?"

"Yes!" Charlie punched the air.

"I suppose you'll be an effective cautionary tale, if nothing else," said my kind and loving husband, chucking me under the chin.

"What's that?" Amy asked brightly.

"I'll tell you another time," I said. "Come on, or you'll be late for registration, then we'll all get a right ticking-off!"

I still remember how eagerly Charlie pulled me over to Dr. Blake when we arrived at the school, how proudly he told her I was interested, and how his face fell with disappointment and confusion and shame when I demurred—said I'd think about it, but . . .

"Don't you want to have a job?" Charlie asked as I tucked him into bed that night.

"I'm not sure I'd be any good at that sort of thing." I pressed a kiss to his head.

"Dad says you're not good at stuff 'cos sometimes you make mistakes," came Charlie's voice as I stood. "But he makes mistakes too. He knocked over that thing in the shop the other day, not you."

My hand flew to the place on my side where Jim had driven his rage and embarrassment into my flesh once we were "safely" back home and the kids were playing upstairs.

"Even if you weren't good to begin with, you'd get better. Like my spelling."

"I'll think about it, OK?"

Charlie rolled away from me. "Night, Mum." He clicked off the light.

"Night, darling," I whispered back, voice choked.

There's no photo of that moment, but it might as well be on home video for all I've replayed it in my mind over the years. Why did I let myself believe Jim when he said I couldn't do this, was no good at that, was no good for anything? Why did I let him make it true by never daring to get a job or even doing some volunteering—anything that would have shown me that I could survive without him?

"Other men worry about their wives leaving them," he said conversationally the morning after the first time he full-on punched me. "But what would you do without me?" He shook the paper out with a snap like a blow. "It's a great comfort."

Why *didn't* I leave? Why did I think it was enough to keep my children safe from violence, but not from the misery of always walking on eggshells when their father was home? His hissed venom was worse than shouting, and underlying it that terrible, insidious tension—the certainty of an imminent explosion.

I let them grow up with that. Let them grow up knowing, despite all my lies and evasions, what was quietly happening in another room when I sent them off "to give their father some peace."

At some point my subconscious must have decided to make a timeline of my life with Jim, or maybe it's the wine, but it feels as if I blink and there it is, laid out in glorious Technicolor before me.

It seems so obvious now. How my smile fades photo by photo. In our last family portrait I almost look as if I'm fading into the backdrop. It's not just that I gradually stopped wearing bright colors; it's as if I've drained of pigment, or the light no longer finds me but passes straight through.

The last truly happy photo I can find shows the kids at about eight and ten. We're playing on the beach. The sun is striking into the shot, setting the three of us alight. Jim lurks at a distance, glaring, his whole posture radiating anger.

Why did I stay? Why did I do that to myself? It seems like madness. But maybe fear, if it's constant enough, is a type of madness. If you're always focused on trying to avert disaster, always looking around for how to solve problems before they can happen and still you fail and fail and fail and fail . . . maybe then it's normal to think failure is the only thing you're capable of.

I reach for the portrait again and start unpicking the back of the frame. Carefully, I slide the picture out and set it aside, then I snatch up the one of me and the kids on the beach and, folding over the edge with Jim, slide it into the frame instead. When I turn it over, happiness instead of misery smiles out at me. It makes my chest clench with grief, but it's a good sort of pain. Clean. Or maybe not clean yet, but cleansing, as if something is washing away with the tears.

It feels like letting go.

Frame by frame, I excise Jim from my life. I can't do anything about the years behind me, but I can refuse to live with him one day longer.

"I thought it would be me, so I can't be sorry it's you instead," I tell Jim's image as I fold him out of yet another family photo. "I didn't deserve that. I didn't deserve any of it."

For a while, I press my hands over my eyes and give in to the tears. Eventually, I smear snot along my arm and carry on. This isn't a job I can leave unfinished: now I've started, I have to see it through. I'm going to see it all through.

AN HOUR LATER, THERE'S a sad little pile of offcuts on the coffee table, but every picture on the walls and shelves makes me smile. Putting all the slivers of Jim in the recycling seems like asking for trouble, so I fetch the metal bin from the box room, dump them in, then collect a box of matches and head into the garden to light it all on fire.

I step back from the resulting rush of colored flames but hover close enough to watch the images curl then fade to black. When the pictures have burned themselves out, I take the bin back inside and run water over the ashes. Picking out the few blackened but unburned fragments, I chuck them away, then wash the sticky soot down the drain.

And then it's done, leaving me empty but triumphant, because while I worked on the pictures, my brain has been busy. Amy's visit hasn't only fired me with determination. It's given me an idea—one that might just work.

I lift my chin and straighten my spine. I'm not brave yet, but I'm learning. Because I'm done with waiting for life to get better. Now's the time to make it so.

44

One Problem Down,
a Thousand More to Go

Although it's Friday and Jim needs to be gone in nine days' time, I am no longer afraid of failure. Or only a little, because I finally know what to do.

Well, most of what to do. There are still a few snags.

Determined to sort at least one, I pop next door and settle on Nawar's sofa with Lionel's iPad. It takes less than fifteen minutes to research why bodies are usually buried six feet deep and whether that's strictly necessary. Turns out there isn't a legal minimum depth for official graves, though the recommendation is to leave one meter of dirt between the top of the coffin and the surface of the ground. Most graves are only deeper so multiple family members can be buried in the same plot with the coffins stacked on top of each other. As I read further, I discover that it's quite common for "green burials" (i.e. ones involving no vault or coffin) in the USA to be just two feet down. Obviously we need extra depth for the bodies themselves, but it means that we can probably get away with a hole three and a half feet deep if that's all we can manage in the time, though four would be better.

Next I look into how accurately the police can track phone signals—not accurately enough to worry about the club's carelessness during those first few days.

Soon I'm back home, proudly pottering around the garden, which is hardly an earthly paradise but at least is no longer an overgrown wasteland. I prune and weed and water as I rehearse how to explain everything to the others.

"**HOW DID TRIMMING THAT** buddleia go?" Edwina calls as I turn onto the street when it's finally time to head to the duck pond.

She's being nice, I remind myself. *It's not her fault you're trying to rush off to a secret meeting with your little murder club.*

I give her a smile and a rather overdone thumbs-up.

Edwina's face is dour as she eyes my happy thumbs. "I don't remember you being this jaunty pre-Lockdown."

"I'm just so happy to be out and about. I never realized how hard it was to be stuck in the house before."

"Really?" she says. "That's not the impression I was under. You should give that serious consideration once this whole Covid situation is over." She casts a narrow-eyed look at the house. "Jim still not venturing out in daylight hours?"

"Doesn't want to risk running into anyone who's not masking properly."

"Well, I can see you're eager to be away so don't stop here, keeping me from my pruning. Off you go."

I give her a salute, then stride away.

When I turn the corner to the park and spot the magenta flash of Leila's hijab it's all I can do not to break into a run, especially when I see that Leila is practically vibrating with excitement.

"What's happened?" I ask as I flop down on the grass.

"You know how I said it'd take something cataclysmic for our family to believe Dad's gone off with your husbands? Well, Uncle Ayaan died!"

Ruth claps a hand over her mouth. "Covid?" she gasps. "Are the rest of them sick too?"

"No! It's even better."

Samira grimaces but presses her lips together to hold back her rebuke.

"He electrocuted himself!" Leila continues with breathless delight. "He got fed up with waiting for someone to fix the electrics at my grandfather's house, so he decided he could do it himself."

Janey snorts. "What a dafty moron," she coos at Ava. "Yes, darling. An evil dafty moron."

"And that's not all," Leila adds, though in a quieter tone. "Without the electricity, the machines went off, so my grand-father's gone too."

Samira squeezes her eyes shut, mouthing something silently—either a prayer for the dead or something very rude.

Ruth's face creases with sympathy. "We are *so* sorry for your loss." She clutches at her necklace, finger caressing the locket.

"What loss?" Leila asks, as Samira says, "Thank you."

Samira heaves a sigh. "Leaving the rest aside, this does change things. With his father and brother dead—and the rest of the family still trapped in Pakistan—people *might* believe my husband would do something as out of character as going off with strangers from outside the community."

"Yeah," says Leila eagerly. "Turns out my dad had a heart of stone where I was concerned, but he loved his psycho siblings. I mean, he wasn't always like that. When I was little . . ." She cuts herself off, shaking her head.

Samira's eyes find mine, full of pain and guilt—for what she did to Yafir, for Leila finding herself part of it, for the fact that none of us can afford to dwell on what we've lost. We have to focus on our freedom or we'll lose it all over again. For now, it has to be about the plan. And to do that we can't think of Yafir and Jim and Keith and Lionel as people—people who sometimes laughed and loved and showed kindness and goodness. Until we're safe, they'll have to stay monsters in our minds.

"How long before Jim's due for his stint in the office?" Ruth asks anxiously. "It must be getting close now."

"Ten days. So it's just as well we've all got our thinking caps on, isn't it?"

The others stare at me morosely.

"OK then, it's just as well *I've* had my thinking cap on."

Janey perks up. "What do you think, darling?" she asks Ava, wiggling the baby's feet. "Do you think Auntie Sally's got a brilliant plan?"

"I'm going to take that as a rousing endorsement," I tell my best friend as she blows raspberries on her daughter's belly. "I've come up with so many complex ideas, but every time it just gets nuts because the more complicated a plan is, the more ways there are for us to get caught, or leave evidence, or for it all to go wrong. So we need a plan that's as simple as possible. Like our little community gardening project—"

"Could you cut to the brain wave?" Janey interrupts.

"Actually, it was Amy's."

Janey gives me a flat stare.

"Just listen, OK? Amy's moved in with a friend who's also going through a Lockdown breakup: the girls have got one flat and their boyfriends have the other."

"We're going to say our husbands have moved in together?" Ruth asks, bewildered.

"How does that explain them disappearing?" Leila shakes her head. "I don't get it."

"We've been using our husbands' phones and their Whats-App group to communicate, so that's the foundation we need to build on. Samira-as-Yafir and Ruth-as-Lionel can commiserate about their brothers and the other losses in the family— how hard it is not to be able to travel to attend the funerals, how it's all getting a bit too much . . . Yafir can whinge about money, then Lionel can jump in about how hard it is to get furlough support when you're self-employed. Then Janey-as-Keith can agree, but also whine about being overwhelmed by Lockdown with an infant. We really need to push the narrative that an hour's walk isn't enough and Keith's looking for a chance to clear his head—he needs to start talking about how they should all go off on a trip together. Then I can message from Jim about our marriage breaking up and how he's been locking himself in his bedroom but is ready to blow his top—"

"Isn't that dangerous?" Samira cuts in. "To admit that you're having marriage problems?"

"I've already told Charlie and Amy that Jim and I are separating after Lockdown, so we might as well use it."

"Go back to you telling the kids. That must've been quite the conversation," Janey says, wide-eyed. "How'd they take it?"

I shake my head. "This isn't the time to get into it. They're happy for me, but *we* need to focus on the plan. We have to milk all the excuses that make it plausible for our husbands to have gone off together on some random mid-pandemic outing ending in disaster."

"But where's the proof they've actually gone on this trip?" Leila asks.

Samira gives me an apologetic grimace. "If we turn their phones off here, and pretend they've gone off grid, that's going to look suspicious."

"That's part of the solution," I tell her eagerly. "Stage one is that we get a vehicle, dress up as our husbands—with masks, that'll be a lot more convincing, since people won't be able to see much of our faces. Then we drive off with their phones on but our own left behind at home."

"And then what?" Samira asks, frowning. "I'm sorry to always be the one poking holes in your ideas and offering none of my own, but we can't pull off pretending to be men if we have to interact with people to get food or petrol or use the toilet."

"We need to avoid going far enough to need petrol—but that's fine. My plan involves the coast and, depending on which bit we pick, that's three hours tops. The difficulty is that we're going to need a different car to get back—public transport or a taxi is too risky. Maybe whoever isn't pretending to be one of the men can drive down separately and pick us up near where we're going to ditch the first car."

Janey gives me an unimpressed—and frankly unencouraging—stare. "So, leaving aside the dozen massive problems with this stunning plan, where are we ditching this car that people are going to believe the men have just vanished into thin air from?"

"And we still have the phone issue," Samira puts in. "If we leave their phones in the car, it begs the question why they would do that—certainly why all four of them would."

"Water," I say. "It's the only thing that makes sense. I realized when Maryam fell in the pond and Leila said she should have left her phone on the bank. If it's reasonable for our husbands to think they might get wet, they'd all leave their phones behind, so we need to focus the plan around water. And it has to be the coast because it's more believable that they could all vanish, and no bodies wash up, than with a river or lake. We just need to make everyone think they've gone into the water."

"For a swim?" Janey says dubiously. "It's not exactly warm yet."

"Swimming, paddling, whatever. The point is that we ditch our outer clothes—their clothes—on the sand . . . and then I'm a bit stuck, because we need to go far enough along the beach that anyone who saw us get in the water won't see us come out again. We'll pack some of our own clothes into a waterproof bag and stash it in advance so we can get re-dressed in this second place, then we get in the second car and come home and bury the bodies in the community garden without raising any suspicions because everyone thinks our husbands disappeared—and presumably died—a hundred miles away at the beach."

There's a pause, then, "That's it?" says Leila. "Not to be unhelpful, but that's more plot-hole than plot."

"I mean, there *is* more. I've got this whole plan about us all bringing hair from our husbands' combs or pillows to plant in the car to show they were there," I add encouragingly.

Samira makes another apologetic face. "I think forensic tests can tell how recently hair has detached from a scalp, not to mention that if we leave their clothes on the beach there will definitely be evidence that we were wearing them, no matter how careful we are, given that the key principle of forensics is 'Every contact leaves a trace.'"

"If there's enough evidence that our story hangs together, will the police really do loads of expensive tests?" I ask, trying (and failing) to keep the desperation at bay. "Surely the tricky bit is the car. We can wear masks and gloves, and of course we'll be in their clothing. Then all we have to do is leave extra gloves and hand gel in the car to explain why the men haven't left fingerprints and other evidence behind."

This is the point at which the others' expressions should be slowly transforming into rapturous admiration. Unfortunately, they don't seem ready to get on board.

Janey crosses her arms. "Even if people buy the disappearance, where is the magic place we can pull this off in a way that won't just incriminate us? Do you know how crowded beaches are at the moment?"

"Look, I never said I had all the details mapped out," I snap, then force myself to steady my temper. "We're working it out step by step. And, yes, there are still quite a few steps left, but we'll get there."

I give Janey an encouraging smile, but her eyes remain fixed on the ground between us, her mouth set into a hard line, and I realize suddenly that she's not angry. She's afraid.

"I'm not trying to criticize. You've come up with more of the plan than the rest of us combined, and I know in time we'll figure out the rest too, but . . ."

She doesn't need to complete the sentence. We all know the rest of the question is, "Can we do it in the next nine days?"

45

Digging for Victory

With no luck filling the holes in our plan, we turn our attention to digging some new ones, getting to work on our garden-cum-burial-plot (double meaning of "plot" fully intended) with grim determination the next day.

No one mentions that it's Saturday and there are now only eight days before Jim is due in the office.

Thankfully, the garden-to-be is big enough for four of us to work socially distanced while the fifth watches Maryam and Ava, so the first hurdle—avoiding censure from Edwina for breaking Covid regs—is swiftly passed.

Ruth and Edwina cordon off the area around the cherry tree so we can't accidentally encroach, then we start clearing the ground. It is much harder work than any of us anticipated. Clearly Edwina is both unsurprised and amused about the degree to which we've underestimated the task ahead of us. Still, there is a look of grudging respect on her face as she realizes that we're determined to rise to the challenge. Once she's confident her cherry tree will remain undisturbed, she takes herself off home with a promise to check in later.

Our next step is to set up a "community garden" WhatsApp

group—now we're all working together, it's important to lay an evidence trail about how we decided that, instead of being jealous about our husbands having a new pandemic friendship group to go on walks with, we'd steal their idea and create our own gardening-focused one.

Digital trail sorted, Ruth and I cut the remaining plants down to the ground while Leila and Samira start hacking away at the roots. Janey takes a turn babysitting, spinning stories out of the air to keep Ava and Maryam mesmerized and the rest of us distracted from the aches and pains of our labor.

"And the girl smiled too as she took the witch's hand, for she knew that, against the odds, she would live happily ever after. And so it is said that, even now, on clear nights when the moon is full, their ghosts appear on the cliffs, beckoning the unwary to their deaths," Janey whispers, making us all strain to hear.

"And then what?" Maryam asks, wide-eyed.

Janey shrugs. "That's it—this isn't a dramatic pause or anything."

"Best ghost-witch story ever!" Maryam says. "But it definitely needs a sequel."

"Haven't I heard this one before?" I ask. "Not that I'm criticizing or anything, but it feels familiar."

Janey laughs. "It should. I've been telling it since we were ten. The ghost-witch part is all me, but the bit about a path through the caves is real, though it's only accessible at certain times of day. My mum told me about it one summer when we were visiting my grandmother's house. She promised to take us, as it's just at the bottom of the cliffs by where she lives, but the thought freaked me out so badly I made up the story so my cousin would throw a fit and I'd be able to get out of it without admitting I was a total scaredy-cat." She sighs. "I thought about going the last time I was down there—conquering old fears and all that— but when I looked through the window at the cliff path I swear there was a woman standing at the edge like in my story and I was just . . . nope."

She stands with a sigh, hefting a spade as Leila takes her place with the kids.

Although we get on faster without the story taking all our attention, it's much less fun just digging with nothing to think about except how tired and sweaty we all are.

"We should sing the baby a song!" Maryam says as Ava babbles away from the pram.

Soon Leila has a YouTube video playing on her phone with a tutorial for easy songs that can be sung in rounds. We laugh, dig, and pant our way through a few hopeless attempts, but soon we're rather chuffed to be belting out a credible effort.

When we finish the latest iteration, we're surprised by the sound of clapping.

Edwina is back. I brace for a telling-off, but *is that a smile on her face?*

"Were we disturbing you?" I ask nervously.

"I was worried you would when I first heard the music, but not at all. This is lovely."

"O-h," I say. "Wonderful." I look around at the others.

Janey mouths "lovely" at me.

Ruth, of course, recovers fastest. Possibly she doesn't have to recover at all because her heart is pure and kind, so she promptly says the obvious thing: "Do you have any suggestions for what we can learn next? I know a few call-and-response songs from my childhood, but they're all Christian." She casts Samira a quick smile.

"Oh, I never let that bother me," says Edwina briskly. "I've never swung from a chandelier any more than I've helped build Jerusalem. Never stopped me engaging with music I enjoy." She moves forward, peering at our excavations as we gawp at her anew. "That's coming along nicely. I came to say that if you need somewhere to put the rubbish, I can take a bit for my compost heap, seeing as the dump is still closed."

"That would be so kind. Thank you," says Ruth.

Edwina inclines her head in that regal little gesture I'm starting to suspect is her equivalent of a hug, then leaves us to it.

"Well, the sun really is shining on our endeavors," I say. "Time to motor, ladies. Daylight is burning, and this ground isn't going to clear itself."

So we slog away and try not to lose heart when we survey all we've accomplished and find it's not a lot: certainly nowhere near enough. Thank goodness we don't have to keep to an hour outside our homes anymore or we'd be scuppered.

"It's only day one," I remind everyone. "No despairing allowed." Still, we bid each other a decidedly solemn goodbye.

Just over a week. One. Week. One. Week, says my brain in time with my feet as I march back home. Though there were pallid shards of sun earlier in the day, now the sky is a blank canvas—like my brain. There are only nine days until Jim's turn on the rota, and I've still got only half a plan for explaining where he's gone. For a moment I consider emailing Jim's boss and saying he's caught Covid, then think better of it. The more complicated we make things, the more that can go wrong and the harder it will be to keep our stories straight. Not to mention that Samira may not have a hard deadline like mine, but Yafir's family won't buy her excuses forever. One way or another, we all need this to be over.

A thin mizzle descends, turning the world dim and fuzzy about the edges.

I *will* figure it out, I tell myself firmly. I haven't come this far to fail the others, the kids, myself when I have more than ever to lose. But what if courage and hope aren't enough? What if I'm not enough?

THE THOUGHT TAKES ME through the house and then straight back out and round to Nawar's, where I fill a virtual shopping basket with wigs to match each of our husbands, plus a bunch of dressing-up stuff so it looks like preparations for a fancy-dress party. I add a men's waterproof watch then check the order over carefully—paying special attention to the delivery dates—and pay with the prepaid card Janey arranged at Tesco and loaded up with cash so there's no paper trail leading back to any of us. Purchase complete, I spend an hour googling beaches where there have been fatal accidents but find nothing that suits our purposes. I try quarries and lakes with exactly the same result.

"I just need a narrower search," I tell the mustachioed catfish eyeing me disparagingly from the corner of the tank.

It whisks around in a fluster of gravel and sand, burrowing into the reeds.

"Oh, very encouraging." I click the power button and the tablet goes dark, but instead of getting up I sit for a while in the silence of Nawar's house. The curtains are drawn, so it feels as if night has fallen. The light in the fish tank makes rippling patterns on the walls, as if I'm underwater.

The first time I crept in through the back for stage one of my illicit googling, it felt like a game of espionage: exciting and frightening in equal measure. Now it just feels small and hopeless.

In books, murderers always have these grand plans. All I've got is a garden and some wigs.

Forcing myself back to my feet, I check everything is in order, then lock up. The glare of the sun as I step out into the garden makes me flinch, shielding my eyes. Around me the world is Technicolor—so bright it's painful. A swallow darts into a neighbor's eaves, and a foxglove nods by the fence.

Taking a deep breath of spring air, I lower my shoulders and stand up tall.

I've got much more than a garden and some wigs. I've got Ruth, Janey, Samira, and Leila. Together, we are everything we need.

We have to be.

46

Hopeful Hearts

he next day the club starts to learn "You'll Never Walk Alone" as we dig, but it's too depressing so we quickly switch to "Raindrops Keep Fallin' on My Head" then "What a Wonderful World" and Soul II Soul's "Joy," on Ruth's suggestion. Despite the cheery music, tension buzzes in the air.

"We could always form a prison choir if it all goes to pot," Janey says encouragingly when we pause for a break.

"Sh!" Ruth hisses, nodding her head in Maryam's direction.

Engrossed in a game on her mother's phone, she's sitting on the edge of the pavement in the shade of Edwina's cherry tree, headphones snugly tucked over her ears.

"I wouldn't worry," Leila says wryly. "The world could end and she wouldn't notice when she's on that game." She groans, arching her back. "I'm taking five."

As promised, Maryam doesn't even look up as her sister settles beside her and, reaching into the bag at Maryam's feet, takes out a water bottle and a sheaf of handwritten notes.

"Homework?" Janey grimaces. "That seems a bit intense on top of . . ." She gestures at our work site.

"Personal statement for my university application—if I ever figure out what's worth putting down for my choices. I know it's super-early, but our teachers wanted us to have a go now so we've time to do some online research even if the Lockdown doesn't ease in time for visiting campuses or doing open days."

Janey frowns. "What do you mean, '*worth* putting down'? You know you can get into anywhere you want, right?"

Leila shrugs one shoulder, ducking her head. "I know most places will look at me, but it's probably a waste having somewhere like Oxford as one of my choices."

"Only if you don't want to go there." Janey grabs the notes from Leila's hands, settling down two meters along the wall as she fishes a pen out of her handbag. "I can help polish the personal statement. As for the interview and special tests and stuff, two of my colleagues are Oxbridge graduates. I can ask them to talk you through the tricks—give you some insider tips."

Leila peers at her shyly. "You don't think I'm being stupid even thinking about it? I mean, before Dad . . ." She breaks off, eyes flying to Maryam, but her sister doesn't even blink. "I probably wasn't going to be able to go anywhere that involved living away—and of course I don't want to be far, what with . . . family responsibilities and everything, but . . . There's got to be something good to come out of all this, right?"

"Exactly," says Janey, but so gently it makes Leila's eyes tear.

"I just . . . Everything feels so . . . so precarious now. I always figured I'd be able to navigate a way through my dad's rules to have the type of independent life I wanted. I mean, it's not like his strictness had never affected me before, but it was stuff like not going to parties and not being able to wear what I wanted. I never thought . . . I mean, it was always there in the back of my mind—would he send me to Pakistan so the family could 'set me on the right path' if I stepped too far out of line? I just . . . I didn't think he'd ever *do* it. You don't, do you? You just don't believe your dad—and half your family—would even consider marrying you off to anyone who'll have you, with no thought to what you want or how you'll be treated or . . ."

Beside her, Maryam stirs suddenly at her raised voice, pulling her headphones down. "Was Dad really going to do that?"

Leila and Samira exchange a worried look.

"Is that why you won't even talk to him through the garage door?" Maryam asks, narrowing her eyes. "And why we're visiting with new friends every day instead of going on walks at the same time as other people in the family?"

"They wouldn't approve of our new friendships, so this has to be a secret, Maryam," Samira says, crouching to cup her daughter's face. "You can't tell anyone at all. Not friends from school. Not even your little cousins."

"We don't want it getting back to Dad," Leila adds warningly. "He'll worry we might start to think we're more than well-trained livestock."

Maryam stamps her foot. "I'm not a livestock! And I like having new friends. It was lonely before, now I can't go to school anymore." She shakes her head mulishly. "I don't want Daddy to come back inside. I hope he has to isolate in the garage forever."

"Let's just focus on keeping our little secret, all right?"

Leila snorted. "Nothing's ever secret when there are always people watching. Always gossiping."

"Why do they *do* that?" Maryam asks. "Why does everyone tell on each other? We're meant to be a family. We're meant to love each other."

"Part of loving someone is helping them be a good person, so if your aunt or your father thinks you're doing something wrong, they have to tell so that the family can guide you properly." Samira's voice is calm and gentle, but there's tightness in her face.

"That's what it's *meant* to be, but it's not what happens." Leila holds her mother's gaze, her expression bleak. "In our family, people tell because they don't want the bad things to happen to them."

Maryam heaves a sigh, fiddling with the buckle on her shoe. "I don't want Dad to sell me to a stranger if I do the wrong thing." Her eyes are glossy with tears when she looks up at her sister. "If I'm not clever enough for university, can I come and live with you instead when we're grown up?"

Samira wraps Maryam in her arms. "No one is selling my daughters to anyone. I am going to make sure you have every opportunity to build a wonderful, happy life with lots of lovely friends and family who only want the best for you."

"But what happens when Dad—"

"You're too little to marry anyone, so that's not even a question." Samira presses a kiss to her hair. "For now, you're going to worry a little more about your homework and I'm going to get back to work on the garden." She pauses to press Leila's shoulder, then busies herself digging.

Passing Maryam a drink, a snack, and her workbook, Leila settles her own notes in her lap again. "With the whole world in crisis, I guess it's not so ridiculous to at least try applying for the places I really want to go."

"We'll whip your application into shape faster than Edwina can spot a rule infraction." Janey's voice is overly cheerful, but Leila smiles all the same.

Samira pauses to flash her a look of strained gratitude. "That would be so kind."

"Did you never think of going to uni?" I ask, as we set to once more. "You're so clever I can't imagine your teachers didn't suggest it."

"I was going to study law before my brother died."

From the corner of my eye, I see Leila look up, surprise written across her face.

"There is this amazing pair of sisters called Hina Jilani and Asma Jahangir who co-founded Pakistan's Human Rights Commission, *and* the first all-female legal aid practice, *and* the Women's Action Forum, which campaigns against discriminatory legislation, *and* they were both on the Supreme Court, and had roles with the UN . . ." Samira's eyes are distant, but her face is alight. "They did so much. Changed so much for the better. When I was a teenager, I said to myself that if I could have even a tenth of their legacy, that would be a life well lived. And it was all because they knew the law, so I—"

She starts, coming back to herself. A flush paints itself across her cheeks as she finds us all staring at her. "I will give you girls the whole story over dinner," she tells Leila and Maryam, "and perhaps one of you will . . ." She shakes her head, digging her spade back into the ground.

"Have you considered a distance learning course?" I ask gently.

When she doesn't answer, just stabs her spade down again, wrenching viciously at a sinewy root, I think I've over-stepped.

"I haven't let myself." Her voice is so quiet I know it's for my ears only.

For a moment our eyes meet. The weight of lost dreams hangs in the air. And then something shifts, as if our shared pain has arced between us like electricity. I see surprise on her face, feel it mirrored on my own.

What if, say Samira's eyes, and mine echo it back at her. *What if we take everything we've learned about strength and courage and apply it to those dusty old hopes? What then?*

As we fall into a silent rhythm of digging and hacking, I can almost hear Samira's thoughts. Can almost believe she hears mine.

When I look round a while later, I find her staring at Leila and Janey with such mingled joy and longing on her face it makes my eyes prick. I turn away again before I start crying at how we've let ourselves be diminished by the men in our lives.

I look at my oldest, dearest friend and see so many things I love missing, and so many sad, angry, hurt things in their place. The Janey Samira knows is often waspish where she always used to be wry, snappish where she used to turn the most mundane and frustrating things into fun. Is it only because of what Keith did to her, or is at least part of it the physical and emotional aftermath of adjusting to motherhood? I adored Charlie and Amy from the start, but the sleeplessness, the endless demand on top of the physical pain—the desperate need to rest to recover from the damage of giving birth and the changes of being post-natal—was an endurance ordeal like nothing else. How much of it will heal with time and freedom from violence, and how much of this new Janey is permanent?

And yet there's hope too. Violence changed us for the worse, but love and freedom can change us back. And maybe we shouldn't want that anyway. Who we're becoming now may be the best yet, and we'll get to do it together.

47

Missing Pieces

U nfortunately, the day goes downhill from there. The four holes in the four corners of the garden seem pitifully small. How long will it take before we can join them into one, let alone start the really difficult stage—digging the whole thing down "enough to get out the worst of the roots," which is what we're using as code to cover our ongoing arguments about how deep is sufficient to accommodate four bodies.

By the time we head home under a dirty gray sky, we're ratty with tiredness and frustration. All the solidarity from earlier seems to have melted away. When Charlie's song of the day pings into my phone—"You and Me Against the World"—it feels all too apt.

Slumping over the kitchen table, I pillow my head on my arms and call Janey, intending to pick her brains about job hunting so at least I can end the day having made progress on something.

"Hey, Courage. Am I interrupting?" I ask, trying to keep my voice light.

"Nope. Absolutely nothing going on here apart from feeding

Ava, brooding, cleaning up after feeding Ava, then fretting until
the feeding starts again. I was in the brooding part of the cycle
so, you know, busy-busy. How about you, Courage? Do I sense
a break in the relentless optimism?"

"Charlie knew about Jim." I didn't mean for it to come out
like that—so simply—but hearing the words draws the rest from
me, like a splinter teasing out of my skin. "He never saw anything, heard anything, but he worked it out, and I . . . I lied to
him. Tried to make him think it was in his head."

"I know," Janey says softly.

"He told you that?" I press a hand over my face, though
there's no hiding from the shame. "When did you talk about it?"

"A while ago," Janey says quietly. "I'd called for his birthday and we were chattering, then he just came out with it and
I couldn't say *nothing*. So I told him the truth—that I didn't
know what was going on in your marriage but that Jim seemed
pretty controlling and it didn't seem healthy . . ." She sighs.
"He needed to talk to someone, and I'm not going to apologize
for doing my best to be there for him, but I never said anything
about our fight, and—"

"I'm glad you told him the truth. At least one of us did," I
whisper, then clear my throat. "The kids say they don't blame
me, but when I think about how I feel about my mother . . ."

"Sally," Janey breathes. "Your kids know how loved they
are. They've never, ever doubted that. You didn't have that with
your mother. You—"

"There's way too much going on for all these feelings." I
shudder, pressing my hands into my eyes. "Talk to me about
something happy. Those song-and-dance routines we used to
make up. Your best summer holiday."

"Sounds like a school essay."

"Janey." I want it to come out teasing. Instead, my voice is pleading.

"'My Summer Holiday' by Janey Halliday aged forty-two and a quarter," singsongs my best friend. "My current summer holiday started in March when plague took over the world, but since things just went downhill from there and now everyone is depressed out of their skulls, I'm actually going to tell you about The Best Summer Holiday EV-er."

She clears her throat dramatically. "The Best Summer Holiday EV-er happened when I was eight years old and my family and I went to stay with The Best Granny in the World in a house by the sea . . ."

I let Janey's voice wash over me, closing my eyes and trying to dream myself into her memories of ice cream on the seafront in the local village and long walks across the cliffs, days split between rock-pooling and building epic sandcastles.

"My mum might tell it differently if she could remember, but because she's literally losing her mind you'll just have to take my word for it." Janey breaks off with a groan. "Urgh. I've still not done anything about her car. When things ease up, will you come down with me and drive *my* car back while I bring hers?"

Yawning, I add it absently to my *When Janey and Ava Move in List*. "I've made a note," I promise. "Now, stop angst-ing about errands for a later date and get back to the carefree days of trying to drown your cousin in the sea."

And then my brain catches up with my mouth. "Janey," I say, voice suddenly tight, "your mum wants you to take her car. She's not allowed to drive anymore because of the dementia, but she keeps forgetting."

"Is there a reason you're playing human echo function? If it's a dementia joke—"

"Your mum's car is our getaway vehicle."

"OK?" Janey says. "I mean, we've got to pick it up first, but sure. I guess that helps with the plan—"

"Your mum's car is *at her house*. Which is a mile or so from a *beach* that has a path through some *caves* to a cove *on the other side of the cliffs*."

"I literally just . . . Oh. OH!"

I laugh. "I love you, but you are such a frigging moron."

"Oh my God. Oh my actual God!"

"How busy is this cave path? It's no good if there are going to be a thousand people telling us not to go in because it's the wrong time of day. Not to mention our disguises are only going to work at a distance."

"Now I really wish I'd gone with Mum when I had the chance. I barely remember what she said about the route."

"We can google it—and I don't even have to go to Nawar's to do it!" Excitement thrums through me as the pieces come together in my head. "If Jim and the others are meant to be going there, then they'd have looked it up themselves, right? So we can too."

"I can pretend to be Keith," Janey cuts in eagerly, "and Whats-App the group about how I was telling Ava the story the other day and it reminded him how much he'd always wanted to go, and he looked it up and it sounds like a proper adventure—"

"Exactly! If we do it just as Yafir is meant to come out of self-isolation, Samira can message as him saying that he's not going to pass up a chance to really get out and away from everything for a day or two."

"Then all we need to do is make it seem like they got their timings wrong with the tide and, hey presto—the perfect explanation for their disappearance," Janey ends triumphantly.

"It has to be a day when the beach won't be busy."

Janey groans. "And this magic day—that needs to happen in give or take the next week—would be . . ."

"One with terrible weather. It won't work for them all to disappear unless they've picked a stupid, dangerous time to go, when it's asking for trouble."

"But if it's actually dangerous, what if it *does* go wrong and *we're* the ones who disappear and drown?" asks my ever-hopeful best friend.

"Then we won't be going to prison, will we? Now, is your mum demented enough that, if you fetch the car to drive the rest of us home at the end, she won't be a reliable witness as to when it happened? You said there aren't a lot of neighbors: would any of them be likely to notice when the car disappears?"

"It's in a garage, so no. And also no to Mum being able to tell one day from the next—she's pretty doolally at this point." The words are flippant, but her tone is taut with loss. "But seriously, Sally. I am not up for death by drowning."

"We're not going to drown."

"You're making a lot of promises. You'd better bloody keep them, or I'm going to come back as a ghost and haunt the shit out of you."

"Can a ghost haunt other ghosts?"

"Try me and see," she says, but she sounds distracted and I can hear computer keys tapping in the background. "OK, I've found a blog post about the caves—it says there's about ten minutes of walking then a tricky bit with a narrow ledge, then a fork, and not to take the path to the right—"

"How recent is the post?"

"Three—no, four years. And, yikes—looks like the person who wrote it makes a habit of breaking into abandoned buildings and old mines and stuff to go exploring. That is categorically *not* the type of person I want to be taking travel advice from."

"But it's exactly the type of adventure we need to pretend our husbands have gone on. See if you can find a second post about the caves. If we compare the two, then look up whether there have been any local news stories about rockfalls or landslides . . . Well, it'll still be a leap of faith, but unless you know any other cave paths that fit our needs it'll just have to do."

"We also have to figure out the timings for the tides—and if they'll be affected by the weather," Janey says darkly. "Get that wrong and we might as well have been digging our own graves these last few days."

48

The Plan Comes Together

After that, things happen so quickly there's a tinge of un-reality to it all. Thankfully, with a week to go, there's time to find a bad-weather day; to our delight, all the forecasts suggest it'll be Friday, which is perfect, both in terms of giving us time to sort the remaining pieces of the plan (including getting far enough with the digging), and in terms of creating a plausible timeline for our husbands' disappearance.

Keith already has a fancy tent that Janey says can sleep three, so I just have to buy a cheap one-person pop-up version for Jim and then we're set. If we leave the tents in the boot of the car our husbands are meant to have traveled in, then when it's found parked by the beach that leads to the caves it will re-inforce the idea that something went wrong early on in the trip. Better yet, if it looks like they were planning to camp, it makes sense that we wouldn't report them missing until after Jim fails to turn up at the office on Monday, and it'll also be harder to pin down exactly when they disappeared.

With renewed energy, I head next door at first light to buy the tent on Lionel's tablet, then realize we need a paper trail that leads back to Jim. Relieved to have spotted the slip in logic before it's too late, I go home and place the order on Jim's credit card instead. Then I sit at the kitchen table and fret over what other mistakes I might be making.

"What am I missing?" I ask Petunia and Rosemary.

They just smile benignly.

THE NEXT STEP IS to plant the story about the camping trip among at least some of our friends and family. Samira and Leila say it's more plausible that Yafir's plans would have been kept hush-hush, but on Wednesday evening Ruth mentions it to her son and Janey to a friend, while I tell Amy and Charlie.

"Guess it's a change from lurking up in the attic," says Amy dismissively.

"He's in the bedroom, Amy."

"Whatever. The point is that you'll be able to focus on you for a few days instead of waiting on him hand and foot."

Charlie just snorts. "I've got the perfect song for you to listen to while he's away."

Which is why the Lockdown Ladies' Burial Club spends the final day's digging session learning The Beautiful South's "A Little Time," though it ends up sounding more like a dirge than a jaunty pop song.

"Well, there's always tomorrow to work on it," Ruth says. Then her face falls when she remembers.

As one, we look at the louring sky.

"Are we sure it's going to be safe?" Ruth whispers.

Janey shakes her head. "Leaving aside the fact I'm still half convinced the caves are haunted, we're about to brave them in a storm. There's an excellent chance that, even if we don't all drown, we'll need to be rescued, then questions will be asked, then we'll all go to prison."

"You'll be singing a new song tomorrow evening," I tell her with all the false confidence I can muster.

"Yeah, with the heavenly choir—unless we all end up in hell," says my ever-optimistic best friend, though the sarcasm is half-hearted at best: a wan attempt to be normal when everything is about to get even crazier. "Just one more sleep and we get to find out which. Yay!"

The clouds are building and darkening, and every so often I feel a tiny drop of the incipient rain on my skin, as if even the weather is announcing its readiness.

Silently, we set back to work. Our gardening project has remained slow going, but bit by bit the hole has been growing bigger and deeper. Some areas of ground are harder to clear than others, but by exploring our various sheds—and getting a helping hand in selecting the correct tools from Edwina—we're now confidently hacking out roots and rocks as if we've been doing it for years. It's sweaty, back-aching, hand-blistering work, but surprisingly satisfying, especially now it's finally big enough for our purposes. It's not quite as deep as we'd hoped, but it'll do, and that's what matters.

"Route checked?" I ask Janey between the thunks of tools hitting the earth.

She stands with a groan, sweeping an escaped curl away with the back of her hand. "I used Google Street View to find a place to drop off our supplies for when we come up the far side of the cliffs so they'll be ready and waiting for us."

"And I've double-checked social media for any reports of police stops to check why people are on the road," Leila cuts in eagerly. "I just wish you'd let me come . . . but I know someone has to look after Ava and Maryam," she singsongs, as we all open our mouths to protest. "I get that it has to be the person who can't swim, so we don't need to go over it again."

I grin ruefully at her. "Trust me. I'd trade puke and poo-ey nappies for slogging through a freezing-cold cave in a storm."

"Not to mention doing it in Lionel's shoes. I've already tried out how to stuff them with socks to make them stay on, but I'm still dreading the blisters," sighs Ruth.

"You're all set with the instructions for looking after Ava, right?" Janey asks Leila anxiously, pressing her hands together as if about to pray. "She's been fine on the bottle, though I know it'll be hard with Maryam to look after too, but—"

"Has she bought the story about you and Janey going to see a lawyer about your uncle's death?" Ruth asks.

Leila shrugs. "She's getting fifteen quid to spend as she wants on Roblox. She doesn't care."

"And she's not going to tell anyone?"

Leila raises an unimpressed eyebrow. "Where would she find the time between deciding which imaginary things to add to her imaginary house?"

Samira sits back on her heels, swiping at her forehead. "The car's got two thirds of a tank of petrol, so we won't have to stop and risk being seen on CCTV filling up, and I've already packed Ruth's bag of supplies, so we're good to go with masks, gloves, and cleaning stuff." She pats her pockets, taking a key fob out of each. "Both of these work, and I even checked the date of the last service, MOT, and vehicle tax: all OK for another two months, so there's nothing we could possibly get stopped for—I hope."

I grin. "Whenever I come up with a plan you can't puncture, I know we're on the right track."

"Still, the chances of it all going smoothly . . ."

"Of course it won't go smoothly. But we'll get through it. And maybe afterward you can think about that law degree."

Samira sighs. "I'll settle for my freedom."

I look away to the far corner of the plot where Ruth is attacking a sapling root as if it has personally wronged her. There's a lot to be said for taking out our grief and rage on the ground where we'll soon be burying the men who caused it.

"We have to try," Samira says, a look of determination stealing across on her face. "Even if we get caught and this is it, then it's joy and friendship we wouldn't have had if we'd called the police at the start, and that makes it a gift. No matter what, I'll always see it that way. Time with my girls. Time with my friends."

"I don't want to let you all down," I whisper. "I'm not clever enough. You should be the planner—"

"I'm the devil's advocate," Samira says. "You have the ideas, and I refine them, and Janey keeps us entertained, and Ruth keeps us good, and Leila . . . Leila and Maryam and Ava, and Ruth's son and your children . . . They are why we have to try."

I pick up my gardening fork again, plunging it down into the ground. For a moment the roots fight me, then give way.

"They're why we have to *succeed*."

49

Here We Go . . .

wake with the light. Curling onto my side, I watch it spill between the curtains, tinged with red at first—shepherds take warning—then bleaching to a murky gray, as if the day has blinked past and it's night once more.

This is it. One way or another, by the end of the day the riskiest bit of the plan will be over.

At half past five, I pull on a shower cap, then a wig—the closest match I could find to Jim's thinning pate. The fact it's a tad shaggy can easily be explained away by a lack of haircuts during Lockdown.

We're going to get caught. We'll all going to prison, says the voice in my head encouragingly.

I blink it away and pull on a double set of plastic gloves, then a set of Jim's clothes with two T-shirts beneath his jumper and coat to bulk myself out.

Heading downstairs, I water Rosemary and Petunia. There's a tarp staked over the dig site at the end of the street so the hole doesn't fill with water when the storm descends. Everything is as ready as I can make it.

The alarm on Jim's phone goes off. Six o'clock. Time to go.

I take a deep breath, then pick up my new waterproof bag, already packed with everything the four of us will need after we safely navigate the caves.

I slip out of the back door, locking it behind me. Samira is parked across the mouth of the alley. We're using Yafir's car because the back windows are tinted so it's all but impossible to see in. Snapping on my mask, I hand-gel my gloves as I march swiftly out of the alley and straight into the back seat, closing the door behind me. We thought about having the pickup point somewhere we could all go to, but decided there's nothing fishy about Yafir picking everyone up from their homes, and it minimizes the time neighbors can spot any of us in our disguises. Tricky enough to fool a stranger from a distance, but it's a much bigger risk with people who know our husbands, so better to keep the window of opportunity to a minimum. With luck no one will even see us, given how early it is.

Samira pulls out the second I'm in. Janey turns from the front to smile at me, lowering her sunglasses below the brim of Keith's baseball cap.

"Everything go OK this morning?" I ask.

"Yup. Samira picked me and Ava up, then she pulled right into her garage so Leila could take Ava inside, then we came straight to you."

"I was worried the timings wouldn't work."

"Well, I hope we haven't used up all our luck on that," says Janey with her usual optimism.

Samira winces, but I just laugh. "Janey's like taking an umbrella everywhere—she sees everything that could go wrong and somehow that seems to confuse the higher powers behind Murphy's Law."

We tense as Samira crawls to a stop at the curb in front of Ruth's, but Ruth is already halfway down her drive. Less than five seconds later we're off again.

"I feel like a spy," Samira whispers, halfway between panic and giggles.

"I love the Le Carré novels, but you know what none of them talks about?" Ruth says mournfully. "Nervous diarrhea."

Samira groans from the front seat. "Don't! I'm trying not to think about it."

Ruth uncaps a water bottle and holds out a pill. "Here, pull in a second and take this. It'll see your stomach right for the day."

Samira dutifully glides to a stop by the park. The only people out and about are at a distance, but still I'm vibrating to get going again as Samira grabs the pill and sloshes it down.

"Here we go." She flicks the indicator and turns the wheel. The engine revs . . . but we don't move.

Samira goes rigid. "It won't go! It's stuck—broken!"

Janey cranes over the central partition to look frantically at the dashboard, then chokes out a laugh more like a gasp. "It's in park."

Samira wrenches the car into drive and a second later we're in motion again.

"It'll be better when we're out of town and on the motorway," Janey whispers to herself.

"No speeding!" I order as Samira accelerates cautiously down the road.

"Are you hot with the wig and gloves?" Samira asks, squirming uncomfortably.

"Sweating like a pig," I promise her.

"But if 'every contact leaves a trace,' won't all this sweat leave DNA?" Ruth asks.

We all freeze.

"How fancy is this car?" I ask, leaning forward to look at the dashboard.

Ruth follows my gaze then reaches between the front seats to hit the air-con button. Cold air blasts out of the vents and we sigh in unison.

"We just need to keep working together."

Janey drops her head into her hands. "Pull over. I'm going to be sick."

"Don't," I tell Samira as she flicks the indicator again. I unclick my seatbelt and lean over, hands on Janey's shoulders. "Deep breaths. In through your nose, out through your mouth."

"God, let me out, Sal. I need to go back for Ava. I need—"

"To calm down. It'll all be over soon."

Janey gives a hysterical laugh. "Yeah. In prison or under the ocean. Great options."

I grit my teeth. "Enough. Come on, Courage. Ava's completely safe with Leila. Now, either we turn around and head to the nearest police station and we all go to prison, or we stick together and focus on the plan."

"Which bit is meant to give me confidence? Today's nightmare or the fact that even if we get through it without a disaster, it's not like it's over. It just means we're free to move on to the dismemberment portion of this jolly adventure. Woo!"

"Actually, I've been thinking maybe we don't all have to do that."

Even Samira turns to look at me before setting her sights back on the road.

"The hole's going to be deep enough to put two bodies in whole," I explain. "The day we do the soil we'll need at least one car for the fertilizer—so why not two, each with a few bags of gravel and compost and one of corpse. We'll get the man-bags in first, then immediately cover them over. If the next layer is just parts, it won't matter that they're not down so deep." I swallow. "It's my plan, so I volunteer Jim for burial-in-parts."

Ruth clears her throat. "As a nurse I'll have the easiest time, so I will be the other."

"We can't ask—" Samira whispers.

"No, but you can accept our offer," Ruth says, reaching across the back seat to squeeze my hand, though we don't look at each other. We don't have to.

We've been in it together from the start. We can weather the worst of the storm if it spares Samira and Janey. Today, they are doing that for us—following us into danger even though their children aren't yet grown. I can't imagine how I would bear it if Amy were still a baby, or Charlie still Maryam's age, and yet here they are. So it's only right that, later, we find the courage for the darkest task of all: the one that will leave the most evidence behind. And the worst memories. It has to happen for us to be free once and for all, so when the time comes we will do what we must.

THE AIR IN THE car is tense and watchful as we drive out of town, ready to duck in case of police cars watching for anyone breaking social-distancing regulations, but we merge on to the motorway without incident.

I'd hoped things would feel more relaxed by this point, but the atmosphere stays silent and tense. When I attempt a rousing chorus of "I Am Woman," it starts off a bit lackluster, but quickly gathers pace and energy until we're all belting out the words at the tops of our lungs, closer to screaming than singing. When we finish, everyone enjoys a nice round of semi-hysterical laughter before the buzzing of Keith's phone provides a welcome distraction.

Janey frowns down at the screen as she scrolls. "Three missed calls and six texts from the in-laws. What on earth—'Why are you on the motorway? Is there something wrong with Ava?'" She turns to me, eyes wide. "How do they know we're not at home?" She stares back down at her phone as a new text pings in. "'Where are you going? Your dad's steaming. I know we're all bored of being cooped up, but just because the weather's bad it doesn't mean the police won't fine you for breaking the rules.' Shit. Shitshitshitshit . . ."

I reach over and pluck the phone out of her hands. "How do they know where we are?"

Janey just shakes her head, then her mouth falls open. "Keith has Find My Friends enabled. They're *tracking* us. Oh my God." She stares round in horror. "I've ruined everything. I'm so—"

"Stop panicking. It's OK."

"How is this OK, Sally?" she shrieks. "Even if I turn the phone off—"

She reaches for it, but I hold it away. "Janey, stop! This is a *good* thing."

"What do you mean?" Ruth asks, voice tight with fear and confusion. "How could it be? They know. We have to turn back."

"Why?" I paint a smile across my face. "They know Keith is in a car heading down toward the coast. They'll watch him make the journey and then the phone stay put in the car park by the beach. It's another digital trail of exactly what we want people to think—right, Samira?"

We all turn to stare at her, watching her tap her left hand absentmindedly against the wheel.

"I can't think of any way it doesn't support our story," she says finally. "I mean, we're not trying to hide where Keith is meant to have gone, or when. And we've all left *our* phones at home, so if Janey's also has Find My Friends it'll show she stayed there."

Janey slumps back into her seat with a groan, hands over her eyes. "I don't feel guilty about Keith," she whispers, "but his parents . . . They'll never know what happened to their son. They'll just have the memory of watching the journey on their phones, then nothing."

Samira's hand creeps off the wheel to squeeze her knee. "The best part of him is your daughter. Let their relationship with Ava be the balm to their grief. We are trying to keep everyone we love safe and spare them what misery we can, but it is too late for a happy ending. And yet when this is done we will have made a garden together. And a new family. And from that more good things will come."

Janey sniffs, wiping her hands across her face, then laughing when a hand-gel bottle appears over her shoulder. "Good thinking," she tells Ruth, obligingly smearing her gloves.

"There's a light!" says Samira in a tiny voice that silences the whole car. "A warning light! On the dashboard."

"Which light is it?" I ask, craning between the seats to look.

Samira grimaces. "I thought it was my imagination, but the steering wheel's been shaking since we got on the motorway."

"Janey, check the glove compartment," I order. "See if the manual's in there."

A moment later it's chucked at my head.

"I know you said the wheel was shaking, but it can't be too bad if you didn't mention it before, right?" Ruth frets to Samira. "We're not going to crash, are we?"

Samira shoots her a comforting smile. "It's a bit tiring, but I've got control."

Next to her, Janey is swearing blue, black, purple, and red murder under her breath.

"It says to seek assistance, but it doesn't say to stop driving immediately." I flick to the back of the manual and check the index. "If we have to stop, I don't think we should turn off the engine, just in case it won't start again."

"Is it dangerous?" Ruth asks.

"The car's not going to blow up, if that's what you mean," says Janey.

"Well, of course it's not," says Ruth sharply. "I'm not stupid."

"Stop it." Samira's voice isn't loud, but we all subside into our seats. "Yes, the warning light is on and the steering wheel is shaking. No, it's not a good sign. But we've come this far. I say we carry on. We're just as stuck if we break down here as if it happens later."

I take a deep breath as the others turn to me for reassurance.

"Let's just hope for the best," is all I can tell them.

50

Are We There Yet?

don't even try to start another round of song, though the lyrics and mournful melody of Nat King Cole's "Smile" go around and around in my head as we sit in tense silence, pretending we're not surreptitiously checking the dashboard every few seconds.

As the forecast promised, the weather grows steadily worse. Ruth uses Lionel's phone to snap shots of a field bathed in yellow light with a purple-gray cloud towering behind.

"He wanted to be a photographer, you know: tried to set up as a freelancer once," she says sadly. "Felt no one appreciated his talents. Used to do poetry readings too. And open-mic nights with his guitar. He just wanted to be good at something—wanted to be admired." She sets the phone down on the seat between us with a sigh. "But every time he wasn't instantly applauded, he stopped putting in the work."

I think of Jim and his bubbling, festering resentment at the world.

"Merge into the left lane and take the next exit," orders the satnav.

"We're going to make it, aren't we?" Ruth whispers. "I mean,

if the light's been on all this time and the car's not conked out
on us . . ."

"It's still ten miles," Samira says tightly.

"We're going to be all right." I meet Ruth's eyes with a smile,
then catch Janey's in the rearview mirror. "It's going to be OK,
and soon this will be over."

"You really need to stop tempting fate," says my oldest friend
in her most helpful and reassuring manner.

We wend our way through the hills toward the coast, the
satnav occasionally dictating a turn.

Suddenly Janey sits forward. "Keep going!" she orders, even
as the satnav reminds us to take the next left. "Ignore it! There's
a queue going up the hill with a police car at the top."

We sail past the turn.

"What if they're on all the roads?" Samira whispers as the
satnav tells us to take the next left.

"Just go really slow, then we can look first," I tell her as
calmly as I can.

Samira slows obligingly.

We all jump as a loud horn-blast sounds from behind us.

"Pull in!" I hiss. "Just let him pass."

Shoulders hunched, Samira pulls on to the verge as the car
behind swerves past with another blast of the horn.

Janey is frantically tapping away on Keith's phone to see if
there's any information on social media about the police traps.
"I think it's OK," she reports as Samira edges us back on to
the road.

We all take a deep breath as she takes the next turn. A bend
obscures the way ahead.

"Please let there be no police," Ruth whispers. "Please let there be no police."

There's no police car beyond that bend. Or the next.

"Nooooooo!" Janey wails as we round the third and there is the dreaded police car, pulled up alongside another vehicle.

Samira slows to a crawl. "Ruth, Sally, duck down so he can't see you."

Peering between the seats, I see the car in front of the police vehicle has a wheel in the ditch. My heart lurches as a police officer looks round from his position crouched at the front of the damaged car.

"Don't stand up, don't stand up," Ruth chants.

He stands up, raises his arm . . . and gives us an open-handed wave. We draw level, then pass on without incident.

"I'm having a heart attack," announces Janey.

51

Beside the Seaside

B eside me, Ruth is bolt upright, trying to peer past Samira's head. "The sea!" she says eagerly, though when I look there are just woods and houses.

Janey leans forward too.

"There!" says Ruth, pointing, but the road has already turned again.

"Are you sure it's not just a field?" Samira asks. "Everything looks so gray in the rain."

Anticipation makes my heart race, though I don't know why I'm so desperate to catch my first glimpse of water. We'll be there soon enough, but, like a child, I can't seem to wait.

Then finally we crest a hill, the shore stretching out before us, and with a rush of triumph I know we're going to make it.

Despite the storm, I was expecting to find glimmers of light reflecting off the water, but the sea is leaden, a murky gray cut through with splashes of white. Bands of rain blend sky and water into one. The wind howls against the side of the car so violently that Samira gives a little gasp, wrenching the wheel to stay in her lane.

"Slow down!" Ruth moans, clutching the back of Samira's

seat as rain sheets across the windscreen, hammering all around us as if a thousand hands are slapping the car.

"Next right, then a left where it forks," Janey says.

I can only just make out her voice above the drumming of the rain on the roof and windows.

"Right here," she tells Samira. "Then we're nearly . . ."

We break over the final hill, and there is the sea. A small road runs along the top of the cliffs. Samira indicates left to join it.

"There." Janey points ahead at a thick stand of trees. "There should be a big oak among the bushes where I can stash our bag of fresh clothes."

She clicks off her seatbelt as I pass the waterproof bag between the seats. Samira slows to a crawl as we pass the footpath we'll be climbing once we're through the caves. Pulling level with the densest part of the thicket, she hits the indicator, easing us to a stop.

"You're clear," I whisper as Ruth and I peer about in opposite directions.

Janey throws open her door and bolts across the empty lane, diving into the bushes as Samira starts an expert three-point turn.

I peer through the rain. "Clear my side."

"Mine too," says Ruth.

"Come on. Come on," I mutter, eyes flicking to the trees before I wrench my gaze back to the road and the opening on to the footpath. A dog bounds out then pauses, quivering. It turns to look at us, tongue lolling, then scampers back downhill.

"Janey, come on," I whisper, tapping my hand frantically against the window.

She dashes out of the bushes, hand on her head to keep her wig and hat in place. Diving around the front of the car, she forces open the passenger door, then staggers back as the wind snaps it shut in her face.

I hold my breath as the dog appears once more—the owner must be nearly on us.

"Get in!" I shout.

Janey wrenches the door open, wedging herself in the gap, then tumbling inside as the wind slams it behind her.

"Go!" Ruth gasps, but Samira is already pulling out.

I force myself to look away as we pass the footpath, only turning back as the road bends. A bedraggled figure is just staggering up the track.

"Did he see us?" Ruth whispers.

"Just the car," I say, nearly dizzy with relief.

Ruth slumps back into her seat, hand on her chest. We exchange a look, then dissolve into laughter.

"And we haven't even started yet," she gasps, closing her eyes.

Samira guides the car round the cliff, indicating left once more. We pull into the empty car park just as the only other car there pulls out. For a moment we sit staring at the brewing storm, gusts buffeting the doors as if trying to get in.

"We're so fucked," says the voice of optimism from the passenger seat.

"This is madness," says Ruth. "Not courage, but madness. At least if we go to prison we'll have lives when we get out."

Samira just stares out to sea, clutching the wheel.

"Done yet?" I ask coolly. "Good. Now that we've got our moment of weakness out of the way, we're going to stop being pathetic about a little rain—"

"It's a bloody gale out there!" Janey hisses.

"So we'll have to hold our hats and wigs on, and we'll get a bit wet," I say dismissively. "We'll dry out."

Samira uncurls her hands from the wheel, stretching her fingers with a wince. "Maybe if we tried a different day—"

"Are people really going to believe that four strong, healthy men disappeared to their deaths on a calm, sunny day?" I shake my head. "We're committed now. And we'll be OK—we *will*, I promise. We just have to stick to the plan."

I look at each of them in turn. "We all knew this would be scary. But prison will be scary too, and it'll last a whole lot longer. A few hours and this is done—we're out the other side and walking away." I check the new waterproof watch strapped around my wrist. "But only if we go now. The tide waits for no woman—and certainly not on a day like this."

I pull Ruth's bag of cleaning supplies across the back seat, fishing out cloths and alcohol wipes. I press one of each into Ruth's hands, but she just sits staring down at them as if she's forgotten how they work.

"Do I seriously need to do some rousing 'All for one and one for all' speech or shall I just go and hope you follow me?" I reach for the door handle. "So much for the sisterhood," I say, then click the door open.

I have to struggle to push it far enough to climb out, but then the wind catches it and flings it out of my hands to quiver against its hinges. Cursing, I turn to my seat and set to with the cloth and cleaner, wiping down every nook and cranny where I could possibly have left DNA.

I don't look up as I work, though soon I can't tell the tears from the rain and sea spray on my face.

The wind changes direction, swinging the car door forward to clap me sharply on the bottom. I shove it back, rubbing my bruised behind.

"Serves you right," says a voice right by my ear.

I spin round to find the others standing in a sodden cluster in front of me.

"Thought you wanted to get a move on," Janey says, a pitiful attempt at a grin drawing up the sides of her mouth.

"Yes, enough dillydallying," adds Ruth.

"All done and ready to go, Captain. We await your command," says Samira.

"All for one?" offers Janey, putting out her hand.

And it's stupid and cheesy and pathetically drippy, especially with all of us needing our spare hands to clamp our hats and wigs on, but I put my blue-gloved hand on hers, then Ruth and Samira add theirs and we all scream, "And one for all!"

The wind whips the sound away.

52

Abandon Hope

I cast one look back at the car. "Everyone left their phone?"

They all nod. We toss our used cleaning cloths into a plastic bag, then wipe the mouths of our water bottles with hand gel, squirt some disinfectant inside, and give them a good shake before Samira runs over to the furthest bin in the car park to chuck them away.

"Everything clean? Nothing left behind except their bags, the tents, and unused cleaning stuff? No fingerprints, no saliva, no snotty tissues? You were all thorough with wiping the phones, right?"

"Check, check, and check," says Janey. "Now are you going to delay all day or are we going?"

There's nothing left to do but turn and march resolutely across the car park to the path down to the beach. Crossing the beach proves harder than any of us imagined. The rain has created a crust over the top of the sand so that one minute it seems firm but the next the ground is sliding under us, not just down but sideways. The wind howls into our faces, buffeting us from unexpected directions.

I turn to see how far we've come and freeze.

A man is standing beside the car, peering at it. After a moment, he moves around and inspects it from another angle. I reach out and grab Janey as she stumbles by.

"What?" she snaps, then turns to look where I'm staring. "Oh my God."

"What is it?" Samira asks, huddling close with Ruth at her shoulder.

Janey raises a hand to shield her eyes, squinting through the rain. "Only my bloody father-in-law."

We all stare up at him as he casts his gaze over the beach. For a moment it seems as if he's staring right at us, then he moves behind the car and disappears from sight.

"That bloody Find My Friends app. So much for it working in our favor!" Janey shakes her head helplessly. "Why is he here? What the hell does he think he's going to accomplish?"

"Who cares why he's here," Ruth says breathlessly. "What do we do about it?"

They all look at me. My mind goes white with panic.

"He's probably seeing if he can spot Keith," Samira reasons, ever the voice of logic. "When he can't, he'll think he didn't recognize him in our group across the distance."

"Being seen from a distance just helps the story, but we need to be into the caves before he can get close enough to be sure there's something wrong with the picture. Come on—" I pull at Janey's arm, but she's frowning up at the cliff again.

"Oh," she says weakly, turning to face me. "Don't kill me, but it seems I might have had a moment of panic and, well . . . It's not him."

We all stare at her. Then at the man on the clifftop. There's now a huge pair of Dalmatians running circles around him as he holds a ball high in the air then lobs it, sending them chasing away, out of sight.

"My father-in-law is massively allergic to dogs. No way he's adopted a pair, no matter how loopy Lockdown has driven him. My bad."

Ruth takes a deep breath, then turns and slogs on toward the caves. Silently, the rest of us follow.

Before long there's a stitch in my side. The air sears my throat with salt. Sweat coats the back of my neck and the skin between my breasts and the backs of my knees.

We've been struggling on forever and it still seems so far. What if we take so long the tide comes up and we all drown? I check my watch: we're only five minutes later than planned, but what if that's the difference between success and disaster? All I can do is tuck my head down and march on, on, on . . .

Finally we stagger from sand onto uneven stone. As one we stumble over to the tumble of rocks at the base of the cliffs and slump down wearily.

Ruth's face beneath the dripping brim of her hat is drawn. "We're not even in the caves yet." She clutches at her neck, where her locket would usually hang.

"I know we're knackered, but we'll just stiffen up the longer we stay here. Come on, Courage." I poke Janey in the side. "If we don't go"—I check my watch—"literally right now, this minute, we really are going to drown. Get up." I poke, poke, poke until she swats me away.

"Bossy, bossy," Janey mutters, but she pulls herself to her feet.

Samira and Ruth do the same, and off we go again, picking our way across the slippery, sharp-edged rocks as the cliff face looms ahead. I can't see any way through the towering gray stone closing in around us as we edge around rockpools, clamber over boulders. Then I slip, my foot skidding down a sheet of wet rock, and there it is ahead of us—a fold in the cliff and a deeper darkness within.

A barbed-wire fence with a series of danger signs bars the way. If we weren't about to ignore them all, I'd be impressed with the sheer range of warnings about the likelihood of meeting imminent death on the other side.

"That's a lot of different ways to say 'Abandon hope all ye who enter here,'" Janey says. Nevertheless, she takes careful hold of a barb-free section of wire with one hand, pulling it upward even as she plants her boot on a straight section of the lower wire to hold it down.

Placing one foot on the far side of the fence, I stoop and angle my body down and through the gap. Ruth and Samira follow while I position myself to take over for Janey. Only when I release the fence do I turn to look ahead into the caves.

The light only penetrates about fifteen meters. Beyond, there is just the faintest outline of cave walls, glistening with water.

"Wigs, hats, masks, gloves off," I order. "We don't need anything to snag or catch as we go."

The next few minutes are devoted to freeing ourselves from our rough disguises and tucking everything into the bum bags Ruth and Janey brought for the purpose.

Then we take out our torches and set off into the darkness.

53

Descent to the Underworld

The rocks are even slimier in the cave, but just as uneven, a sudden ridge making Janey stumble while I stub my toe and Samira turns her ankle painfully. We hobble steadfastly onward until I lurch down into a hollow, gasping at the furious cold of the water within. Ruth nearly stumbles into me from behind as our shouts of surprise bounce off the walls.

"It's OK," I call breathlessly. "Just watch for rockpools."

Janey looks over her shoulder. "Do any of you hear voices?" she whispers.

"It's just echoes and the wind. Don't start going all superstitious on us now," I tell her firmly, but I can't help my own nervous glance back. *It's just the wind*, I tell myself. *The wind and the waves and the others' breathing*.

Then Janey gives a squeak of terror.

"What is it?" I gasp, shining my torch beam on her. She looks fine—well, bedraggled and terrified, but unhurt.

She points a shaking hand into the darkness. I train my torch along it until it flashes on a column of white.

My breath catches . . . then whooshes out when I realize it's just a stalagmite.

I sweep the torch up and down. "There's your ghost, Janey."

"I am too scared to be rude to you right now," she whispers. "But when this is over, I am going to have words to say."

"Yeah, yeah, blah, blah, keep walking."

It's only another few minutes before we hit the first of the big hurdles the blog posts by previous trespassers warned us about. The cave narrows and deepens, a stream of rushing white and black water filling the space, except for a hideously narrow ledge along one side.

"Samira, you light my way across, then I'll shine my torch back for the rest of you," I say, even though we all know the plan.

Putting my back to the slimy cliff wall, I tuck my heels in tight to the rock and start edging carefully along, arms outstretched to either side. Halfway along the ledge has given way and I have to reach, spread-eagled, across the gap. The moment I have to push off to transfer my weight feels like falling as I struggle for purchase on the slick rock, but then I'm over.

Janey comes next, cursing the whole way. She waits for Ruth at the gap so they can help each other, then Janey comes to join me while Samira follows.

Everything is fine until the moment Samira steps across to clasp hands with Ruth and Ruth leans out just a little too far.

For a terrible moment, they waver. Janey clutches at my shoulder so hard I know I'll have finger-mark bruises tomorrow.

Ruth's hands scramble for purchase as Samira's foot skids into hers . . . and anchors there. We all freeze, gasping.

"Come on. Get across, then you can take a minute to calm down," I snap, voice sharp with fear, but it does the trick.

Janey and I reach out the moment they are close enough, pulling first Ruth then Samira to the safety of the wide, flat space on the far side of the ledge. We cling to each other, shaking.

"It feels as if we've been in here for a week," whispers Ruth. "What's the time? The tide—"

"Is rising, so let's not dawdle," I say, refusing to check my watch again as I lead the way deeper into darkness. It's too late to go back, so there's no point.

For a while the noise of the storm and waves was deadened by the rock, but now it's starting to build. I want to believe it's because we're approaching the far side of the caves, but I know it means the tide is coming in.

We slip and slide, stumbling around a bend, and there is our last challenge: a fork in the caves. The floor of the right-hand branch is level and inviting, but I know it leads only to a sharp drop into the sea. The floor of the other crumbles away on all sides. On the right the water runs deep and dangerous, narrowing as it rushes around the bend behind us to become the torrent below the ledge we just navigated. To the left, the water is shallower—for the most part. But below the surface are hidden dips and pockets.

The latest blog post we could find about the path through the caves was two years old. The water is likely to have worn away even more of the floor by now. What was up to the thigh for those trespassers may be higher for us—and they went on a fine day with a low tide.

This time I can't help myself checking my watch. We're ten minutes late—it's not much, but we can all see that the water on the shallower left, where we will be forging our path, is not just rushing in one direction but moving back and forth, meaning we'll have both the current of the tide and the current of the stream to contend with.

And the cold. It's the cold I'm most afraid of. Exhausted, in heavy, waterlogged clothing, we'll have to fight our way across fast enough not to lose our strength to the freezing sea but slow enough to feel our way across the treacherous floor with just the help of the slippery, water-smoothed wall for balance.

I had a speech prepared for this moment about how this is the last hurdle: how we've got this far and can literally see the light at the end of the cave . . .

All of it sounds hollow and hopeless now.

And then something rises in me, firing my aching muscles, allowing me to straighten my shoulders and raise my head as I turn to my friends—the women I've brought here and must bring through this last danger.

Putting my torch away, I turn to the cave wall and force my right leg down into the water. My breath hisses out in pain at the stabbing, tearing cold as my foot goes down and down . . . and finds purchase. Gritting my teeth, I bring the other foot into the water, then step out sideways, then again and again, clinging to any crevice and crack I can find in the cave wall as I ease myself along.

Only once I'm beyond arm's reach do I turn back to the others, still frozen at the edge of the water. I can't make out their features in the dimness but catch the glint of Janey's eyes, wide with fear as she stares blankly toward the faint light at the end of the caves.

"Janey."

Her eyes lock on mine, but though she knows it's her turn she shakes her head.

I hold out my hand. "Courage calls to courage," I say.

Janey heaves in a breath, tears standing in her eyes. Then she snaps off her torch, stowing it away. But as she starts to lower her leg into the water, she wrenches it back with a cry.

My stomach turns over. What do I do if they won't follow me? Is there even time to make it back out the other side before the tide rushes in?

Then Janey lifts her head and meets my eyes. "Courage calls to courage," she whispers, her voice shaking as tears spill onto her cheeks. But she clenches her jaw and steps into the water, lowering her leg down and down and down until she finds the floor. She moves out to join me before turning back to Ruth and Samira. "Courage," she says, her voice suddenly strong and clear.

Ruth's breath comes out as a sob, but she follows, splashing down so recklessly I think she'll fall, but she steadies, holding her hand out to Samira.

Samira raises her head proudly. "Courage," she pledges.

And then we're all in the water, with time running out.

54

Rolling in the Deep

The water gets deeper and deeper, the cold biting through flesh into bone. I thought we'd just go numb. Instead, my feet are stiff and swollen with pain. I have to fight for every inch. The air tastes of blood and salt, my throat scoured raw.

Behind me, Ruth is sobbing. Over the sound of the rushing water on our right, and the seductive, terrible whispering of the tide pulling in and out, I catch a moan from Janey, a whimper from Samira.

We're only halfway across and still the water gets deeper, even as we slow and tire. The cold feels as if it's opened a vein and is pouring itself inside in place of my blood.

"We have to h-hurry!" I try to shout it, try to make my voice commanding, but it comes out hoarse and thin and scared.

We gain a meter, then another and another, then we're slowing again because the water is still getting deeper and deeper, up to mid-thigh now. The current is growing stronger.

A cry echoes against the stone and I whip my head round to see Janey clutching the wall, her head pressed against the rock.

"Fine. I'm fine," she gasps. "Just hit a deep bit. Felt like someone grabbed my leg and tried to pull me down."

"It's the tide. I know we're all tired, but we've got to fight. It can't be more than ten meters now."

I don't check my watch. All we can do is keep going.

Then my foot goes down and down and there is no floor.

"Sally?" Janey whispers, huddling against my back. "The blog posts said the l-last b-bit's the deepest. We won't b-be able to walk against this current if it's up to our waists. We're too cold, too t-tired."

I stare across the darkness. The floor emerges from the water about eight meters away, dull gray light making the stone glint like metal. Beyond, the cave mouth beckons.

"Sally?"

I turn back to the others. Samira is sheltered under Ruth's arm as she tries to keep them anchored to the wall.

I swallow my fear. "Take your jackets off. They're not keeping us warm now, just weighing us down."

"H-how's that g-going to h-help?" Janey grinds out between chattering teeth, even as Samira starts wriggling clumsily out of her husband's coat.

I hold Janey steady while she does the same, then we switch, Janey acting as my anchor against the tide while I reef-knot the arm of Samira's coat with Ruth's, then add mine and Janey's.

"Even if we can throw one end across, there's nowhere for it to wedge to hold our weight," Ruth says hopelessly. "We need a hook or—"

"We just need me," I tell her, tying the end of the jacket-rope through Jim's belt. "I'm going to swim across, then you're going to catch the loose end and I'll pull you over."

Ruth shakes her head, clutching past Janey at my arm.

"The current's too strong. You can't swim and hold on to the wall. You'll get swept away."

"Not if Janey gives me a good shove. I just need to time it right. Now, stop talking. The colder we get, the harder it'll be."

I turn my back on Ruth's pleas, moving my feet to the very edge of the drop. Only my hand against the wall stops me toppling over. There's going to be no lowering myself into the water and pushing off. I'm just going to have to put my arms out and dive.

I stagger into Janey as a vicious wave surges over my waist then tugs me forward so sharply I nearly plunge over the drop.

"Sally," Janey whispers, her voice little more than a sob.

I force breath into my lungs. "We're going to be OK. I promise. Five minutes and it'll be over. Ready?"

Her lips are quivering, but she clenches her jaw and puts her hands against my back as I turn away, bracing my feet as I lean into the tide. It pushes harder, harder, harder, then suddenly the force dissolves. For a frozen moment everything is calm. Time seems to stop.

The tide curls around me and, as it drags me forward, Janey's hands shoot out, driving into my back as I leap, propelling myself into a long, shallow dive.

My front hits the water, the cold squeezing my chest as if I'm being crushed. I clench my jaw to stop myself from crying out as I reach, reach, reach, letting the tide pull me toward the far side of the cave, the rope of coats dragging out behind me like a tail. Then the wave slacks. As the water settles around me, I see the cave floor rising up only a few meters ahead . . .

Frantically, I drag my arms to the side and back, thrusting

myself forward. Closer, closer, closer . . . I force my arms across my chest and up, ready for another stroke . . .

The tide snatches me backward, hurtling me away from the cave wall and into the deeper current. I move my arms desperately, kicking with all my strength, but the wave has me, bearing me inexorably into the darkness, away from the light of the cave mouth.

I watch it grow further and further away and know that if I don't break free in the next few seconds I'll be swept into the stream on the right and from there into the depths of the caves, where there will be no way back in time to beat the tide.

Screaming, I force my head above the waves, saltwater foaming into my mouth as I drag my arms back in one last desperate stroke.

The tide's pull is too great. Instead of lunging through the water, I thrash in place.

The sea gentles, but it's too late. I'm too far out into the middle of the cave. The stream has me. I feel it dragging at the rope of coats tied to my belt, drawing me even further into its grip.

There is no breath left in my lungs. The cold has taken it.

There is no strength left in my limbs.

Then the tide seizes me. I feel the rope of coats concertina into my back, then I am flung forward, back toward the light.

The rock is three meters away. It's too far. Still I reach, reach, reach . . .

Pain erupts in my shin, my mouth opening in a reflexive cry. I thrash as water rushes down my throat.

As the tide gathers, I grope frantically beneath the surface for whatever scraped my shin. My hands find stone. I take a gulp of air then force myself down, curling my body around the rocky outcropping on the cave floor. Scrabbling for something to brace against, my foot wedges against a shallow ledge.

Waves rush over me, pulling, pulling, pulling. I need to breathe, but there is no air, only water, pulling, pulling, pulling . . .

And then it releases. With the last of my strength, I launch myself up, scrambling for purchase with my feet, hands, knees . . .

The cave floor rises up to meet me, the waves calming in the shallows. I grab at the slick stone, heaving myself up and out of the water to lie face down on the icy ground. Wind howls through the cave mouth, cutting straight through my wet clothes and into my bones as I gasp and cough.

I think my leg is bleeding. Every muscle feels torn. The cold is so terrible I am practically retching as pain wracks me. Still I force myself to my knees, fumbling to untie the rope of coats from my belt, sobbing when my frozen fingers refuse to work.

Desperately, I wrench at the rope, and finally the sleeve of Jim's coat comes free.

I look back across the cave at the others. Whatever happened while I fought my way over the deep part, all I see now is utter faith. Samira is clutching Ruth, who is clutching Janey, her feet planted at the edge of the drop, already leaning out into the water, hands outstretched.

I shuffle forward to the place where the cave floor drops away, then plant myself between the rocks, forcing my knees into a narrow trench. The tide shoves against my bum, then turns and pushes on my stomach.

I lock eyes with Janey and, when the water stills around me, I fling the rope out across the cave with the last of my strength. My vision goes black at the edges with the force of the throw.

I watch the heavy, waterlogged fabric sail out, out, out . . . It strikes down meters from Janey's fingers. My heart clenches as I see it drift sideways, the current trying to snatch it away.

Then the tide grabs it and casts it forward.

Janey lunges into the water, Ruth stretched between her and Samira. My heart clenches with fear.

Then there is a sharp tug on the rope. I blink my stinging eyes, forcing them to focus. Samira has pulled Ruth back to the cave wall and together they are dragging Janey with them. A moment later, they are all huddled together, panting, the rope clutched safely in Janey's hands.

"Janey, go!" Ruth screams, voice torn and tattered.

I throw myself backward, wedging my bum in a shallow dip, feet braced against a lip of rock. Hunching over my end of the rope, I hug it to me against the push and pull of the tide washing ever higher against my back then splashing up my front. I moan at the pain in my hands, arms, shoulders, back. The rope tugs and drags as Janey fights her way toward me, churning the water around her into white froth as she drags the others forward. Finally there's enough rope for Ruth, then Samira to grab, as they struggle across the gap.

Squeezing my eyes shut, I hold on and hold on and hold on . . .

Then finally there are gasping, gulping breaths in front of me. Finally, a wet body pulls itself up out of the water beside me. But my hands are so cold as the wind howls around me, searing against my wet clothes and every strip of exposed skin. I don't think I can hold on any longer.

Then suddenly there's a weight against my shoulder and the rope grows lighter.

"I've got it," Ruth grits out. "Sally, I've got it. You can let go. Janey will help with Samira."

I nearly topple sideways as I turn and belly-crawl up the rocks till I'm out of the water. Crumpling forward, I pillow my head on my arms as I fight to breathe through the agonizing leap of my heart, pumping so hard and fast it feels as if it's trying to break through my ribs.

Behind me, Janey is cursing, Ruth and Samira grunting, but though there's fear and urgency in the sounds, there's no panic. Then they're crawling up the rocks around me, coughing and spluttering and gasping for breath. All I want is to give in: just sink into the waiting darkness and sleep.

But we can't stay here. We may be across, but the cave is filling with water. If we don't get up, we'll be cut off from the beach by the tide.

A hand, clumsy with numbness, drives under my shoulder on one side. Through my dripping hair, I squint my eyes open and find Janey's gray-white face inches from mine. Samira staggers past, leading the way toward the light as Ruth bends to grip my shirt on the other side. Together, they haul me to my feet.

I sway, the cave reeling around me. My legs buckle, but they wedge me between them.

Their skin is chill and clammy as meat, but their breath is warm, sparking a last flare of adrenaline as I lock my knees, taking back some of my own weight.

"Walk!" Janey snarls in my ear, then together we're stumbling across the rocks.

Trudging so wearily our feet barely lift from the ground, we list one way, then the other, balance gone.

I nearly rear back when light falls on my face. Ahead of me

is the sea, waves shattering against the side of the cave and showering us with spray. Ruth and Janey force me along the cliff wall, then we tumble down a slide of rocks and onto the sand. I almost go to my knees again, but Ruth holds me up, groaning with exhaustion.

"Above the tide line," she gasps, voice breaking on every word.

My vision is fading, but I put my head down and drive myself forward. I know we must be moving by inches, but it feels as if we are sprinting across the sand, churning it under our shoes as we stagger up to the top of the beach.

Ahead of us, Samira drops to her knees, then collapses forward. A moment later, Janey thumps down on my right, spilling over onto hands and knees and vomiting into a drift of seaweed.

I try to get a hand out to brace myself as my vision goes to black, but I know it's hopeless. My last thought is that I'll just have to trust Ruth to turn me over so I don't drown in the sand when I pass out.

55

Homeward Bound?

Someone is shaking my shoulder.

"We have to change out of these wet clothes," Ruth is saying, her voice thin with weariness. She shakes me again, shoving at me till I roll onto my side. "You can't sleep here."

I make a pathetic whining sound. Everything hurts, but if I can just drift off again I'll feel better when I wake.

"You're on the verge of hypothermia, Sally. Get. Up!"

But I can't. My eyelids are too heavy, my limbs too numb. My fingers and toes burn with returning sensation. I just need to rest: to sink deeper into the beckoning void where nothing hurts and I'm no longer cold or scared or . . .

Hands drag me up so I'm sitting propped against someone who is shivering so hard her breath shudders on both the inhale and exhale. "You don't get to quit on us now. WAKE UP!"

I turn my face into Janey's neck, then sway back at the strange feel of her cold, cold skin. When I force my eyes open, the world drifts around me.

"We have to start moving, Sally."

I pull back, nearly toppling to the side before I get a hand down into the sand to brace myself. My vision tilts as I turn to look for Samira. She's huddled with her back to the rock wall that surrounds us, and I realize we're not out on the open beach but sheltered in a little fold of the cliff, protected from the sea spray—and from view. She gives me a wobbly smile, teeth chattering so frantically her jaw bounces. But though her lips are a startling, terrible purple, her eyes are clear and alert.

I look back at Ruth and Janey. There are shadows like bruises under Janey's cheekbones and her hands are greenish-gray with cold, but she moves with stubborn purpose as she fights her way to her feet then leans down to offer Samira a hand up. Beside me, Ruth has her face to the rocks as she uses them to pull herself up. She totters as she stands, bracing herself, yet a moment later she's reaching for me.

With her help, I stagger to my feet too—then keep staggering as the world threatens to turn upside down. Ruth and Samira lunge to hold me up.

"Deep breaths," Samira says, rubbing her hands up and down my arms, my back.

I bend forward and vomit down the rock face.

Wiping my mouth on my sleeve, I take a deep breath, then another. Finally, I look up and nod.

Ruth's lips quirk as if she's trying to smile but can't find the energy, then she turns and starts up the beach to the treeline.

I trudge after her, wanting to speak but too shattered to do more than put one foot in front of the other. I don't even think to check the sand is empty of other people till we reach the bottom of the path up the cliff, but we're alone. If anyone else was mad enough to be out in the storm, they'd have chosen the bigger, flatter beach on the other side of the cliffs, not this tiny, rocky cove.

Although the rain is down to a drizzle, wind still buffets the cliffs as we stumble onto the path and start climbing. I'm surprised to find I almost don't feel the cold anymore, but I suppose it's all relative to the shock of the water in the caves. At least now we're out and moving we're drying out, though it will take longer to be anything close to warm.

We're halfway up when the shivers start. I think it's just the adrenaline leaving me, but then my muscles start clenching and jerking and I have to sink down on a rock as it wracks through me. Janey presses in on one side, Samira on the other, while Ruth crouches in front of me, blocking the wind as she rubs at my arms.

"It'll pass," she whispers as I convulse, feeling as if every part of me is trying to leap apart. The others join in the rubbing and soon I realize how cold I am.

It seems to last forever, and I'm just despairing of how we're ever going to get off the cliff—and what we'll do if someone comes down and sees us and everything is ruined because of me—when the shuddering finally ebbs into shivers. When I'm just shaking, teeth knocking together, but no longer feeling as if my whole body is about to fly apart, Ruth nods and the others lever me up once more.

"Moving will help," she promises, keeping a steadying hand on my back as Samira sets off in the lead.

It's only when I walk into Samira, bouncing backward into Ruth, that I realize we've reached the top. Samira peers around to make sure we're alone, then darts along the road to the stand of trees where Janey left the waterproof bag earlier. At the place where the weeds on the verge are bent back, she holds the branches aside and beckons the rest of us through.

We emerge in a hollow space under the shelter of a massive, gnarled oak. The bag is stuffed beneath a protruding root, curtained by ferns. I drop down beside it, flexing my still-tingling fingers. Janey nudges me out of the way. In a second, she has the bag open and is passing out clean, dry clothing.

"The coats!" I gasp.

She blinks at me, then we look back at the others. Everyone's hands are empty.

"Shit!" says Janey.

"I know it's bad to litter, or whatever you call abandoning a rope of coats after nearly dying in a cave," Ruth says, "but under the circumstances . . ."

Samira shakes her head. "What if we left something in our pockets?"

"Then it'll have been washed in saltwater, so no DNA," I say, flapping a weary hand. "You've got your bum bags, right?" I ask Janey and Ruth.

They immediately scramble to set everything out. Four wigs. Four hats. Four masks.

"Four gloves," says Ruth, slumping in weary relief.

"Three."

We all stare at Janey.

She holds up a handful of gloves. "I've only got three."

She and Ruth check, then check again.

"Could it have been washed out?" Samira asks, wringing her hands.

Ruth shakes her head. "My bag was zipped up tight."

"Mine too. At least I think it was." Janey swallows hard. "I don't remember."

"It's only one glove. There must be loads in the sea and on the beach at the moment with the pandemic."

"It'll have fingerprints from one of us on the inside," Samira says in a tiny voice.

"Well, so what if one of our husbands had an old glove of ours from . . . whatever? Before Covid it'd be a flashing 'guilty' sign, but now it's not suspicious at all. Anyway, it's probably wafting out to sea as we speak, never to be seen again." I wriggle out of Jim's jumper and T-shirts before attacking the sports bra I'd used to flatten my chest. "It's too late now, so let's fix what we can—not freezing to death."

Janey mutters under her breath but begins shimmying out of Keith's jeans.

I expect the cold to strike into me even more viciously as I struggle out of Jim's wet clothes, but it's a relief to be free of the sodden, leaching weight. Too tired for shame, I pull on dry knickers and a bra, then a long-sleeved top and my favorite chunky-knit cardigan before working myself into leggings and a skirt: we all agreed to go for dresses and skirts to make sure we look as different as possible on this leg of the journey.

By the time I've folded Jim's stuff back into the bag, Ruth is distributing provisions. I pull a face as she passes me a bottle of Lucozade.

"Drink," she orders, uncapping it for me.

"Should've brought alcohol," I huff, aiming for laughter but too tired to make it.

"It makes hypothermia worse." Ruth watches me drink.

Then, when I lower the bottle, she raises my hand, obliging me to take another swallow before she finishes the rest, while Samira and Janey share a second bottle between them.

Plopping down onto the driest bit of ground, we huddle together, Samira's head drooping onto my shoulder as Ruth passes out chocolate bars.

"Don't argue," she says. "Just eat."

It nearly comes straight back up, but after the first two mouthfuls I find myself wolfing the rest down.

"So much for social distancing," Janey says wryly as she puts her head on my other shoulder.

I give her the finger.

Ruth tuts but has to suppress a smile.

"Maybe the saltwater will help disinfect us all," Samira offers hopefully.

"Yes, that's definitely going to work," Janey drawls.

"Is there nothing that can dampen your ability to inject pessimism into a situation?" Ruth asks, exasperated, but there's fondness in her eyes.

"We've all got our parts to play. You're Jiminy bloody Cricket and I'm the doubting Thomas who has a mile-long walk to make while you lot sit about dozing," Janey says as she drags herself up again.

"I'd go if I could," Ruth says.

Groaning, I pat Samira's shoulder apologetically as I struggle to my feet.

"What do you think you're doing?" Janey snaps at me.

"I'm coming with you, because if I sit here and fall asleep, it's not going to end well. I need to keep moving—at least till I can crawl into a car with the heaters blowing."

Janey turns to Ruth, who shrugs, giving me a worried once-over.

"Picking up the car is a one-person job." Janey crosses her arms. "Anyway, I thought the whole point of splitting up was that a group would attract attention."

"Which is why Samira and Ruth are staying behind." Stiffly, I bend to retrieve the tote containing the supplies we'll need at the cottage. "Four people out in the Lockdown is unusual, but one or two won't get a second glance. Stop arguing, lump. It's time to go."

"I knew I was going to regret pulling you off that beach," Janey grouses as she leads me through the bushes.

We peep out, looking both ways along the road, then quickly turn left, staggering along as fast as our exhausted bodies will allow. Somewhere below us are the caves, filled with water now.

When we hear a car, Janey pulls me across to the other side of the road, pressing me into the bank behind a straggly gorse bush. A wet wildflower goes up my nose.

As soon as the sound of the car fades, we're up again, stumbling around a bend and on to a footpath that leads us swiftly out of sight of the road.

I am so tired the world seems to float around me as I follow Janey up the hill and into a narrow lane. On tarmac now, she picks up her pace, and I do my best to follow, tripping over pebbles and sliding on patches of mud. At one point we hurry, bent over, past a garden wall. On the other side we can hear people talking, but a moment later we round a corner into a stretch where the lane is hemmed in by hedges on both sides.

I promptly catch my foot in a pothole and go flying, scraping my palms raw and cutting a hole through the knee of my leggings. Janey helps me up, gently brushing off the dirt and gravel.

"Are we nearly there yet?" I groan.

It forces a laugh from her. "Just round the corner."

Thankfully, it's not a lie. Soon Janey is marching up the side of a charmingly ramshackle cottage to a listing garage. She reaches behind a drainpipe, bringing out a little pouch. Unzipping it, she tips a set of keys into her palm.

Unlocking the garage, we slip inside. Janey beeps the car open to check the battery isn't dead.

"Where are you going?" I hiss when she quietly unlatches the door at the back of the garage to slip into the garden.

"We're dead on our feet. Mum never locks the kitchen door, so I'm going to make us a Thermos of strong, sweet coffee. If she sees me, she won't be able to tell anyone what day it was." She gives me a flat look. "Sal, your lips are still blue and I am going to crash the car if I don't have some caffeine. Now, get on with your job. I'll be right back."

I give her a sloppy salute, then crouch with a pair of scissors and a roll of black tape to alter the license plate. Next, I add a bright bumper sticker, a decal on one side panel, then a prominent National Trust sticker to the side of the windscreen. For my final flourish, I hang a big blue jelly-bean air-freshener from the rearview mirror just as Janey slips back into the garage with the Thermos. Tucking her hair under a scarf, she snaps on a mask while I open the garage doors. As she pulls out on to the drive, I lock up then crawl quickly into the footwell of the back seat to hide as we bump down the narrow, rutted lane.

When we turn on to the clifftop road, we see that the car park is empty apart from Yafir's car. Rounding the corner of the cliff, we slow to a stop by the footpath sign as Ruth and Samira tumble out of the bushes, throwing themselves into their pre-agreed seats. Then finally we head home.

Soon we're merging onto the motorway, passing Janey's pilfered Thermos back and forth to keep us going as the vents blast out a blissful stream of hot air.

Janey drops Ruth home first, then leaves me at the mouth of the alley. I stumble through the back gate and into the house, shedding shoes and clothes as I go. The last thing I know before I plunge into the deepest sleep of my life is the ping of my phone, freshly set to charge on my bedside table. I drag it toward me. There on the smudged screen is the last piece of news I need before I can let myself rest.

Janey: All good. Ava fine. Love you. x

56

Burial Ground

Sheer exhaustion means I don't edge out of the front door until mid-morning, wincing and hunched over with the strains of yesterday's exertions. Ruth and Janey are already at the garden, guiding Samira as she backs her car up to the hole. My pulse jumps when Edwina steps onto her front path.

"Morning!" I call, voice husky with tiredness. "We're putting in some topsoil and the fertilizer you recommended. It's so heavy Samira's bringing half and Janey's got the rest, but we should get it all in today."

Edwina frowns. "Are you quite well, Sally? You look positively peaky. If you're symptomatic at all—"

"Didn't sleep well and . . ." I take a deep breath, fixing my eyes on Edwina's hedge so I don't have to look her in the eyes as I lie. "Jim and I are separating. We decided weeks ago—hence him holing himself up and only going out at night, and me trying to get out in the day as much as possible. Then yesterday he went off on this mad road trip with Janey's husband. I told him it wasn't allowed, but he wouldn't listen, so I understand if you have to report them, but I just can't, OK? I—"

"Sally?"

Bracing myself, I move my gaze from the hedge to Edwina's face. The kindness nearly floors me.

"You are not responsible for him. You are only responsible for yourself. And your friends' work on the garden, of course," she adds pointedly. "I will definitely be holding you to account for any flaws and failures in *that*."

It breaks me into a laugh. We both look toward where Samira and Leila are now dragging something heavy from Janey's boot.

"I should go and help. Don't want them lifting all those bags alone."

"Indeed. It's not a task anyone should have to tackle by themselves." Her tone is distant, as though she's thinking of something else. Then she shakes herself. "I am sorry about Jim, Sally, but this . . ." She gestures at the garden. "At the end of the day, it's about whether you're alone or you have love. The type of love doesn't really matter."

She turns back to the house before I can think of a single thing to say. I find myself hoping she'll look back so I can smile or nod or *something*, but her door shuts without any such opportunity. And yet I feel warm. Sad and touched and . . . warm. Because she was speaking about both of us as if, in some important way, we're the same.

When her curtains stay placid and still, I drag myself away down the street to help the others.

As I near the hole, I see several bags of soil and fertilizer lined up by the edge, with one big parcel remaining in Samira's boot. The cars are parked bonnet to bonnet along the curb beside the garden, blocking the view from the street.

"This is going to get messy," Leila says, reaching out to

grab Maryam's hand as they loiter at the edge of the garden. "The last thing anyone needs is you underfoot, and I've got a bag of rubbish that needs a bin." She tips me a nod, lifting a plastic bag through which I can just see the outline of the bum bags. "It's super-stinky, so let's go and find a bin far away so no one ever knows it's ours."

Maryam pulls her hand free, making a face. "I don't want to do stinky-rubbish things."

"Not even if we get an ice cream afterward as a reward?"

Maryam instantly seizes her hand again and tugs her off down the street.

I crawl into Samira's car boot before anyone can object. Solemnly, Janey and Samira take their places at either side of the opening, Samira's breath picking up as her hands grab the tarp.

"Let me do this for you?" Ruth asks. Then, with a glance that takes me and Janey in, "Let us do this for you."

Samira wheels away, hands over her face. With one last check that there's no one coming down the pavement toward us, no cars approaching, I give the others the nod.

Though we try to be quiet, the strain of lifting Yafir out of the car sees us all groaning and puffing and, more than once, cursing. We aren't gentle—it's simply not possible as we lever the package out and let it topple into the hole. I jump down from the car and slither in after it, shoving till it's pressed against the far wall of the hole so Keith can fit easily alongside.

By the time I've crawled out again, Ruth and Samira are opening the boot of Janey's car. With a weary groan, I climb inside and we start work on Keith.

We're making good progress when someone hammers frantically on the side of the car.

"Sally! There're people coming down the street!" Janey hisses.

Ruth and Samira peer around, tipping me off balance so I bash my head on the car roof. Cursing under my breath, I haul myself up to look. An elderly couple are sauntering down the far pavement.

"Janey, you get the soil bags open and positioned so we can tip them over the packages as soon as we're done," I order. "Quick now."

My muscles quiver with strain, but we grunt and shunt and soon Keith is almost out.

"Janey, come and stand so you're blocking the view," I pant.

As soon as her shadow falls over me, we tumble Keith out. I sag over the back of the boot as Ruth jumps down into the hole and heaves until Keith and Yafir are side by side.

The moment they're level and flat, Janey tips the first soil bag over. Samira is already tearing open the next bag, then they tip that in too.

I drag myself out of the car to find the elderly couple are just a few houses away.

Throat tight with panic, I look back at the hole. The top half of each package is covered. As I watch, Janey tips another bag to start covering the lower torsos and Ruth wrestles with a fourth for the feet.

"Keep it going," I call, aiming for cheerful, though I just sound terrified.

I maneuver so I'm blocking as much of their work as possible, flashing the approaching couple a smile.

When they draw to a socially distanced stop, Janey spares a moment from folding empty compost bags to wave, while Samira nods as she wipes a hand across her forehead, streaking grime below her hijab.

"It looks like a big, muddy mess now," I tell the couple, "but come back in a week and we should have the first set of plants in."

"Good luck with it!" the shorter woman says.

"Great to see the community pulling together," adds the taller one.

We grin and wave till they're four houses along and have stopped glancing back.

"Two bags of husband down, two to go," announces Janey brightly.

"REMEMBER TO SMEAR SOME Vicks below your nose before you open your package tonight," Ruth tells me as we pin the tarp over the hole at the end of our day's gardening.

There's enough room in the hole to add the bulkier pieces of Jim and Lionel whole, so the dismemberment isn't going to be as physically hard as it could be. Emotionally . . .

I give her a tight nod.

She nods back, pursing her lips.

"Thank you," Janey says quietly.

"Yes, thank you both for . . ." Samira's eyes flick to Leila and Maryam.

Then we all go our own ways.

57

A Life in Pieces

plod up my front path with the house seeming to loom over me, as if it's suddenly grown tall.

For a moment I teeter on the doorstep, hand outstretched with the key an inch from the lock. Then I open the door and prepare myself for my final confrontation with Jim.

Just pretend you're jointing a deer carcass, I tell myself as I pull on two sets of disposable gloves. I've already followed Ruth's advice about the Vicks, but still I set a brand-new air freshener diffusing from the nearest socket before I hook a mask over my face.

Taking another leaf out of Amy's book, I've bought a cheap little tent, lined the bottom with a sturdy groundsheet, and dragged the Jim-parcel inside to minimize the spread of evidence.

"As soon as it's done, I'll drink myself silly," I tell Rosemary and Petunia cheerfully.

I just hope it'll be enough to dull the memories of what I'm about to do.

I know that if I pause I'm done for, so I don't. Just kneel before the Jim-parcel and start picking at the gaffer tape sealing it shut.

"Ruth's doing her part, you're doing yours," I chant in time to the *pick-pick* of my nails against the plastic and the tearing sound of the gaffer tape peeling off the tarp. "You're doing it for Charlie and Amy and Samira and Leila and Janey and Ava and Maryam."

Although my brain is screaming, *NO! I CAN'T!* the reality is that I can. I just don't want to.

I open the parcel.

AFTERWARD, I CAN'T QUITE remember how Jim looked or smelled or felt. I'm fairly sure my mind just turned itself off from the horror. There's the odd thing—the sound of the cat litter grating against the tarp as I work, the exact color of the handle of the knife I'd chosen to sacrifice to the task. Those moments are crystal clear in my memory and yet there are so many gaps—so many things that left not a single trace.

I know that after I opened the parcel, I paused to look out of the tent window. I remember thinking how comforting it was to see the normal world of the kitchen beyond. It looked oddly distant though—soft about the edges, as if nothing were real anymore.

I remember marveling at how there seemed to be no thoughts in my head even as my hands worked steadily away, as if they knew what to do. Instead of being scared and horrified, I wasn't anything at all.

The truth is I remember that evening as the deepest calm I've ever felt. No thoughts or images chased my hands as they went about their business. I just felt very still inside. Peaceful.

It probably helped that I didn't have to deal with "the big bit in the middle," because we'd left room for it to go in as one piece.

I don't remember a single moment of the task itself, and yet I know that I put my husband's torso into a series of large compostable bin bags, each sealed within another. Afterward it went into the wheelbarrow, then I covered it over with two forty-liter bags of potting soil, ready for the next day's work on the garden.

I don't remember giving the other parts the same treatment, the quadruple-bagged head going into a bucket, disguised between a couple of rocks from the garden, for burial the day after.

The tent, groundsheet, tarp, and cat litter were parceled up in a series of black bin bags, one within the next.

I don't remember it, and yet I know it happened.

I do have a vague memory of shedding my clothes—some of Jim's old stuff—onto a stretched-out bin bag, then adding the gloves and mask, before shoving the lot into yet another bag.

Finally, I put on fresh clothes, tossed the lot into Nawar's non-recycling bin, then dragged it out to the curb for the refuse collectors to take away on Monday.

That bit I remember properly, just as I remember collecting Rosemary, Petunia, and the bottle of Grand Marnier I'd bought to make the process of deadening my memories with alcohol as pleasant as possible. Obviously, it worked a treat because I don't remember anything else. Not really.

The one memory that comes back to me again and again is the quiet in my head, and the terrible, terrible peace.

58

Almost Done

A bsolutely nothing goes wrong with our gardening endeavors on Sunday, except Janey tearing a nail painfully down to the quick as we dispose of the torsos and make a start on the limbs. We fill in as much of the hole as we can, layering with compost, sand, and extra pieces of husband as we go. The most unnerving bit is just how mundane and anticlimactic it all is.

That evening we flood our new community-garden WhatsApp group with messages asking if anyone's husband has been in touch to say they're staying away another night. Of course no one's heard a thing from them at all. We make a grand show of worried unconcern but agree to meet first thing for some more work on the garden.

And then it's Monday. Jim-in-the-office Day. The moment of triumph or truth.

We meet early for our gardening session—if anyone asks, the story is we're worried about why our husbands weren't home, as planned, the night before.

"You're sure all the fertilizer you're using is natural?" Edwina asks as she inspects the ground. "Nothing in there that isn't biodegradable?"

"We've done our level best," I tell her with complete honesty and an entirely straight face.

Her mouth bunches up at one side, but she lets it pass. "You've done good work here. It'll be ready for planting soon. I know you've already bought the lily-of-the-valley bulbs, as we discussed, but remember that the bigger plants have to suit the soil and the amount of exposure too. Why don't you do a bit more research, then you can show me your short list?"

"Will I get a gold star if I do a good job?" It slips out before I can stop it.

A smile—a definite, actual smile—curls the corner of Edwina's lips, lighting her eyes up so that for the first time I can see the little gold flecks in the irises. "Only if you are very, *very* lucky," she says primly, then turns and marches off while I'm still laughing.

Janey appears by my elbow. "Well, that's a nice surprise."

I look behind me to Edwina's memorial cherry tree. "After all this is over, we need to do our best to be kind to her. We owe her that much at least."

Janey sighs. "I know. Another thing for the endless to-do list."

I groan. "Speaking of . . . Ruth? Samira?"

They look up from where they've been tramping down the soil in the bit of the hole that's almost filled in now.

I take a deep breath. "We promised that if we came out the other side of all this, we'd hold each other to account about living good lives, so it's time we started working on that just as hard." I turn to Janey. "You need to figure out the whole moving-in-with-me thing. And Ruth"—I flash her a smile—"for you that's signing up to go back to nursing. Leila's got her uni applications, and Samira's going to look up online courses. As for me . . ." I swallow hard. "I'm going to apply for some jobs."

"Well, I'm available for CV and cover-letter prep sessions." Janey grins, and I can see she means it. Like me, she really *wants* to do something to help.

Samira smiles round at us all. "The club's next stage of evolution."

THE DAY'S BURYING—HEADS AND feet—done, we head home early "to see if Jim and the others are back yet," on the basis that it'd seem suspicious if we just carried on as normal. I'm in the kitchen, Charlie's song of the day, "Running Up That Hill," playing in the background when Jim's boss calls.

"Sorry to bother you again, Sally, but our handyman arrived this morning to do some repairs while the office is empty, only everything was locked up tight, no sign of Jim, and I can't get hold of him. Did he forget it was his week on the rota? I know we're all out of practice, so it's not the end of the world, but I'd love a word if you could pass the phone over."

"He's . . . he's not here." I swallow audibly. "He went on a trip with some friends who've . . . well, they've all been having Lockdown problems, and I know they shouldn't have, but they went off to . . . relieve some stress, I guess. Grieve for loved ones. I . . . I assumed when he wasn't back last night he was going direct to work."

There's a pause. "I had to go in myself, and he's definitely not here."

"The other wives said their husbands weren't back either,

so we figured they'd decided to string it out another night. Maybe they had car trouble on the way back, because it's definitely not just Jim."

A sigh the polite side of enraged echoes down the phone. "I'm sure that's it. Car's dead. Phone's out of battery holding for roadside assistance. I'm sure he'll be here—or back with you— soon. Could you drop me a line if he heads home first, just so I know what time I can get out of here?"

I let the silence stretch for an awkward moment, then realize that the iPad is still playing in the background and the track has rolled disconcertingly over to Kelly Clarkson's "Stronger." I snap the music off.

"Jim and I . . . we're separating. Have separated. I mean, obviously we can't separate-separate until after the restrictions are lifted, but that's why he went off. Said it was too hard being stuck in the house together knowing it's over, so . . ." I sniff. "I'll text him your number, but could you let me know if . . . if you see or hear from him, just in case he's not planning on coming back here after all? I'm sorry to dump this on you on top of you being in the office when it's not your turn, but . . ."

"In the scheme of problems, I really shouldn't complain, should I?" Jim's boss says, his voice softer now with sympathy. "I'm sorry about you and Jim, Sally. Tough business, this Lockdown."

"Yes. Yes, it has been. Anyway," I say briskly, "I'll go and text Jim, then try the other wives again and see if there's any update."

I tap the end call button, then fetch myself a fortifying mug of Baileys and ring Janey.

"Hey, Janey," I say when she picks up, sounding tense and

breathless. None of us can see how anyone would be able to re-trieve a copy of our calls later, but if ever there was a time to be paranoid . . . "Have you heard from Keith yet about when they'll be back?"

We go through our rehearsed script—surprise, concern, at-tempts to reassure each other, then Janey goes to call Ruth, while I call Samira.

Surprise, surprise, they haven't heard from their husbands either.

59

An Inspector Calls

t unfolds pretty much as we'd hoped. I call Jim's boss again mid-afternoon—still no word at his end. Samira contacts Yafir's family. Janey calls her in-laws, who promptly check Find My Friends and report that Keith's car is still in the clifftop car park. At six o'clock, Janey calls the police. The next morning, the local force confirms that the car is there—no sign of damage, but also no sign of our husbands. Thanks to the Lockdown, no friends or family can come round to console us.

I am heading home from planting Jim's lower legs when I realize there's a police officer walking along the street toward me, checking house numbers. Dread churns in my stomach as she stops by my drive, even though of course I was expecting it sooner rather than later.

I hurry forward. "Hello?" I call.

"Sally Baldwin?"

"Yes," I say breathlessly. "Is there any update yet on Jim and the others?" I let my hand curl white-knuckled over the edge of the gate post. "I know they've broken Covid regulations, and we'll pay the fines, really we will, and I'm so sorry . . ." I heave in a breath.

The officer gives me a smile. "We don't have any news yet. I'm just here to get a little more information."

I drag in a breath, folding down to sit on the garden wall. "OK. Yes. Thank you." I don't have to try to make my tone tight with worry.

"Can you tell me about why your husband isn't at home right now?"

My shoulders hunch automatically. "We're separating," I say hoarsely. "We decided weeks ago, but we were trying to keep to the rules, only it's been . . ." I close my eyes. "Jim wouldn't come out of his room for weeks. Then one of his friends, Keith—he's my friend Janey's husband—decided to take off for a few days. They've got a new baby, and it's just been a lot with no help from grandparents or friends. Anyway, Jim and Keith made this WhatsApp group with a couple of local mates and they've been doing socially distanced walks together, but Keith's been pushing for a proper adventure since restrictions eased a bit—he was dead set on this cave route near where Janey's mum lives, and they all decided to go together. The other two—Lionel and Yafir—both lost brothers, and Yafir lost his dad too . . . They've been struggling with the grief on top of being isolated from their support systems . . ."

The officer looks up from scribbling in her notebook with an encouraging nod.

I swallow then make myself go on. "I know it's not really allowed, even now, but I think they felt they'd explode if they didn't get away from it all. So they picked a day with bad weather—Jim's idea. Said the cops . . ." I flash her an apologetic look. "He said the police were less likely to be giving out fines in the pouring rain, so they could get to the beach and just be away from everything for a few days, even if it was pissing down."

"And where were they planning to stay?" the officer asks.

My palms are sweating. I quickly fold them under my arms. "They were going to camp, but I don't know where exactly. We haven't really been talking much . . . You know, with him being holed up in his room."

"And when did he leave on this trip?"

"Early Friday morning. I assumed he'd be back on Sunday, but when he wasn't I figured they'd just decided to drive back in time for Jim's stint in the office on Monday, so I didn't . . . I tried not to worry. I mean, I checked in with the other wives and we were all concerned that none of us had heard from them at all, but Ruth suggested maybe their phones were dead after camping for two nights. Janey figured that maybe they were wrapped up in having fun and didn't want to have an argument about staying another night, and . . . Well, we just . . . we talked ourselves into believing that, since they were all together, nothing too bad could have happened and it was silly to get het up until at least Monday."

"And when did you start to suspect there might be a problem?"

"When Jim's boss called yesterday morning to say he hadn't shown up at the office for his week on the rota."

"And how about the other wives—you said one of them is a friend?"

I shrug. "Well, all of them now—we decided that if the boys were going to have a Lockdown walking club, we'd have a community gardening one, but we only know each other through our husbands. Except for Janey, of course—she's been my best friend forever. That's how Jim knows Keith. Keith and Lionel know each other through work—Lionel's a decorator and Keith's a surveyor. Lionel is the one who dragged Yafir into the group." I look down at my hands, clamped together in my lap.

The officer nods. "And you said your friends hadn't heard from their husbands during the trip either—did you mean at all or just on the Sunday?"

"At all. I guess it seems mad that we didn't panic sooner, but we thought they were just trying to switch off . . . Janey was furious. At least she was trying to be, instead of being scared. Samira was the most worried, but she said Yafir's been so un-like himself since his brother and father died, nothing would surprise her. As for Lionel, Ruth says he never does updates when he's out with mates, so . . ." I shrug helplessly. "We hoped they were all having such a good time they'd come back more themselves if we just left them alone."

"So your last contact with Jim was when he left?"

I nod, pressing my hands together so tightly the knuckles show white.

"And what would you say Jim's mood was when he left?"

I'm fully rehearsed for this exact situation, yet my stomach seems to be trying to fold itself into some complex work of origami.

"Our marriage had fallen apart and there's a worldwide pan-demic, so . . . not great." I shake my head. "Janey says the local police found the car near the start of the cave walk. It's close to her mum's house, so did anyone check if she—"

The officer nods. "She's an older lady, as you know, and it seems her memory isn't what it was. She doesn't remember seeing them and the officers who visited saw no sign they'd been there, but it's not definitive. Is there anyone else who might have an idea of where your husbands were planning to camp?"

I look away. "He doesn't get on well with our son, but I'll give you my daughter's number . . . Do you think they could have got lost in the caves? Has anyone been able to check?"

"The local rescue services are looking into it. Was Jim aware that the route was cordoned off to the public? Would it be out of character for him to ignore a series of warnings signs?"

"Jim thought trying Thai food was a leap," I say weakly.

"Given he was with a group of mates, does that make it seem more likely?"

I shake my head, then shrug. "Who knows right now? I didn't expect any of this," I say quietly.

The officer bites her lip and I know I have her. She produces a slip of paper and scribbles a few notes before handing it over. It tells me Jim's missing person reference number and her work mobile. "Try not to worry. We're exploring all possibilities, but hopefully it's just some misunderstanding or minor misadventure. If you hear anything or find unusual activity on your bank account, please let me know, otherwise we'll be in touch soon."

I *think* it's a promise rather than a threat.

60

How Does Your Garden Grow?

The minute the policewoman is out of sight I WhatsApp the others—we'd agreed that it would be more suspicious not to.

"Everything quite all right?" a voice calls behind me.

I manage not to yelp as I spin round to find Edwina watching me from the opposite pavement.

"Not bad news, I hope," Edwina says, eyes drifting down the street after the police officer.

"I'm sure it's nothing. I just haven't heard from Jim since he went off on his trip."

Edwina's eyes narrow. "Snuck off, you mean."

"He didn't show up at the office for his week on the rota, and the other wives haven't heard from their husbands either. We all assumed that, since they were together, it wasn't a problem, but now . . ."

"I'm sure the police will have news to set your mind at ease soon. Have they discovered any leads as to where they might be?"

My lungs squeeze as, for a second, I think Edwina's sharp eyes move to the hole at the end of the street, then I realize she's glaring at a car approaching too fast, radio blaring.

"What a pity the police missed *that* little display." Edwina sniffs, giving a furious little shake of her head.

I give her a pathetic attempt at a smile.

Edwina meets it with one of her patented down-the-nose looks. "Now we're allowed to socialize with one other person outside the house, it's about time you had a gardening master-class. And you look as if you need someone to make you a cup of tea. Come on," she says. "Spit spot."

Too shaken to argue, I follow her down the narrow path along the side of her house. The paving slabs are neatly swept, and the fence freshly sealed with wood preserver, but there's nothing much to remark on except an arch at the end with a rose rambling over it.

Then I step through into the garden and my breath stills.

Edwina turns with a smile. "Welcome," she says. "I've wanted to show you this since we . . . Well, since we started talking like proper neighbors. I might even presume to call it a friend-ship. Of sorts," she adds gruffly.

Although the idea would have horrified me a month ago, I find myself smiling. "I'd love to think we're friends now, Ed-wina. That would be the most wonderful compliment."

"Because someone as stupid as you would never be of in-terest to a woman as clever as me?" she asks, then shakes her head. "You really will have to stop thinking such daft things, Sally. I won't have it. Not in a gardening mentee, and certainly not in a friend. Now, sit down and enjoy the view while I fetch us some tea."

As she marches off, I turn a slow circle, taking it all in. I can't believe this was here and I never knew it. Does *anyone* know?

Ahead of me is a cluster of small, artfully pruned trees like in a Japanese garden. Beside them is a pond ringed with what I now know (thanks to Edwina's book) to be miniature tête-à-tête daffodils, anemones, and irises. There's a path of flat rocks leading across the water at one end and a tiny wooden bridge at the other, sweet peas hanging from its balustrade.

A nearby bench is shaded by two arches—one of wisteria vines twisted together and the other of filigree metal supporting a clematis dripping lemon-yellow bells. In another corner, a second bench rings a magnolia tree on the verge of bloom, tulips poking up between its mossy roots. Over by the house there's a patio with a wrought-iron table surrounded by potted plants—alstroemeria and day lilies—and a trough brimming with herbs.

A fence rises up from a sea of poppies and Canterbury bells in white, blue, and mauve on one side; on the other, it's all lavender and periwinkle and aquilegia. A path meanders through the middle, with violets poking up between the dappled gray paving stones.

As I look around, a blue tit wings its way between a series of delicate bird feeders hanging from the lower branches of a burnished copper beech. Peering closer, I realize that above one of the lower boughs a tiny blue door is set into the tree trunk. In shaded nooks all around are little lanterns of stained glass, a stone hedgehog, and a matching seat shaped like a mushroom. A pewter fairy peers between the branches of the bush behind.

Laughter bubbles out of me.

"You should sell tickets! Children would love this," I say, as Edwina sets a tea tray in the middle of the nearest bench.

"Only children?" she snaps. "Why should they get all the fun?"

I just grin. I'm starting to understand this eagle-eyed woman, with her tone sharp as cut crystal. Now I see the humor behind the gruffness, the whimsy behind her glares.

"We wanted children," Edwina says suddenly, voice so low I can barely make it out. "My fault we couldn't." She swallows. "I'd have adopted—I wouldn't have minded at all—but he wouldn't even discuss it. 'I'm not raising some other man's child, especially with you off at work all hours and me home before you, doing a wife's work.'"

"Didn't he know who he'd married?"

Edwina's face is oddly tender. "Do any of us?"

I have to look away.

"It is hard to be a clever woman. Men may claim to admire us, but they don't. Not when it makes them feel small in comparison. And heaven forfend that they should do their share of the work in the home because we wish to do our share outside it."

"I've started job hunting," I tell her. "The supermarkets are all hiring, so I'm hoping they'll at least consider me. I mean, it's not a *career*, like being a teacher then running a whole school—"

"Everyone's career starts somewhere," says Edwina. "Now tell me how your garden is coming along."

"Well, it looks like a wasteland in comparison with this, but not in comparison with what it was like three weeks ago. Thank you."

Edwina looks over at my tone. When our eyes meet and she sees the weight of gratitude in my face, the tightness goes out of her own and suddenly the kindness, the surprising softness, is on full display.

"I used to garden with Granny and my mum. It was the best bit of my childhood," I whisper. "I wanted to give that to Amy and Charlie, but I just let it go and . . ."

Edwina reaches out across the bench as if she's about to take my hand, then stops, shaking her head. "Bloody Covid," she says, jolting a watery laugh out of me. She waits till my eyes raise to hers again. "If there's one thing life's taught me, it's that there is always time to rediscover happiness, and a garden is a fine place to start."

We sit together, in her fairy-tale wonderland, drinking our tea and eating our biscuits. Maybe it's my imagination, but it feels as if we're having a whole conversation without any need for words.

I don't know if I can ever repay her for quietly teaching me that there is joy after loss and pain, along with how to make irises thrive. The guilt that I've used her lessons to plant Jim and the others so close to her memorial aches below my ribs, but there's nothing to be done about that apart from ensure she never, ever knows.

"I am attempting to grow these lovely cream-colored California poppies. Perhaps, when they're ready, you might come over and learn how to pot seedlings on," she says diffidently.

I make sure to meet her eyes with a smile in mine. "I'd love that, Edwina."

A month ago, I all but hated this woman. Now I think maybe she was the missing piece of my *Be Happy List* all along.

61

Curiouser and Curiouser

Although I'm a font of positivity and reassurance whenever the others start to panic, my heart is in my throat every time the doorbell or phone rings, especially when it's an unknown number. It's bad enough during working hours, but when it happens as I'm cooking dinner the next day—Day 3 of Jim's official disappearance—I take a slug of the cooking sherry before I accept the call.

It's Jim's boss.

"I just got off the phone with the police," he says grimly, "and thought I'd better let you know what I just told them."

My heart clenches.

"I had our techs check Jim's online activity, and the last day he logged into his email was the day before his trip. Obviously it doesn't mean much, but I thought you should know. We're all thinking of you—and Jim, of course." He clears his throat. "There's just one thing that I can't get out of my head. When our IT team was checking Jim's activity, it seems he was looking at his email now and then during Lockdown, but the day after I called—that time I spoke to you about the rota—he started checking every day. Sometimes several times a day."

My breath catches. In trying to avoid suspicion have I ruined everything?

"I'd hate to think he took my call to mean his job was at risk. I can see how, with everything else going on, that might make a man panic—"

"Please don't worry about that. He didn't say anything to me about it, and I can't think it would have made the slightest difference to . . . to whatever's happened."

"Right," he says, sounding relieved. "Well, I'll leave you in peace. Do call if there's anything we can do."

I've only just put the landline down when my mobile beeps.

Charlie: **Any news?**

I've just been talking to his boss, and no activity on his email since before he left, I text back.

The phone pings again a second later. **This is just his way of punishing you for leaving.**

Ping. **He's trying to make you feel guilty so when he comes home you'll take him back. Don't do it.**

Ping. **This isn't your fault.**

Ping. **You did the right thing, Mum. We're both behind you. x**

I set the phone aside with a sniff and cast a look at the cupboard under the sink. Behind a bucket of cleaning supplies are two sets of quadruple-bagged Jim-parts, waiting their turn for burial. I could have moved them to Nawar's in case the police decide to search the house, but that seemed equally risky. In two days, the garden will be finished, then it won't be an issue anymore.

I may not sleep well tonight, but I will sleep. And tomorrow I'll get up and do everything I have to for life to slowly get better now that Jim is finally out of the way.

Well, most of him anyway.

62

Loose Ends

Another bucketful of Jim-parts is disposed of the next day without incident as Leila and Samira tell us about their phones ringing off the hook with family and the wider community in both the UK and Pakistan demanding answers.

"So then my cousin called, and *she* said, 'What sort of son and brother goes off to party with strangers when he should be in mourning?' and then Yafir's aunt heard about it, and *she* called to tell me she'd never forgive him for the way he has ignored all pleas for help when she—'his blood family'—is stranded in a foreign country during a plague," Samira tells us wearily.

"I missed that bit," says Leila as she shovels topsoil over Jim's and Lionel's arms. "But I caught the part where she went 'Now he is too ashamed to show his face before his community—and rightly so! But to allow the police to become involved is beyond what can be borne. You girls will never find husbands now,' which is obviously music to my ears."

I sprinkle fertilizer over the top of the freshly planted limbs. "And no one's come round?"

"Well, a few people came to the door, but now the word's gone out about the police being involved they're kind of giving us the cold shoulder—mostly because they're so bewildered they don't really know *what* to say. But even though it's so out of character for him to just leave all his responsibilities and forget all propriety, everyone's sort of buying it too, because of the pandemic—and then losing my uncle, on top of my grandfather." Leila grins. "Of course the police stuff also means they can't even think about doing *anything* to me."

Samira just sighs as she pours soil over Lionel's quadruple-bagged thighs. Is the guilt worse or just different because of her beliefs? How does it all fit together for her, or is it the same as for me—it doesn't: it's simply this mad, impossible, horrific thing that happened? I still brush my teeth every day and somehow life goes on, so I have to at least *try* to think of myself as a good person, because what else is there to do?

"In happier news, I have a meeting with my old boss next week to see if they'll let me back to work at the hospital." Ruth can't hide her smile, hand stroking her locket. "Did you get your job application in, Sally?"

I nod, then turn back to Samira. "Are you ready to give it a go too?"

She sighs, shaking her head. "I shall have to wait. It would be too suspicious right now for me."

"Well, how about we look at Open University stuff together on Zoom tonight?" I blurt out. "At least, you could look at the law stuff and I could just look?"

Samira flushes but smiles shyly. "That sounds wonderful. I don't have anything to be frightened of now, other than my own disappointment, and I'd rather be disappointed in myself for trying and failing than for doing nothing." Her eyes drift to Maryam, sitting on the wall, playing on Leila's phone. "I've showed my daughters what a woman may do for love and duty. Now I want them to see what she can do with freedom and courage."

She reaches out then, and for a moment we clasp hands, but we don't cry because there's still too much to do before we're really, truly free.

"Let's each apply to our favorite course and see what happens," I say when I can speak without sobbing. Then I distract myself ladling fish, blood, and bone over the freshly spread soil. "Well, they'll take you, so I guess that's a moot point, but—"

"They'll say yes to you too, Sally," Samira tells me firmly.

"I guess we'll see. If I ever figure out which course I want to do," I grumble, wiping sweaty hair from my face.

Samira smiles. "It'll come to you," she says. "Something always does."

I shrug. "Well, for now we can look and plan. What's the worst that can happen?"

We both pause, then dissolve into giggles. After all, when you're standing over an illicit grave there's not a lot that measures up.

THE NEXT AFTERNOON I am overjoyed to find an invitation in my inbox to interview as a supermarket home-delivery packer. I can't help thinking that fate approves of the whole situation. Well, Fate and Justice are generally depicted as women, so it makes sense that they'd get it.

This is the day we finish the grave. The day Ruth and I bury our husbands' hands.

I find myself restive, prowling the house until it's time to meet the others.

Although I'm ten minutes early, when I step outside I see Ruth already standing over the hole, fingers clasped about her locket.

Something in the set of her shoulders stops me from calling out as I go to meet her. Instead I simply step up to her side and take her hand in mine.

"My son called," she says after a moment, voice hoarse as if she's been crying, though her cheeks are dry. "He's trying to bear up for my sake, but he's . . ." She swallows heavily, as if it takes effort. "I'm just . . . I'm so angry," she bites out. "I never hated Lionel before, and now that's all I can feel. But how can I hate him after what I've done? I'm the reason my son is never going to hear from his stepdad again, and I'm not even telling him the truth—I'm leaving him in limbo, letting him hope and worry, even though I know Lionel's gone and . . . And I'm the one doing that. Me."

For a moment her breath shudders in and out as she tilts her head to the sky. "At night, when I can't sleep, I hear my mother whispering that she can't bear what I've become. And every night I swear I would turn myself over to the police if not for you, and my son, and the others. Every night I lie to her memory."

"It's not a lie, Ruth," I tell her gently. Then I snort. "Hell, half the time I'm worried you'll confess to someone else's crime just so you can get the punishment you think you deserve. Bet you would too, if it didn't mean someone else—someone dangerous—going free."

"Are we not dangerous?" she whispers, looking down at her bucket sitting next to mine at the edge of the hole.

I squeeze her hand. "Only to those who'd have killed us otherwise. We have to allow ourselves that, Ruth. We'd allow it to anyone else."

"But that doesn't make it OK. It doesn't mean we shouldn't be punished or . . . It was one thing to do what we did, in the moment. But this." She stares down into what's left of the hole. "This is different, Sally. Not letting those who loved them ever quite know what happened. Leaving them wondering if somehow, someday . . ."

"It's this evil versus the evil of us all in prison, and for what? They're dead, Ruth. We can't take that back."

"If only we'd known each other before. If only we could have helped each other leave."

I lace her fingers with mine and hold on tight. "There is love here, Ruth, not just evil and violence. It will have to be good enough because it's all the good there is."

From the corner of my eye, I see her chin tremble. But then she closes her eyes and peace steals across her face. She nods once, silently, squeezes my hand back then bends to pick up her bucket.

"Should we wait?" she asks, looking around for the others.

"Not today," I answer.

She takes a ragged breath but manages something almost like a smile when she turns to me as I pull back the tarpaulin then pick up my own bucket. "Together?" she asks.

Shoulder to shoulder we stand at the edge of what's left of the hole and tip the contents of our buckets into the earth. Our husbands' hands, in their layers of composting bags, look far too small for all the pain and misery they've caused.

As one, Ruth and I move to the mound of earth waiting to

be packed back into the hole and set to work with our bare hands. When we're done, we lace our muddy fingers together again and stand in companionable silence as we wait for the others to join us.

When they arrive, we finish filling in the hole. It is bitter instead of triumphant.

Surely this is the climax of our adventures, yet it feels so small and empty.

If the police decide to search our homes, there's nothing left there now to find. It would set my mind at ease, if not for the fact that more than once I look up from shoveling earth to find Maryam watching us intently. Every time I catch her, she just smiles sunnily and makes a zipping-her-lips motion.

Although I don't think for one minute she has any idea about the garden's secret purpose, the last thing anyone needs when trying to hide a set of corpses is a clever, curious child watching the proceedings.

Still, I can almost persuade myself that the worst is over. Which is, of course, the same as asking for trouble.

63

The Other Shoe

Ruth goes back to work at the start of the following week, taking on all the worst jobs and picking up every extra shift going as her self-enforced penance. I watch as she lightens and hope that eventually she'll find peace with what we've done. The relief is potent, but I soon have new and urgent things to worry about.

It starts with a call from the police.

"It's Detective Constable Jurek—we talked when your husband first went missing. I just wanted to let you know we searched the car your husband was traveling in, and the report's back from the lab," she tells me.

I press a fist to my breastbone, trying to force my breathing level.

"They didn't find much. It seems your husband and the others were quite conscientious about wiping down surfaces—maybe a concession to breaking the social-distancing rules? Does that sound right?"

"No," I admit, because it would be stupid not to. "None of it makes sense." If they aren't asking for hair or DNA or fingerprints from us now, then whatever evidence we left in the car obviously seems perfectly plausible.

"According to your last statement, Jim wasn't quite himself. Have you thought any more about that and how it might all fit together?"

I shake my head, then roll my eyes as I remember I'm on the phone. "Did you find anything else?"

"Their belongings, including tents, were in the car, which suggests that they're not camping nearby." She pauses for a second. "Their phones were there too. All four of them. We're working with local colleagues to search the area around the car park, including the caves, but the location—and the weather—are complicating factors."

"Do you want us to come down and help?"

"I understand the urge, but there's really nothing you can do. Just sit tight, and we'll update you again as soon as we can."

This turns out to be a few days later.

"A resident from the town near where you husband and his friends left their car has responded to appeals for information," DC Jurek says without preamble when she calls again. "He reported seeing four men—two white, one Asian, and one Black—heading across the beach toward the caves at roughly the same time as the car's satnav records them parking. The witness's description of the men's clothes matches what you and the other wives told us they were wearing when they left."

She pauses ominously. "I'm afraid a picture is starting to emerge. We will, of course, continue to pursue all leads and information. Local officers have found some clothing in the vicinity—"

Bile rushes up my throat and I completely blank the rest of

the call. Have they found the coats? Should I tell the others or leave them in blissful ignorance? There's nothing we can do about it either way.

I'm still undecided when we meet that afternoon, though none of them notices I'm distracted. Samira, as head researcher of the legal ins and outs of our situation, has the others enthralled as she explains how a coroner's inquest and declaration of presumed death work, and what else happens when a death is suspected but there is no body. Now that the men have officially disappeared, it's perfectly reasonable for her to be looking into it from her own laptop, so it's been easy enough for her to answer our most pressing questions.

"The coroner's inquest is likely to be immediately adjourned while the police keep investigating, though unless there's new evidence there will probably be a finding that they're presumed dead by misadventure—eventually. I'm trying to figure out what sort of timeline we should expect. For now, all we can do is wait."

"Or we could panic," Janey says, voice strangled.

We turn in unison to follow her gaze and there, stepping out of a car a few meters away, is DC Jurek. Beside me, Janey starts to tremble.

"I'm afraid it's not the news we were hoping for," DC Jurek tells us. "Two of the garments found on the beach near where your husbands were parked match the descriptions you gave of Jim's and Keith's coats. Are you OK to look at a picture?"

I nod as she slips a photo printout from a file under her arm. When she passes it to me, the page ripples in my hand as if turned to liquid. Janey makes a wounded noise.

"Do you recognize the coats in this picture?" DC Jurek asks.

I nod. Janey clutches my arm, but I can't move even to comfort her as my heart lurches then starts to pound so hard my shoulders curl inward.

Did they find the missing glove? If they did, will they check for fingerprints?

DC Jurek purses her lips. "Can any of you think of a reason your husbands would tie the sleeves together like that?"

"Mummy?" Maryam's piping little voice makes us all jump.

"Hush a moment, darling," Samira says tightly. "This is very important—"

"Daddy said he'd rather be dead than have a disgrace in the family. He was on the phone to Auntie Kiran, but I heard him through the door before he got Covid and had to isolate."

"Shut *up!*" Leila hisses, grabbing her sister's arm to pull her away, but Maryam shoves her off, turning mulishly back to DC Jurek.

DC Jurek crouches down so she can meet Maryam's eyes. "Did your father say anything else about that?"

I exchange a worried look with the others. It was never the plan to make anyone think they'd gone off on some suicide pact. We tried to make it look like a foolish adventure that ended in disaster. Still, I suppose it doesn't matter what the police think—as long as it doesn't lead back to the five of us.

Maryam fixes DC Jurek with a determined stare, twisting her whole body from side to side. "He wouldn't just go away with strangers when we're in mourning, and now Mummy and Leila have all these secrets. They think I'm too little to understand, but I'm very clever. If he doesn't want us anymore, then he can stay away forever because I don't want him either." The words are full of anger, though her chin quivers with hurt.

As DC Jurek stands again, Samira pulls Maryam close, face a mask of despair.

"I believe your husband was also grieving a close relative," DC Jurek says to Ruth, then turns to me. "And you'd agreed to separate from yours?"

"Well, I wasn't separating from mine, and he wasn't dealing with any bereavements," Janey snaps, her pale skin flushing in angry patches. "He'd been struggling, sure, what with being cooped up with a new baby and not having any sleep and no one to help because of the Lockdown. And, OK, he was worried about money, but we have my maternity pay, and *everyone's* having trouble right now. *Everyone* must be having low moments, and . . . and . . ."

DC Jurek looks from Samira's and Leila's wild-eyed faces to Ruth clutching her locket and Janey trembling by my side.

"That—what you're suggesting . . . we don't believe that," I say. "It just . . . it doesn't make sense. Not if you knew them." I stop, swallowing the swirling panic because this, right here, is the moment that makes or breaks us all. "I know the whole world is mad right now. Jim would never usually do any of this, but when there is no normal anymore . . ." I look round at the others, then turn back to DC Jurek. "Jim, Keith, all of them . . . They were just trying to blow off steam. Whatever's happened, that's . . . that was the intention. That's what I believe."

DC Jurek glances at the others, but all I see in her eyes is a guarded sort of pity. "I'm very sorry to have to ask such difficult questions," she says quietly. "Can I put you in touch with a family liaison officer before I go?"

No one speaks.

After a long moment, I step forward and hand back the photo. "We'll be OK," I say.

DC Jurek smiles. "It's important to have good friends at times like these."

"I'm sorry we're not social distancing," I blurt out. "I promise we're usually very good when we work on the garden. Please don't write us up."

"I wouldn't dream of it. Take care of each other now. We'll be in touch."

We stand watching as she walks back to her car.

I reach for my spade. "I feel a sudden urge to get our garden finished as quickly as possible."

64

An Unexpected Gift

We wait for the call that the police have found suspicious fingerprints on the inside of a glove in Jim's or Keith's coat, but it doesn't come and doesn't come and doesn't come, and I tell myself that, since there's a plausible explanation, they won't be looking anyway.

It doesn't stop the nightmares, but there's plenty to keep busy with. My interview goes well, and the supermarket not only gives me a job but asks me to start at the end of the week.

So here I am—off to my first day of work.

I was up far too early, fussing with my hair, my makeup, changing outfits, then checking and re-checking my handbag.

A text pings in just as I finish washing up from breakfast.

Amy: I'm so proud of you, Mum. xxx

I am sniffing over the message when another flashes up.

Charlie: Have the best day. You deserve it. Love you! x

It tips me over the edge, but thankfully there's still time to fix my makeup after I finish crying. Then it's time to go.

Across the road, Edwina's curtains swish, then her door swings open. When she gestures at my feet, I look down to find a tiny plant poking up out of a terra-cotta pot on my doorstep.

"An acer seedling—Japanese maple—for good fortune on the first day of your career."

I have to clear my throat before I can thank her. Putting the pot inside, I lock up and, with a grateful wave, set off before I can lose my nerve.

I AM BEAMING AS I saunter out into the sunshine at the end of my shift, thinking happy thoughts about the celebration dough-nut I am going to scoff in the park on the way home.

Everything is perfect until I walk into my next challenge.

Unfortunately, I do this literally, sending us both stumbling backward: me into the nearest wall and her into a rack of trolleys.

"I'm so sorry!" we say in unison.

"Are you OK?" the woman asks.

That would have been in unison too, but the words have frozen on my lips. Her collar is askew, revealing a dark bruise.

When the woman draws back into herself, I realize I'm star-ing and force a smile onto my lips. It may be hidden by my mask, but it's funny how it shows in the eyes all the same.

"Are *you* OK?" I ask softly. "I don't mean running into each other. I mean—and please don't take this the wrong way, but—there've been times in my life when I needed help and people just walked by like they didn't notice, though I know they did, and . . . maybe I have a chance to be different from those people—if you'll let me?" I shrug, giving her a wan little smile. "Would you maybe have a sec to just . . . sit somewhere and talk?"

The woman blinks, leaning back as if she's about to hurry away.

"I promise I won't pry—I won't even ask any questions—but could we just go and sit at the edge of the park together? I've got a doughnut we can share—socially distanced, of course!"

She stares at me, so many emotions crossing her face—need, confusion, conflict, fear—and suddenly I know that something important is about to happen.

"Just five minutes," I coax. "We don't have to talk at all if you don't want. We could just sit together and have a friendly little moment. I don't know how your Lockdown has been going, but I could use the company." I tip my head toward the street. "Plus there's half an apple crumble doughnut in it, which is nothing to sniff at. It's my first day of work, you see, so I've bought it with my own money, and I . . . I'd really like to share that with someone."

AS OF THIS EVENING, the Lockdown Ladies' Burial Club is expanding its remit.

I'm meeting the woman—Marianna—on the park bench again tomorrow after my shift at the supermarket and, if all goes well, we'll meet there every day until I've persuaded her to leave her husband. Somehow I'll help her find a place in a shelter if there's no family or friend she can go to and, when it's time, I'll take her wherever she needs to go. Maybe I can even buy a few things to make the first night of her new life just a little more comfortable: a little less bleak.

I'll write a letter too—something inspiring, hopeful, heartfelt. If it were me, I'd feel beholden, but it won't be like that. Somehow, I'll find the words to make sure she knows she doesn't owe anyone anything for helping. That she doesn't have to give back or pay anything forward unless she chooses to, because nothing I do for her could ever compare with the gift she'll have given me by letting me help.

I've found the thing I want to do with my life. Though I wouldn't know where to start if I were alone, I'm not. With the club's help, I'm going to make a plan. And that plan is going to take me step by step from today's realization to a career helping other women do what I couldn't. I want to look back on my life and know that though creating the club was the only option for me, Janey, Ruth, and Samira, I didn't just keep inducting women into it—I found a better way.

The desire wars against the knowledge that I didn't make the choice I'm urging on Marianna. I was so afraid of what Jim might do—to the kids even more than me—that I never even tried to leave. But more than once I hovered by the display of charity leaflets at the library, picking up this one, then that one, then—with a titter of laughter to the woman on the desk and a casual "Thinking of volunteering, now the kids are bigger"— finally picking up one on dementia and one on domestic violence. I memorized the number of the helpline, repeating it in time to my steps all the way home. But I never rang it. Never asked any of the questions I wished I knew the answer to, because what if Jim checked the call log on the phone and I hadn't deleted it properly? But maybe, with someone to help me like I am determined to help Marianna, it would all have been different.

I blink as I realize I've walked myself to the club's garden.

The first plants are in now, spurts of green in the raw soil. I want today to be like that—not just the start of my new life as a woman with a job and colleagues and money of her own, but something even better. Jim made me feel as if I were nothing. But, from here on, I'm going to have a purpose.

Even if I can't help Marianna, one day I'm going to be the reason a woman doesn't spend twenty years with her Jim. It won't fix the past. And who knows if it'll weigh in the balance against what I've done. But I do know that when it happens—and I *will* make it happen—it'll feel as if I've rescued myself. I don't fully understand if I mean past-me or present-me, or both. All I know is that today I figured out what life I want to live now: one where I turn pain into power, weakness into courage, and helplessness into strength.

65

Responsible Horticulture

Day by day our garden grows. Janey proposed forget-me-nots, but even I agreed that was in poor taste. In the end we chose pear for lasting friendship and lilac for love between women, with lily-of-the-valley bulbs all around for returning happiness.

The day the planting is finished, Janey puts her house on the market.

"Are you sure about this?" she asks as she dumps the first of a thousand boxes on my front step—the start of the slow process of moving her things across so that, when the restrictions ease and she's allowed to move in, it's all ready for her.

"Don't get cold feet on me now," I say as I drag the boxes inside.

"Thank you, Courage," she whispers, and we both smile tremulously at the old joke, imbued now with so much new meaning.

We occupy the afternoon setting up for a socially distanced party in my back garden to celebrate ticking the last items off the *Get Rid of Jim—et al—List*. Now it's all about the *Be Happy* one.

I wear my new dress, Janey a rainbow-hued evening gown,

Ruth her beloved *wob dwiyet*, and Samira, Leila, and Maryam their finest *shalwar kameez*. There's Mum's sherry trifle, gulab jamun rosewater doughnuts from Samira, brownies from Janey, and coupe coconut cake from Ruth. Every bite tastes of happiness and hope. As afternoon becomes evening, we talk and laugh and sing and talk some more about plans and hopes and dreams—things we've always wanted to do and are now pursuing. Things we've always aspired to and are now working toward.

Ruth teaches us Estelle's "Conqueror" and we belt it to the skies.

A few months ago, life felt so small and sad, with just more of the same ahead. Now it's big, and full, and happy. Not just because we're finally free, but because of what we have together—what we've given each other. I never realized before that friendship—real friendship—is one of the raw ingredients of courage, but here we are.

As the sky turns lilac and Maryam dozes in a deck chair, I fetch a bottle of champagne—fizzy apple for Samira—then we fling open the back gate and sing our way down the alley to watch the sun set over our community garden.

We're so busy laughing and looking at the sky that we're only a few meters away when first Janey, then Ruth, then Samira and Leila stumble to a sudden stop. I am the last to follow their horrified stares.

And there is Edwina, standing on the pavement beside the garden with a little cascade of soil strewn at her feet. In one hand is a limp lavender plant and, in the other, an arm.

Beside me, Ruth gives a low moan. Janey claps a hand over her mouth, sinking down onto her knees in the road.

And just like that everything comes crashing down. All our

hopes and dreams: the wonderful future we'd just begun building for ourselves.

For a moment all I can do is let it cut through me.

Then I raise my chin and step forward. My life may be over, but I can still save the others. It will still be a life well lived if I've traded myself for my friends.

"That's my doing," I say, the strength of my voice surprising me. "They have nothing to do with it."

Edwina gives me a sharp glare, casting her eyes over each of us in turn before returning her gaze to me. "You may be chief mischief-maker among this little bunch of horticultural hooligans, but they've as much responsibility for this as you. I was here, remember. I watched you. Gave advice throughout, and what did you do with it?"

"I killed four abusive men and used my friends—without their knowledge—to create an impromptu grave to bury them."

Edwina does that thing where she manages to look down her nose at me even while looking up. "Do you know what I found when I came to look at my tree ten minutes ago?" she continues, as if I hadn't spoken. "I found a fox digging up your shoddy, lackadaisical efforts and pulling out this."

She brandishes the arm, and I take a moment to be impressed by her complete unflappability.

"Honestly, Sally, after all my help, your dilatory attempts at a proper burial are most disappointing. Heaven knows how we're going to get this sorted before the light goes—and we certainly shan't manage to do it with proper social distancing. It's really too bad."

"Edwina, please . . ." I gasp. "Whatever you feel you have to do, please, *please* leave the others out of this."

"Oh, for goodness' sake. Pull yourself together. Your generation needs to learn some respect for your elders. As if you're the first women to ever have these problems. But did you think to ask for the help you needed?" She shakes her head. "It's been seven years, and has even one little toe of my husband surfaced from beneath his tree? No, it has not. Whereas your husband didn't even last the week!"

"Your husband . . ." I look from Edwina to the cherry tree, then back to Edwina.

She must be recording us. It's a ploy to get me to confess. Rule-loving Edwina would never . . .

But then why is her memorial cherry not in her beautiful, beloved garden? Why would she plant it in the scrubland at the corner of the street? And why has she been so blasé about the depth of the hole we dug for the garden?

It would also explain why she's been strangely lax about our little end-of-street gatherings to carry out the work. We've done our best, but of course we've mucked up the social distancing at times. I wanted to think it was a sign of her mellowing, despite her strict scruples.

The point I've blithely failed to recognize until now is that Edwina's scruples apparently extend to mentoring us in our body-burying endeavors as well as our gardening ones. She must have enjoyed pretending to be oblivious while really we were the ones who couldn't see what was under our noses—or our feet.

Edwina looks at the arm in her hand, then holds it out to me.

"Now, shall we get to work, or are you going to stand there all night, staring like lemons?"

So what can I do but take the arm and the lavender, then turn to the others. "Janey, take Ava back home and stay there with Maryam. Leila, go with her and bring back the tools we need from the shed." I take a deep breath and square my shoulders as I face Edwina once more. Then I pause. "Actually, we need something else."

"And what's that?" Edwina asks tartly.

"Another glass." I raise the champagne bottle. "Under the circumstances—and as the resident expert in the proper technique for illicitly burying one's husband—it seems only right that you be inducted into the Lockdown Ladies' Burial Club forthwith."

"That is a most frivolous and repellent idea," snarls Edwina.

I just grin. "You're going to love it," I tell her.

SO THEN THERE WERE six, and they all lived happily ever after.

Acknowledgments

I owe a thousand thanks to my family for always being so wonderful and supportive. My mother has demanded specific credit for nurturing my homicidal tendencies, so thanks, Mum. And thank you for lending me your awesome criminological and human rights expertise, not to mention being a fantastic sounding board for whenever I got stuck on the plotting. I'm so grateful for all the hours you spent helping me ensure there were no gaps in my deviousness. Biggest love and hugs to my dad; I'm so lucky to have grown up with a father who never for a second thought I was less because I was female, and who always encouraged and supported my ambitions . . . and also made a lovely corpse at every murderous birthday party of my entirely normal childhood. Tons of love to all the Anglo-Italian-American hordes: Auntie Liana (with love for Uncle Benito), George, Auntie Mira and Uncle Bym, Rich and Josie, Sophie and James, Lori and Jim, Erin, Alice and Ella, Aidan and Kieran, with a shout-out to Auntie Ann and all in Wales. A big hug to Simon and love to my Ros—you would have liked this one even more than SING. Thank you to my wonderful Aunty

Pat, who reads and edits everything a million times, and sends cake to boot. And to my amazing godmother Dany, who gave me a home to adventure from and always supports me. A special, massive thank-you to Giudi and Julian, who make the world better and safe, and also kindly did a specialist policing read to ensure that the story remained plausible. I'm so grateful to know I've been as accurate as possible.

There wouldn't be an acknowledgments section to read if not for agent extraordinaire Dr. Kristina Pérez. Thank you for believing in my writing and for being the most wonderful editor. My books are so much better for your clever, insightful input and advice. I am so grateful to work with you. Thank you for seeing the potential of this one and telling me to drop everything to write it—and then making the time, in a hectic year, to get it edited at lightning speed. I couldn't ask for a better partner and advocate in my career. It is a joy to know and work with you.

I owe so much to my wonderful friends, without whom I'd have far less fun and definitely not have managed to slog through the writing and editing of this book. Big thanks to my amazing author friends who help me navigate the wonderful but mad world of publishing: massive thanks to Karen (hugs for Naomi and Will!), Christi and Jack, Louisa, Anna (hugs for Ally!), Gina, Kate, and Liz, and all the other wonderful writers who make my life (and everyone else's) so much better. Huge hugs and thanks to my non-author friends who help me keep track of the world outside the bubble, particularly the amazing Dr. Emma Milne; Lizzie (with hugs to Micah and Phil); Andy, Fauzia and Stuart; my godbrother Malcolm; Tony (with love for Aoife); Riki and Fran (with love to Katja and Alexia); James and Myrren (with love to Toby and Amber); Chris (with love for Carmel); Katie (with love for Peter); Ian and Kitty; Katie (with hugs to Isabella Lily) and everyone I'm too blotto from editing to remember if I forget to come back to this! Big thanks to my blogger friends, especially Luna. Big thanks to the fab London Screenwriters' Festival team, particularly Chris Jones, with a wave to Bob's Sunday Morning Lockdown Gang, and with particular thanks to Paul Higgins for all the kind career advice when the going was tough! Massive hugs and thanks to Gavin Whenman for stonkingly insightful feedback on the initial (script) version of the start of the story. I could not have done it without you! And a huge, enormous hug for Holly for amazing critique, right at the start of this book, when I was about to go off in exactly the wrong direction—I love you tons and I am so grateful for your friendship, support, and brilliance (PS: extra hugs for Connie and Will).

I am so grateful to my wonderful editors at Viking—Harriet Bourton in the UK and Pamela Dorman in the US. Thank you for choosing my book; it has been the most enormous honor to work with you both. I have learned so much and having this opportunity to develop my craft with your guidance and support has been the most tremendous gift. Thank you for all your wonderful feedback, from the big stuff to the small; it's made the book so much stronger and deeper. Huge thanks to the fantastic Lydia Fried in the UK, and Marie Michels in the US, for being the glue keeping it all together! Many thanks to my fab copy editor Sarah Day for not only catching all my stupid missteps and finding extra ways to add nuance, but also sorting out the hyphens—*shudders*! Huge thanks to Amelia Evans in rights for being so kind and trundling me around in the midst of such a busy, busy time,. and to lovely Monique Corless, for her amazing work and for looking after me at LBF with Amelia; many thanks to the rest of the wonderful rights team too: Ann-Katrin Ziser, Penny Liechti, Elizabeth Brandon, Catherine Turner, Annamika Singh, Laura Milford, Jonathan Herbert, and Mary Akpeki. Big thanks to Natalie Wall in editorial; Chloe Davies in publicity; Annie Underwood in production; Ellie Hudson, campaigns manager, and Jasmin Lindenmeir, campaigns executive; Beau Merchant for the brilliant book trailer; Sam Fanaken, Ruth Johnston, Eleanor Rhodes Davies, Kyla Dean, and Autumn Evans in sales; and Linda Viberg in international sales. Many thanks to Jane Glaser, Elizabeth Brando and Jeramie Orton in the US. Huge thanks to Lucy Schmidt (art and illustration) and Charlotte Daniels (cover design) in the UK and Elizabeth Yaffe in the US for my stunning covers. In the US, thank you to Brian Tart, Kate Stark, Andrea Schulz, and Patrick Nolan in publishing; Matt Giarratano and Nick Michal in managing editorial; Norina Frabotta and Nicole Celli in production editorial; Emma Brewer in production; Sabrina Bowers in interior design; Mary Stone in marketing; Lindsay Prevette in publicity; and Lauren Monaco and Andy Dudley in sales. Biggest thanks to Nadine Jendrusch and everyone at dtv in Germany—Nadine, it was so wonderful to meet at LBF!

I am so grateful to Clarence for the brilliantly insightful final sensitivity read: it really helped take the book that final step to be the best I could make it. I hope I've done your input justice. Thank you so much for all the music recommendations too! Thanks to Sheeba Arif for all the detailed feedback on the first sensitivity read, particularly on points of language, what concerns would be foregrounded at different times, and the order a mask and hijab need to be put on. The details about St Lucia, and its rich culture, are largely from Hattie Barnard's *Saint Lucia: An Inspiration for Art*; the paintings described are all inspired by her artwork, so do check it out! (Hattie, it's been such a pleasure to know and work with you.)

Thank you to Alice, Ama, Beth, and everyone at Faber for helping me balance everything during The Year of Nonstop Work.

Thank you to my lovely friends and colleagues at BSU, particularly the team marching through 2022–23 with me: Lucy, CJ, Karen, Anna, Louisa, Gina, Annalie, Sam, Alex, Rachel, and Dashe, and to Sarah, Alison, Richard, Robin, Mike, Giles, and everyone I've been so lucky to get to know these past two years. Many thanks to my fabulous students—I can't wait to read your published books. It is such an honor and pleasure working with you all and being part of your journeys as you've been a part of mine.

Thank you to Paul and Catriona for helping me figure out all the financial stuff, to Simon, Sue, and Katharine for fun and amazing presents, and to Viv, Cindy, Stephanie, Andrew, and all who helped keep the house from falling/burning down mid-edit. Shout-out to friends and family in Italy, particularly everyone in Sarnano—Maura, Luca and Roberta, Gabriella and Fabio, et al. Thank you to Melvin Lobo, Gavin Wright, Vikram Khullar, Alan Hakim, Rita Mirakian, Nick Gall, Helen Walton, Qasim Aziz, and Prof. Matthias for keeping me ticking over.

I am so inspired by all my amazing colleagues and clients in human rights, but particular thanks and admiration must go to those I've worked with on issues of male violence against women and girls. I have been so lucky to work with such brilliant people from international bodies to national charities, and from academics to frontline workers supporting those in desperate situations. I hope I have done justice to all I've learned from working with you.

And finally, thank you to those who've bought, read, and reviewed this book. I wouldn't have the career I love without you and your support.

Author's Note

On average, a woman is killed by a man every three days in the UK: in the vast majority of cases, that man is a current or former partner. At the start of the Covid lockdown, the femicide rate doubled—in the first three weeks, fourteen women were killed where a man was suspected of, or charged with, the crime.

I have worked as a specialist human rights nonfiction editor for more than twelve years, focusing on violence against women and girls, and working particularly with academics and frontline activists in the Black and minority ethnic (BAME) community. (NB: I use the term BAME here because it was the prevailing term during the relevant period and no agreement had coalesced around a replacement at the time of writing.) Work exploded for all of us during lockdown. My small part involved helping clients prepare funding applications to obtain the necessary resources to set up new ways of working in the context of lockdown restrictions and social distancing.

During the lockdown, 67 percent of victims told Women's Aid that the abuse they were suffering had escalated, while Refuge saw a 65 percent increase in calls to their helpline and a 700 percent increase in visits to their website, reflecting victims' difficulties in accessing support when trapped with abusers. Significantly, the police saw a more moderate increase in calls from victims—but a big increase in calls from third parties: this resolved as the lockdown eased, demonstrating that the disparity was a result of restrictions preventing many victims from contacting official sources of support themselves. Indeed, Women's Aid reported that 72 percent of victims said their abuser was able to exert more control over them during lockdown.

Many charities focusing on BAME communities reported a significant increase across a range of forms of male violence against women and girls (MVAWG). Karma Nirvana, which focuses on so-called "honor"-based violence, saw a 200 percent increase in calls to their helpline, including a 150 percent increase in teenagers calling in relation to forced marriage. Similarly, the charity Iranian and Kurdish Women's Rights reported a doubling of forced-marriage cases, while the Middlesbrough-based Halo Project reported a 63 percent rise in referrals, cautioning that with schools closed many victims were slipping through the net.

As ever, I was struck by the fact that while women killed by men have often suffered long-term domestic abuse, in the rare instances women kill male partners the pattern of long-term violence doesn't reverse: instead, it is *still* the woman who, in the majority of cases, has suffered long-term abuse. Given that women are just as capable of terrible, long-term violence as men, I am astounded by how infrequently women, as a group, commit such crimes.

My editorial work is centered on helping clients drive change, though this takes many forms, including polishing funding bids to support frontline activities, and revising research articles and news stories to increase knowledge and understanding. However, there is often a feeling of shouting into a void. Especially now, with Covid having turned the world upside down, people don't want to hear about the grim reality of male violence against women and girls.

This novel is an attempt to use humor to cut through people's reluctance to engage. The idea that four women in one moderately sized town would kill their husbands—even in self-defense—within one week of each other is laughably implausible. We can laugh unproblematically because it's never going to happen in real life. The reverse (four men killing their wives within one week in a small geographical area) is merely unlikely and, as such, wouldn't be remotely funny, even as the basis for a black comedy.

All the women in this story kill in self-defense in the context of long-term violence: they are now perpetrators of violence as well as victims, but that is the point—their situation is complicated, and that complication introduces a window for sympathy and emotional engagement while we go on this most unlikely adventure. The book in no way glorifies female violence—at most it quietly asks what is the right way to represent women who have suffered years of serious abuse and can see no other way out? Indeed, I set the book in the lockdown to demonstrate that the women in the Lockdown Ladies' Burial Club don't have the usual avenues of escape, even with all their attendant dangers, given that many women are killed by ex-partners, not just current ones.

In trying to authentically and respectfully portray the different characters, cultures, communities, and religions represented in the club, I was grateful to have detailed advice and input from two sensitivity readers, and also an expert policing perspective with a focus on domestic violence. I hope I have managed to convey a strong sense of how men from all backgrounds, communities, and cultures use what is at their disposal to attempt to excuse their violence—and that often this involves warping positive cultural and/or religious values into oppressive ones or purposefully eliding the distinction between religious requirements and patriarchal custom.

In a work of fiction, it's hard to clarify the truth of these complex issues while also capturing different characters' perspectives and beliefs, without ending up writing a treatise. For instance, the *mahr*—paid to a bride by the groom—is a religious requirement for an Islamic marriage to be valid, whereas what most Westerners would consider a dowry, paid by the bride's family to the groom's family, is a matter of cultural custom. A further complication is the huge disagreement about where the line between religion and cultural custom lies: such sincere differences in belief and faith are a key cause of friction between different sects, branches, and denominations within religions.

A further challenge is that, as all the families portrayed in the book are dealing with domestic violence and abuse, I am seeking to write about versions of *un*healthy family dynamics within cultural contexts outside my own: a highly sensitive task. The alternative, though, was to write five main characters just like me, which would have been a dereliction of responsibility when the whole point is that too many men do these things to too many women across the world. Although MVAWG dresses up in different clothes and excuses in different places, it is the same problem at heart. There's a tendency in Western media reporting about MVAWG to blame cultures and communities when victims or perpetrators are from BAME backgrounds, but to blame individual factors when white people are involved. If culture weren't a factor in cases involving white victims and perpetrators, why would MVAWG be so common? If MVAWG were just an issue of violent and abusive individuals, how come there are so many men displaying such similar patterns of behavior across families, cultures, communities, religions, and ethnic backgrounds? It's just not plausible, is it? Indeed, I chose to make Janey and Sally white, and long-term friends, to make the point about how ubiquitous MVAWG is.

Different patterns of MVAWG are more common in different countries, cultures, and religions, and these differences are vital to efforts to prevent MVAWG, and to understand how to help individual victims. But the core of the problem is always the same: sexism.

I have no answers to any of the questions the book raises, but then I'm not trying to provide them. I'm trying to make people laugh—and then think. Male violence against women and girls is a pandemic on a greater scale even than Covid, but it receives only a fraction of the attention and effort. Changing that will require our whole society to engage—and in these grim times, comedy may prove an effective way forward.

FOR THOSE READERS IN America, it's worth mentioning that the national context is rather different, not least because there are around 3,000 intimate-partner homicides per year in America, versus around 100 in the UK. Current figures from the National Coalition Against Domestic Violence show that the majority of domestic homicides involve a firearm in the USA—almost none do in the UK, and of those that do, all are male crimes. The ease with which a person can be killed with a firearm, and the prevalence of firearms, changes the situation substantially.

Nevertheless, in America one in two female murder victims is killed by a domestic partner versus only one in thirteen male victims—and of the male victims, many are killed by other men. Overall, women account for roughly three quarters of domestic homicide victims. Although the statistics don't clarify exactly how many male victims are killed by men versus women, 48 percent of male victims identify specifically as gay; since the statistics also include other non-heterosexual victims in addition to murders of other (non-partner) family members, it is reasonable to assume well over half of the male victims were killed by other men. Best estimates suggest that in 70–80 percent of domestic homicides involving heterosexual couples, the male partner abused the female partner, irrespective of which partner became the homicide victim: in other words, as in the UK, whether a man kills a female partner or a female partner kills a man, it is the man who is overwhelmingly likely to have committed prior long-term abuse. The statistics also show that women in America are roughly five times more likely to experience domestic violence than men and that, when women are violent, it is often in self-defense. As such, the same general trends prevail in both the UK and the USA.

THE CASE SAMIRA REFERENCES about the teenager killed by her parents some months after drinking bleach to save herself from being forced into marriage on a family trip to Pakistan is, tragically, a real one. Even after her injuries, Shafilea continued to be a dedicated student who longed to become a solicitor. The National Day of Memory for Victims of Honour Killings is organized by Karma Nirvana and takes place on her birthday, 14 July. If you are reading this, please take a moment to remember Shafilea Ahmed, 1986–2003.